In S

JD Kirk is the author of the best-selling DCI Logan series, set in the Highlands of Scotland. He also does not exist. Instead, JD is the pen name of former children's author and screenwriter, Barry Hutchison, who was born and raised in Fort William. He still lives in the Highlands with his wife and children. He has no idea what the JD stands for.

Also by JD Kirk

DCI Logan Crime Thrillers

A Litter of Bones
Thicker than Water
The Killing Code
Blood and Treachery
The Last Bloody Straw
A Whisper of Sorrows
The Big Man Upstairs
A Death Most Monumental
A Snowball's Chance in Hell
Ahead of the Game
An Isolated Incident
Colder than the Grave
Come Hell or High Water
City of Scars
Here Lie the Dead
One For the Ages
In Service of Death
A Dead Man Walking
Where the Pieces Lie
A Killer of Influence

JD KIRK

IN SERVICE OF DEATH

CANELO CRIME

DK Penguin Random House

First published in the United Kingdom in 2023 by Zertex Crime

This edition published in the United Kingdom in 2025 by

Canelo, an imprint of
Canelo Digital Publishing Limited,
20 Vauxhall Bridge Road,
London SW1V 2SA
United Kingdom

A Penguin Random House Company

The authorised representative in the EEA is Dorling Kindersley Verlag GmbH.
Arnulfstr. 124, 80636 Munich, Germany

Paperback ISBN 978 1 80436 832 9

Printed and bound in Great Britain by Clays Ltd, Elcograf S.p.A.

Look for more great books at
www.canelo.co
www.dk.com

Chapter 1

The worst day of George Rodger's career started much like all the others.

Badly.

He used to be an early riser, back when he was working on the bins. Now that he'd set up business for himself, though, he struggled to summon the energy to get up in the mornings, and it'd take two or three goes on the snooze button before he'd finally give in to the nebby wee bastard that was his alarm clock.

It had seemed like a good idea at the time, the whole window cleaning lark. He got to be his own boss, he was out from under his wife's feet all day, and all that up and down ladders and lugging his kit around helped keep him fit.

And, more importantly, it let him set his own schedule. His one-man window cleaning business provided a weekday-only service. Monday to Friday, he covered the Lochaber area in his van, earphones in, audiobook playing, washing windows and scrubbing skylights.

Weekends were a whole different kettle of fish, though. Weekends were when he came alive.

At weekends, George Rodger was a rock star.

He'd take to the stage—or the corner of one of the busier local bars, at least—and let his fingers fly along the fretboard as the drunken punters danced and sang along to his band's repertoire of classic anthems.

On weekdays, he was a man up a ladder with a squeegee.

Come Friday and Saturday night, though, he was Jimi Hendrix. Eric Clapton. Eddie Van-fucking-Halen.

Unfortunately, today was Monday, and the weekend felt like a very long way away.

That morning, once the protests of the alarm became too much to bear, he got up, made himself breakfast—the last of the bacon and a slightly stale roll—then tried to shower off the remnants of Friday night's hangover.

It was a persistent bastard of a thing that had hit hard on Saturday morning, intensified on Sunday, and was now hanging around like that last guest at a party who steadfastly ignored all hints that he should fuck off home.

Shower done, he gathered up his gear from the garage, dumped it in the van, then slid in behind the driver's seat and consulted his appointment system. It wasn't a particularly complicated system, being just a list of addresses and dates scribbled on the back of an envelope, but it did the job.

He swore below his breath when he realised that today was a Spean Bridge day. He had a few customers up that way now. Because they were a bit spread out, and he only got up there once a month, it meant he'd be up that way all day.

Maybe he could swap it. Stay local today. Rattle through a dozen houses by lunchtime, then call that a job well done, and sleep the afternoon away.

Then again, the wife would be home by then. She'd have a list of things for him to be getting on with, and getting a couple hours of extra kip was unlikely to feature prominently on it. She'd be at him to clear the guttering, or empty all the shite out of the shed—both jobs he'd assured her he was going to take care of some months previously.

But you couldn't rush these things. They took time. You needed a run-up at them.

'Spean Bridge it is,' he announced to the empty van.

He fired up the engine, joined and crawled along with the slow-moving morning high school traffic, then floored it north up the A82 the moment he made it to the roundabout at Lochy Bridge.

The first house wasn't bad. It was a bungalow. A wee one bedroom. The guy who lived there was in his forties, and while he looked perfectly capable of washing his own windows, he didn't. Instead, he seemed content to wander from room to room in a baggy T-shirt and boxer shorts, eating cereal from a bowl with a handle on the side and steadfastly avoiding George's eye.

That suited George fine. There was nothing worse than when they kept smiling at you. It freaked him right out, and he never knew how to react. Sometimes they'd just watch him the whole time, smiling encouragingly and occasionally nodding or raising their eyebrows.

It made him feel like he was a monkey in a zoo, although he'd so far stopped short of flinging handfuls of his own shit at them.

He'd only have to clean it off again, anyway.

The second house was a bit further out towards Roybridge. It was much bigger, with an upstairs, downstairs, a couple of VELUX loft windows, and some solar panels that he generally gave a bit of a once-over.

It was set back from the road, and while the front was paved and slabbed, the back was more or less straight onto bumpy, uneven ground laid with sparse, patchy grass. It meant the ladder was always shoogly, no matter how many times he tried to get it balanced.

Not really what you wanted when you were fifteen feet in the air in the middle of nowhere, hidden out of sight of passing traffic, and with nobody home.

That was one of the good points about this place, though. The occupants—a guy in his fifties and his girlfriend, wife, or maybe even grown-up daughter—were hardly ever in. There were no awkward looks or cheerful waves. No having to pretend he couldn't see through the glass. No need to first acknowledge, then try to ignore any stares or nods.

He could just get on with it. Crack on. Job done.

At least, that was how it usually went.

But not today.

He was around the back, grunting his way up the shaky ladder towards a bedroom window, when the hose of his brush trailing behind him snagged on the corner of the house. He gave it a couple of tugs, then a flick that freed it from where it was caught on the masonry, and then continued the unsteady climb.

He saw it as soon as his head rose above the sill.

A woman's bare arse, both barrels pointed his way.

'Oh, Jesus Christ,' he muttered, dropping back down a step. The metal rung creaked beneath his weight.

He pressed the back of his hand against his mouth, stifling a schoolboy snort.

This was new.

He'd heard about this sort of thing happening, of course. Everyone had. There was an assumption that window cleaners were constantly getting an eyeful of nude women, or couples shagging, or whatever else people's sordid imaginations might conjure up.

The reality was, though, that the closest George had ever come to an erotic encounter while on the job was a naked, red-faced, nineteen-stone man having a shite in a downstairs bathroom with the window wide open to let out the smell.

Their eyes had met as George appeared at the gap with his brush in hand. The shock had worked wonders for the lad sitting on the toilet, though, and whatever blockage he'd been struggling with cleared in one explosive instant.

Other than that, though, *what the window cleaner saw* was generally just lazy bastards lounging around with their feet up.

His eyes crept back to the window above him. He shouldn't look, of course. Looking would be wrong.

Peeking, though? Peeking would be all right. Just a quick one to make sure he hadn't imagined things. Maybe a quick photo. Nothing perverted, just to show the wife. She'd never believe him otherwise. He'd delete it right away.

He balanced there on the ladder for a moment, considering this.

No, a photo would be out of order. But a quick look would be all right, just to be certain of what he'd seen.

He carefully inched his way back up a rung, head lowered so he wouldn't be seen just yet. Not until he was ready.

He got himself into position, gripped the side of the ladder with his free hand, then popped up quickly.

Sure enough, there she was. Head down, arse up on the bed. George bit his lip, stifling the rising urge to giggle again. She was wearing silky black underwear that had been pulled down to just above her knees.

There were handcuffs, he noticed, securing her wrists to her ankles. This kept her arms down by her sides, and meant her face was pressed against the bed.

Unnaturally against the bed.

A reflection in the mirror at the side of the room caught his attention. The woman's reflected image stared back at him, her eyes and mouth open, a dark swell of blood and bruising staining the ice-white skin of her face.

George recoiled as he realised what he was looking at.

He recoiled fifteen feet in the air, balanced atop a shoogly ladder.

And with the look of terror in the woman's eyes burning brightly in his brain, George Rodger—weekday window cleaner, weekend rock star—plunged, screaming, towards the ground.

Chapter 2

Detective Chief Inspector Jack Logan sat on one of the high stools in his kitchen, slurping on tea and munching his way through something that could, with a bit of imagination, be described as an omelette. There were definitely eggs involved, judging by the smell of the thing, although their fluffy yellow colour had been turned a shade of ash grey by the oily residue of the mushrooms he'd fried in the same pan.

He swivelled away from the breakfast bar as the door opened behind him, and flashed a smile at a sleepy-looking Shona Maguire.

She'd been on a late shift at the hospital the night before, and had decompressed when she got home by slumping in front of the telly and channel surfing.

Her surfing had brought her to the Keanu Reeves and Patrick Swayze movie, *Point Break*, on ITV3, and she'd been left with no choice but to watch the remaining seventy-odd minutes in their entirety before finally heading to bed.

It was, after all, a stone-cold classic. So she'd insisted, anyway. Logan hadn't really seen the appeal, and had cleared off to bed shortly before midnight.

'Morning,' he said, and the upbeat timbre of it made Shona pause.

She blinked in surprise when he leaned over from the stool and planted a kiss on her forehead.

'Someone's cheerful this morning,' she said, suspicion sharpening her up a little.

Logan shrugged. 'No more than usual.'

'Ah, come on now, *any* level of cheerful whatsoever from you in the morning is more than the usual. On a *Monday*, too. God Almighty. What's brought this on?'

'Nothing,' he said, quickly birling himself back around to the breakfast bar and changing the subject. 'You want an omelette? I could rustle you one up.'

'Is that what that is?' Shona asked. Her Irish accent was always a fraction stronger when she was tired, and today was no exception. She scrunched up her nose as she peered at the shapeless, discoloured lump on Logan's plate. 'I thought it was, like, a placenta or something. Or, like, you know, a cancerous organ.'

Logan regarded his breakfast in silence for a moment.

'Well, cheers for that,' he eventually replied, before immediately getting stuck back into it.

Shona crossed to the kettle and clicked it on. 'I mean, fair play to you for eating it,' she said. 'And, coming from me, that's saying something.'

'You will usually eat any old shite,' Logan conceded.

'Famously so,' Shona agreed. 'It's like my whole thing.' She shrugged. 'Well, that and being an excellent pathologist and all round just fantastic person. But that?' She pointed to his plate. 'I wouldn't even feed that to the dog. Speaking of which…?'

'Back garden,' Logan said, jabbing a fork in the direction of the door. 'He was being a mooching wee bastard.'

'What, for a bite of that thing? That's concerning. Maybe he's got distemper, or rabies, or something.' She glanced out of the window, searching for him. 'You check the gate was closed?'

'Does it matter?' Logan asked.

'Well, he might run away.'

'Chance'd be a fine thing. Anyway, you've that bloody GPS tracking system on him. We'll get him back.'

Shona rolled her eyes. 'It's not a GPS tracking system. It's an AirTag collar. Which means, yes, I can track where he is.'

'How does it work?'

7

'Well, sure, yes, granted, I assume it probably uses GPS, but it's hardly what I'd call a GPS tracking system!'

Logan nodded slowly. 'What would you call it, then?'

'Well, I mean, it's a—' Shona hesitated. 'Does it matter? It won't stop him getting run over if he's escaped outside and… Oh. No. There he is.' She grimaced and turned away from the window. 'Great. He's taking a shite. Just what I wanted to see first thing in the morning. And does he have to hold eye contact like that?'

'Pity your tracking system didn't warn you about that.'

'What are you talking about? How would that even work? That's not how they work. Sure, you wouldn't be tracking some fella lost in the mountains going, "Here, we'd better not swoop in and rescue him yet, lads, he's taking a dump."'

A yawn almost split the pathologist's head in two across the middle. She rubbed her eyes with the back of a hand.

'Man alive, I'm tired,' she muttered.

'Maybe you shouldn't have stayed up so late watching that film.'

Shona scowled at him as the kettle rolled to a boil. 'You take that back. Not watch *Point Break*? What am I, an animal? Keanu Reeves? Patrick Swayze? God rest his soul.' She glanced briefly towards the ceiling, then held her hands up as if to fend off any further discussion. 'I had no choice in the matter. It was out of my control. Could've done without being so knackered today, though.'

'Why? What's today?' Logan asked, juggling a wobbly lump of grey egg around inside his mouth. He took a swig of tea that quickly took care of the problem.

'Today's Neville day,' Shona announced.

'Oh. Aye. Course. The new assistant. I'm sure he'll be fine.'

'Well, I'm sure he won't be.'

'How come?'

'He's called Neville, for a start. The only Neville I was previously aware of was in Harry Potter, and he was a big useless bastard, then he died. Is that what I've got in store?'

'That'd be a hell of a first day.' Logan chewed thoughtfully. 'Neville Chamberlain. He's another one. Former Prime Minister.'

'Oh, yeah?' Shona picked up the kettle, then paused. 'He's not the potato famine one, is he? Because that'd be all I'd fecking need.'

Logan ran his tongue around his teeth, dislodging bits of omelette while he gave this some consideration. 'No. He's best known for appeasing Hitler, I think.'

'Oh, great! Well, that's ideal, isn't it? A bumbling Nazi apologist who ups and dies on me out of the blue. That'll help tremendously with the old workload, so it will.'

Logan laughed. He scooped up a final forkful of the grey egg-based monstrosity on his plate, shoved it in his mouth, then rose from the chair.

'Aye, well, good luck with it. I'd better be getting off,' he announced, and Shona noted for the first time that he was fully dressed in his work shirt and tie.

'Jesus, you're keen. It's barely eight. Has there been a shout or something?'

'What?' Logan shook his head as he dumped his plate in the dishwasher. He swallowed the last morsel of his breakfast. 'No.'

'Right. So, why the rush?'

Logan's hesitation went on for just a moment too long. 'No reason. Just thought I'd get a head start.'

Shona's eyes narrowed in suspicion. 'You're up to something, Jack Logan. I can tell.'

'I'm not,' Logan protested. 'What would I be—'

Shona inhaled sharply. 'Wait!' she cried, stabbing an accusing finger at him.

Logan tensed. He watched the realisation spreading across Shona's face, before settling into something deeply smug and patronising.

Shite.

'Aw, bless. You're all excited,' she cooed.

'Excited? To get to work? Why would I be excited?'

'It's today, isn't it?'

Logan made a show of patting his pockets, checking for his keys and his wallet.

'Today?' he said. 'I don't know what you're on about. What's today?'

'Ah, come on!' Shona took a jar of instant coffee from a cupboard, tried unsuccessfully to twist open the lid, then passed it across to Logan. 'You know full bloody well what today is. That's what all this, this'—she pointed at him with a teaspoon, waggling it up and down—'*keenness* is about.'

Logan pulled a thoughtful face, then opened the jar with a single effortless twist, and handed it back. 'I honestly don't know what you're on about,' he told her.

Shona dumped two big heaped teaspoons of coffee granules into a mug, then sloshed on the hot water, grinning at Logan the whole way through.

'Fine. We'll play it that way, then,' she said. She replaced the kettle on the worktop with a *clunk*, and reached for the open bag of sugar. 'But, for what it's worth, I think it's fecking adorable…'

–

Detective Constable Tyler Neish was having a bit of bother with his tie. Specifically, he'd forgotten how to tie the bloody thing.

In his defence, it had been almost three months since he'd last had to wear one, and he'd previously always just left it slackened off enough so he could pull it over his head.

Not only was he out of practice, but he was having to tie it from scratch, and while he had a vague idea of what he was doing—wrap, under, over, loop and pull—the more intricate details of it were proving elusive.

There was no point in asking Sinead. She had her hands full with the twins this morning.

Then again, she always had her hands full with the twins.

Being a parent was a joyous and magical adventure, but Lauren and Cal were being a right pair of gurning wee arseholes today.

It probably didn't help that Tyler's alarm had woken them both at just after six o'clock—a mere eighteen minutes after Sinead had successfully wrestled them back to sleep—but it was his first day back to work, and he didn't want to be late.

'Maybe you should get one of them clip-ons.'

Tyler shifted his gaze in the hall mirror until he spotted Harris standing in the kitchen doorway. He was leaning against the frame, slurping his way through a bowl of cereal, grinning like he'd just cracked the ultimate funny.

Sinead's wee brother was now nothing of the sort. He was half an inch taller than Sinead, which made him more or less level with Tyler. His vocal cords, which had been going bananas over the past year, had now bedded down into a near-monotone low drone that worked wonders for sending the babies to sleep.

It had a similar effect on Tyler, too.

'I don't need a clip-on,' Tyler insisted. Hoping to prove his point, he attacked the tie again, twisting and contorting it in a big sudden rush of activity, like he might be able to catch it off guard.

He grimaced as he twisted his thumb and forefinger together in the material, then muttered below his breath while he unravelled it all again.

'Seriously, get a clip-on. I've still got that one Sinead got me for school.' He inhaled some more cereal and his grin widened. 'But I don't need it, because I'm not a div.'

'Shut it, you,' Tyler warned. 'And have you seen the time? You're going to be late!'

Harris twisted his wrist to check his watch, then jumped back and cried out as he sloshed a big splash of sugar-infused milk down the front of his trousers.

'Can't believe you fell for that.' Tyler smirked and turned back to his reflection in the mirror. 'Now who's the div?'

While Harris mumped and moaned his way upstairs to get changed, Tyler manipulated both ends of the tie into something that very nearly looked correct. It wasn't perfect by any stretch of the imagination, but unlike the previous six attempts, it didn't look like it had been tied by someone who'd recently lost both thumbs in an industrial accident.

Sod it. It would do.

He headed for the living room, then stopped when he heard the approaching footsteps and tuneless whistle of the postman.

A quick glance at the stairs confirmed that Harris wasn't watching. Tyler rushed to grab the letters that came slithering in through the slot in the door.

There were six in total, two of them junk. The other four had his name on them, red 'Urgent' and 'Final Demand' stamps marking the top right corner. He folded them all in half and shoved them hastily into the inside pocket of his jacket, which hung from a hook on the wall by the front door.

He spent a moment composing himself, then plastered on a smile and went strutting through to the living room.

'Right, that's just about me,' he announced, throwing open the door.

He froze when he saw the look on Sinead's face, balanced as it was between horror and hatred. She sat in the middle seat of the three-seater couch, a baby asleep on either side of her.

Well, they had been asleep, at least. Tyler's entrance made them both kick their legs and jerk their arms in fright, and their petted lips warned him of what was to come.

They might be small, but by Christ, they could make a racket. Their screams were ragged and hoarse, a night of endless crying having taken its toll on the soft lining of their throats.

'Sorry!' Tyler whispered, though the damage was already done. 'I forgot!'

'You forgot what? That you had children?' Sinead shot back.

She looked tired. That was fair enough, though, because she *was* tired. She had to be. It had been months since she'd had a full night's sleep.

The all-night sobbing was new, but the babies hadn't seemed particularly keen on sleeping since day one, and even the power of Harris's post-puberty monotone had its limits.

Sinead had breastfed on her own for the first month, until her increasing rage at the sight of Tyler sound asleep in bed beside her had made her invest in a pump and some bottles.

Now, they were both in a near-permanent state of exhaustion, sniped at one another constantly, and couldn't sit down for more than five minutes without falling asleep.

But Tyler wouldn't change it for the world.

'Off you go, get yourself a cup of tea and some breakfast,' he said, offering her a hand. 'I'll deal with this pair.'

'It's fine. You need to get sorted for work,' Sinead replied, but he beckoned her with a curve of a finger, like he was inviting her onto the dance floor. She sighed, smiled, then let herself be dragged to her feet. 'I could do with something to eat, right enough.'

'Aye, well, I hope you're not after cereal. I think your brother's wolfed his way through that.'

Sinead rolled her eyes. 'I'll find something.'

Tyler slid onto her spot on the couch, put a hand on each of the babies' bellies, and *shh-shh-shhh'd* as he rocked them.

'Thanks. Won't be long,' Sinead said. She started to move away, then stopped and pointed at his neck. 'You know your tie's messed up, yeah?'

Tyler fixed a smile in place. 'Yeah. I know. Just threw it on. I still need to fix it properly.'

Sinead raised an eyebrow. Then, she bent down and spent all of three seconds fiddling with the knot before straightening up again.

'There,' she announced. 'All done. What would you do without me?'

'Look like a div,' Tyler replied.

Sinead snorted out a laugh. 'Aye, well, come on. I'm not a miracle worker.'

She lowered her voice as Tyler's rocking eased the grumbling twins, then gestured towards the kitchen as their eyelids grew heavy.

'Two minutes,' she whispered.

'Take your time,' he urged, still gently rocking the dozing infants back and forth on the couch.

She mouthed out a silent *thank you* then crept out into the hall and tiptoed to the kitchen.

A plate sat on the table, a stack of slightly burned and oddly oblong pancakes piled up on it. Beside it sat a glass of orange juice with droplets of condensation clinging to the sides, and a big mug of lightly steaming tea.

In the middle of the table, in a narrow vase, was a single red rose.

Sinead beamed as she pulled out the chair and lowered herself onto it. She took a gulp of the juice first, the sharpness and the cold helping to take the edge off her sleep deprivation.

The pancakes smelled good. So good, in fact, that she was prepared to overlook the stack of dishes that hadn't quite managed to make their way to the dishwasher, and what looked like half a bag of flour that lay scattered across the worktops and floor.

Through the thin walls of their home, Sinead heard her husband singing softly to their son and daughter.

'What would I do without him?' she whispered, then she picked up her knife and fork, and got stuck in to her breakfast.

Chapter 3

Tyler paused to take a breath at the double doors of the MIT offices at Burnett Road Police Station. He straightened his tie, then grinned in anticipation of the rush of activity that Sinead had been certain would await him when he stepped inside.

Instead of the expected cheers and party poppers, he was met by the slow, steady, *clack-clack* of PC Dave Davidson's one-fingered typing. He sat in his wheelchair at his desk near the door, logging something or other in the system.

The rest of the room was empty, the computers off, the chairs pushed in under the desks.

Tyler's gaze returned to Dave, who still hadn't looked up from his screen.

'All right, mate?' the detective constable ventured.

Dave held up his typing finger, indicating he'd be right with him, then went back to pecking away at the keys.

Tyler looked around again, just in case he'd missed anyone.

Nope.

It suddenly occurred to him that the bastards would be creeping up the corridor behind him! They'd probably have a cake!

Not wanting to ruin the surprise, he kept his back to the door and braced himself for the excitement.

Across the room, the unsteady rhythm of Dave's typing continued.

After almost a full minute of waiting, Tyler stole a glance back at the door. There was no movement beyond the frosted glass. No sound of footsteps or whispering from out in the corridor.

Nothing.

He shrugged off his jacket and hung it on the back of his chair. His mug was there on his desk, and as he leaned over, he saw a moss of blue mould clinging to the bottom.

'Jesus,' he remarked, picking it up by the handle. He turned to Dave. 'Did nobody think to wash this out for—'

Dave raised his finger again, indicating that he wasn't yet done.

Tyler sighed. So much for his triumphant return.

He moved towards the door, mug in hand, then was stopped by the sound of Dave clearing his throat. When he looked back, the constable was still staring at his screen, but was now waggling his mug around to make it clear that he'd appreciate a top-up.

With a tut of annoyance, Tyler took the mug, and was thanked with a raised thumb from the man in the wheelchair.

Both mugs in hand, Tyler left the office, hung a right, and trudged along the corridor in the direction of the tea room.

On the way, he passed a couple of the CID boys and smiled hopefully in their direction. They were deep in conversation about how their respective weekends had gone, though, and didn't so much as glance his way as they swept past.

No great loss. They were a couple of arseholes, anyway.

But, still. Was a nod in his direction really too much to ask?

He found the compact tea room exactly where he'd left it. There was a tea trolley outside, stacked high with cups and saucers. That was new. When had they brought that in? How did it work? Did the tea now come to them? That would save his legs a bit. Maybe he'd no longer have to listen to shouts of, 'Oi! Tea Bitch!' from any of the senior detectives.

Or, when she came back to work, from his wife.

He was still wondering about the technicalities of the new scheme when he opened the door to the tea room, and was immediately assaulted by a roar, and the blinding flash of an explosion.

'Jesus Christ!' he yelped.

Something hit him in the face, and he staggered backwards, arms flailing, the echo of a bellowed, 'Surprise!' ringing in his ears.

The voice of Tammi-Jo, the DC brought in to replace Sinead while she was on maternity leave, rang out.

'Oh, God! Oh my God!' she squealed. 'I shot him in the face!'

Tyler stumbled backwards into something. He heard Dave Davidson shout, 'Careful, mate!' from somewhere beside and below him, then he toppled into the tea trolley, sending himself and several dozen cups, saucers and teaspoons crashing to the ground.

The noise was something extraordinary, a hundred or more individual smashes, clunks, bangs and bumps all erupting at almost exactly the same moment.

When his vision cleared, Tyler looked up to see DCI Logan, DI Ben Forde and DS Hamza Khaled all standing over him, looking down. DC Tammi-Jo Swanney stood behind Ben, one hand over her mouth, the other still clutching a discharged party popper.

On the wall of the tea room, the words, 'Welcome Back!' hung on a shiny silver banner.

Logan raised an eyebrow. It pulled the corresponding corner of his mouth up into a suggestion of a smirk.

'Well,' the big man intoned. 'That didn't quite work out as expected.'

'You all right, mate?' Hamza asked.

Tyler nodded. 'I mean, I'm on the floor with a load of broken cups, and I'm half-blind…'

'My fault. Totally my fault. I got over-excited,' Tammi-Jo announced, the words spitting out of her like bullets. 'Sorry, sorry, sorry!'

'It's fine,' Tyler said, shuffling himself up onto his elbows. 'I mean, who needs both eyes, anyway?'

He grabbed onto the toppled trolley to pull himself up the rest of the way. His weight made the whole thing tip over again, raining the last of the saucers and teaspoons and half a bag of sugar down on top of him.

Logan let out a chuckle. 'And to think,' he said, extending a shovel-like hand in Tyler's direction, 'some of us actually missed you.'

He heaved the DC to his feet, brushed some broken crockery off his shoulder, then patted him on the back and steered him towards the canteen, where a big plate of bacon, square sausage, and black pudding rolls awaited.

Despite the indignities of the last few moments, Tyler smiled. 'Is that for me?'

'Well, no' bloody all of them,' Logan said. 'But, aye. Some of the others thought it would be good to do you a wee welcome back breakfast. Seemed a bit over the top to me.'

DI Forde shot Logan a sideways look. 'That's no' quite how I remember it, Jack,' he said, then he put an arm around Tyler's shoulders. 'And don't you worry about this mess out here, son,' he continued, glancing back at the pile of smashed crockery.

'Cheers, boss,' Tyler said.

Ben pulled him in closer, turning the shoulder grab into a hug. 'There'll be plenty of time for you to clean it up later.'

'Eh, cheers, boss,' Tyler said again, although with a bit less enthusiasm this time.

They all grabbed rolls, poured the teas and coffees, and shuffled into the closest they could get to comfortable positions in the compact room.

There were only two chairs, both ancient and uncomfortable things. The tea room wasn't meant for hanging about in. Usually, you came in, made a brew, and left. But, they made the most of it, leaning against walls, or sitting on the counter as they ate and caught up on what had been going on over the past few months.

Not that there was a lot of catching up necessary. Most of them had been round to the house two or three times while Tyler was on his paternity leave. Hamza's whole family had paid a visit. Logan had brought Shona round, too.

She in particular had fussed over the babies to the extent that Tyler could've sworn he saw Logan breaking into a sweat.

Even Tammi-Jo had popped in to drop off a couple of teddies she'd bought. The twins had seemed quite taken by her—Cal in particular. He'd sat there in his bouncy chair, staring at her, seemingly smitten by her shining blonde curls and bright blue eyes.

Either that, or he was just wondering if she was ever going to shut the fuck up.

But, still, even though none of them had really been strangers these past few months, this was good. Catching up like this? Laughing together? This was nice.

Of course, it couldn't last. It never did.

'There you are,' said Detective Superintendent Mitchell, appearing in the doorway with ninja-like stealth. It was a simple three-word statement, yet she managed to make it sound like a reprimand.

'Just throwing a wee welcome back party for DC Neish, ma'am,' Logan said, indicating the banner on the wall with a tilt of his head.

Mitchell's gaze flitted to the sign, darted around the room, then settled back on Logan. 'Why not do it in the office?'

'Because that wouldn't have been a surprise,' Logan reasoned.

Mitchell indicated the carpet of broken crockery on the corridor floor.

'And I take it this was?'

Tammi-Jo gingerly raised a hand. 'I shot him in the face, ma'am. It was my fault. I've never been allowed party poppers before, and I got a bit carried away. I thought I'd killed him. Well, not killed him, but blinded him, maybe. Which, you know, I'd have felt really bad about, and—'

Beside her, Logan quietly cleared his throat. It had taken a bit of training over the past few months, but she picked up on the signal and stopped herself from saying any more by cramming half a dry bread roll into her mouth.

'We'll clean it up,' Ben promised. 'Just didn't want the food getting cold.'

'Forget it,' Mitchell said, dismissing the suggestion with a shake of her head. 'You've got more important things to worry about.'

Logan groaned. 'Oh, God. Seriously? Today?'

'Afraid so.' Mitchell thrust a torn-off page of a notebook in his direction. 'Just north of Spean Bridge. Woman. Window cleaner found her.'

She turned to Tyler, who hurriedly forced down a half-chewed mouthful of bacon roll in anticipation of having to respond.

'Welcome back, Detective Constable,' she told him. Her smile was businesslike, but genuine. 'But I'm afraid the celebration is going to have to wait.'

Chapter 4

They made the trip south alone, for the most part, each of them in their own cars, with the exception of Tammi-Jo, who Logan had somehow found himself saddled with.

He liked the lassie. He did. She was… sweet. That was generally something he didn't have much time for, but on her, it worked. More importantly, she was shaping up to be a promising detective.

But by Christ, she could talk.

Even Taggart, who usually sat up attentively on long journeys, the fur of his head just visible over the top of the back seat, was lying down out of sight. Probably with his paws over his ears, Logan reckoned.

'I mean, for a horrible minute, I genuinely thought I'd blinded him. Or disfigured him, anyway. Imagine that! First day back at work and your colleague has your eye out with a party popper. Some start to the day that would've been. I'd never be able to look him in the face again. He'd look like a pirate. And what would I have told Sinead? She'd hate me. His babies would grow up thinking I'm a right cow. And rightly so!'

'Aye. Still, all good,' Logan said. He turned the radio up a notch or two, hoping she would take the hint.

She did not.

'Would he have got compensation? For losing an eye? I mean, it wasn't exactly in the call of duty, was it?' She gasped so deeply Logan would've sworn the oxygen level inside the car dropped sharply. 'Would I have had to pay it? That'd probably be millions. Getting your eye shot out. You probably get millions for that. I couldn't afford that! I'd have to get a second job, and even then, that wouldn't make a dent in it. Unless I got a job, you know...' She made a sort of beckoning motion with one hand, like she was trying to draw the rest of the sentence out of the ether somewhere. 'Being Rihanna.'

And so it went for most of the journey. She lurched wildly from talk of Tyler's eye to the cost-of-living crisis, then onto what she'd had for dinner the night before, a round-up of her six favourite TV shows, and why she'd never wear a green hat, even on special occasions.

Except maybe St Patrick's Day. Apparently, the jury was still out on that one.

By the time they pulled up at the cordon tape blocking the driveway of the house where the body had been found, Logan's head was so fit for bursting that he all but fell out of the car in his rush to get away.

He was unsurprised to see Shona's car already parked just inside the flapping line of blue and white tape. She'd texted him shortly after Mitchell's announcement, letting him know she was heading to the scene.

The van that ferried the Scene of Crime team around was a little further up the drive, the sliding side door open despite a smirr of fuzzy rain. A trio of figures in white paper suits poked around in the house's expansive garden, a few plastic yellow marker tents indicating where they'd noted points of interest.

An ambulance sat parked up and waiting, ready to move the body once everyone had done their bit. A couple of paramedics sat up front. They were both eating, but since Logan had no idea what shift they were on, he didn't know if it was breakfast, lunch or even a late supper.

He nodded to the two Uniforms standing guard at the tape, then tossed one his keys. 'There'll be more of us coming. Park that up somewhere, will you, son?'

The constable caught the keys, then tapped his hat and nodded. 'Will do, sir.'

Tammi-Jo turned to watch the officer heading for the BMW. 'How come you let him drive it, and not me?'

'Because to the best of my knowledge, he's never shot a colleague in the face with a party popper at point-blank range,' Logan replied, then he lifted the cordon tape, motioned for her to duck under, and followed behind.

The house wasn't grand, exactly, but it was aspiring towards it. It was a big grey block of a thing, with a porch dead in the centre that housed a double front door. Oak, Logan thought, studded with decorative metal rivets.

Ivy covered some of the wall at the front, and crept around the sides. It meant that, at first glance, the place looked stately and impressive, and it distracted from the slightly sagging roof and the rusted metal guttering.

As Logan and Tammi-Jo approached the house, one of the front doors opened. Shona emerged with the SOC head honcho, Geoff Palmer, trailing in her wake like a bad smell.

She picked up the pace when she spotted Logan, and Palmer's stubby legs were forced to work overtime to keep up.

'Oh. There's Shona,' Tammi-Jo whispered, as if Logan could somehow have missed her.

'Aye,' he confirmed.

'Should I look away? Are you two going to want to, you know, kiss or something?'

Logan fired a look back over his shoulder at her. 'Eh?'

'I don't want to just be standing there watching. That'd be weird. I mean, not that there's anything wrong with it, even at your age, I just… I don't want it to be awkward.'

'We're not going to kiss,' Logan replied. He scowled. 'And what the hell do you mean, *even at my age?*'

The two groups met on the path before she could answer, much to her relief. Logan could tell from the strain on Shona's face that the inside of the house had been rough, though he

23

wasn't sure yet if that was because of the body, or the company she'd been forced to keep.

Palmer noticed the detectives for what appeared to be the first time—for a man tasked with finding evidence, he could be worryingly unobservant sometimes—and his focus immediately switched from Shona to Tammi-Jo.

'Well, hello,' he said, beaming at her. 'We meet again!'

As usual, he had the hood of his white paper suit up, the elasticated trim gripping his face so all they could see of him was a circle of greasy skin and yellow teeth. He'd secured it badly under his chin, so it pushed up a roll of fat that curved like a smile around his long-lost jawline.

'First on the scene, I see,' he continued, still leering at the young DC and completely ignoring the senior officer by her side. 'Keen. That's nice to see. Rare in a young person, too. It's really quite refreshing.'

'Cut the shite, Geoff,' Logan said. 'You're old enough to be her father. Or, actually, no, more like her creepy uncle that nobody in the family likes to talk about.'

Tammi-Jo nodded, her nostrils flaring, her eyes taking on a faraway sort of look. 'Uncle Clive.'

Logan shot her a sideways look. 'What?'

'Hm? Nothing. Carry on,' she urged, beaming brightly from ear to ear.

Palmer didn't need telling twice. He snorted, finally raising his eyes to meet Logan's scowl. His smile stayed plastered in place. 'That's rich. I'm younger than you.'

'Fuck off!' Shona cried, then she slapped a hand over her mouth, her eyes silently screaming an apology. 'I'm so sorry. That just came out. I meant… Are you? Honestly?'

'Course I am!' Palmer replied, with a note of incredulity in his voice. 'Of course I'm younger than him! Look at him!'

Both women turned to look at Logan, then back at Geoff. From their expressions, both remained wholly unconvinced.

'Yeah, but seriously, though?' Tammi-Jo asked.

'Yes! Seriously!' Palmer was still holding onto the smile for the young detective's benefit, but it was starting to slip through his fingers. 'Why? How old do you think I am?'

'Fifty-eight,' Tammi-Jo guessed without a moment's hesitation.

'*Fifty…?!* Shut up. You do not!' Palmer cried. 'I'm forty-three.'

Tammi-Jo's laugh was a short, staccato sort of thing that died away almost as quickly as it had started. 'Oh. You're being serious.'

'Yes! Of course I'm being bloody serious. I don't look anywhere near fifty!'

'Well, no. I know. That's why I said fifty-eight,' Tammi-Jo reasoned.

Palmer's smile had been consigned to the annals of history now. He crossed his arms petulantly across his chest. This made the suit ride up, further pancaking the roll of flab against the underside of his chin.

'Well, you're wrong, actually. Because I don't look fifty-eight,' he insisted. 'So, there. Joke's on you.'

A silence hung in the air between them. Finally, Logan sucked in his bottom lip, spat it out, then raised both eyebrows.

'Aye. She's definitely the laughing stock in this situation, right enough,' he said.

Behind him, back beyond the cordon tape, Hamza and Tyler pulled up in their cars.

Logan gave them a quick wave, then asked Tammi-Jo to go and meet them and follow Hamza's lead.

Palmer watched her hurry back down the path towards the new arrivals. He shook his head, a disgusted expression on his face. It was very clear from the angle of his eyeline, though, that he was checking out her arse.

'I mean, *fifty-eight*. Of all the bloody cheeks,' he mumbled, somewhat distracted by the view. He shook his head. '*Cheek*, I mean. Of all the cheek. Anyway, she's one to talk about ages. How old is she meant to be? Twelve?'

'I bloody well hope not, the way you're perving at her,' Logan said, shifting his weight to one side, blocking the Scene of Crime man's view.

He turned to Shona, and made it very clear that he was now pretending Palmer wasn't even there.

'Right, then,' he began, shooting a look to the house at the head of the path. 'What have we got?'

Palmer, apparently, could not take a hint.

'Oh, God,' he said before Shona could get a word in. His face lit up, his eyes widening. He stopped just short of rubbing his hands together with glee. 'This one's an absolute belter!'

Chapter 5

She'd been crying. That was what hit Logan the hardest.

Not how her semi-nakedness exposed her to the world, or how her position on the bed robbed her of any dignity in death.

The fact that she'd been crying.

He could see the dried tracks of her tears rolling sideways across her nose and over her temple. Little crusts of white that would go unnoticed by most people, but which made something writhe in the pit of his stomach.

Her wrists and ankles were badly bruised, and marked by deep red welts where the metal of the cuffs that bound them together had been cutting in.

She'd cried. She'd struggled. Begged, probably.

And none of it had done her any good.

'See!' Palmer ejected. 'What did I tell you? Arse to the wind! Don't see that every day, do you? Quite an unfortunate ending to what looked like an otherwise thoroughly good time!'

'Jesus, Geoff,' Shona muttered.

'Well, I'm just saying! She must've got into that position herself in the first place, so clearly she was right up for it at some point.'

'Fuck off, Palmer,' Logan barked, the words rising unbidden from the pit of his stomach. He didn't look at the man. He couldn't. Didn't dare.

Even so, he could almost picture the bastard's big red plook of a face puckering up in outrage. 'I beg your pardon? You can't talk to me like that.'

Logan lunged. The movement would've been swift and sudden for a man half his size. Palmer recoiled and let out a whistling yelp through his nose, like the sound of a dog having a nightmare.

'Here! Here! Steady on! It was just a joke! That's what we do, isn't it? We make jokes, even at times like these! That's how we deal with this stuff!'

'Get out,' the DCI growled. 'Now.'

'Jack…' Shona began, trying to soothe his rising temper.

'I've got a job to do,' Palmer protested.

'And you can come back and do it when I tell you,' Logan told him. 'Now, get the hell out of this room, before I compromise the scene by driving you head first through that bloody window, you creepy, disrespectful, boil-headed bastard.'

Palmer glanced over at the window like he was picturing this turn of events playing out. From his expression, he clearly didn't like the looks of what he was seeing.

He huffed out a sigh. Then, without saying another word, pulled a crisp about-turn and marched out of the room.

He was halfway along the upstairs landing before he started muttering his defiance below his breath. Logan waited until his footsteps on the stairs had faded into silence before turning back to the body on the bed.

'You OK?' Shona asked.

Logan sighed and ran a hand down his face. 'Aye. That bastard just rubs me up the wrong way sometimes.' He gave this a moment's thought. 'And by sometimes, I mean all the time.'

'Oh, I hear that,' Shona said.

'What are we looking at?' Logan asked, gesturing to the dead woman. He turned away when Shona started to reply, taking in the bedroom around them.

'Suffocated, I think. Though her neck seems to be broken. I'll need to X-ray to confirm, but it's pretty much a given, going by the angle her head's at. There's some hair missing from the

28

back of her scalp there. Someone pulled out a handful. Probably while they were…'

Logan had been looking out of the window into the back garden. A ladder was leaned up against the sill. A brush and an upturned bucket lay on the grass at the bottom.

He turned back to the pathologist.

'You think she was sexually assaulted?'

'I mean, I suppose it could've been consensual. To start with. Geoff has a point. Not easy getting someone into that position against their will.'

'You'd be surprised what people will do when they're scared,' Logan said. 'Someone could've coerced her.'

'Well, whatever happened, it looks like whoever was with her got violent.' She coughed quietly, like she was struggling a little with the next part. 'There's bleeding that suggests anal intercourse took place. Quite aggressively, too. I'll know more when I get her back to the hospital.'

'Jesus Christ.' Logan squeezed his temples, a headache already starting to form. 'Any thoughts on time of death yet?'

Shona indicated the colouring of the dead woman's face, and the way the capillaries on the cheek closest to the bed had bloomed red and purple beneath her skin.

'I'd say she's been dead around ten to twelve hours. So, between eleven last night and one this morning.'

Logan nodded slowly, then went back to checking out the room. Palmer's team hadn't given it a going over yet, and he and Shona were both wearing protective footwear and gloves to reduce the risk of contamination. Small stepping mats had been placed down to further protect the integrity of the scene.

The room was nothing much to write home about. A large, old-fashioned dressing table was cluttered with perfumes, deodorants, face creams and assorted hair products. Beside it, a single chair was stacked high with clothes that hadn't quite made it to the drawers or wardrobe yet.

There were two bedside tables. Lamps on both. A Kindle eReader sat on one, a battered paperback copy of *Bravo Two Zero* by Andy McNab on the other.

Logan turned back to the dresser and plucked a can of Lynx Africa deodorant from the mass of bottles and canisters with his gloved fingers. He set it down again, then crossed to the other side of the bed and checked the victim's left hand.

'She was married.'

'Right. Well, I guess you've got your chief suspect, then,' Shona reasoned.

Logan chewed on his bottom lip, looking around the room again. 'Aye. Maybe.'

There was a painting on the wall of a beach, the azure water cresting as foamy white horses against the yellow sand and smooth grey rocks. Logan could see the ridges of the paint, and the strokes of the brush that marked it as an original.

It was also not very good. He was no artist, but give him a couple of weeks' run-up and a selection of brushes, and he reckoned he could do something to a similar standard.

Was it the woman's work? Her husband's? More likely that, than them having paid anyone for the thing.

Some fingerprints were visible on the glass around the edges, where the pane met the frame. Probably nothing, but he'd flag it to Palmer, anyway.

He was about to turn away when something else caught his eye. It was just below the painting, sticking out from the wall but almost invisible. Had he not been looking so closely at the picture, he'd never have spotted it.

'Sellotape,' he announced.

Shona was down on her haunches, studying the body. She looked up at him, confused. 'Sorry?'

'There's a bit of Sellotape here. Stuck to the wall.'

'Could've been there for ages.'

'Looks new,' Logan said. He bent towards the pillows and twisted his neck so he was looking up. 'Can't miss it from down here. They'd have seen it.' He straightened again. 'You wouldn't leave that there. Take half a second to pull it off.'

'So, what are you thinking it is?'

Logan scratched at his chin, the rubber gloves creaking as the fingers flexed and stretched.

'Don't know yet,' he admitted, looking around the room again. 'But I think maybe there was something stuck there. Recently.'

Shona frowned. 'How recently are we talking?'

'Don't know. But, at a guess, I'd say within the last ten to twelve hours,' Logan replied, echoing her comment on the time of death.

He crossed the room again and opened the wardrobe. A few summer dresses were hanging up, along with several near-identical pale blue shirts, and an assortment of his and her coats and jackets.

He nudged a few of them aside, half-hoping he'd find a killer hiding in there. All he saw was the back of the wardrobe, though, and he let the clothes swish back into place.

Closing the door, he gave the room another once-over, then directed his attention to the victim. Her head was turned away from him, revealing the bald patch on her scalp. Her reflection stared back at him in the dressing-table mirror.

She'd begged for her life, he thought. Now, it felt like she was begging him to avenge the loss of it.

Even from that distance, even in the reflection, he thought he could see the salty white tracks of her tears.

'Jack.'

His name was an urgent and breathless whisper on Shona's lips. He looked down to find her still on her haunches, shuffling back away from the bed.

'What is it?' he asked. 'What's wrong?'

'Jack, look.'

She pointed to the floor just below the bed, eyes locked on something lurking just beyond the curtain of shadow down there.

Logan joined her. His knees cracked as he lowered himself into a squat.

'What?' he asked, lowering his head to peer into the darkness. 'What are you… Oh. Jesus.'

There, on the floor, among the little balls of dust on the carpet, lay a plump, slug-like used condom.

–

DI Forde stood in the entrance foyer of Fort William Police Station, regarding the woman on the other side of the glass. She smiled at him, a big wide beamer of a thing that welcomed him in, and immediately made him feel right at home.

That wasn't right.

'Where's Moira?' he asked, the question coming out like a demand. 'Moira should be here.'

The woman, a willowy forty-something with a bob of brown hair, continued to smile, undaunted by the DI's reaction to her presence.

'I'm afraid Ms Corson is currently unavailable,' she said, her voice a lilting lullaby that danced from word to word.

Even as she spoke, the smile remained nailed in place. It looked genuine, and yet there was something unsettling about the sheer eagerness of it.

'What, is she off sick?' Ben probed.

'She's unavailable,' was all the woman would say, and Ben thought he detected a slight emphasis on that second word. 'But my name is Jennifer—hi—and I'm more than certain that I can provide any assistance you might need.'

Ben tapped a finger on the edge of the counter, then ran it along the length of the wood, like he was checking for dust.

'Eh, aye. DI Ben Forde. I'm here to set up the Incident Room for—'

'The incident up at Spean. Of course,' Jennifer said.

She thumbed a button, and a buzz indicated that the security door leading through to the station proper was now open.

'Just head on through, Detective Inspector,' she said, her voice still the same sing-song as before. She ratcheted her smile up another few notches. Ben winced at how painful it looked. 'And please, don't hesitate to call on me if there's *anything* you need.'

Hamza had things well in hand by the time Logan emerged from the house. They'd called Palmer back in, and Shona had hung around to point out what they'd spotted, for fear that Logan might yet throttle the bastard.

Tyler and Tammi-Jo had already been dispatched to talk to the neighbours. They lived several hundred feet away on both sides, though, so the chances of getting anything useful from them were slim.

Luckily, one of the local Uniforms had been able to provide some background. Hamza filled Logan in as they made their way towards the cordon tape at the bottom of the driveway.

'Victim's name is Sharon Simpson,' the DS announced, reading from his pad. 'Teacher at a primary school down in Fort William. We checked, and they confirmed that she didn't show up for work this morning, and no one has heard from her since yesterday.'

'Yesterday?' Logan frowned. 'Sunday?'

'A lot of the teachers are friends. They were out for lunch yesterday afternoon.'

'You get their names?'

Hamza nodded. 'I assumed you'd want us to talk to them.'

'Anything on the husband?'

'Watch where you're standing, sir,' Hamza warned. He pointed down at a smear of mud on the ground, where a yellow triangle marked the patterned imprint of a bicycle tyre.

They gave the tread a wide berth, then continued on towards the fluttering tape.

'Husband's name is Isaac,' Hamza said, flipping a page. 'He's a bit older than Sharon. She's late thirties, he's in his fifties, the constable reckons. Ex-army. Big bugger, from what I hear.'

Logan looked back at the house, then around the garden. There was one small hatchback car parked in the drive, with a window cleaner's van sitting behind it.

At the end of the drive, fixed to the wall of the house, was a small black box with a blue ring of light on the front. A charging point for an electric car.

'What's he do now?'

'He runs a travel website. About the Highlands, mostly. Where to go, what to see. That sort of thing. Mostly camping, I think.'

Logan turned back to the detective sergeant. 'Aye? And that's a full-time gig, is it?'

'Apparently so, yeah. Does pretty well at it, by all accounts.'

'Aye, well. Certainly bought him a big lump of a house. Do we know where he is?'

They didn't. No one had been able to get a number for him that didn't ring out in the living room of the house. They had an email address, and were working on finding a mobile number, but so far they were drawing a blank.

'We do have a car reg for him, and we've got an ANPR search running to see if he's been picked up anywhere.'

Logan nodded, but there wasn't any particular enthusiasm behind it. The automatic number plate recognition system was a powerful tool in the cities. Up here, though, the infrastructure that would make it useful just didn't exist. Unless he'd driven past a police car on a straight stretch of road, there was almost no chance of him popping up on the system.

'Who found her?' Logan asked, though the van and the abandoned ladder had already given him a pretty good idea.

'Window cleaner, sir.'

Logan nodded, his suspicions confirmed. 'Where is he now?'

'Hospital. When he called it in, he was screaming about having a broken arse,' Hamza explained. 'He fell off the ladder when he saw her. They took him in to get him checked out. Unlikely he'll be able to tell us much, but I said one of us might swing by A&E to talk to him.'

'Put Tyler on it. Nice easy one to break him back in.'

He looked over at the cordon tape. The two Uniforms were chatting away, shoulders hunched against the fine drizzle. Beyond them, a couple of cars slowed to ogle the scene as they passed, before speeding up again and continuing up the road towards Roy Bridge.

The detectives' cars were lined up at the side of the road just outside the tape. All but one of them.

'Where's Ben?' Logan asked. 'I thought he was right behind you?'

'DI Forde went straight through to the station in the Fort, sir,' Hamza said. 'He thought he'd start getting the room set up.'

Logan let out a pained-sounding grunt. 'And go and check in with his fancy woman, no doubt.'

'He didn't mention, sir,' Hamza said. He shuddered slightly at the thought of Moira Corson, the dragon-like guardian of the Fort William Police Station's front desk. 'But aye, maybe.'

Logan ran a hand down his face, sweeping away the water that had begun to accumulate in the crags and ridges.

'Not a lot more we can do here for now,' he said. 'When Tyler and Tammi-Jo get back, get Uniform checking the other neighbours further up the road. Maybe someone's got a doorbell camera or something. Give us a view of the road.'

'Fingers crossed, sir. I don't hold out much hope, though. I think this is more a "leave your door unlocked" sort of neighbourhood.'

'Aye, well. There's nosy bastards everywhere. Hopefully, one'll turn up. Send both DCs down the road, if you're all right hanging off here until Palmer and his team piss off.'

'No bother, sir,' Hamza confirmed, then something back up the path near the house caught his attention.

Logan followed his gaze and saw Shona coming hurtling towards them, pulling on her jacket, her car keys clutched in her hand.

'Neville!' she cried, as she raced past. 'I forgot about Neville!'

She stumbled down the driveway, got momentarily tangled in the cordon tape, then disappeared around the corner.

'Who's Neville?' Hamza asked.

They heard Shona's car engine roaring into life. The screeching of tyres was followed by the blast of a horn and a shouted apology from the pathologist that faded as she sped off.

'New assistant,' Logan explained. 'Today's his first day. I'm guessing he's currently sitting in an empty mortuary, reconsidering his life choices.'

'Whoops!' Hamza said. He flipped his notebook closed, but before he could pocket it, Logan held up a hand.

'Here. Wait. The plate you ran on the husband's car? Was it a Tesla?'

Hamza didn't need to check his notes for that one. 'Aye. It was, sir. Why?'

Logan nodded past the detective sergeant, to where a dark grey vehicle had silently drawn up to the tape. A man with a greying beard and thinning hair stared at all the police activity through eyes bulged wide by alarm.

'Because, unless I'm very much mistaken, I think we just found him.'

The man threw his door open and was half out of the car before Logan had finished talking. He was big—Logan-sized, even—and dressed in a range of mismatched army surplus gear, making him look like a soldier in some ragtag, post-apocalyptic war.

He didn't emerge from behind the car door, and instead stood gripping it like it was a shield that would protect him from dangers not yet known.

'What the hell's this? What's going on? What's happened?' he demanded. The quaver in his voice said he had already guessed it was something terrible.

He looked past the detectives as they approached, scanning the front of the house and the upstairs windows, searching for movement.

'What the hell is this?' he asked again, the pitch of his voice rising. 'Is it Sharon? Oh, God. Is it Sharon? Has something happened?'

'Mr Simpson?' Logan said, closing in. He and Hamza stopped a few feet from the man, their faces sombre.

'What? Yes. Yes, that's… Yes. Why? Who's asking? Who are you?'

'I'm Detective Chief Inspector Jack Logan. Police Scotland Major Investigations.'

He felt a heaviness settling down in his gut. The same one he always felt at moments like this. He used to think he'd stop feeling it someday. That the weight of it would eventually lessen, then disappear completely.

He'd long since come to accept, though, that it wasn't going anywhere.

And maybe that was how it should be.

'I'm sorry to have to say this, Mr Simpson, but I'm afraid I've got some bad news.'

Chapter 6

The detective constables had split up at the bottom of the drive, Tyler taking the house on the right, while Tammi-Jo took the one on the left. The one on the left was closer, so giving it to Tammi-Jo felt like the gentlemanly thing to do.

Also, it meant Tyler had a bit more time to clear his head while he walked along the road towards the house on the right.

Knocking on doors and sticking his nose into other people's business had been second nature to Tyler for years now, since back on his beat days. And yet, following his almost three-month break, he felt a fluttering of butterflies in his stomach as he headed up the driveway of the victim's next door neighbour.

It was a nice house, bigger and better kept than the one Tyler had just left. The garden was well maintained, the walls were recently painted, and vegetables grew in raised beds over by a greenhouse that was the size of Tyler's living room and kitchen combined.

There was a lovingly maintained dark green 2003 Rover 75 car parked on the driveway, the metal all buffed and shiny, a damp shadow on the ground revealing it had recently been washed.

Beyond it, a 1950s Morris Minor sat in the shade of a carport, raised up on blocks to keep its wheels off the ground. The bonnet was open, but there was no sign of anyone working at it.

Tyler had never been much of a car guy. He appreciated the purpose they served, but he'd never been one to get excited over torque, or horsepower, or...

His knowledge of motoring terms fell away sharply there.

'Boot space,' he muttered, after some thought.

He wondered how much a car like that cost. It might be a few hundred quid, or it could be tens of thousands, he had absolutely no idea.

The thought of money reminded him of the stack of final demands in his jacket pocket. His heart fluttered in his chest, kicked into high gear by the first stirrings of panic.

He pushed the thought of his pocket full of bills back down into the darkest corners of his mind, and turned his attention back to the matter at hand.

After a quick check under the Morris Minor to make sure that nobody was lying beneath it, Tyler continued on to the front door of the house and rang the doorbell.

A circle of blue light illuminated around the button, and Tyler saw himself reflected in a small round lens just above it.

A doorbell cam. That was a pleasant surprise. He turned and tried to estimate the extent of the camera's view. It probably took in a chunk of the drive, but was unlikely to show anything of the main road. Still, could be handy. If the killer happened to take a somewhat convoluted scenic route while fleeing the scene of the crime, they'd have him bang to rights.

There was no response to the doorbell, so Tyler knocked. His official Policeman's Knock would never be up there with the likes of Logan's, but it had been decent enough. Today, though, it sounded weak. Flimsy. Like a schoolboy chapping on the headmaster's door.

He wanted to try again, do it better, but knocking again so quickly would make him seem desperate.

Or was he overthinking it?

'Jesus Christ. It's just knocking on a door,' he muttered, chastising himself for his nerves.

He raised his hand to give it another go, with a view to putting some real welly into it this time. Before he could, though, a voice crackled out at him from the doorbell.

'Yes?'

'Eh. Hello,' Tyler said, shuffling closer. 'Are you the homeowner?'

'You don't need to lean in,' the voice replied. It was a man. An unhappy one, by the sounds of him. 'I have no desire to look right up your nose, thank you.'

'Oh. Right. Aye. Sorry.' Tyler took a hurried half-step back. 'Are you the—'

'What business is it of yours who I am? What do you want?'

An apology started to take shape on Tyler's tongue. He pulled himself together before it had a chance to get out.

He drew himself up to his full height, remembering who he was and what he was doing here.

'Detective Constable Tyler Neish,' he said, with as much authority as he could muster. 'Can you come to the door, sir? I want to ask you a few questions.'

He held the beady black gaze of the camera lens, standing his ground.

There was silence from the doorbell at first, then a sigh that sounded exaggerated for Tyler's benefit.

'I'm around the back. Come round.'

'Will do,' Tyler said, feeling quite pleased with himself. He descended the front step, looking for the best route around to the back of the house.

'And don't look at the dog,' the voice added.

Tyler's head whipped back towards the camera. 'What? What dog? Hello?'

No answer came.

Tyler winced, muttered a quiet, 'Shite,' then crept around the side of the house, making his way towards the rear.

He had nothing against dogs. Not really. It was just that quite a lot of them seemed to have something against him. On a number of occasions over the past few years, he'd been chased, knocked down, and bitten on the arse.

He'd also almost been hit by a train, though that was completely unrelated to the whole dog thing.

And anyway, he didn't really like to talk about it.

There was a tall fence and gate around the side of the house, the wooden slats staggered so it was impossible to see through into the back garden. A big sign on the gate declared 'BEWARE: DOG' in a serious-looking red typeface.

The sight of the sign on that big barricade of a fence stopped him in his tracks.

It didn't even say, 'Beware of the Dog.' He'd have much preferred 'Beware of the Dog.' 'Beware of the Dog,' he thought, sounded comparatively much friendlier and less terrifying than simply, 'BEWARE: DOG.'

'BEWARE: DOG' suggested that the fraction of a second wasted by reading the words 'of the' might well spell the difference between life and death.

'Hello? Anyone there?' he called.

The same voice he'd heard through the doorbell speaker called back to him. 'Yes. I'm here. Come in. It's not locked.'

Tyler approached the gate. There was a thumb-operated latch just below chest height. He gripped it, but didn't yet depress the lever.

'What about the dog?' he asked.

'Just don't look at her, and you'll be fine.'

Tyler felt like pointing out he didn't know where the dog was, and therefore, had no idea where not to look, but he was worried he was already struggling to maintain any sort of authority.

'I'm coming in,' he announced.

The gate's latch *clacked* as he pressed the button down, then he stepped into a backyard that favoured function over style, with two large metal sheds standing side by side up the back, and a paved area criss-crossed by sagging lengths of washing line.

Both sheds were secured with industrial-grade padlocks. They were the sort of locks only someone in possession of a top-of-the-range angle grinder and a considerable amount of patience had any hope of cutting through.

Tyler noted the locks, then continued to look around. He couldn't help himself. His gaze alighted briefly on a man in an oil-streaked sleeveless vest, then continued on until it settled on a white shape that seemed to be crouching in the strip of overgrown grass between the sheds.

He tensed when he spotted a pair of dark eyes peering back at him. From inside the tangle of greenery, he heard a growl.

'Christ Almighty. What did I literally just say?' the man in the vest spat.

And then, before Tyler could say a word, a four-legged ball of fury exploded out of the undergrowth and launched itself in his direction.

–

The woman standing in the hallway tore her eyes away from the detective on her doorstep just long enough to check her watch.

Only a couple of minutes had passed since the door had been knocked. It felt like longer. Much longer.

'...not that I'm saying you're involved in anything. I'm not saying that at all. Don't think that. Please,' Tammi-Jo told her.

The woman shook her head. 'I didn't.'

'Good! That's good. Because you're not a suspect or anything. You didn't do anything. I know that, you know that.' The detective constable shrugged. 'Well, I mean, I don't *know* know, maybe you did, but I don't think so, and even if you did, that's not why I'm here.'

'Did what?'

Tammi-Jo smiled apologetically. 'I'm afraid I can't say. I'm sure you'll hear soon enough, though. These things get around. People talk, don't they?'

The woman in the doorway slumped her weight onto one hip. 'Some of them certainly do, aye.'

'So, did you see or hear anything last night?'

'What, in general?'

'Out of the ordinary, I mean,' Tammi-Jo clarified. 'Not, like, *Inspector Morse* on the telly, or whatever. Or…' She chewed her bottom lip. 'What's another one?'

The woman frowned. 'Another what?'

'TV show.'

They both looked at each other in silence for a few moments.

'*Great British Bake Off?*' the woman finally suggested.

'Yes! Not anything like that. Anything out of the ordinary, I mean. Did you see anything strange?'

There was another moment of silence.

'What, like aliens?'

Tammi-Jo's eyes narrowed. 'I mean, not really what I was aiming for, but I suppose that would count.'

'No. Nothing,' the woman said, shooting another look at her watch.

'Didn't hear anything? Didn't see anything unusual?'

'No. Why? Has something happened? Is everything all right?'

Tammi-Jo made a weighing motion with her head, tilting it left and right. 'I mean, they've been better. So… nothing, then?'

The woman shook her head. She straightened up, sensing the conversation might finally be drawing to an end.

'Sorry I couldn't be more help.'

'No problem. Just quickly, though, do you have a doorbell camera?'

'No.'

'CCTV system?'

'Of course not.'

'Right. No.' Tammi-Jo closed over her notebook. 'What's your frog made of?'

This caught the woman in the house off guard. Her brow furrowed, and her lips moved as she silently replayed the question in her head.

Going over it a second time still didn't do her any good. 'What?'

Tammi-Jo turned and pointed to a bright green frog statue that stood near the edge of a garden pond, over by the hedge that divided this garden from the one on the other side. It was about the size of a large Labrador, and had been sculpted to look like it was wearing a little black top hat and matching waistcoat.

'Your frog,' she said. 'What's it made of?'

The woman leaned out of the house and looked over towards the pond, like she still had no idea what the detective was on about.

'Oh. That. I don't know,' she said, leaning back in. 'Concrete?'

'Heavy?'

'I'd imagine so. I can't say I ever tried to lift it.'

'Don't blame you. Looks like it weighs a tonne. Anyone else in the house moved it recently?' Tammi-Jo asked.

The woman shook her head. 'It's just me and my daughter. And she's six.'

Tammi-Jo nodded sagely. 'Probably not strong enough to lift a chonky big lad like him,' she said, then her face brightened into a big beamer of a smile. 'Anyway, thanks for your time. Good luck with the frog, and if you think of anything...'

She produced a business card and held it out between the first two fingers of her left hand.

'I'm always happy to chat!'

—

The dog was a fucking maniac. That much was clear.

It was all bulging eyes and slavering jaws, its teeth gnashing at the air, strings of saliva flying from its chops as it barked and howled at this invader who had dared enter its domain.

It was also, to Tyler's immense relief, less than a foot high.

44

With its puffy plumes of fluffy white hair, the dog looked a bit like a cloud with legs as it darted back and forth around his feet, *yipping* aggressively.

Tyler had been braced for something far worse. The dog that had taken a nibble of one of his buttocks a while back had seemed like the Hound of the Baskervilles at the time. Compared to this ball of wool, though, it had been more like Godzilla.

Had that thing fully turned on him, it would've eaten him alive. The only way this thing could hurt him would be if he sprained his ankle while dropkicking it over the fence.

Not that he ever would do such a thing, of course. At most, he might hook a foot under her belly and flick her out of the garden. But even then, he couldn't see it happening.

Although, it was nice to know that it was at least an option.

The man in the oily vest had put down the old car radiator he had been cleaning, and marched over to join Tyler and the dog. His fists were clenched and his arms were held straight down by his sides, like he was one wrong word away from stamping his foot and running home to tell his mum.

He was tall and lean, and while there wasn't a lot of bulk to his biceps, the cut of his muscles showed he kept himself in shape—even if the shape he kept himself in was ever so slightly odd.

It was his arms, Tyler thought. Though he was tall, the arms seemed a little too long for his body, like he had an extra elbow halfway down each forearm.

There was a tattoo of a dagger on one of his arms, the DC noted, though it had faded with time so it looked a little washed out.

Further up the same arm, near the shoulder, was a blob of solid black. At first, Tyler had thought it was just another oil stain, but up close, he could see that the guy had clearly had another tattoo covered up at some point.

The dog was still barking away like a lunatic. Since there was no danger of it ripping his throat out, though, Tyler was able to more or less block it out.

The dog's owner, though, was not having it.

'Polly. Polly. *Polly*. Polly. Po*ll*y. Polly!' he said, glaring impatiently at the yapping dog. Each time he said her name, he used a different intonation—some sharp and shrill, some drawn-out and disappointed—like he was trying to crack the code which might deactivate her.

The dog clearly didn't give a shit how he chose to say her name, as she showed equal amounts of indifference towards every variation of it.

'It's fine. I can just ignore her,' Tyler said.

The man in the vest met his eye. There was contempt in that look, the DC thought.

'No, we can't just ignore her. How will she learn if we just ignore her?'

Tyler was pretty sure that was how you were meant to train a dog. Ignore behaviour like this, then reward them when they eventually shut up. The dog's owner clearly hadn't read the animal's operating instructions, though.

He rattled through another repertoire of varying pronunciations.

'Polly. *Po*lly. Polly! Poll-eee! Polly. Polly!'

Still, the dog ignored him. Her eyes were practically out on stalks now, the pitch and volume of her barking steadily rising. Tyler was now sorely tempted to try the foot-flick thing.

Fortunately for all involved, the vest wearer's last attempt to silence the dog worked. Her name rolled from his mouth as a venomous roar that made Tyler jump and sent the dog scuttling back to her spot between the sheds.

Her owner rolled his head around, stretching his neck, then slowly let out a long, unsteady breath. He moved to run a hand through his close-cropped grey hair, then remembered the oily stains, and thought better of it.

'There. Isn't that better?' he asked Tyler, in a tone that dared him to argue.

'Eh, aye,' Tyler said. He found himself turning to look at the dog again, but a sharp cry from the other man stopped him.

'Well, don't look at her! For Christ's sake, you'll just set her off again.'

He marched past Tyler, headed for the back door of the house, leading the detective away from the dog. As he walked, he wiped his hands on the front of his vest, marking it further with oily streaks.

'Come,' he urged.

Tyler wasn't sure if he was talking to him or the dog. Since Polly didn't show any signs of shifting, though, he concluded it was probably him.

He started to follow, then stopped after a few paces. This guy was completely setting the tone of the conversation. Would Logan allow that? Would Hamza?

Hoon would likely already have shoved the guy's dog up his arse.

Maybe even vice versa.

'Could you just stop there, sir?'

The guy in the vest did as asked, though he didn't look happy about it.

'I was going to wash my hands,' he said, holding them up to demonstrate quite how filthy they were. 'Is there some sort of problem with that?'

'No problem, sir,' Tyler said. He smiled, but he didn't go overboard. He was usually eager to please, but something about this guy made him hold back. 'This'll only take a minute, then you can get back to your day.'

The sighed response was a petulant and childish-sounding thing. 'Fine. What is it now, then?' he asked, planting himself down on the step by the back door. 'Has there been another incident or something? Jesus Christ. I thought you lot were meant to be doing something?'

Tyler's forehead furrowed in confusion. 'Another incident? What do you mean? And sorry, can I take your name?'

'It's Holburn. Armand Holburn.'

Tyler smirked as he wrote. 'Like Bond, James Bond?'

'What the hell are you talking about?'

The DC shook his head. 'Nothing. You were saying something about other incidents?'

Armand sighed again for effect, and rubbed a particularly stubborn stain on his left hand with the thumb of his right.

'Yes. All the hassle that's been going on. All the bloody nonsense. The harassment.'

He gave a wave of his hand that suggested this should all mean something to Tyler. When it was clear that it didn't, he tutted so sharply his dog pricked up her ears.

'The funny calls. The eggs and stones thrown at the bloody window. Clothes nicked off the washing lines. God, don't you people talk to one another?'

'How long's this been going on for?' Tyler asked.

Armand shot to his feet. 'Seriously? It was reported months ago, and you've done nothing. I thought maybe you were actually taking it seriously last time, when that girl came round. The policewoman. I told her everything. She seemed to actually listen for a change, though clearly she hasn't bothered her arse to pass it on!'

'I'm sure there'll be a report on it, sir,' Tyler said. 'Nuisance calls and the like aren't really my department.'

This made the other man pause. His eyes narrowed and his face appeared to elongate as he considered Tyler's response.

'Oh. So, what is your department, then?' he probed. 'What's all this about? Is it about Molly? Have you found the bastard?'

Once again, Tyler didn't have the faintest clue what the man was on about. 'Molly?'

Armand groaned and shook his head. 'Forget it. Clearly that's not why you're here. So, what is it? As you can see, I'm a very busy man.'

Tyler considered the dented and dirty old radiator Armand had been cleaning. It didn't feel like a particularly important task for a Monday afternoon, but maybe it was how the guy made his living.

'Could you tell me if you saw or heard anything out of the ordinary within the last twenty-four hours or so?'

Armand stared at him. It was quite an intense look, with perhaps just a hint of defiance to it. 'No.'

'Nothing at all? No strangers knocking around? Unfamiliar cars…?'

'I'm perfectly aware what 'out of the ordinary,' means, son. You don't have to break it down.'

Tyler smiled thinly. He took a breath, then channelled his inner Hoon.

And then, because he wanted to keep his job, he channelled his inner Logan, instead.

'It's Detective Constable.'

'What?'

'It's Detective Constable,' Tyler said again. 'It's not "son".'

For a moment, it looked like Armand was going to laugh it off, but instead he gave a nod. 'Apologies.'

Tyler blinked in surprise, and only just managed to stop himself saying, 'Bloody Hell, that worked!' out loud. He stood a little taller as he continued.

'I want to make sure we're on the same page, Mr Holburn. There's been quite a serious incident in the area, so we're gathering all the information we can.'

'Serious?'

He looked to his left, where a tall fence marked the boundary between his garden and the patch of empty land beyond. It was a ten-second sprint to the grounds of the victim's house next door, and all the activity over there was hidden from view.

'How serious? What do you mean? Has something happened to Isaac and Sharon? Are they all right?'

Tyler chose not to answer, and steered the conversation in a more useful direction.

'The doorbell camera. Does that show the road, at all?'

Armand hesitated, taking a moment to catch up with the shift in subject. 'No. It's a pain in the arse. It's triggered by movement, so any time anything drove past I'd get an alert on my phone. I moved it. It just shows the path and part of the drive.'

'Gotcha,' Tyler said. 'Much call for it out here? Pretty peaceful, I'd have thought.'

Armand ejected a scornful laugh. 'Well, it was. But if you'd take the time to go look up all those incidents I mentioned, you'll see why I felt the need.'

'I'll do that,' Tyler assured him. 'But if you don't mind, maybe you could give me a quick rundown of the highlights now.'

He clicked the button on the top of his pen and held it ready above a blank page of his notebook.

'Quick question to get us started,' he said, watching for the man's reaction. 'Who's Molly?'

Chapter 7

Isaac Simpson was holding himself together remarkably well. He sat across the table from Logan and DI Forde in the nicest of the interview rooms at the Fort William Police Station.

Logan had gone to lengths to stress that he wasn't a suspect, and that interviewing him under caution was just standard procedure. He'd been offered a solicitor, but had declined.

Lawyers, he'd insisted, were for people with something to hide.

'When can I see her?' he asked, his voice flat and controlled. It wasn't devoid of emotion—far from it—but he was keeping it on a tight leash.

He sat with his fingers interlocked and his back straight, a picture of composure. It was only whenever he reached for the mug of hot, sugary tea he'd been provided with that the tremble in his hands became apparent.

'We'll arrange that for as soon as we can, Mr Simpson,' Logan said. 'We'll need you to confirm her identity for us.'

Isaac scraped his teeth across his bottom lip. 'Is it bad? Is she bad? Does she look in a bad way?' he asked, and a crack in his voice almost betrayed him.

Logan shook his head. 'No. No, she doesn't.'

This seemed to give the man an injection of strength. He breathed out slowly and tightened his grip on his emotional leash.

'I know it's a very difficult time, Mr Simpson,' said Ben. 'And you have our full sympathies. We're going to do everything we can to find out what happened to Sharon, and to bring the person responsible to justice. You have our word on that.'

'Thank you. I, uh. Thank you,' Isaac said.

He took a shaky slurp of his tea. From the way he looked at the detectives over the rim of his mug, it was clear that he was bracing himself for the question he knew was coming next.

'Do you mind telling us where you were last night, Mr Simpson?' Logan asked. 'Just to help us build a timeline of events.'

Isaac stopped drinking, but didn't put down his mug. Instead, he wrapped both hands around it, like he was drawing energy from its warmth.

'I was camping. Up near Dalwhinnie.'

'What time did you leave home?'

'About… I don't know. Six yesterday evening. About then. I wanted to get some photos for the website before it got too dark.'

'You were alone?'

Isaac confirmed this with a nod.

Ben offered a smile of encouragement. 'Was it a campsite, or…?'

'No. I avoid those. I was wild camping, as they call it now. But just camping, as far as I'm concerned. And, to save you time, aye, I was on my own, no, I didn't see anyone, and nobody saw me. And yes, I know that doesn't look great.'

'Like I say, Mr Simpson, just putting together a timeline. That's all. You're not a suspect,' Logan assured him.

'What? Of course I am,' Isaac shot back. 'I mean, I hope I am. If not, you're not doing your bloody job, and if you're not doing your job, you're not going to find the bastard who—'

His voice did let him down then. It shattered like glass, and he quickly buried his chin into his chest, hiding his eyes and his shame.

The detectives gave him a moment to pull himself together.

'Just ask your questions. You don't have to mollycoddle me,' he said, once he'd sat up straight again. 'I understand it's necessary. So, go on. Ask me.'

Logan shot a sideways glance at Ben, then fixed the man on the other side of the table with one of his sterner looks.

'Did you kill your wife, Mr Simpson?'

Isaac didn't rush to answer. Logan couldn't quite interpret the meaning of the pause, and it was over before he had time to dwell on it.

'No. I didn't.'

'OK. Well, that's a good start,' said Ben, his tone far softer than the DCI's. 'Can you think why anyone would want to hurt her?'

'She's a primary school teacher. She teaches five-year-olds to count to ten and spell their names.' Isaac skipped a beat again, although this time the reason for the hesitation was clear. 'Taught,' he said, and his vocal chords wobbled again. 'She *taught* them to do those things. Oh, *God.*'

He dropped the mug. It hit the table bottom first, bounced once, and landed on its side. He'd drunk most of the contents, so only a dribble of the milky tea trickled out onto the tabletop.

'Sorry. Sorry,' he said, immediately grabbing for it.

His face almost crumpled up at the sight of the spillage, like it was the worst thing that had ever happened to him. Logan assumed there was some emotional transference going on. Either that, or he was the world's biggest neat freak.

'It's fine. Don't worry about it,' Ben said. He pulled a handkerchief from his pocket, gave the table a wipe, then offered the victim's husband a smile of reassurance. 'See? All sorted. Not a problem.'

Isaac cleared his throat several times, like there was some-thing stuck there he couldn't dislodge. The armour he'd constructed around himself for the interview was rapidly rusting and falling away.

'Would you like some time, Mr Simpson?' Logan asked, but Isaac dismissed the suggestion with a curt shake of his head.

'This is the important time, isn't it? Right after you find the body. This is when you're most likely to solve the case, isn't it?'

'It's when a lot of the progress happens,' Logan confirmed.

'Then come on. Crack on,' Isaac urged. 'What do you want to know?'

'Are you sure, son?' Ben asked. 'We can take a break.'

'Get on with it. Please.'

'Some of this might not be easy to hear,' Logan warned.

Isaac replied through gritted teeth. 'I suspect I've seen things that would stop you sleeping for the rest of your life, Detective Chief Inspector. I don't care how gory the details are. Just get it over with.'

A look passed from Logan to Ben, and an almost impercept-ible shrug was returned in the other direction.

'When did you and your wife last have sexual intercourse, Mr Simpson?' Logan asked.

Whatever line of questioning Isaac had been bracing himself for, this wasn't it.

'I'm sorry? What the hell's that got to do with anything?'

'If you could just answer the question, please?'

Isaac started to smile at the DCI, like he was making a joke, but then shook his head, his mouth curving downwards again. 'I don't know. I don't keep track.'

'Roughly,' Logan urged. 'Yesterday?'

'No. A week, ten days, maybe.' His gaze flitted from one detective to the other. 'Why?'

'Did you use contraception?'

'How is that relevant? Or any of your business?' Isaac demanded.

'I know it's not nice, son,' Ben said. 'Talking about all this. But it'll help us build up a picture. It'll help us find who did this.'

Isaac looked doubtful. He gave another shake of his head before replying. 'She was on the pill. We'd agreed we didn't want kids. I'm too old, and she has a son from an earlier relationship. She didn't want any more.'

'A son?' Logan asked, eyebrows creeping upwards.

'Struan,' Isaac said, and a suggestion of something unpleasant darted across his face. 'He's twenty. She had him young. He's off somewhere doing God knows what.'

'Do you have a number for him?'

'I will have, yes. At the house.'

'And that's it for contraception? You weren't using condoms?'

Isaac frowned. 'No. Why?'

'Like we said, Mr Simpson, just putting together a picture.'

Logan checked to make sure that Ben was making a note of everything Simpson had just said, before he hit Isaac with a sucker punch.

'Was she sleeping with anyone else?'

Isaac's body language had suggested he was prepared for some tough questions. He'd probably already anticipated most of them, but that one came at him out of nowhere.

'I… What?! I beg your pardon?!'

'Sorry, I thought I made myself pretty clear,' Logan replied. 'Let me rephrase it. To the best of your knowledge, Mr Simpson, was your wife having sex with other men?'

'I don't… What? No! Christ! No, of course she wasn't!'

'You're sure?' Logan pressed. 'You didn't have any suspicions? She hadn't been acting differently?'

'She wasn't shagging someone else! Of course not. She wouldn't!' Isaac cried. His eyes darted between both detectives, first narrowing, then growing wider. 'Why? Why are you even asking me that? Why would you say that?'

Logan tried to phrase the response as tactfully as he could.

'When Sharon was found, there was evidence that she'd been involved in sexual activity.'

Isaac clamped both hands over his mouth, just a little too late to trap the sob that came rolling out of it.

'She was raped, then. That must be it. Oh, God. That's what happened. She was raped. Oh, Christ. Sharon,' he whispered. 'She must've been raped. She wouldn't cheat on me. She wouldn't.'

'That is a possibility we're investigating,' Logan confirmed.

Isaac slapped a hand on the table. The bang it made rolled around inside the compact room.

'It's not a possibility! That's what's happened! That has to be what happened!' he cried, his mask of control falling away completely to expose the teary-eyed, snot-nosed grief of the man hiding behind it. 'She wouldn't do that to me! We loved each other!'

'Of course you did, son,' Ben said. 'And I'm sure you're right. But, like you said yourself, we have to ask these questions. It's the only way we'll get to the truth of it all.'

Isaac sniffed and ran his sleeve across his eyes and nose. And like that, the mask was back.

'Sorry. Of course. Carry on. I'm fine to continue. It's just… It was a shock.'

'We understand, son,' Ben assured him.

Logan turned back to the matter of Isaac's whereabouts the night before. He'd taken his own car, turned down a narrow side track just before Dalwhinnie, and parked up in a layby a couple of miles further along.

Or so he claimed, anyway.

'And nobody saw you? You didn't speak to anyone?'

'No,' Isaac admitted. 'But I took some photos. On my phone. They'll be time-stamped.'

'We'll look at those,' Logan said. 'But, to be honest, unless you were taking them every half hour on the dot, a few photos are unlikely to prove your whereabouts.'

'Sentry mode!' Isaac yelped, leaning forward.

Ben raised his eyebrows in surprise at the sudden outburst, then dropped them again in confusion when he realised he had no idea what the man was on about.

'Sorry, son?'

'The car. The Tesla. It's got Sentry mode. The cameras on it watch for any movement around the car. I left it on all night.'

'Not a lot of movement out in the middle of nowhere, I'd have thought,' Logan reasoned.

'There were eighteen clips saved when I went back to the car this morning. Couple of passing vehicles. Some deer. Between that and the photos, that should cover most of the night.'

He sat back and ran his hands through his thinning hair, his sense of relief at having an alibi palpable all the way across the table.

'We'll look at that, too,' Logan said. 'Though, that might prove the car didn't move. Since you weren't in it, it doesn't necessarily help you.'

'You've a point there, Jack,' Ben said.

Logan kept watching Isaac, while aiming the next question at the DI beside him.

'I'm not actually all that familiar with that neck of the woods. How far would you say it is from there to Mr Simpson's house, Detective Inspector?'

Ben blew out his cheeks. 'God. Now you're asking. Thirty miles? Give or take.'

'About forty, forty-five minutes by car, then,' Logan reasoned. 'Three hours by bike.'

'Bike? What do you mean? Where does a bike come into anything?' Isaac asked.

'I'm just saying, given how long you were away, it would've been possible to cycle back and forth.'

'Well, maybe, but I don't have a bike,' Isaac replied.

'Don't you?' Logan asked.

'No. No, I don't,' Isaac replied. There was a hint of venom in it. 'Sorry to ruin whatever theory you've been busy concocting.'

'No theory yet, Mr Simpson. But I'll get there,' Logan said. 'Did Sharon own a bike?'

'Just a Peloton.'

'Is that a kind of bicycle, is it?' asked Ben.

'Not one with wheels,' Logan explained.

Ben's frown asked the question before he did. 'Then what the hell is—'

'Exercise bike,' Logan said. 'One of the fancy ones with the big screen. I hear it's quite like being outside.'

Ben sat back in bewilderment. 'Why not just go outside?'

'Because it's always pissing down,' Isaac said. He smiled fondly. 'That was her reasoning. She wanted to get the miléage in, but hated going out in the rain. So, I bought her the Peloton. Signed her up for the subscription. Forty quid a month.'

Ben nearly choked. 'To pretend to be cycling outside?!'

'That's the theory. It's been a clotheshorse for the past six months. She kept saying she was going to get back to it.'

The smile hung around for a moment longer, then fell away.

'And now she never will, will she?'

That was the thought that did it. The idea that his wife would never get back on that exercise bike. Never fulfil another goal or hit another target again. That was the thought that broke him.

He shook at first, a whole body tremble that started in his bottom jaw and spread down through the rest of him. Two perfectly synchronised tears broke through his defences and rolled down his cheeks, taking very different routes through the wrinkles and old acne scars, before being lost in his greying stubble.

'Can we take a break, please?' he asked. His throat sounded narrow, like it was gripping the words and holding onto them. 'I don't... I can't... Can we just take a break?'

Logan tapped his pen on his pad a few times, then nodded. 'Course we can, Mr Simpson. If that's what you want.'

'I can go, can't I? I don't have to stay here?'

'You're not being held,' Logan told him. 'Right now, you're free to leave. But I'd ask that you don't go far. And you won't be able to go home yet until we're done at the scene.'

'Is there somewhere else you could go? Locally, I mean?' Ben asked.

Isaac nodded. 'My neighbour. He can… I can get him to pick me up.'

Logan consulted the notes he'd been handed by Tyler and Tammi-Jo. 'Is that…' He squinted as he tried to decipher Tyler's handwriting. 'Armand Holburn?'

Another nod from Isaac confirmed this.

'OK. Fine. I'm going to assign you a police liaison officer to go with you. They'll be able to keep you up to date with the investigation, and bring you back in if and when we need to interview you again.'

'That really isn't necessary,' Isaac said.

'I'm afraid it is, Mr Simpson,' Logan insisted. 'We all want to find out who's responsible for what happened to your wife. This is one way we do that. I'm afraid the liaison is non-negotiable.'

'So, they're spying on me? Is that it?'

'They'll be there to help,' Logan told him. 'That's their only purpose.'

Isaac wiped his eyes on the heels of his hands, then straightened himself up again in his chair.

'Right,' he said. 'Though, I notice you didn't specify which one of us they're going to be helping…'

Logan and Ben stood looking out of one of the station's upstairs windows, peering through the blinds as Isaac clambered into the front passenger seat of a dark green Rover 75.

It wasn't until he was in the car with his belt on that he leaned forward and looked back at the building he'd just left. He didn't glance up in Logan and Ben's direction, though even if he had, he likely wouldn't have spotted them behind the window coverings.

'Thoughts?' Logan asked as they watched the vehicle pulling away. He caught a fleeting glimpse of the driver, but not enough to rush to any sort of snap judgement of the man.

He thought he might be wearing a cravat, though, and if that was indeed the case, then he disliked him already.

'He seemed awfully keen for his wife to have been raped,' Ben remarked, still watching as the car paused at the roundabout to let another vehicle pass, then pulled away.

'Aye, I noticed that, too,' Logan said. 'Certainly seemed to prefer the idea of that than the thought that she might've been having an affair.'

The car disappeared from view, and both men turned away from the window.

'Takes all sorts, I suppose,' Ben said, though his expression said he wasn't happy about it. 'I've started setting up the room for us,' he continued. 'Dave's come down to handle Exhibits. The Big Board's being sorted now.'

That stopped Logan in his tracks. 'The Big Board? Is Hamza back?'

Ben realised he was now walking alone, and turned to look over his shoulder. 'Not yet, no. Why?'

'Then who's…?' Logan began, before a terrible thought struck him. 'Wait, you've not let that pair loose on the board, have you?'

'Tyler and Tammi-Jo? Aye. Why?'

Logan scowled. 'Christ. Well, on your own head be it,' he muttered, then he carried on walking with the DI towards the door. 'You see your fancy woman yet?'

Ben tutted. 'How many times do I have to bloody tell you? She's no' my fancy woman, Jack. She's just a friend.' He adjusted the collar of his shirt, like it was suddenly too tight. 'And no. She's not around.'

'Aye, she is.'

It was Ben's turn to suddenly stop. 'Eh?'

'She was on the front desk when I brought Simpson in. That's why it took me so long, with all the bastarding paperwork she had me filling out. I thought she was going to ask me for a bloody stool sample at one point.'

'She's in?' Ben asked. 'Moira? She's in now?'

'Well, she certainly was half an hour ago,' Logan replied. 'But I don't know. Maybe she's away back to her cave and her big pile of gold by now.'

If Ben heard the comment, he didn't rise to it.

'Sorry, Jack,' he said, distracted. 'Would you excuse me for a few minutes?'

Chapter 8

'So, what's it like, then? Being a dad, I mean?'

Tyler looked up from the computer screen, then gave a little jump when he saw how close Tammi-Jo was standing. She was right by his desk, leaning down like she'd been studying the top of his head.

'Eh, aye. It's good,' he said, then a yawn betrayed him. 'Tiring, though.'

He yawned again, stretched, then went back to studying his screen. Tammi-Jo, however, didn't move.

'What else?' she pressed.

Tyler met her eye. 'What?'

'What else is it like? That can't be it. It can't just be "good" and "tiring". There must be more to it than that.'

Tyler sat back in his chair. 'I mean, aye. Of course. There's loads more to it than that. There's dirty nappies, and crying, and feeding, and then winding them, and then they throw up down your back, and you spend every waking moment worried you're going to somehow accidentally kill them.'

Tammi-Jo's delicate features arranged themselves into a frown. 'Wow. No wonder my dad was always moaning about having kids,' she muttered.

'But it's brilliant, too,' Tyler continued, and his eyes seemed to sparkle at the thought of the babies he'd left at home. 'Just seeing them smiling. Hearing a wee giggle. Feeling their head on your shoulder as they fall asleep. And just, like, I don't know, sniffing them. Is that weird?'

Tammi-Jo shook her head. 'No. I sniff a lot of things,' she said. A distant, faraway sort of look settled momentarily on her face, like something was troubling her. 'A *lot* of things.'

Tyler's smile faltered a little. 'Aye. Well. Fair play,' he said, because he had no idea how else to address the remark. 'But yeah, it's all that, and it's way more, too. It's like someone's taken the heart right out of your chest, wrapped it in a blanket, and made you responsible for it.'

Tammi-Jo drew a deep breath in through her nose, like she was getting a good whiff of this conversation, too.

'My dad's never mentioned that bit,' she said. 'I like that. Someone's taken out your heart and made you responsible for it. That's nice.'

'They've also made it a greeting-faced wee pain in the arse that shites and throws up everywhere,' Tyler added. 'But that probably doesn't sound that nice, I suppose.'

The other DC wrinkled up her nose, considering this. 'Not *as* nice, no. Anyway, what do you think?'

Tyler's eyes narrowed. 'Of what?'

'Of that,' Tammi-Jo replied. She stepped aside and gestured behind her. 'Of the Big Board!'

Tyler looked past her and saw for the first time what she'd been doing on the board. He rose slowly to his feet. Were he a hero in an action movie, he'd have chosen that moment to pull off a pair of sunglasses in a dramatically laborious fashion, and mutter a quiet, 'Son of a bitch,' below his breath.

Since he wasn't, though, he just stared in blank-faced confusion at what he could best describe as 'an arrangement of nonsense' on the board.

And coming from him, that was really saying something.

A photograph of the victim, Sharon Simpson, had been pinned to the board on the left-hand side. It was a low-resolution image, clearly scraped from a social media profile, then printed out on the office's old inkjet printer, which was clearly—*clearly*—badly malfunctioning.

The photo looked like it had been a bit dark and blurry to begin with, and the printing process had only degraded it further.

As a result, it looked more like a vaguely female blob than the late Mrs Simpson, and had it not been for the word 'VICTIM' written on a piece of paper underneath—every letter a different colour—Tyler would've had no clue who, or perhaps even what, he was looking at.

Tammi-Jo had also, for reasons best known to herself, attached the photo to the board by sticking a pin through the poor woman's forehead.

At the other end of the board, on the right-hand side, the detective constable had written 'AND THE KILLER IS!!!!' across two sheets of A4 paper, taped together. Arrows had been drawn on half a dozen Post-it Notes, which all pointed towards an empty space where, presumably, a photo of whoever had murdered Sharon Simpson would be placed.

She had also added a few sticky notes with question marks on them between the ones with the arrows, presumably just for style points.

Between those two extremes were a smattering of printouts, handwritten notes and a colourful drawing of an upside-down frog. They seemed to have been fixed in place without any rhyme or reason, as if someone had loaded them all into a shotgun and just blasted them at the board.

Tammi-Jo chewed on her thumbnail, closely watching his reaction.

'It's probably not the way you usually do it.'

'No,' Tyler admitted. He thought for quite a long time, searching for something more to add, but eventually settled for a second, 'No.'

'Is it OK, do you think?' DC Swanney asked. She stole a glance at it, and didn't immediately recoil, which made Tyler wonder if she was seeing something he wasn't. 'I think it makes sense.'

Before Tyler could respond, the door to the Incident Room was opened, and Logan entered.

'Right, then,' he began.

The rest of the sentence failed to materialise, the sight of the Big Board stopping the DCI dead in his tracks.

'What the f...?'

'Oh, God,' Tammi-Jo whispered. From the corner of his eye, Tyler saw her cringe. 'I knew I should've just written the word "frog" instead of drawing it.'

That, Tyler reckoned, was the least of her worries.

It *was* still fucking weird, though.

'What the hell's happened here?' Logan asked, gesturing to the board. 'Who did this?'

Tammi-Jo opened her mouth, but Tyler stepped in front of her, taking the bullet.

'I did, boss,' he declared.

Logan held the DC's gaze. 'You did it?' he intoned.

Tyler nodded, just once. He could feel Tammi-Jo's eyes on him, but didn't dare glance her way.

'Aye, boss,' he insisted. 'It was me.'

Logan squared his shoulders and narrowed his eyes, like a cowboy getting ready for a shootout at High Noon.

'All right then, son,' he said. The words were innocuous enough, but there was a note of menace in his voice. 'How about you talk me through it?'

Tyler swallowed. His mouth made a strange clicking noise, his throat suddenly very dry. 'Sorry, boss?'

'The Big Board. What you've done,' Logan said. He kept his eyes trained on the younger officer, even as he gestured to the board. 'Talk me through it. Step by step. Show me your working.'

Tyler did his best to keep his nerve. He stole a quick look at the arrangement of notes and images. The wrong-way-up frog smiled encouragingly back at him.

'Well, I mean… You know, obviously this bit over there is…' He pointed at a few random spots on the board, moved his finger around, then croaked out the word, 'Frog'.

'I did it, sir,' Tammi-Jo said, stepping past him.

'Oh, thank Christ,' Tyler wheezed, slumping down into his chair. He pointed to his fellow DC. 'Aye, boss. She did it.'

'Really? Well, it's a good thing you came clean, DC Swanney, or I'd never have guessed,' Logan told her. He fired a withering look in the board's direction. 'You want to explain it?'

'Which bit, sir?'

'Just in general.'

'It's a chocolate machine,' Tammi-Jo said, and both men looked at her like she'd lost her mind.

'It's a what?' Logan asked.

Tammi-Jo rushed over to the board. 'You know Willy Wonka? You know he had the chocolate factory?'

Logan continued to stare at her, saying nothing.

'It's a book, boss,' Tyler said.

Logan sighed. 'I know it's a fu… Forget it. What the hell are you talking about, Tammi-Jo?'

'Well, I'm just saying, it's a bit like that. Like a chocolate machine. Or a cake machine. Or a crisps machine. Or any sort of machine, really. But a food one. Not a car one or something. You feed in the ingredients…' Tammi-Jo was babbling as she pointed to the left side of the board. She could feel a rash of embarrassment creeping up her neck. 'Victim, suspects, other stuff…'

'The three key ingredients to any investigation,' Logan mumbled.

'Exactly!' Tammi-Jo said, her desperate smile suggesting she'd missed the sarcasm. 'All those ingredients just sort of swish around a bit here in the middle, and then—BING!—the machine spits out a chocolate bar here.'

She rapped her knuckles against the empty space that all the arrows were pointing to.

'Or, I don't know, some magic toffee or something,' she concluded.

'Or the chief suspect in a murder investigation?' Logan suggested.

Tammi-Jo lowered her arm and smoothed the front of her shirt, her pale cheeks reddening.

'Or that. Yes. Or that,' she said. 'Sorry, I should've done it the normal way. It's stupid.'

She reached for the pin that had been shoved through Sharon Simpson's pixelated forehead, but Logan stopped her.

'Why's there a frog on the board?'

'Hmm?' Tammi-Jo glanced at the various notes, like she had no idea what he was on about. 'Oh! It's not a real frog, sir.'

Logan tutted. 'Jesus Christ,' he whispered. 'No, I know it's not a real frog, Detective Constable. Believe me, I'd be even more concerned if you'd pinned a real frog to the board. I get that it's just a drawing of one, but why's it there?'

'Sorry, sir, no. I mean, it's not a drawing of a real frog. It's a drawing of a concrete frog.'

Logan turned to look at Tyler, in the hope that DC Neish had something more sensible to add. He realised then quite how desperate the situation had become, when he was hoping that Tyler might be the voice of reason in the room.

Tyler, however, looked just as bewildered as Logan.

'All right. Why have you done a drawing of a concrete frog, then?'

'And why's it upside down?' Tyler added.

Tammi-Jo looked at them both like they were thick. 'Well, so I remember it's in the wrong place.'

Logan waited for more, and somehow managed to suppress a sigh when it failed to arrive.

'And what does that mean?' he pressed. He was determined to get to the bottom of the frog picture. Suddenly, getting to the bottom of the frog picture felt like the most important thing in the world.

Assuming there even was a bottom. Knowing DC Swanney, the frog picture might well lead him in a continuous downward spiral into insanity that went on forever.

'In the neighbour's garden, sir,' she explained. 'The frog was near the pond, and the pond was near the hedge. I noticed, though, that the frog used to be nearer to the pond than it was when I saw it. There was an imprint of it in the mud. Fresh, too. But, when I saw it, it was nearer to the hedge.'

It took both detectives a moment to find some meaning in that. To everyone's surprise, not least his own, Tyler got there first.

'So someone moved it?'

Tammi-Jo looked down at him with something like sympathy. 'Well, unless it moved itself…'

'What are you saying?' Logan asked. 'You reckon someone used it to get over the hedge?'

Tammi-Jo shifted uncomfortably, like she was sensing a trap that she had no choice but to walk straight into.

'Yes, sir. I do.'

Logan took a few faltering steps closer to the board. He spent a few moments taking it all in.

'A chocolate machine, eh?' he muttered.

He raised his eyebrows and shook his head, in much the same way DI Forde did whenever he encountered some new piece of technology. He tapped the frog picture like he was *booping* it on the nose, then turned to Tammi-Jo.

'Good work, Detective Constable,' he said. 'Well spotted. Did you mention it to Hamza?'

Tammi-Jo seemed to gain an inch in height. Her cheeks, which had already been skelping, reddened even more.

'Thank you, sir. And I did, sir, yeah. He got Scene of Crime to check it out, and in fact, he's just sent through…'

She marched past the DCI, swept dramatically across the room, then grabbed a sheet of paper from the ancient inkjet.

'*This!*' she cried, holding the page aloft.

Logan and Tyler both squinted and cocked their heads, trying to figure out what the blurry smudge of blown-up blacks and greys was supposed to represent.

Tammi-Jo deflated a little and glanced at the page.

'It's a footprint,' she said. 'And, I'd just like to say, for the record, that moment would've been *way* more impressive if we'd had a better printer.'

Chapter 9

Moira Corson held up a withered finger, making it clear to the person approaching the police station's front desk that she was busy. She heard footsteps stopping on the other side of the counter, then licked the end of the finger she'd been holding up, and used it to very deliberately turn the page of the local newspaper she was reading.

Only when she'd finished skim-reading a story about a strong man competition, and glanced at an advert for conservatory renovation beside it, did she bother to look up.

DI Ben Forde stood smiling at her. She saw the slight look of concern on his face as her sigh clouded the glass between them.

'How can I help you?' she asked.

Across the counter, Ben's smile faltered. 'Eh, hello! How're you doing? I brought you something,' he announced, rallying as best he could. 'Been holding onto it.'

He stifled a little giggle of excitement as he raised a copy of a tabloid magazine called *Love It!* into view, holding it up beside his head.

The magazine had been a little shared vice of theirs since Ben had gone to visit the receptionist in hospital following her stroke a year or so back. Moira had a reputation for being, as Logan put it, 'a dour-faced bastard,' but she'd laughed as he'd read her the ludicrous 'real life' stories.

'It's a belter, this one,' he announced. 'There's a woman that's supposedly turned her daughter into a bedside table! I mean, how the hell does that work?!'

His face lit up in anticipation of her glee, but Moira continued to stare back at him, stony-faced.

'How can I help you?' she asked again.

'Moira!' Ben said, lowering the magazine.

There was a note of laughter to his voice, like he thought she might be winding him up. She didn't laugh along, though. Far from it.

'Unless there was something you wanted, Detective Inspector, I'd ask you to leave the reception area. We're very busy.'

'Moira, come on. What's this about? What have I done?' Ben asked.

'Are you deaf, Detective Inspector? I said we're *very* busy.'

She held eye contact while she licked the yellowed end of a nicotine-stained finger, then lowered her head and went back to turning the pages of the newspaper.

There was silence for a moment, then the squeaking of shoes on the vinyl flooring.

'Could you buzz me—?' Ben asked, then the door let out a sharp squawk to announce it was unlocked.

'Here, hold up!'

Ben turned, the door in hand, just as Constable Dave Davidson wheeled himself across the floor, headed for the open doorway. Dave eyed Moira as he raced across the reception area, arms pumping, expecting her to order him to *stop right there* and fill out a stack of paperwork.

Instead, Moira just sniffed loudly, and cast her gaze across the newspaper's letters page.

'Cheers!' Dave said, ducking under Ben's arm and wheeling himself through the door.

'No bother, son,' Ben said. He glanced back at Moira, then lowered his head and followed the PC through into the station proper.

It was only when the door had finally clunked closed that Moira allowed herself to look over at it, and, through the glass, at the sagging outline of DI Forde as he shuffled away along the corridor.

A moment later, the willowy forty-something woman who had welcomed Ben to the station popped her head out from the office door at Moira's back.

'You all right, Moi?' she asked, in her bright, cheerful sing-song.

'Oh, piss off, Jennifer,' Moira muttered.

Jennifer's smile only widened. She gave the dragon at the desk a double thumbs-up.

'Right you are, Moi,' she said, then she disappeared back into the office, leaving Moira Corson all alone at the front desk.

–

'Who's pissed on your chips?' asked Dave, while he and Ben waited for the lift.

'Hmm? Oh. Sorry, son. No one, doesn't matter,' Ben said. He looked down at the magazine in his hands, then twisted it into a tight tube. 'Doesn't matter.'

Dave looked back towards the door they'd come through. He adjusted himself in his chair, mentally preparing himself for the conversation to come.

'Woman trouble, is it?'

Ben blinked. 'What?'

'You don't need to tell me. Head-wrecks, the lot of them,' Dave announced. 'They're impossible to figure out. They say they want one thing, and you do it, and then it's wrong, and they tell you they never actually wanted that thing in the first place, and they wanted the opposite thing all along, and you were somehow supposed to have known that the whole time.'

'Who are we talking about here, son? Me or you?' Ben asked, smiling down at the man in the wheelchair.

'Ha! Sorry,' Dave said. They both looked up at the lights above the lift. They hadn't yet shifted. Someone must be getting in on the upper floor.

'It's nothing like that,' Ben said. 'Moira and me, there's nothing romantic about it. We both agreed on that. We made that very clear. We're friends, that's all. We were emphatic about that.'

Dave nodded. 'Good. That's good. I mean, as long as you're both on the same page,' he said.

'Exactly,' Ben agreed. 'And we are. We very much are. On the same page, I mean.'

He regarded the scrunched-up tube of the magazine in his hands, then pressed the button again, like this might make the lift move faster.

'Who wrote the page, though?'

Ben frowned. 'Eh? What do you mean?'

'The page you say you're both on. Who wrote it?' Dave asked. 'Who said it first, I mean? Who laid out the rules that there was nothing romantic about it?'

Beyond the sliding doors of the lift, the mechanism finally started to move.

'Does it matter?' Ben asked.

'Probably, aye. I mean, if one of you said it, and the other one just went along with it, but doesn't really feel that way...' Dave shrugged. 'Then again, don't ask me. What do I know about relationships? It's not like my love life has exactly been going great guns lately.'

He stopped talking when the elevator door opened, revealing a young uniformed officer with hair just long enough to hide her hearing aids.

Dave stared, slack-jawed, at Constable Beatrice Niddrie. Nidds, for her part, just stood there staring back.

It was only when the door began to slide closed again that Ben felt compelled to intervene. He thrust a hand forward, forcing the door to beat a retreat.

'Sorry,' Nidds said, stepping past them into the corridor. She nodded to Ben, 'Detective Inspector,' then flashed an indecipherable smile at the man in the wheelchair. 'Dave.'

'All right? How's it going?' he asked her. 'Long time no—'

'Busy, busy!' she declared. Then, she scuttled along the corridor, pulled open the door, and hurried out through reception.

'See?' Dave declared. 'What do I know? Don't listen to my advice. If you're both on the same page, that's all that matters.'

He rolled into the lift and turned around. Ben remained standing outside, squeezing the magazine between both hands like he was throttling a snake.

'You coming?' Dave asked.

'Actually...' Ben turned to his left, looking at the door to reception. 'No, son. Not yet.' He straightened his tie. 'There's something I need to do first.'

–

There was some sort of commotion over by the ambulance. Good timing, too, as Hamza had just spotted Geoff Palmer sidling out of the house towards him. Any excuse to delay talking to that bastard was fine by him.

Jogging along the drive, Hamza saw two Uniforms trying to put themselves between Isaac Simpson and a lanky, long-armed man, who both seemed determined that Isaac was getting in the back of the ambulance.

Hamza was a little surprised to see Isaac back this soon. He'd expected him to still be giving a statement at the station in Fort William.

He noticed that the paramedics were out of the vehicle and standing off to one side, out of harm's way, but ready to jump in should the need arise. They relaxed a little when they spotted Hamza approaching the scene.

'I just want to fucking see her! She's my wife! I want to see my wife!'

'Just give him a bloody minute with her,' the other man barked.

He wasn't upset like Isaac, but sounded outraged that the two uniformed officers weren't doing as they were told.

'She's not in there, sir,' one of the constables said. 'And even if she was, we couldn't let you in.'

'You're lying! She's in there, I know it!'

Isaac barged through the gap between the officers and hurled himself against the ambulance's back door. He fumbled for the handle with one hand, while slapping the darkened glass with the other.

'Open up! Open this fucking door!' he wailed.

The larger of the two Uniforms grabbed one of his arms and twisted it behind him, pulling him away from the vehicle. He struggled, twisting and thrashing so violently in the officer's grip that the other constable jumped in to help restrain him.

Seeing his chance, Isaac's pal strode right past them, grabbed hold of the ambulance's back door handle, and pulled.

It was only when Hamza slammed a hand against the door and held it closed that any of the four men noticed he was there.

'Right! Enough!' he snapped. 'Everyone get a bloody grip of themselves.'

The man holding onto the handle gave it another tug. Hamza didn't feel the door move, and realised it was locked. He kept his hand there, all the same, for effect.

'Please step away from the vehicle, sir,' he said, in a tone that made it clear this was not a request.

The other man regarded him with thinly veiled contempt, then made a show of releasing his grip, raising his hands, and stepping back.

'Isaac. That's enough,' he said, still eyeballing Hamza.

Behind him, Isaac let out a throaty sob, but immediately gave up trying to wrestle with the uniformed constables.

'I just want to see her. That's all,' he wheezed. 'I just want to see my Sharon.'

Hamza let his hand drop away from the door, then fired a nod over to the paramedics.

A moment later, the ambulance's lights flashed, and the horn gave a sharp *beep-beep*.

Hamza opened the door, to reveal an empty interior.

'Like the constable said, Mr Simpson, she's not there.'

Isaac buried his face in his hands and whimpered. Through gaps in his fingers, he looked up at the house, but made no move to try and get to it.

'She's being taken care of, Mr Simpson. We've got a great team in there'—now that Palmer had left the house, Hamza felt comfortable saying this—'making sure everything is done properly. Once they're done, Sharon will be taken up to Inverness. She'll be treated with nothing but respect.'

Isaac's mystery mate let out a snort at that. 'Oh, sure. She'll be laid out on a slab and gutted like a bloody fish.' This earned him a cold stare from Hamza, and another sob from Isaac. 'Well,' he said. 'There's no point sugarcoating it, is there? That's what's going to happen.'

'Sorry, sir, I didn't ask your name or what it is you're doing here,' Hamza said. 'I'm Detective Sergeant Hamza Khaled. And you are?'

The taller man brought his face a little closer to Hamza's, which involved him stooping slightly. A smirk tugged upwards at a corner of his mouth. 'Wouldn't you like to know?'

'For God's sake, Armand, will you just *stop*?' Isaac yelped. He wiped his eyes and nose on his sleeve, and turned away from the house. 'I want to go. I don't want to be here. I can't... I can't do this right now.'

'Armand Holburn,' Hamza said, staring up into the other man's face. He was grateful that Tyler had taken the time to check in with him about the door-to-door before heading down the road. 'The neighbour with the annoying wee poodle thing. That's you. Right, sir?'

Armand continued to loom over him, but Hamza didn't appear remotely intimidated.

'She's a bichon frise,' the taller man eventually said. Then, with a shake of his head, he wheeled around and set off at a marching pace towards a Rover 75 that was parked on the road behind one of the police cars.

'Come on then, Isaac!' he called, snapping his fingers like he was summoning his dog. 'Let's leave these *gentlemen* to their work.'

—

Moira Corson looked up from her crossword, and once again found herself eye-to-eye through the glass with DI Ben Forde.

'I'm sure I remember stressing how busy we are, Detective Inspector,' she griped. 'Is there something I can do for you?'

'Yes,' Ben said. He was smiling, but it was hanging by a thread. He swallowed, and the magazine gave a creak as his hands tightened further around it. 'You can come out for dinner.'

Moira's face remained completely motionless. Her fingers interlocked as she clasped her hands on top of the newspaper.

'A proper dinner this time,' Ben continued. 'With, you know, candles? And nice wine. And maybe dancing.'

Moira's top lip drew up into the beginning of a sneer. 'Sounds like you're describing *a date*,' she said, spitting the last two words out like they were laced with arsenic.

Ben steeled himself.

The magazine groaned in his grip.

He nodded.

'I am,' he said. 'That's exactly what I'm describing. A date. Me and you. You and me. The two of us. I know I said—we said—that this was just a friendship, and nothing more, but…'

His breath ran out on him there. He took a moment to get it back, then straightened up again.

'I don't want that. Not really. I want us to be more than that.'

'Well,' Moira said, flatly. She tapped a finger on the news-paper. Her gaze flitted up and down, taking him in. 'Well, well, *well*.'

The shape of her mouth changed, the sneer shifting into something altogether less menacing.

'And here was me thinking you were never going to bloody ask.'

Chapter 10

An hour later, once the body of Sharon Simpson had been taken up to Inverness, Hamza joined the others in the Incident Room at Fort William Police Station.

The detectives were all gathered by the Big Board, which Hamza immediately guessed had been set up by Tammi-Jo. Nobody else would've drawn the dot of the first letter 'i' in 'murder investigation' as a smiley face.

Constable Dave Davidson was sitting at a desk near the door, his wheelchair angled to face the board. Taggart, Logan's dog, slept soundly in the corner nearest the window. His tail occasionally thumped, suggesting he was enjoying a dream.

'Just in time, Detective Sergeant!' Ben cried, meeting Hamza as he entered the room.

He patted the DS on the shoulder, his face alive with warmth and good humour. For a moment, Hamza thought Ben was going to hug him, but instead the DI just winked, then took a seat.

Once seated, Ben reached into his overnight bag and produced a full packet of Tunnock's caramel wafers, which he set on the table beside him.

'Fire in, everyone,' Ben urged. 'Help yourself to one.'

All eyes turned to stare at him. As one, their gazes shifted to the packet of biscuits, before returning to the detective inspector.

'The hell's up with you?' asked Logan.

Ben's eyebrows dipped a little, but his smile remained unaffected. 'What do you mean?'

'You usually hoard them things like that wee doughball-faced goblin fella from *Lord of the Rings*.'

Ben laughed and leaned back in his chair so that his feet briefly lifted off the floor. 'Well, maybe I'm just in a generous mood. Still, if nobody wants one…'

There was a rabble of protest, and a rush of movement as everyone scrabbled to grab one of the foil-wrapped biscuits. Logan tossed one over to Dave, who caught it and responded with an appreciative raised thumb and a, 'Cheers!'

Ben, despite his self-professed generosity, pounced and slapped Tyler's hand away when the DC tried to treat himself to seconds.

'Here! Help yourself to *one*, I said!'

Tyler rubbed at the back of his hand, clutching his solitary caramel wafer. 'Sorry, boss. Thought I'd bring one home for Sinead.'

'Oh well, in that case, don't worry, son,' Ben said, his tone softening. 'I'm sure you'll pass a shop between here and there.'

With biscuits on the go, it was agreed that they needed tea. Tyler and Tammi-Jo were dispatched to get it sorted, and returned a few minutes later carrying three mugs each.

That done, they all took their seats, raised their various drinks in toast, and spent a couple of minutes just enjoying their biscuits.

'I just have to say something, Tyler,' Logan announced, once he'd finished eating and had rolled his biscuit's foil wrapper into a little red and gold ball. 'You've no' been with us now for close to three months.'

Tyler grinned. 'I missed you, too, boss.'

A few chuckles went around the room. Logan waited for them to fade away again before continuing.

'Well, I must say, it's certainly been a lot less interesting without you. I mean, during the course of those months, we didn't have a single murder across the whole of the Highlands,' Logan said. 'Then, your first day back comes around, and we get a shout in the first fifteen minutes.'

80

He took a slurp of his coffee, then set the mug back down with a *thunk*.

'I've always suspected this, son, but I've never had enough evidence to say it. Not until now. But, I think the evidence is there, now. I think it's undeniable.'

Logan pointed to the detective constable, who was starting to look a little worried.

'You're a fucking jinx.'

He smirked, and Tyler ejected a relieved-sounding groan. 'Jesus Christ, boss. I thought you were going to peg me as a secret serial killer or something!' he cried.

Hamza snorted. 'Aye, like you'd be able to get away with it.'

'What do you mean?' Tyler demanded. 'I reckon I could be a brilliant serial killer. I could be one of the really big ones.'

Tammi-Jo nodded sagely. 'Like that giant in *Jack and the Beanstalk*,' she said, and nobody could tell if she was winding them up or not.

'Well, maybe don't try and put that theory to the test, son, eh?' Ben suggested. He neatly folded up the wrapper from his caramel wafer, and reached for a second biscuit.

'Here, what was all that about just taking one?' Tyler objected.

Ben grinned at him. 'My biscuits, my rules,' he said, making a show of unwrapping it. Once fully unsheathed from its foil, he used the biscuit to point to the Big Board. 'Now, can everyone else see that cartoon frog, or is this me having some sort of mental breakdown?'

—

It took a few minutes for Tammi-Jo to explain her chocolate machine analogy, and several more for her to answer all the questions that arose from it.

Once that was out of the way, Hamza took the floor to recap where they currently were with the investigation.

'Sharon Simpson, aged thirty-seven, seen here looking like a photocopy of a monster with a drawing pin shoved through its forehead,' he said, indicating the picture that Tammi-Jo had put up.

'This place really needs a better printer,' the DC pointed out.

'Cause of death yet to be confirmed. Suffocation is a possibility, though she also had her neck broken. We'll know more after the PM,' Hamza continued. 'She was in a state of undress, and handcuffed in a position that could generously be described as "compromising". Evidence of sexual intercourse, and a condom was found at the scene.'

'What, used?' asked Ben, leaning forwards in his chair.

'Used,' Hamza confirmed.

'I wondered why you were asking the husband about that,' Ben said. 'Bloody hell. That's a find.'

'Someone was helluva careless,' Tyler said.

Logan's grunted response gave very little away.

'We're running forensics on it now. We'll need to get a DNA sample from the husband to check against it.'

'He claims they hadn't had sex in over a week,' Logan said.

'Probably not his, then,' Tammi-Jo reasoned.

Dave piped up from his desk by the door. 'Unless they're a right pair of clarty bastards.'

'He also said they never use them,' Logan continued. 'She was taking the contraceptive pill.'

Ben took a sip of his tea. 'Got to be the killer's, then?' he said, but he sounded like he was already questioning the theory.

'Seems likely,' Logan confirmed. 'But something feels off. He clearly had the foresight to use one in the first place. To then just leave it lying on the floor...'

'Could've panicked, boss,' Tyler suggested. 'He might not have meant to kill her. When he saw he had, maybe he freaked and ran.'

Hamza nodded along with this. 'It's a possibility. It could've been a consensual thing that got out of control.'

'Did we get her phone?' Logan asked.

'We did, sir. Scene of Crime's going to bring it to Tech Support. That might give us some insight into whether she's been seeing someone else.'

'We'll need a warrant to access it,' Ben reminded them. 'I can run that up to Mitchell and get her working on it.'

'What about the frog?'

Everyone looked at Tammi-Jo, who had asked the question. She, in turn, was staring at the upside-down drawing in the middle of the board.

'Eh, what about it?' Tyler asked.

'Well, someone moved it. There's a footprint,' DC Swanney said. 'We think someone used it to climb over the hedge.' Her eyes searched the room for confirmation. 'Right?'

Hamza regarded the frog for a moment. 'If it was a consensual hook-up, why sneak in over the hedge? If he knew the husband was out, why not just come up the driveway? It's shielded by trees and the hedge on both sides. None of the neighbours would see anyone coming or going.'

Logan scratched at his chin, his mind whirring through all the possible explanations, and finding only one.

'The only way you'd be seen was if someone was looking out of the windows of the house,' he realised. 'And if you knew they were expecting you, why would you bother your arse to hide?'

Silence fell while they all gave this some consideration. It all pointed in one direction.

'So, an intruder, then,' Ben said. 'That's our theory?'

'For now,' Logan said. 'But let's not get hung up on it.' He turned his attention back to DS Khaled. 'Any more info on the footprint or the bike tread?'

'Not yet, sir. Palmer's team has catalogued them, and will give us what they can. We might need to draft in Uniform to run comparisons if we want to find exact matches for them.'

'Did Palmer give any idea of shoe size?' Tyler asked.

'Vaguely. It's only a partial print. Size eight to ten is the best we've got. Trainer of some sort, he reckons. Wearer is probably male.'

Ben scribbled a note on his pad. 'Just the one print?'

'That's all they could find, sir, aye,' Hamza confirmed.

Logan swivelled his chair until he was aiming at Tyler. 'What about the neighbour on the other side? The one that came and picked the husband up. What did you make of him?'

'I'm not personally a big fan, boss,' the detective constable replied. 'Something off about him, but couldn't put my finger on what. He seems very security-conscious, which felt odd for the area. Big padlocks on his sheds and gate. Doorbell cam at the front.'

Everyone in the room perked up.

'Only shows his front path,' Tyler said, dashing their hopes. 'He didn't get any alerts the night before.'

'Bollocks. Let's see if we can get footage, anyway,' Logan said. 'Never know, there might be something on there from the days leading up to the attack.'

'Anything else jump out at you when you were there?' Ben asked Tyler.

'Aye, boss. His dog.'

Over in the corner, the sleeping Taggart raised an ear, but kept his eyes shut.

'Annoying wee shite of a thing,' Tyler continued. 'And he's been getting a lot of harassment lately. Nuisance calls. Some property damage. And his dog was killed in a hit and run.'

'What, the dog that jumped out on you?' Tammi-Jo asked.

'Eh, no,' Tyler said, after a pause.

'No. No, of course,' Tammi-Jo said. 'I was going to say, that would've been weird. Spooky.'

'Another dog, I mean. He used to have two,' Tyler explained. 'One got knocked down a couple of weeks back. Molly, her name was. He seemed to be pretty attached. Think she was his favourite. Motorbike hit her, he reckons, though nobody saw anything. Other than that, he didn't say much interesting. Except…'

He reached behind him, lifted a folder from his desk, and opened it with some dramatic flair.

'I went ahead and followed up on something he mentioned, boss,' Tyler announced. He rocked back in his chair. 'It made for some *pretty interesting* reading.'

Logan sighed at the DC's dramatic pause. 'Jesus Christ, son. You're no' Columbo. You don't need to try and build up the bloody suspense.'

'Sorry, boss,' Tyler said. He consulted the printouts in his folder. 'So, a few months back, Armand started reporting all the harassment stuff on 101. The calls. Windows being egged. Car getting scraped, bins knocked over. All that stuff. Apart from the dog getting run over, which he admits might not even be connected, it was nothing major, but he was understandably pissed off about it all.'

'And?' Logan asked, sensing there was more to come.

'And he wasn't the only one, boss. Isaac Simpson—the victim's husband—he reported similar things happening around the same time. There are multiple reports from both of them, four by Armand, two by Isaac.'

'Local kids pissing about?' Ben guessed.

'Aye. Could be that. Except…' Tyler flicked through the pages until he found what he was looking for. He tapped his pen against the page. 'Norman Todd.'

Glances and shrugs passed between the others in the room.

'Who's Norman Todd?' Logan finally asked.

'I'm glad you asked that, boss,' Tyler said, with a note of triumph, then he quickly rattled off all the information he'd been able to dig up.

Norman Todd was a fifty-four-year-old man who lived in the tiny village of Appin, somewhere between Oban and Ballachulish. He'd reported similar harassment starting at almost exactly the same time as Armand and Isaac, despite living an hour's drive south.

The reported incidents were all similar. Windows pelted with eggs, tyres slashed, bins scattered across the garden, dogshit on the doorstep. That sort of thing.

A couple of local Uniforms had popped round and taken a statement. After that, things had gone from bad to worse. He'd started getting phone calls at all hours of the day and night. There had been a man on the other end of the line. He had insisted it was a man, although the caller had never said a word.

'Well, there are kids everywhere,' Ben reasoned. 'And some of them can be right wee bastards.'

'There's no saying it's connected,' Hamza agreed.

Tyler grinned, and interlocked his fingers behind his head, relaxing further into his chair.

'Except they're all friends. All three of them. Armand, Isaac and Norman. They're all ex-army buddies.'

The atmosphere in the room changed subtly. Chairs creaked as everyone sat forward a little, paying closer attention now.

'They served together in the war in Bosnia,' Tyler continued. He flicked through his pad. 'Back in…'

'Sixth of April Nineteen-Ninety-Two to the Fourteenth of December Nineteen-Ninety-Five,' said Ben.

Tyler found the page he was looking for, then scanned his notes. 'Bang on, boss! Check out the history buff.'

Ben shook his head. 'I was there,' he said, and all his earlier joviality was notably absent. 'For some of it, anyway. Last tour I did.' He rubbed his hands together slowly, like he was running them under a hot tap, trying to get them clean. 'One tour too many.'

He gave himself a shake, then cleared his throat and sat up straighter, aware that everyone else in the room was watching him.

'They'll have had it rough. Everyone did. They'll have seen things that…' He couldn't find the words to describe whatever long-buried images were forcing themselves upon him. 'They'll have seen some things.'

A weighty silence lingered for a moment, before the tension was broken by Tammi-Jo springing to her feet and crossing to the Big Board.

'This is all good stuff,' she announced. 'I'll start sticking it up.'

'Good idea,' Logan said. 'And we should arrange to go and speak to this Norman fella. See if he can tell us anything else.'

'No can do, boss,' Tyler said. 'He's missing.'

Logan's fingers tightened on the armrests of his chair. 'Missing? How do you mean?'

'Just, you know, in the traditional sense of not being where he's supposed to be, boss.'

Logan tutted. 'Since when?'

'Just over five weeks, boss. He left a voicemail on his sister's mobile that made her think he was going to do away with himself. She lives down south, called it in to 999, and Uniform went round to check on him.'

'And he wasn't there?' Hamza guessed.

'No sign. Door unlocked, wallet, phone, keys, bank cards, all that stuff's still in the house. The house is near the water. A loch. So, when he didn't turn up, the divers went in for a look, but couldn't see any sign of him. He's down as a missing person, but the assumption is he's done himself in.'

'Any history of mental health problems?' Logan asked.

'Oh, aye, a whole catalogue, boss. PTSD, depression, anxiety... And they're just the ones I can pronounce. He'd attempted suicide a couple of times before. Overdose both times, but he came to his senses and called an ambulance. Last time was a couple of years back. He was still on the waiting list for additional counselling.'

This wasn't a huge surprise. The detectives rarely had to deal with it, but the uniformed division was slowly becoming an ad hoc care service for those with mental health issues. At least one shout in three involved someone off their medication, or long overdue an appointment to be put on some in the first place. It was a bloody pandemic.

'There's a couple of other things of potential interest, boss,' Tyler continued. 'When I spoke to Armand, he mentioned a female officer had come out to see him a few weeks ago about all the harassment stuff. Reckons she was the first one to take it seriously.'

'And?'

'There's no record of it.'

'What, nothing?' Ben asked.

Tyler shook his head.

Logan frowned. 'So, what are you saying? Whoever it was didn't get around to writing up their report? Not unheard of.'

'Not even that, boss. There's no record of anyone being dispatched,' Tyler explained. 'I mean, it's still an open case, and he was certainly making enough noise to get a home visit, so someone probably did go out. I just can't find any evidence of it.'

'Dig around a bit more. Someone's bound to know,' the DCI replied. 'If it comes to it, ask your man himself again. He might've written down a name.'

'I can do that if you want?' Dave volunteered from the sidelines. 'Doing hee-haw else until the Exhibits start coming in.'

'Nice one!' Tyler said. 'You're a star.'

Logan looked over at the board, but Tammi-Jo was still adding to it, and blocking most of it from view as she buzzed around from side to side, scribbling notes and sticking them up in what appeared to be a completely haphazard manner.

He got up from his seat and crossed to the window. It looked out over the car park, and at the big empty wasteland across the road that had once been earmarked for a supermarket. That deal had fallen through, though, and now it was rumoured that the new hospital was being built there.

There had been some signs of work happening last time they were here, but the site was once again bare.

He watched a couple of birds circling in the sky and ran over everything he'd just heard. Three men, all connected, all getting harassed at the same time, but in different parts of the country.

'Any of the other neighbours mention problems?' he asked, not turning around.

'No, boss. Just those three.'

Targeted, then. Someone had a bone to pick with those men. Someone wanted to be a thorn in their sides.

But was it the killer? It was a big jump from knocking over someone's bin to raping and murdering their wife.

'There was something else,' he said, a detail from the house popping into his head seemingly out of nowhere. 'Sellotape on the wall. Above the bed.'

Nobody quite knew what to say about that. Hamza eventually answered with a hesitant, 'OK…?'

'New or old?' asked Tammi-Jo.

Still facing the window, Logan's lips twitched fleetingly upward into a smile. 'New.'

'Gotcha.'

Logan heard the squeaking of a marker pen scribbling on a card.

Ben fiddled with the rolled-up ball of his second biscuit wrapper. 'You think it's connected?'

'No idea,' Logan admitted. He turned his back on the window. 'Palmer's lot are going to look at it. Might be nothing.'

Ben's eyes narrowed. 'I know you too well, Jack. That's not a 'might be nothing' face.'

Logan shrugged. 'It probably is nothing. It's just a theory. Christ, it's barely even that. It's a hunch, that's all.'

Ben looked around at the rest of the team. 'Are you going to share it, then? We're all ears.'

Logan thought about this for a moment, then shook his head. 'Not yet. We'll see what pans out. Like I say, it's probably not worth wasting any thought on yet.'

'OK, cool,' Tyler said. He tapped the folder with his pen again. 'So, all right if I finish my bit, boss? You sort of cut me off before my big moment, there. I had a big finale planned that was going to blow you all away, and then you started talking some shite about Sellotape.'

Logan raised an eyebrow and looked the detective constable up and down. 'Someone's got cocky on their time off.' He took his seat and gestured for Tyler to continue. 'Fire on then, son. Blow our minds. I'm sure we're all excited to see what you've dug up.'

Tammi-Jo stopped writing and joined the others in staring at Tyler. Normally, this level of attention might have made the DC nervous, but from the smug look on his face, Logan realised that he must actually have something major.

'Like I said, boss, there were a lot of similarities in the reports made by all three of the guys. There was one difference, though. One thing about Norman's stood out.'

He stopped there. He wore the expression of a man holding a royal flush, who knew that everyone else around the table was bluffing.

'You're going to make me say it, aren't you?' Logan sighed. 'What's the difference?'

'All three of them were being harassed by someone,' Tyler said. He picked up a sheet of glossy paper from the open file and held it aloft for the others to see. 'But Norman was the only one who got a photo of the guy.'

Chapter 11

Shona stumbled, red-faced and sweating, into the mortuary office, tried to blurt out an apology to the man standing behind the counter, then ran out of breath before any words could make it out of her mouth.

She held up a finger to let him know she'd be with him in a moment, then bent with both hands on her knees while she waited for her heart rate to slow, and her lungs to begin accepting oxygen again.

'I'm hoping you're Dr Maguire.'

She raised a thumb to confirm this, then spent a few more moments wheezing until she'd gathered enough strength to straighten up again.

'Sorry. Got called away. Forgot you were—'

She stopped talking when she saw him properly. The wind and rain had whipped at her hair, giving her a distinct 'wild woman' look. Without realising she was doing it, she reached up and smoothed it down.

'Are you Neville?' she asked.

He wasn't. He couldn't be. Surely not?

From past experience of Mortuary Technicians—Neville's official title—she'd expected a gawky, pale-skinned, and unrelentingly awkward twenty-something. Not the swarthy, square-jawed Adonis standing before her.

He had the look of an Italian film star about him. A proper A-Lister, too.

When he smiled, his teeth were so perfectly straight that Shona could only assume they'd been set into his gums by some internationally renowned master jeweller.

He was dressed in a shirt and tie, with the top button undone, and the tie loosened rakishly. He also wore a pair of light grey Chinos that were so tight they left very little to the imagination.

Practically nothing, in fact.

'I am. Neville Knox.'

'Does he? Shona says, "Come in!"'

He stared back at her, an amused sort of confusion chiselled into his face.

'Sorry, rubbish joke. You said "knocks" and I said…' Shona swallowed. 'Forget it. I sometimes make terrible puns when I'm nervous.'

He smiled, and the usually chilly room suddenly felt uncomfortably hot. As he took a step closer, the smell of his cologne encircled her. Aniseed and warm spices.

'Why are you nervous?' he asked.

Shona shook her head. 'I'm not.'

'You just said you were,' he reminded her.

'Oh. Right. Yes,' Shona said. Her eyebrows crept up her forehead while her eyes narrowed. To the casual observer, she looked like she was straining to pass a kidney stone. 'I left the car parked on double yellow lines.'

'Ah. No wonder you're worried,' Neville said, though it was clear from his smirk that he wasn't buying it.

'I know! Totally boxed in an ambulance, and everything,' Shona said, doubling down. 'Hence any apparent, you know, anxious behaviour on my part.' She clicked her fingers, as if only now remembering something. 'Also, I don't like meeting new people.'

'God, nor me!' Neville laughed.

It was quite a nice laugh, Shona thought. Strong and manly, but not over the top, and not for anyone's benefit but his own.

'I get really awkward around new folk,' he continued, leaning in a little and whispering like they were sharing a secret. He shuddered, then his smile broadened, like the shared secret had graduated to become an inside joke. 'I'm a total introvert.'

He didn't seem like an introvert. He exuded confidence, which only served to put her even further on the back foot.

'You don't look like a Neville,' she said, grasping for something to say. She was still sweaty and flustered—perhaps even more so than when she'd first arrived—and thinking straight was proving problematic.

His smile only grew, and her eyes were drawn to his mouth. God, those teeth! They belonged in an art gallery somewhere, not shoved in the gums of a mere mortal man.

If, indeed, he was mortal.

'What does a Neville look like?'

Thoughts collided in Shona's brain. Harry Potter. Adolf Hitler. She couldn't very well mention either of those.

'Just, you know, smaller,' she said.

Her gaze accidentally fell on the crotch of his trousers, then shot back to his face in horror.

'I thought you were going to be a big useless bastard who'd die!' she blurted.

Neville regarded her through narrowed eyes. He smiled. It was a little lopsided, and all the more perfect for it.

'Sorry?'

'You know, from Harry Potter? Neville. The big oaf of a lad. I was saying to my… partner. Boyfriend. Man friend. You know? We're very much an item. Anyway, I was saying to him, that the only Neville I know is the one from Harry Potter, who's a useless bastard, then dies.'

'Neville doesn't die.'

Shona stared back at him, her lips moving silently. 'Doesn't he?'

'No. He kills a big snake, and saves the day. He's pretty heroic, actually.'

'Right.' The pathologist swallowed. 'Who am I thinking of, then?'

'Don't know. I can't read your mind,' Neville told her.

'Thank Christ,' Shona whispered.

She accidentally glanced at his crotch again, let out a little cheep of embarrassment, then wheeled around so she was facing the door.

'My car!' she cried. 'I need to move it before I get started here.'

'I can move it, if you like?' Neville suggested.

Shona shook her head. 'You don't know what it looks like.'

'You could tell me.'

'No. I can't,' she said, tripping over the words.

Neville frowned, but his smile hung around. 'Why can't you?'

Shona looked back at him over her shoulder, her mind racing. Why couldn't she tell him what her car looked like? What possible explanation could there be for saying that?

'It's… a secret,' she said, in a slightly hysterical whisper.

Then, without another word, she hurried back out of the mortuary, strode to the end of the corridor, and leaned herself against the wall, out of sight.

'It's a fecking *secret*?' she muttered. 'Jesus Christ, Maguire, what's wrong with you?'

She slouched there for a few moments, calming herself down and getting her breath back. She tried giving herself a couple of slaps on the face for good measure, but couldn't bring herself to make the full contact necessary to have any real effect.

It was almost a full minute later, when her breathing and heart rate had slowed to more reasonable levels, that she noticed the figure standing along the corridor.

She must've emerged from the adjoining corridor that fed into this one, and now stood staring at Shona with eyes that were ringed and made puffy by circles of red.

It had been a month or two since she'd seen the girl, but Shona recognised her at once.

'Olivia?' she said, stepping away from the wall. 'Are you OK? What's the matter? You look like you've been crying.'

Olivia Maximuke, teenage daughter of the feared—but long since incarcerated—Russian mobster, Bosco Maximuke, stood shaking in her school uniform and staring in Shona's direction.

Though she'd clearly been crying recently, her face held almost no expression now, like all her emotions had been wrung out of her through her tear ducts.

'Olivia? Are you all right? What is it? What's wrong? Has something happened?'

As she spoke, Shona started to walk towards her, but the girl took a sudden step backwards so she was right in the mouth of the connecting corridor, a look of panic igniting across her face.

The pathologist realised Olivia was going to run at the exact same moment she set off.

'Olivia, wait!' she cried, breaking into a jog.

There was an angry shout from an orderly as Olivia shoved past him, and then she was racing around the corner at the far end of the corridor, moving far too quickly for the still partly breathless Shona to stand a chance of catching her.

'What the hell was that about?' Shona muttered, slowing to a stop.

Olivia could be unpredictable. Since Shona had somehow been roped into babysitting the girl a few years back, she'd been through quite a lot with Bosco Maximuke's daughter. She'd seen her angry. She'd seen her scared.

But she'd never seen her looking like that before. Something had happened to the girl.

Something awful.

'You OK?'

'Jesus!' Shona gasped, jumping at the voice that came from right behind her.

Neville smiled his fabulous smile and held his hands up in apology. 'Sorry, didn't mean to startle you. I just heard shouting and wanted to make sure everything was OK.'

He glanced at one of the corridor windows. 'You, uh, you get your car shifted?'

Shona looked back in the direction that Olivia had run. The hospital was a maze. Even if she was still in the building, the chances of Shona finding her were almost non-existent, especially if she didn't want to be found.

'Yeah. All done,' she said.

'That was quick!'

Shona turned away from the corridor and shrugged. 'It's not a very big car,' she said.

Then, she set off past him towards the mortuary before he could figure out that her reply made absolutely no sense whatsoever.

'Now, come on, this poor woman's not going to dissect herself.'

Chapter 12

'Cheers for this, mate,' Tyler said, sliding his bundle of notes onto Dave's desk. 'Not sure what you'll be able to find out. Holburn might've just got his dates wrong about when the house call was made. No saying there's even anything to find.'

'It'll give me something to do,' Dave said. 'I'm just sat twiddling my thumbs until Palmer is finished looking over the stuff up the road.'

Tyler tapped a finger to his forehead in salute and started to roll away in his chair. Something about Dave's demeanour made him stop again, though.

'Everything all right?'

Dave took a moment to reply, as if he hadn't realised the question was directed at him. 'What? Oh, aye. Just peachy.'

He didn't sound peachy. Not unless it was a mouldy one lurking undiscovered at the bottom of a fruit bowl.

Tyler used his feet to pull his chair in closer to Dave's desk. 'I saw Nidds knocking about earlier...' he said, leaving the rest of the sentence hanging.

'Aye, me too,' Dave said wearily.

'I take it things aren't going great?'

'They were. It was great. For a while. But now, they're not going at all,' Dave said. 'They're gone.'

'Shit. Sorry to hear that, mate. I thought you were good together. She seems really nice. Funny, too.'

Tyler hadn't actually spent all that much time with Constable Niddrie. Most of his first-hand experience of her had come from one conversation they'd had in the canteen up in the

Burnett Road station in Inverness, when they'd bonded over their shared love of pickled onion-flavoured Monster Munch.

He'd liked her, though. And, from what he'd been able to gather in that fifteen-minute conversation, she really liked Dave.

'She was. I mean, she is. Nice. And funny. Smart, too. Really smart. She did a degree. Before signing up.'

'In what?' Tyler asked.

Dave pulled a face like he was straining with a particularly stubborn bowel movement. 'Science things,' he replied, though it sounded like he was asking Tyler for confirmation. 'Not sure. But she's really clever.'

'What happened?' he asked. 'What went wrong?'

'Dunno. She just liked the idea of being in the polis, I think.'

Tyler shook his head. 'No, with the relationship, I mean.'

'Oh!' Dave shrugged. He was a big man and usually filled out his wheelchair. Right now, though, he looked like a little boy sitting there in it. 'Not sure. But it's not me, apparently. It's her. So, that's something.'

Tyler nodded sagely. He'd been there. He didn't know any man who hadn't.

'Damn. That's shite,' he said.

'It is what it is,' Dave said. He shrugged again, though he forced some positivity into it this time. 'Honestly? I reckon she's just scared of getting attached. Commitment and stuff. She had a pretty tough time growing up, being adopted, and all that.'

Tyler's eyebrows rose in surprise. 'She's adopted? I didn't know.'

Dave's face contorted into a rictus of horror, then froze there. 'Shite. I'm not supposed to say.'

'Don't worry,' Tyler assured him. He rapped his knuckles on the side of his head. 'Memory like a goldfish. Already forgotten.'

Logan's voice rolled across the room like a peal of thunder. 'Right, you two, enough with the bloody chit-chat. Constable Nidds' family situation is no business of either of yours. You've both got stuff to be cracking on with. Dave, I want to know who went out to the neighbour's house. Tyler, why haven't you found me that guy in the photo yet?'

'Sorry, boss,' Tyler said, hurriedly rolling his chair back towards his desk. 'I'm jumping on that right now. Me and Dave were just taking a minute to catch up.'

'Oh, you were, were you?' Logan snapped. 'Is that all you were doing?'

Ben looked up from the printout he was studying and peered at the DCI over the top of his reading glasses.

'Someone pissed on your chips, Jack?' he asked. He hadn't heard the phrase in a while, and Dave's use of it earlier had reminded him how much he liked it.

Logan managed a one-note chuckle. 'Aye. Something like that,' he intoned, rising to his feet. 'I've got a call with Palmer for an update in a minute, and the way I see it is, if I have to be miserable, then so does every other bugger.'

Tyler grinned. 'Oof. Aye, that's fair. Tough break that, boss. Still, on the positive side, if it's just a call, at least you won't have to look at his annoying wee pug face…'

–

Geoff Palmer's annoying wee pug face filled the screen of Logan's laptop, his pock-marked skin and blackhead-infested nose smoothed over by some unconvincing technical wizardry that made him look like a twelve-year-old. Albeit, a twelve-year-old who'd seen things no twelve-year-old should have to see.

The Scene of Crime man's camera was down low and angled upwards, so the first three things Logan saw on the screen were all chins. The next two things he noticed were the hairy caverns of Geoff's nostrils, which he was staring straight up into.

The sound quality was thin and reedy, and unpleasant on the ears. Although, to be fair, that pretty much described Palmer's voice at the best of times.

'I hope you've got your wee policeman's notebook out, Jack, because there's quite a bit here you're going to want to write down.'

'Or you could just do your job properly and send me the report,' Logan suggested.

Palmer huffed a sigh out through his nose. The audio was slightly out of sync with the image, so it took his on-screen nostrils a moment to catch up with the whistling sound. They flared wider, giving Logan an even more detailed view of the man's nasal passages.

'Obviously, we'll send the report. I just thought you might want a sneak preview. I thought that might be useful. But if it wouldn't be, if you'd rather wait until it's all typed up, just you say the word, Jack, and I'll end this call quicker than you can say...' His face went momentarily blank, like he'd forgotten all the words he'd previously known. He eventually settled on, 'End call,' but it was clear from the sourness of his expression that he wasn't happy with it.

'Cut the shite, Geoff,' Logan replied. 'Tell me what we've got.'

Palmer smirked, like he'd just emerged victorious from some battle of wits Logan hadn't been aware he was even competing in.

'Right, then. The big headline first.'

The condom, Logan assumed, so he was surprised when that wasn't the case.

'Your Sellotape.'

Well out of sight of the camera, so Palmer couldn't see him doing it, Logan opened his notepad and held his pen poised ready to write.

'What about it?'

'You were right. It was new. We found the roll in the kitchen, with a pair of scissors beside it.'

'Prints?' Logan asked, then he winced when Palmer shook his head.

'That would be nice and neat, wouldn't it? But no. Clean. Mostly.'

Logan's ears pricked up. 'Mostly?'

'There was residue from a piece of paper on the bit of tape in the bedroom,' Palmer said.

Logan was hit by a surge of excitement. Maybe his hunch about the Sellotape was right.

'A note,' he said. 'There was a note stuck to the wall.'

Palmer looked disappointed. 'Yes,' he mumbled, his big moment ruined. 'That's what we reckon.'

'Any sign of it in the room?'

On-screen, the SOCO shook his head. 'No sign in the house.'

'Bugger it.' Logan leaned back in his chair. 'That makes things more complicated.'

'It does. But don't worry, your old pal Geoff's got something up his sleeve. It's quite something, actually. If this doesn't impress you, nothing will.'

'Just get on with it,' Logan urged. 'What have you found?'

Palmer swivelled from side to side in his chair, enjoying this feeling of glory, however fleeting it might be.

'I don't know if you noticed the little notepad in the drawer in the bedside table?'

Logan admitted that he hadn't, and Palmer rolled his eyes in a show of exasperated amusement.

'Not to worry. I had the foresight to check.' He reached off-camera for a moment, then returned with an evidence bag that held a cheap rectangular note block with the logo of some hotel or other up the top. 'This is it. It's been there a while, by the looks of it. Not a lot of pages left.'

'Is it a match for the residue on the tape?' Logan asked.

'Bingo,' Palmer said, drawing the word out and emphasising both syllables. 'Everyone else was just going to file it, but I had a feeling, you know? Like a hunch? I knew there was more to this pad than meets the eye. I could sense that there was something—'

'For fuck's sake, Geoff, you're no' narrating your autobiography here. Get to the point!'

Palmer fell silent. What Logan could see of the face beyond the chins looked utterly dejected, his big moment having been snatched away from him.

'There was an imprint on the top sheet,' he revealed. 'After we ran forensics on the pad, we did a rubbing. It revealed some text.'

He reached off-camera for another evidence bag, and held this one up for Logan to see, too. There was a single sheet of paper inside, with the same hotel branding at the top. The side of a pencil had been rubbed across the page, revealing the faint outline of some lettering Logan was just about able to make out.

'"I know what you did",' he read.

Palmer said something, but he was no longer listening. Instead, he was slotting the note into the mental picture he'd been building up, working out exactly what had gone on in that room, and why.

'The underwear,' he said, cutting Geoff off. 'Is there a brand name on the label or anything?'

Palmer smirked. 'I don't think they're exactly your style, Jack. I'm not sure you could carry them off.'

'Aye, very good,' Logan said, sighing.

'Or maybe they're going to be a gift for—'

'Cut your shite, Geoff, and just get me the details,' Logan told him. 'I want to find a match and show the husband. See if he recognises them, or if they were for someone else's benefit. And get me anything you can on the handcuffs, too. There should be a make and maybe a model number. I'll get the team here following up. I want to know where they came from.'

'It'll all be in the report,' Palmer said. 'The shoe print, the tyre track, the condom, it'll all be in there. And no, before you ask, there's no word on a DNA match yet. These things take time. But, what I *can* tell you now is that your *rather attractive*'—he waggled his eyebrows suggestively—'new detective constable was onto something with the frog statue. Someone definitely came over the top of that hedge. Probably got himself a fair few cuts and scratches, too, unless he was wearing a lot of protective layers.'

'Right. Good to know,' Logan said, making a note.

'I know she's just filling in until the other one gets back,' Palmer continued. From the way he said 'the other one', Logan assumed he couldn't remember DC Sinead Bell's name. This wasn't any real surprise. 'But I hope you keep her around. She seems... fun. Brings a bit of life to a murder scene, if you know what I mean?'

He winked, and that one tiny movement made every last inch of Logan's skin crawl.

Logan opened his mouth, preparing to share his thoughts on what a slimy, weasely, Play-Doh-faced wee runt the Scene of Crime man was.

But then, he shook his head, muttered, 'Ah, fuck it,' and clicked the button that ended the call.

—

DI Forde held the photo that Norman Todd had taken out at arm's length, alternating between looking at it through and over his glasses.

'It's, eh, it's not your eyes, boss. It's a bit blurry,' Tyler told him.

'Oh! Thank Christ for that. I thought I was needing a new prescription,' Ben said. 'Be worth running this by some of the local guys. Maybe he's a *kent face* around here.'

'Worth a shot, boss,' Tyler agreed.

'I'll maybe run it by the front desk first,' Ben suggested. 'They see everyone coming in and out. Maybe they can give us a few pointers.'

Tyler wrestled to keep his face straight. He knew full well what the detective inspector was angling for.

'Good idea. Maybe someone there'll be able to point us in the right direction.' He reached for the photo. 'I'll run it down now.'

'It's fine, son,' Ben said. 'I'll take it. I could do with the exercise.'

Tyler's grin fought its way to the surface. 'Whatever you think yourself, boss.'

The door to the office opened, and Logan ducked through it, clapping his slab-like hands together to draw the attention of everyone in the Incident Room. Even Hamza, who had been on a call, spoke quietly into the receiver, then pressed the button to put the person on the other end of the line on hold.

'Right, everyone listen up,' Logan boomed, his voice filling the room. 'That hunch I mentioned, it's now graduated up to being a full-blown theory. The tape on the wall in the victim's bedroom—I suspected there had been something stuck to it, and I was right. A note. A note which, by the looks of things, said "I know what you did."'

'Bloody hell, boss,' Tyler said. 'That's huge.'

'How come? What does it mean?' Tammi-Jo asked, looking around at the rest of the team for an explanation.

'It means Sharon Simpson's murder may well have been a message,' Logan continued. 'A message that could've been intended for her husband.'

'Connected to the harassment, maybe?' Ben said.

'Likely, but too early to say for sure. We know what the note said because whoever wrote the message used a pad in the bedroom, and left an imprint on the page below. That tells me they weren't prepared. They may not have planned the murder in advance, or at least not planned to leave the note.'

'What about the note, boss?' Tyler asked. 'Any sign of it?'

'No. The note itself wasn't anywhere in the room. No trace of it in the house, in fact, or in the bins outside. It wasn't found in the garden, either.'

Hamza, still holding the phone, was the first to grasp the significance of this.

'Someone took it,' he said.

Logan pointed to him and nodded. 'Bingo. I can't be sure, but my theory is that our killer raped and murdered Sharon Simpson as some sort of act of revenge on the husband, then left a note for him to find. And that note is nowhere to be found, meaning...' He shifted his attention to Tammi-Jo. 'Detective Constable?'

Tammi-Jo snapped to a clumsy sort of attention, her eyes darting left and right as her mind whirred into top gear. 'Meaning... someone else had to have been there. Someone had to have found the body and taken the note before the body was found.'

'Exactly,' Logan said, and the young DC smiled brightly, pleased with herself for passing his test. 'Which means that, as of right now, we're no longer looking for just one person of interest, folks. We're looking for two.'

Chapter 13

The Morris Minor was still sitting in the carport outside Armand's house, although the bonnet had now been lowered. The sun was on the wane, but the evening was yet to start tightening its grip. It had been a few weeks since the clocks had gone forward, and the days were starting to stretch.

'You want my advice, boss?'

Logan looked across at the detective constable sitting in his passenger seat. 'Generally speaking, no, but go on.'

'Don't look at his dog. It's a right pain in the arse.'

Logan glanced in the rearview mirror. Taggart sat behind the back seats, stretching up so his chin was lying in the gap between the two headrests. He perked up when he sensed he'd been noticed, his ears rising, and his tongue rolling out.

'Aye, well. I've plenty experience of that,' Logan said. He glared into the mirror, ejected a warning, 'Wait!' then opened the door and got out of the car before Taggart could even start to scrabble for freedom.

He set off up the driveways towards the house, then realised he hadn't heard DC Neish's door closing. Looking back, he saw Tyler still sitting in the passenger seat.

It took a moment for the penny to drop.

'For fu—' he muttered. Then, louder: 'I was talking to the bloody dog, Tyler. No' you.'

The passenger door of the BMW was quickly opened. 'Oh. Sorry, boss. Thought that was meant for me.'

There was a rush of movement behind him, and Tyler hurriedly shut the door just in time to stop Taggart jumping out.

'Wait!' he said, trying to emulate Logan's tone but falling well short.

The little dog just stared up at him with sad eyes, and placed a pleading paw on the glass.

'It's not up to me!' Tyler protested, backing away. 'I'm sorry!'

Logan turned and continued towards the house. 'Heel, boy,' he barked, then he shot a look back over his shoulder at the detective constable. 'That one *was* meant for you, by the way.'

By the time he'd passed the Rover 75 and the Morris Minor and reached the front door, Tyler had just about caught up. There was a doorbell, but Logan didn't use it, preferring to knock instead. A knock was an announcement. A knock said a lot about the person waiting to be let inside—things that an electronic *ding-dong* couldn't even begin to convey.

Logan's knocks generally announced that some big bastard from the polis was standing on the front step, and how it would be in everyone's best interests if the door was answered sooner rather than later. Today's was no different.

'Right, leave the talking to me, son. I want you taking notes, but eyes and ears open. Watch for his reactions. Watch for the reactions he doesn't make, too. And if you get a chance, speak to the liaison. See if she's picked up on anything.'

'Got it, boss. You can count on me,' Tyler said. He patted his pockets, then winced. 'You got a pen I can borrow, though? Think I left mine on my desk back in the—'

Without a word, Logan produced a brand new biro and held it up.

'Cheers, boss,' Tyler said, taking the pen and tucking it into his shirt pocket.

At the sound of footsteps in the hall, both men straightened and faced the door.

'Eyes and ears, son,' Logan muttered, then the door was opened and Tyler let out a surprised little squeak that made Logan shoot him a sideways scowl.

The woman standing in the doorway hadn't seemed to pick up on it.

'All right, sir?'

'Constable Niddrie,' Logan said, nodding at the uniformed officer.

'Nidds?' Tyler flashed her one of his better smiles, but it was tempered a little by his confusion. 'What are you doing here?'

'Constable Niddrie's the acting liaison officer,' Logan said.

'Oh? I didn't know. You didn't tell me that, boss.'

'Sorry, Tyler, I forgot you were the one running this investigation. I'll be sure to report everything directly to you from now on.' Logan turned to the officer in the doorway. 'He in?'

'They both are,' Nidds replied. 'They're in the living room. They've, eh, they've had a few drinks. Not many, but a couple.'

Logan nodded. 'Fingers crossed it helps loosen their tongues a bit, eh?' he said, then Nidds stepped aside to let both the detectives into the house, and closed the door behind them.

–

Ben stood on the opposite side of the reception counter to Moira, talking to her through the glass. He had the photograph from Tyler in one hand, and waved it about as he spoke like he was conducting a very low-key orchestra.

'So, I've been having a think. I thought we could go somewhere tomorrow. For our, you know, our *date*,' he said. 'You know, get it over and done with. No point putting it off.'

Moira scowled at him. 'You're making it sound like a bloody hernia operation.'

Ben's smile faltered. 'I know. I heard that as I said it, but… God. I don't know. I'm not good at this. The last time I was winching was decades ago. I don't know how you're supposed to go about these things.'

'Aye, well, I'm not exactly an expert myself,' Moira said. 'But at a guess, I'd say that phrases like "get it over and done with" are generally to be avoided.'

Ben ran the edge of the photograph between his fingertips and chuckled. 'Aye. That's probably a pretty good bet.' He took a deep breath. 'I thought we could do it tomorrow because I'm so looking forward to the pleasure of your company.'

On the other side of the glass, Moira's face puckered up in distaste. 'God. I think I preferred your first try. That just felt creepy.' She chewed on her bottom lip for a moment, then shook her head. 'No.'

'No?' Ben frowned. 'What do you mean? I thought you were right up for it?'

'I beg your pardon?'

'The date, I mean, not… Jiggery-pokery. I thought you were right up for us going on this date.'

'Tonight,' Moira said.

'Tonight? But we're right in the middle of—'

'And you can get back to it afterwards, if you must,' Moira told him. 'You might think you're important, but I'm sure they can get by without you for a couple of hours. It's not like you're doing anything useful up there that the rest of them couldn't be get getting on with. If anything, they'll probably get on better without—'

'All right, all right! Jesus!' Ben cried, cutting her off. 'I get the message, no need to go bloody overboard.' He nodded. 'Fine. Tonight it is.'

'Good. I like a man who knows how to do what he's told,' Moira said. She nodded down to the printout the DI was clutching. 'What are you after?'

'Eh?' Ben looked down and seemed genuinely surprised to find he was holding the photo. 'Oh, aye. That's why I came down. Well, that and to see your beautiful—'

'No. Enough of that shite,' Moira said, holding up a hand to silence him. 'It's already weird, don't make it worse.'

'Weird?' Ben blinked. 'How's it weird?'

'Just show me the bloody photo,' Moira snapped. 'It's nearly knocking off time, and if you think I'll bother my arse to help you with anything after the stroke of five o'clock, you're in for a big disappointment.' She tapped her watch. 'Four minutes.'

Ben slid the photo through the slot at the bottom of the glass screen. 'Right, aye. We're trying to trace him,' he said, once Moira had snatched the printout away. 'He might be local. This was taken down near Appin, but we think he might've been active up this neck of the woods, too.'

Moira sniffed as she considered the man in the photograph. The picture had been taken from an upstairs window, so the angle wasn't great. It was blurry and dark, too, and as Moira turned her head this way and that, trying to work out what she was looking at, Ben felt the urge to apologise.

'We could probably get Tech Support to try enhancing it. Maybe Hamza could even do something with it. Brighten it up a bit.'

Moira continued to stare at the picture, not acknowledging that the DI had spoken.

'Where are we going?'

'Eh?'

'Is this dementia kicking in? Is this what that looks like?' Moira asked. She shot him a scathing look, before turning her attention back to the photo. 'On the date. Tonight. Where are we going?'

'Oh! I don't know. I hadn't really thought about it yet.'

'It'd better be somewhere decent,' Moira said. 'Don't even think about trying to palm me off with a bacon roll at JJ's.'

'I wouldn't dream of it,' Ben said, even though a bacon roll from JJ's sounded just the ticket right about then.

'Fish.'

Ben's gaze flitted to the photograph on the counter in front of Moira. 'Fish? What, is that his name?'

Moira tutted. 'I like fish. Seafood. For dinner.'

'Oh! Aye!' Ben chuckled, then frowned. 'Do you, though? When you were recovering, I offered to fry you up a bit of haddock, and you told me—and I remember this quite clearly—to shove my haddock up my arse.'

Moira rolled her eyes. When she spoke, it was like she was addressing a child. And not a particularly bright one, at that.

'That's because the house would've stunk of fish for days. I don't like fish made at home. I don't like fish brought in from the chippie either, for that matter. But, I like fish in a restaurant. Good fish. Properly done. Not whacked in a load of Ruskoline and fried to within an inch of its life.'

'Right. Fair enough. That's me told,' Ben said.

He dimly recalled there being a seafood restaurant over-looking the loch at the back of the town. White building. Red roof. He couldn't remember the name.

'The Crannog,' Moira said, as if reading his mind. She raised her gaze from the photo, just for a moment. 'And that'll do nicely.'

'OK. Cool. I'll get that booked,' Ben said. 'Eight o'clock?'

'Don't be so bloody daft! I'll be starving by then. Seven. And none of this picking me up nonsense. I don't need you ferrying me about. I'll get a taxi. And you can, too, because we'll be having wine. I'll be choosing it, because you won't have a bloody clue.'

Ben was momentarily taken aback by the rush of information, but he couldn't help a smile spreading across his face.

'That sounds perfect,' he declared. 'Seven. I'll get that booked for us.'

'I'll do it. You'll only forget,' Moira said.

'No, I will not. I insist. I'll book it,' Ben said.

'Aye, well, you can pay for it, and all,' Moira retorted.

She slid the photograph back through the gap at the bottom of the glass. Ben picked it up and shrugged. 'Worth a try. Thanks for looking. I'll see if Hamza can do anything with it.'

'Shayne Feasey.'

Ben's brow furrowed. 'Eh?'

'Your lad there. Shayne Feasey. Shayne *Faeces*, I call him. Aye, to his face, I mean, not behind his back. I'm not a complete cow. And anyway, where's the fun in that?' Moira asked. 'He's your typical pain in the arse. Moved up this way middle of last year from down south. He's from somewhere abroad, originally, but been in the UK for decades. Brought over as a kid from one of them old Russian countries or something. Annoying wee bastard. In and out of here a few times. Fighting. Peeing in the street. Just making a nuisance of himself. Suspected of nicking a couple of bikes a month or two back, but they couldn't pin it on him.'

'Bikes?'

'Aye. You know? Bikes? They've changed a bit, but back in your day, they would've had one big wheel at the front and one wee one at the back.'

'Funny. But you're just as bloody old as I am,' Ben reminded her.

Moira's face darkened. The glower she fired his way almost froze him where he stood. 'You don't talk about a lady's age, Detective Inspector. It's not the done thing.'

'Sorry,' he mumbled, then he looked down at the photograph again and steered the conversation back onto safer ground. 'You sure it's him? You can't see much from this angle.'

'It's him. It's the ears. He's like the lovechild of Dumbo and the BFG.'

'Do we have an address?'

'Probably, aye,' Moira said. She tapped her watch and wrestled herself down from her raised chair. 'But that's five o'clock, so you can bloody well figure it out for yourself.'

Chapter 14

'Sorry to bother you again so soon, Mr Simpson,' Logan said, as he and Tyler took the seats they'd been directed to at Armand Holburn's dining table. Isaac joined them. He had a glass of Scotch in one hand and looked ever so slightly unsteady on his feet as he pulled out one of the other chairs and plonked himself down in it.

Nidds sat on the couch, her hat in her lap, her fingers splayed on the domed top of it like she was a fortune teller with a crystal ball. Logan had asked her to observe the interview. Another set of eyes didn't hurt, and having grown up mostly deaf, Nidds had developed a real knack for reading body language.

Armand remained seated in a throne-like armchair, staring into a glass of malt whisky, and trying very hard to look like he wasn't earwigging in. A fire was burning in the hearth beside him, making the room feel stiflingly hot.

'It's fine,' Isaac said. 'Armand reckoned you'd come. Have you got anywhere yet?'

'We're following up a few leads,' Logan said.

'So that's a "no", then,' Armand said. He raised his glass towards the window that looked across the field onto Isaac's garden hedge, then took a sip.

Logan ran his tongue around inside his mouth, like he was trying to get rid of a nasty taste.

'You sure you wouldn't rather do this somewhere private, Mr Simpson?' he asked. 'There may be some personal details that come out during our conversation, so I think it'd be better if we were to discuss this without Mr Holburn present.'

Isaac sniffed indignantly. '*Mr Holburn* is the reason I'm still this side of the soil. If it wasn't for him, I wouldn't be here. I'd be dead on some backwater battlefield. That man has saved my life, Detective Inspector.'

'More than once,' Armand added.

'More than once,' Isaac confirmed. 'I owe him everything. And this is his house. As far as I'm concerned, he can stay right where he is.'

Armand raised his glass again, this time in Isaac's direction, then took another drink.

Logan wasn't happy, but there wasn't a lot he could do about it. He glanced at Tyler to make sure he was ready with his notebook, then launched straight into it.

'Why do you think you're being targeted, Mr Simpson?'

Across the table, Isaac hid his hesitation by taking a sip of his drink.

'Targeted? What do you mean?'

He didn't look at Armand. He *very deliberately* didn't look at Armand, Logan thought, and he hoped that Tyler had caught that, too.

'You mean the harassment stuff? The eggs. The bins. The calls? That what you mean?' He shook his head. 'I don't know. Kids. That's what your lot said, so I just assumed...'

'What about Norman?' Logan asked.

The fire crackled in the hearth, but the silence from both men was almost deafening. Logan was glad that Armand had stuck around. There was a lot to be gleaned from his and Isaac's furtive looks—or lack thereof.

'Norman Todd?' Logan said. 'Friend of yours. Both of you. That's right, Detective Constable, isn't it?'

'Far as we know, boss, aye,' Tyler said.

'DC Swanney found a newspaper article about a wee memorial service that was held for him. You two spoke at it. Very touching, by the sounds of things,' Logan said, looking at each of the men in turn. 'No' a dry eye in the house.'

'What about him?'

It was Armand who asked the question, Isaac having apparently been struck dumb.

'Did he reckon it was kids? You know, hassling him?'

When Armand didn't reply, Logan turned his attention back to Isaac.

'Mr Simpson?'

'I, uh, I don't know,' Isaac said. 'I assume so.'

'That's one hell of a patch for them to cover, isn't it?' Logan mused. 'Forty miles, thereabouts? Long way on a skateboard.'

Armand knocked back the rest of his whisky, then reached for a crystal decanter that sat on a small side table near his armchair.

'What's Norman got to do with anything?' Armand asked. 'He's dead.'

'Technically, he's missing,' Logan corrected.

'Oh, come on. We're all grown-ups. We know he's done away with himself,' Armand said with a sneer. 'He's dead. So, how is he in any way connected to what happened to Shazz?'

Shazz. Quite familiar, Logan thought. Especially as her husband had only ever referred to her by her proper name.

Armand must've known her well. It would be interesting to know precisely *how* well.

'Maybe nothing,' Logan admitted. 'Maybe everything.'

He met Tyler's eye, then glanced at Armand. The detective constable was refreshingly quick to pick up on the hint. He watched Holburn closely while Logan turned his attention back to Isaac.

'I know what you did,' the DCI said.

He'd been interested to see what the reaction was going to be. Would there be blank looks of confusion, or flashes of obvious guilt? Would Isaac try too hard to feign ignorance, or break down into big, gulping confessional sobs?

That last one would've been nice, though he'd known it was a long shot.

What Logan got, though, was almost as good. Isaac's breath caught somewhere deep in his throat. The sound it made was soft and quiet, but Logan had been listening for it.

His eyes began making incremental left and right motions, like they were searching for a way out. Finally, they alighted on Armand, and though they lingered there for just a fraction of a second, that was enough to tell Logan what he needed to know.

'What are you talking about?' Isaac asked, his voice a croak through his narrowing throat. 'What's that supposed to mean?'

'You tell me, Mr Simpson.'

The look of panic on Isaac's face was going nowhere. Every part of it seemed to shift around independently, like each individual feature was a sentient thing, and every one of them was currently shitting itself.

'I don't know. I don't...' His hands wrung together, the palms glistening with sweat. 'I mean, I think... One of the calls. One of the late-night calls I reported. I think it said something...'

He stole a quick look at Armand, then thought better of continuing the sentence.

'But maybe not. I can't remember. I'm not sure.'

'I see. And what do you think he meant?' Logan asked. 'When the man on the phone called and said that, what do you think he might have been referring to?'

Isaac shrugged. 'I don't... I'm not even sure he said it.'

'You seemed to think so a moment ago, Mr Simpson. I'm sure I don't need to remind you why we're here.' Logan leaned a little closer. 'It is very much in your best interests to be as open and honest with me as possible.'

'I know. I am. I just... It was late. The calls. I was half asleep. I don't think he said anything.'

Logan continued to stare at him for a few moments, then nodded. 'OK, then. But, here's the thing, Mr Simpson.' Logan clasped his hands on the table, his thumbs tapping together in a slow, steady rhythm. 'Those words—that message—"I know what you did."—We've come across them again.'

'What? Where?' It was Armand who asked the question, though he seemed to regret it the moment it came out of his mouth, and quickly took a sip of his drink as if to stop himself saying anything more.

'We'd rather not disclose that yet,' Logan said. He redirected his attention back to Isaac. 'But what I will say is that, while it's early to say for sure, from where I'm sitting, it's starting to look a lot like your wife's murder was meant as a message.'

'A message?'

'A message for you, Mr Simpson.' Logan turned to Armand. Tyler was still watching the man like a hawk. 'Maybe a message for both of you, in fact.'

Armand remained stoic and silent, though his hand trembled lightly as he took another sip from his replenished glass of Scotch.

'So, what I want to know,' Logan said, turning back to Isaac, 'is what *exactly* it is that you did?'

—

Ben strode into the Incident Room, announced the name, 'Shayne Faeces', then corrected himself once he saw all the confused looks.

'Feasey, I mean. Shayne Feasey. He's our man in the photo.'

Hamza shot to his feet. 'The guy Norman Todd got the picture of?'

'The very same,' Ben confirmed, slapping the photograph down on the DS's desk.

'Bloody hell. That was quick? How did you find him?' Hamza asked.

Ben tapped the side of his nose. 'Friends in high places, son. Friends in high places!' He spun on the spot, checking that Dave Davidson and DC Swanney were both paying attention. 'What are we all working on?'

'The report came through from Scene of Crime,' Hamza told him. 'We're working through that. Tammi-Jo's trying to find a match for the victim's underwear.'

'It's from an online-only brand,' DC Swanney explained. 'I should have an image we can share with the husband soon, although there are a lot of pants on the site. A *lot* of pants. Weird ones, too. Like… sexy ones. But, you know, *too* sexy? Like, full on. Shiny ones. Frilly ones. These sort of—I don't know what you'd call them—mesh ones? Like fishnets for your fanny.'

She clamped both hands over her mouth, her eyes widening in horror.

'I just said "fanny" to a detective inspector! I'm *so* sorry!'

Ben chuckled. 'Believe me, I've heard a lot worse.'

Tammi-Jo's hands slipped off her face and back to her sides. She still looked mortified, and while she'd liked nothing more than to have changed the subject, she found herself slipping straight back into the previous one.

'There are some pairs that are basically just all straps. Like, elastic or whatever? They don't look comfortable *at all*. Or warm. You wouldn't want to be wearing them in the winter, I'll tell you that for nothing.'

She hesitated, like she wasn't quite ready to share the next part.

Her mouth had other ideas.

'And there's some that have no underneath to them. Literally no gusset. Just a big…' Her eyes darted around the room, searching for an alternative to the word that had lined itself up at the end of her sentence. 'Hole,' she said, failing to find one.

'What, crotchless?' asked Dave, who'd been growing increasingly interested in the conversation over the past few seconds.

'Uh, yes. That sort of thing.' Tammi-Jo put her hand on the back of her neck and rolled her head around awkwardly. 'I feel a bit pervy looking at them all, if I'm honest.'

'I'll swap, if you want?' Dave suggested. 'I've got no problems with feeling pervy.' He gestured to his screen. 'Anyway, I've hit a dead end. Can't find anything to say who could've called round to talk to the neighbour a few weeks back. Either he's got his dates wrong, or he's making it up.'

'Or someone didn't do the paperwork,' Ben added. This would be unusual, but by no means unheard of. He clapped his hands. The bang was like the firing of a starting pistol. 'Sorry, Tammi-Jo, I want you to stick with the underwear. Find a match, quick as you can.'

'Operation Crotchless Panties is underway, sir!' the DC said. She fired off a crisp salute, but even as her hand was raising, her face was starting to wince. 'Sorry, that was meant to be an internal voice thing. Forget I said that.'

Cheeks burning, she hurried back to her computer, and returned to scrolling through images of women's underwear.

'Hamza, keep going through the SOCO report,' Ben continued. 'Dave, I'm assuming if Palmer's team is done, we're going to start getting Exhibits coming through soon. Once they come in, I want you to prioritise that. It'll make it a late one, but I want it all checked in before we leave here tonight.'

'But until then…' Dave prompted, sensing what was coming next.

Ben picked up the photo from Hamza's desk, and placed it on the constable's instead.

'Until then, get me everything you can on Shayne Feasey. I want to know who he is, where he came from, and where we can find the bastard.'

He started to turn away, then a thought made him turn back.

'And, more importantly, I want to find out how the hell he's connected to Norman Todd, and if there's any link to Isaac Simpson. Everyone know what they're doing?'

'No bother,' Dave said.

'On it, sir,' Hamza confirmed.

'All the pants, all the time,' Tammi-Jo added.

'Good. Right.' Ben smoothed down the front of his shirt and adjusted his tie. 'Now, I'll be back in a few minutes. I need to go sort out a restaurant for my hot date!'

He grinned expectantly at them, like he was waiting for some big reaction. Hamza, however, just stared at him in a vaguely horrified way. Tammi-Jo made an adorable *aww* noise below her breath and clasped her hands together.

It was only Dave's response that really fit the bill. 'Gaun yersel', big man!' he called. 'There's life in the old dog yet!'

Ben felt a little surge of pride. 'Aye,' he said, with a smile and a wink. 'I'm starting to think that maybe there is.'

Chapter 15

Tyler stood in the kitchen with Nidds, waiting for the kettle to boil. Isaac had asked for a break from the interview after denying any knowledge of what the 'I know what you did' message could be referring to, and Logan had reluctantly agreed. Sharon's husband wasn't currently under arrest, and Logan didn't yet want to haul him back down to the station for a full interview under caution. Not while he was essentially getting two interviews right now for the price of one.

Isaac now stood out in the front garden, a cigarette wedged between the first and second fingers of his left hand, held down near his hip. He'd taken one or two shaky draws from it, but otherwise seemed content to just let it burn down.

Logan had stayed with Armand in the living room, and suggested to DC Neish and PC Niddrie that now would be the perfect time for a cuppa.

'They been saying much?' Tyler asked.

'Everything and nothing,' Nidds told him. 'I'm pretty sure they're whispering when I'm not there, but they shut up as soon as I'm in the room, or they change the subject. From what I can gather, they go way back. They were in the army together. I get the impression Armand was in charge at the time, because Isaac still seems to be intimidated by him.'

'You reckon he's scared of him?' Tyler asked.

'I'm not sure. More sort of… deferential,' Nidds said. 'You know, like we would be with a senior officer?'

Tyler nodded. There was a certain familiarity with DI Forde and DCI Logan that meant he probably didn't show them quite the levels of respect he otherwise would, but he knew how he felt around Detective Superintendent Mitchell, and any of the *High Heid Yins* who occasionally put in an appearance.

'They haven't said anything that makes me think either of them killed Sharon, though,' Nidds continued. She shrugged. 'But they also haven't said anything that makes me think they definitely didn't.'

She picked up the kettle as it clicked off, and tipped the boiling water into Armand's surprisingly dainty teapot.

'That's probably not that useful,' she said, smiling weakly.

'What? No, it's great, it's…' Tyler looked down at his notes, then returned her smile. 'No, you're right, it's shite. Thanks for nothing.'

Nidds laughed at that, then took the lid of the teapot that Tyler handed her, and slotted it into place.

'Now, the waiting begins,' she said. 'Armand likes his tea strong, I've discovered. Moans like a bastard if it isn't half-stewed.'

Tyler glanced over at the kitchen door, like he could see around the corners and into the front room. 'He seems half-stewed himself. Fairly tanning that whisky.'

'Aye. He's been on it since before I arrived,' Nidds confirmed. 'Knocking it back. It's expensive stuff, too. I looked it up on my phone. Six hundred quid a bottle.'

'Fucking hell. My first car didn't cost six hundred quid,' Tyler said, whistling through his teeth. 'Mind you, third gear didn't work, the passenger door didn't open, and it smelled like a fisherman's welly, so it wasn't exactly a steal.'

Nidds went wide-eyed with surprise. She swept her hair back from her hearing aids and stared intently at his mouth. 'What did you say?'

'Eh, just that even at that price, it wasn't a steal.'

'No, before that. What did it smell like?'

'Like a fisherman's welly,' Tyler said.

Nidds snorted out a laugh and put her hand on her chest. 'Oh. *Welly*! Thank God for that! I thought you said it smelled like a fisherman's *willy*, and I had so many questions.'

'Haha! Jesus. No. *Welly*,' Tyler stressed. 'Although, I'd imagine they probably smell quite similar, to be honest.'

Nidds shuddered, her tongue sticking out as she mimed her disgust at the thought.

She picked up the teapot and moved it in a little circle, swirling around the liquid inside.

Talking about the ludicrously overpriced whisky made Tyler think, once again, about the pile of unpaid bills in the inside pocket of his jacket, so he quickly moved on from all talk of money.

'So, eh, I was talking to Dave,' he announced.

Nidds stopped sloshing the tea around. She tensed, but tried not to show it. 'Oh? I saw him earlier.'

'I hear you two are... Or, you know, that you're *not*...' He made some vague hand motions, hoping she might finish the sentence for him. When she didn't, he concluded with, 'A thing.'

Nidds turned away, fetched five mugs from one of the wall cupboards, then slid open a drawer that contained the teaspoons.

'No. We're not. It wasn't him, though. Dave's great. Really, he's... He's just a great guy. It was me. It was all me,' she said. She sounded hesitant, like she was carefully choosing her words, but at the same time seemed pleased to be able to get it off her chest. 'I'm just... It was getting serious. We started talking about marriage at one point. Kids were mentioned. I wasn't ready for that.'

Her mention of children made her turn quickly on the spot.

'Kids! God, I'm such an idiot!' she said. She poked him playfully with a teaspoon. 'How's it going? How are the twins?'

'They're great! Hard work, but...'

'Sinead does all that?' Nidds teased.

'I was going to say, "but totally worth it",' Tyler replied. 'I'm actually a master at changing two nappies at once now. Can't do one at a time, for some reason. They always fall off. But two? I'm your man.'

Nidds laughed. 'That's great. That's really good. They're lucky to have you.'

'Aye, well, we'll see if they agree in a few years,' Tyler said, chuckling. 'Not that they've got much choice in the matter, of course. The one thing you're stuck with is your parents, I suppose.'

An alarm had started to flash in Tyler's brain somewhere around the midway point of that last sentence. The edited highlights of his earlier conversation with Dave replayed, before settling on the bit about Nidds being adopted.

'I'm sorry. I didn't mean...'

'What?' Nidds asked, visibly confused. 'You didn't mean what?'

'Nothing,' Tyler said. 'What? Nothing.'

Constable Niddrie's face contorted in horror. 'Wait. Hold on, hold on. He told you?'

'What? No. Told me? Who? Nobody tells me anything. What do you mean?' Tyler said, his mouth streaking ahead of his brain.

'I can't believe he told you! He promised me. He promised me he wouldn't tell anyone.'

'He didn't. Tell me what? I don't know what...' He pointed past her suddenly, looking out through the window at the garden beyond. 'Hey, wait. Who's that?'

Nidds tutted. 'Seriously, Tyler? Do you actually think that's going to work?'

'No, look. Out there,' Tyler insisted. .

Just then, from the back garden, the yapping of an annoying wee dog rang out. Nidds turned to the window, while Tyler went barrelling towards the door.

There, standing in the back garden, was a stocky male figure in a dark hoodie and jacket. He was kicking his foot out, trying to shoo the barking dog, but as soon as Tyler pulled the door open, the stranger made a break for the back gate and went racing out into the deepening gloom.

'Bollocks,' Tyler muttered. Then, with all the authority he could muster, he bellowed, 'Stop! Police!'

And with that, the chase was on.

—

Sinead held her breath, eyes darting left and right as she backed slowly towards the door of the nursery. The twins were both sleeping in their cots, but one wrong move—one squeak of a floorboard—would be enough to wake them.

Putting them down this early was madness, she knew, but they'd struggled and gurned through their afternoon naps, and hadn't slept a wink. Tiredness had turned them into a right pair of grumpy wee shites, though she couldn't exactly blame them for that, considering she felt much the same herself. After they'd been changed and fed, they'd both flaked out immediately.

Of course, this probably meant they'd be wide awake by midnight, but maybe if she woke them for another feed around half ten, she might be able to get a reasonably solid night's sleep.

Or a handful of hours, at least.

Before then, she'd have to tidy up. Do the dishes. Empty the tumble dryer, then fill it again with the load from the washing machine.

Or… she could not.

Harris was staying over at a friend's tonight. She hadn't heard yet if Tyler was coming back up the road or not. It was entirely possible that she might be able to have an evening to herself, slouching in front of the TV and munching on the packet of Jaffa Cakes she'd gone to great lengths to hide behind the Kellogg's Special K box in the cereal cupboard.

She knew it was a safe hiding space, because the cereal had been there for about six months now, and neither Tyler nor Harris had touched it once during that time.

Although, to be fair, neither had she.

She reached the hall without incident, and both babies were still fast asleep when she tiptoed out of the room and pulled the door over until it was open just a crack.

The sense of relief was immeasurable, and she just stood there for a moment, bathing in the peace and quiet.

Bathing.

God. Maybe she could have a bath. An actual bath. With bubbles.

Or was that too much to hope for? She'd had a shower on— her lips moved silently while she calculated—Saturday night. Was a bath just pure decadence? Should she make do with a fistful of chocolate biscuits and a couple of hours of vegging in front of the telly?

Or should she go wild and treat herself, just this once?

To hell with it. She knew what she was going to do. Tonight, she was going to live recklessly! Tonight, she was going to have a bath *and* eat chocolate biscuits.

The thought of it almost made her giddy. She didn't have to settle for one or the other. She could do both things.

And she would've done, too, had someone not chosen that moment to hammer a fist on the front door like they were trying to batter it down.

From the nursery came the high-pitched wail of a baby woken from a peaceful slumber. This was followed a second later by more of the same.

The knocking on the door came again, and Sinead felt something go rushing through her all the way from head to toe. It was something she very rarely felt.

She was feeling it now, all right. She was feeling it perhaps more so than ever.

Rage.

'What the hell are you knocking like that for?' she hissed, pulling the front door open without bothering to peek through the spy hole first.

Two men stood on the step, one with his hand raised like he had been just about to knock for a third time.

She didn't recognise either of them. As far as she could tell, she'd never seen the men before in her life.

But she knew exactly what they were. Most of them had the same look—dark clothing, stocky builds, faces that knew how to take a punch, and fists that were plenty experienced in dishing them out.

She'd been called in to deal with situations involving men like these several times when back in Uniform, sometimes by the men themselves, sometimes by the folks whose houses they had called at.

Sinead knew a Sheriff's Office debt collector when she saw one.

'Sorry to bother you, Mrs… Neish?'

The smaller of the two—the one standing further back—was clearly going to be doing the talking. The hesitation and questioning way he said her name told her he wasn't sure he had the right person.

Maybe he didn't. Maybe this was all just some misunder-standing. It was bound to be.

It had to be.

And yet, the knot in her stomach told her otherwise.

'What do you want?' she asked, holding onto the door, making it very clear that they weren't getting inside. Not easily, at least. Not without a fight.

Behind her, in their room, her children cried.

Outside, across the road, she saw the twitching of curtains in the neighbour's windows.

'Sounds like you've got your hands full.'

The smaller man—comparatively, at least—smiled quite kindly and nodded past her into the hallway. She could see now that he was older. Late fifties, maybe tipping over into sixty.

'We won't keep you. I remember what it's like having little ones. You're probably run off your feet. Last thing you want is us two arseholes on your doorstep. Pardon the language.'

Sinead wasn't about to argue with any of that. She glanced at the larger man. His hand was still raised, like the signal to lower it hadn't made it all the way from his brain yet.

Probably struggling to force its way past his biceps, she thought.

'What do you want?'

The older man opened a black hardback notebook that he'd been holding down at his side. It was A4 sized, and its pages were covered in neat, densely packed handwriting. He raised a foot onto the step as he flicked through the pages. When it gave a metallic *chink*, Sinead's gaze was drawn down to the ornate black leather cowboy boots he wore.

The crying of the twins became higher. Sharper. More piercing. The invisible cord tying her to them both tightened and tugged at her, drawing her towards them.

'I have to go. Whatever this is, it'll have to wait,' she said, starting to close the door.

The bigger man stuck a foot out, stopping her shutting it all the way.

'Of course, of course,' his marginally shorter companion said. 'We'll be out of your hair in no time,' he assured her.

His finger traced down the page he was on, then he gave it a tap as he found the note he was looking for.

'Just as soon as you tell us where we might be able to find a Mr Tyler Neish.'

—

Things were not going well for Tyler.

It had taken him all of ten seconds to realise he was out of shape.

In the past, he'd always been the running guy. The chaser. The one dispatched to pursue some fleeing suspect or other when they made a mad dash for freedom.

And he'd been good at it, too. He'd been quick out of the blocks and, once he'd got going, he was fast. Not *athlete* fast, but fast enough to catch up with the average jakey, and capable of keeping up with neds half his age.

He'd even once outrun a train, although it had been a very close-run thing.

But that was the old him. That was the pre-fatherhood Tyler.

For that guy, running had been second nature. All his limbs had moved like clockwork, all the various bits of his body working together in perfect harmony.

Or functional mediocrity, at least.

Now, though, nothing seemed to be working correctly. His legs and arms were all moving, but the timing felt way off.

By the time he was through the back gate, aches and pains he'd never felt before had already started to make themselves known. One of his knees hurt. His lower back grumbled every time a foot hit the ground. He wasn't out of breath yet, but a faint burning in his lungs was making him aware that this was a distinct possibility.

The man he was chasing had his head down and was powering ahead. He was twenty yards in front, and didn't seem to be suffering any of the issues Tyler was facing. The guy was fast, perhaps even faster than the old Tyler. Certainly faster than the *all-new and diminished* version stumbling after him now.

There was no danger of the DC catching him. None.

Fortunately, he didn't have to.

As the suspect ran past the Morris Minor, Isaac Simpson stepped to the side and held an arm straight out at his side, perpendicular to his body. It caught the other man across the throat like an iron bar. His legs continued running, but his top half was already toppling backwards.

For a moment, he appeared to run straight up an invisible wall, and then gravity made itself felt, and he landed heavily, flat on his back, on the driveway.

'Oh, thank Christ,' Tyler muttered.

The downed man lay there for a moment, all the breath knocked out of him by the impact. When he tried to sit up, Isaac pressed a foot against his chest, pinning him back down.

'Cheers for that,' Tyler panted, slowing to a stop beside the men.

'No bother,' Isaac told him. 'Who the hell is it, anyway?'

'No idea,' Tyler admitted. 'Saw him in the garden, and he legged it.'

Down on the ground, the fallen man pushed back the hood of his hoodie to reveal dark, shoulder-length hair, and a carefully sculpted beard that immediately made Tyler think of one of the Three Musketeers.

Isaac kept his foot in place, but let out a little gasp of surprise. 'Struan?' he whispered.

Down on the ground, the bearded man grinned. It was an unfriendly sort of smile that immediately turned him from a Musketeer into an evil stage magician.

'Hey, *Dad*,' he said, going heavy on the sarcasm. 'You miss me?'

Chapter 16

Shona Maguire had been dead against the idea of an assistant. An assistant, she'd reckoned, would just get in the way. An assistant would be more trouble than they were worth. It was hard enough running the department on her own without saddling her with babysitting duties, too.

And yet…

Neville knew his stuff. He'd made good use of his time alone, and had already prepped the mortuary for the post-mortem before Shona had even arrived back at the hospital.

He'd been fully up to speed with the process itself, too. Any time Shona needed a tool, it would be right there waiting for her hand. He took care of all the photographing and video work, and when she didn't need him, he just blended into the background, making notes of everything she said.

Literally everything, in fact. And, after momentarily forgetting she wasn't alone, she'd had to ask him to scrub the first verse and chorus of 'I'm in the Mood for Dancing' by the Nolan sisters from the record.

'Don't worry,' he assured her, as he drew lines across the page. He winked and smiled, and it was all so dazzling she would've sworn one of her legs actually passed out, forcing her to hold on to the edge of the operating table for balance. 'Your secret's safe with me.'

Once they were done, and Sharon Simpson was all sewn up again, she'd felt confident enough to leave him to finish up the paperwork.

After scrubbing up and placing a quick call to the lab to arrange for them to pick up the samples, she'd set off into the hospital in search of answers.

Olivia wasn't answering her phone. It was on, Shona reckoned, because there was no pattern to how long it took to go to voicemail. The first couple of times, it had rung out. The third, it had gone straight to the messaging service, and she'd thought maybe Olivia was calling her back.

When her phone didn't ring, she tried again a few times, and listened to varying lengths of ringing tones before the stock, robotic-voiced greeting had instructed her to leave a message.

A lap of the hospital building didn't turn up any sign of the girl, and nobody at the Outpatients Reception had any information to share. Nobody, it seemed, had clocked a crying teenager roaming the hospital corridors.

It couldn't have been an accident that Olivia had been so close to the mortuary. There was very little else around that way. She had to have been looking for Shona. It was the only explanation.

So why run away?

And why the tears?

Shona tried the girl's number again. It rang four times, then the messaging service kicked in again.

'Shit,' the pathologist whispered.

She stood in the empty corridor, bumping the top of the phone against the palm of her hand. Olivia could be anywhere. Even if she was still in the hospital, it was too sprawling, with too many hiding places. She was a resourceful girl. If she didn't want to be found, then she wouldn't be.

Shona didn't like it, but she'd just have to wait. Hopefully, once Olivia was ready, she'd come back, and they could deal with whatever the problem was together.

Three steps back in the direction of the mortuary, Shona stopped.

Olivia's tears had been fresh, her grief recent. Raw.

Maybe there was still one place left to look.

—

The Accident and Emergency Department was on the brink of chaos when Shona wandered in through the front door. She had access to enter via another door through the back, but that would bypass the waiting room, and though she'd looked in through the window on her circuit of the building, she wanted to give the place a proper once-over.

Most of the seats were full. Trembling old women sat jammed in beside young men gingerly holding injured ankles or wrists, while mothers rocked screaming toddlers and shot anxious looks at the heavily fortified front desk. A backing track of rattling coughs and pained groans completed the soundtrack, and the radio presenter wittering from the ceiling-mounted speakers had no chance whatsoever of making himself heard.

Shona turned on the spot, taking in the faces of the people in the waiting room. All human life was here.

Just not the specific part of it she was looking for.

Approaching the counter, she rang the bell and waited for the window hatch to be opened. She didn't know a lot of the A&E staff, so she was relieved when a familiar face appeared in the opening.

'Millie. Hi!'

'Shona?' The nurse—a greying fifty-something woman whose eye bags had been packed with the weight of a thousand double shifts—frowned in concern. 'You OK, love? Something happened?'

'No. I mean, yes. I mean… I'm fine,' Shona said. 'I'm, um… Bit of a weird one. I'm looking for a girl. Teenager. About yay high.'

She held a hand up to just about her own head height.

'Wearing a school uniform,' Shona continued. 'Name's Olivia. I saw her earlier. She, uh, she seemed upset. I'm trying to find her.'

Millie stuck out her bottom lip like she was thinking hard, then slowly shook her head. 'Not ringing a bell, sorry, love. If I see her, I'll give you a shout.'

Shona tapped her hands lightly on the edge of the counter, then nodded. 'Thanks. Please do.'

'But listen, since you're here, one of the juniors was going to give you a shout. We've got one for you. Woman. Mid-forties. Overdose, by the looks of it.'

'Right. I'll go start getting…'

Her eyebrows crept upwards, even as the rest of her face fell.

'Where?'

'Sorry?'

'I want to see her,' Shona said. She pointed to the door leading through to the back. 'Can I see her?'

'Uh, yeah. Sure. Come through.'

Shona hurried over to the door, danced on the spot for a moment while she waited for it to be unlocked, then shot through the moment it was opened.

'Last one on the left,' the nurse called to her as she marched past the blue-curtained cubicles, her stomach tying itself into increasingly complicated knots.

'No. No, please, no,' she whispered as she made for the final cubicle on the left-hand side of the hallway.

The body lay on the bed, covered by a thin sheet that clung to all its bumps and curves. Shona couldn't recall how many corpses she'd seen over the years. She'd been able to recall them all a few years ago—not their names, but their faces—but at some point she'd lost track.

At some point, it had all become normal. Seeing the shell that had once held a person had stopped being something of note.

Now, though, there in that room, she wasn't sure if she was ready for this one. If she was ready for all the pain and suffering it was going to cause.

Slowly, steadily, with a tremble in her hand, Shona lifted the sheet from the dead woman's face.

'Oh.'

She swallowed.

Shook her head.

Felt a burning way at the back of her eyes.

'Oh, God, no.'

There, her lips blue, her skin pale, lay the source of Olivia Maximuke's grief.

There, on that bed, in that cubicle, lay the body of Olivia Maximuke's mother.

Chapter 17

Tammi-Jo stood back from the Big Board and admired the placement of all the new ingredients in her chocolate machine. The type of trainer that had left the footprint in the neighbour's garden had been identified. Unfortunately, they were Adidas Sambas, an incredibly popular shoe that was probably worn by a third of the men in town.

Still, it was good to have the information, and she'd pinned it next to the frog drawing because… Well, because that felt like the right place for it to go.

The bike tyre was still a mystery. Uniform was out talking to the local bike shops to see if they could offer any help. Going by the width of the tread, it had been left by a mountain bike, and the depth of the imprint in the mud suggested someone reasonably heavy had been riding it.

It also, though Tammi-Jo wasn't sure how they figured this out, indicated that the rider had been cycling away from the house, and probably at speed.

Shona Maguire's initial post-mortem report had come through, confirming suffocation as the cause of death. The broken neck had happened during or after, but hadn't been the killing blow.

It was all useful information, but not enough to make a chocolate bar with, so her 'And the killer is…' section remained empty for now.

She'd found the underwear on the website, and had printed off a photo. It was another low-resolution image, and the printer hadn't miraculously improved since the last time she'd used it, so the picture she'd pinned to the board only looked like women's underwear if you knew what you were trying to see. Otherwise, it was a bit like an inkblot test. From certain angles, it looked like a butterfly.

Or maybe two men about to kiss.

Dave had found out quite a lot of information about Shayne Feasey, the man who had been photographed outside Norman Todd's house. It wasn't up to Tammi-Jo to declare a chief suspect, but if it was, she'd be putting her money on him.

He had been arrested half a dozen times in Fort William alone. Prior to that, he'd been living in and around Manchester for ten years, and had spent time in prison. Never long—a few months here and there—but enough to paint a picture of a young man with a knack for getting himself in the shit.

His early years had been spent in the care system. A couple of stints with foster families hadn't ended well, particularly for one of the foster fathers, who'd been left with life-changing injuries.

The army had welcomed him with open arms in his late teens, and then ridded itself of him again just four years later, dumping a leaner, meaner, more highly trained version of an angry young man back on Civvy Street.

It wasn't clear what had brought him to the Highlands. When questioned about it, he'd implied there were some people in Manchester very keen to speak to him. The sort of people who largely communicated through broken legs and missing fingers.

Manchester may have been in the north of England, but getting there involved driving several hours due south from Fort William. It would be a determined bampot indeed who would travel all that way just to give a toerag like Shayne Feasey the kicking he almost certainly deserved.

One thing they didn't have on him yet was a fixed address. Officially, according to his last few arrest sheets, he was home- less. He'd used a couple of different addresses before that, usually of lassies he'd been shacking up with. Uniform was following up on them, and asking around to see if anyone knew where he might currently be found.

If he was still in the area, they'd catch him, she reckoned. If he wasn't…? Well, then they'd still catch him. It just might take a little while longer.

'Either way, that no-good varmint is going down!' she drawled in a Deep South American accent. She glanced around to make sure nobody had heard her talking to herself out loud, then went back to arranging the board.

It was the, 'Whoa!' from Hamza a minute later that made her turn away.

'What's up?' she asked, turning away from her colourful display of notes and printouts.

Hamza held up a hand for her to wait a moment, and she noticed his frown deepening as his eyes tick-tocked from his screen to a sheet of paper on the desk beside him.

'Whoa,' he said again, and his frown flipped itself in the opposite direction. 'Holy shit.'

'Don't keep us in bloody suspense!' Dave called over. 'What is it?'

'I pulled up Norman Todd's phone records. We had them on file from when he was getting the harassment calls. They all submitted them, actually, Norman, Isaac and Armand. The harassment numbers have been highlighted.'

He angled the screen for Tammi-Jo to see. Dave wheeled himself over and both constables studied the scanned images.

'They're all withheld numbers,' DC Swanney remarked.

'Most. Not all,' Hamza corrected. 'Look.'

He pointed to a string of digits down near the bottom of the list. A mobile number had made one call at three in the morning several months previously.

'Norman flagged it as someone heavy breathing,' Hamza said, consulting the printout on his desk. 'Nobody spoke. Because it was a one-off, it looks like it was just sort of dismissed.'

'Doesn't feel like it warrants a "whoa",' said Tammi-Jo. 'I'm guessing there's more.'

Hamza leaned forward, clicked and scrolled with his mouse a few times, then settled on a different scanned document. This showed a similar list of late-night calls from unknown numbers, all highlighted in yellow.

'This is Isaac Simpson's report. Same deal. Lots of calls from withheld numbers, then this.'

He indicated the screen. Tammi-Jo and Dave both studied it for a moment.

'That's the same number,' the detective constable said.

'You sure?' Dave asked.

Tammi-Jo rattled off all eleven digits from memory without looking at the screen. Dave followed along, his amazement increasing with each number she said.

'Bloody hell,' he said.

'I'm good at remembering numbers,' the DC said.

'That's handy.'

'I can also remember the names of all the Sylvanian Families families,' Tammi-Jo told him, and she seemed prouder of this than she was about the numbers thing.

'Probably less useful,' Dave reasoned. 'But, you know, well done.'

'I thank you,' Tammi-Jo said, bowing graciously.

DS Khaled quietly cleared his throat. 'Aaaanyway,' he said, really drawing the word out. 'Yes, you're right. Same number. Called both Norman and Isaac, just once, a few weeks apart. Isaac reported the same thing. Someone breathing heavily until he hung up.'

'What about the other fella?' Dave asked.

'No. That's what's interesting. Only called those two.'

'Want me to run a check on the number?'

'Already done it,' Hamza replied. 'It's a pay-as-you-go SIM. Unregistered.'

'That's annoying,' Tammi-Jo said.

'The sergeant looking into the harassment already ran a search on the database, too,' Hamza said. 'But what he didn't do was stick the number into Google. If he had…'

The DS turned his screen back for a moment, then brought up his web browser with a couple of taps of the keyboard.

'They'd have found this.'

He pointed the screen to face the constables again. There was a web forum on the screen, one of the old-style bulletin boards where people could post messages to each other. They'd been mainstays of the Internet for a while, before Facebook had come along to end their reign.

This one seemed to be aimed at military types, both past and present. From the amateurish design, it clearly wasn't an official MoD site.

'"Highland Soldier",' Tammi-Jo said, reading the username displayed near the top of the page. Underneath the name was his location—Spean Bridge, Scotland—and the same mobile number that had appeared on both sets of records. 'Hang on…' she began. 'So, wait a minute, you're saying…?'

Hamza nodded. He tapped another key, and the browser tab switched to show a post on the same website. It had been written by *Highland Soldier* in reply to someone called *BingoW-ingo623*, who had given her real name—Janet—and invited others to share their own.

She'd also posted an animated GIF of a cartoon kitten, for reasons best known to herself.

And there, in his reply, *Highland Soldier* had outed himself.

'It's a pleasure to meet you, Janet,' the reply read. 'My name is Armand. But you may call me Army.'

'It was Armand,' Hamza said. 'Armand Holburn made those calls.'

–

Tyler stood at the top of the drive, watching the police car pulling away with Struan Ward sitting in the back seat.

The reunion between Struan and his stepfather had started badly with the wrestling-style clothesline across the throat from Isaac, and then had got steadily worse from there. Tyler had inserted himself between both men in an attempt to stop them coming to further blows, but it was only when Logan came storming out of the house like some vengeful God that they stopped squaring up to one another.

Struan had announced that he had information related to the murder of his mother, but insisted he would only divulge it in private at the station. Since Logan and Tyler hadn't been quite ready to leave, Nidds had called for a car to swing by for the victim's son.

Tyler had waited with him while Logan went back inside to finish his conversation with Isaac, then the DC had instructed the Uniforms to make Struan comfortable back at the station.

It was only once the squad car had pulled away that Tyler took out his phone. He'd felt it buzzing a couple of times in his pocket, one after the other, and his heart had leaped up into his throat.

He knew what it was about before reading it. Somehow, though he couldn't explain how, he knew.

Sinead's texts were brief and to the point.

I just had bailiffs here, read the first.

What the fuck is going on?!? read the second.

Tyler let out a groan through his nose, and rubbed at his jaw, his fingers pressing grooves into the flesh, drawing red lines across his skin.

Shit.

Shit, shit, shit.

His jacket felt heavy on one side, the weight of the overdue bills throwing it off balance.

He hovered his thumb over the phone's on-screen keyboard, but no reply popped into his head. What could he say to her?

How could he tell her just how badly he'd messed up?

Shoving the phone back in his pocket, he returned to the back garden, and muttered a, 'Piss off' to Armand's dog when it started barking.

'Charming.'

Tyler stared in disbelief at the animal, then spotted Nidds standing by the back step, chucking some foil wrappers and half-eaten biscuits in the big green wheelie bin.

'Sorry, not you,' Tyler said, managing a half-smile.

'I guessed,' Nidds replied. She shot the dog a dirty look. It was darting around Tyler's feet, head back, eyes bulging as it continued its high-pitched barking frenzy. 'Arsehole of a thing. He used to have two of them, apparently, but one got run over.'

Tyler clutched at his head. 'Aye. I heard. Imagine that in stereo.'

He remembered the cock-up he'd made in the kitchen, and found himself striving to repair the damage he'd done. He had a feeling he'd be doing a lot of that in the near future.

'Listen, Nidds, Dave didn't mean to say anything. He was saying how much he missed you, and it just sort of slipped out. He felt really shite about it. Made me promise not to tell anyone.' Tyler winced. 'I guess I've fucked that up, too.'

Nidds tipped half a sandwich off a plate and into the bin, let the lid fall shut, then set the plate on top of the recycling bin and slouched back against the wall with her hands in her pockets.

'What do you mean, "too"?' she asked. 'What else have you been fucking up?'

Tyler puffed out his cheeks. 'Nothing. Not really,' Tyler began. 'I mean, it's just—'

'Wait!'

Nidds straightened suddenly and opened the bin lid again. She peered down into the morass of black bags and festering rubbish, then reached inside.

Tyler watched as she carefully lifted out a crumpled-up piece of paper. At the top, just visible in amongst the creases and folds, was the same hotel logo as the pad in Isaac and Sharon Simpson's bedroom.

'Here, hold on,' Tyler said.

Fishing in his pockets, he produced a sealed pack of rubber gloves, opened the packaging, and slipped them on.

Nidds continued to hold the ball of paper by one corner until he plucked it carefully from her grasp. She watched over his shoulder as he slowly unfolded it, opening it up until five words were revealed.

'I know what you did.'

—

'Got a minute, boss?'

Logan turned away from Isaac and saw Tyler hovering half in the living room, half in the hallway. The look on the DC's face made him get quickly to his feet.

'No bother, Detective Constable. We were pretty much done here for now.' He smiled at Isaac and Armand, and there was a hint of menace behind it. 'This has been a very enlightening conversation, gentlemen. You can relax, though. For now.'

He stalked out of the room, and found Tyler pacing back and forth in the kitchen. The lad looked agitated, like something major had happened.

'What's up?' Logan asked. 'What have we got?'

'Check this out, boss,' Tyler said.

He thrust out an evidence bag containing a sheet of note-paper, the writing visible through the clear plastic.

Logan read it.

Then, to be on the safe side, he read it again.

'Where did you find this?'

It was Nidds who chimed in with the reply. 'The bin outside, sir.'

'The bin?' Logan shot a look at the back door, his brow furrowing. 'Armand's bin?'

Both constables nodded.

'Aye, boss. Nidds spotted it.'

'It was just lying there, sir. Scrunched up.'

Logan turned his gaze on the liaison officer, then nodded his appreciation. 'Good work, Constable. This is a major find. This could be the key to this whole case.'

Nidds shrugged self-consciously. 'I don't know about that, sir. I just… I spotted it and thought it looked interesting.'

'It's that, all right,' Logan agreed. He took the evidence bag from Tyler's hand, and turned it over, checking the notepad page from all angles. 'It's definitely interesting.'

'There's something else, boss. Text from Hamza. Two of the dodgy harassment calls came from a number he was able to identify. Unregistered pay-as-you-go, but he did a bit of digging, and you won't believe who it belongs to.' Tyler rocked back on his heels, savouring the feeling of knowing something the DCI didn't. 'Only a Mr Armand Holburn!'

He'd expected the DCI to be blown away by this revelation, but Logan simply nodded and tucked the evidence bag into his coat pocket.

'Aye. That makes sense,' he said.

Tyler blinked, bewildered. 'What? How?'

'I'll explain later,' Logan said. He scratched at his stubble for a moment, then leaned in closer to Tyler and lowered his voice so the men in the next room wouldn't hear. 'Get me two cars here, quick as you can. We're bringing them both in.'

Tyler's eyes widened. 'Both, boss?'

'Aye. We'll ask Armand about the note and the phone calls. And, about his relationship with the victim. I want DNA samples from both of them, too.'

'Got it,' Tyler said, taking out his phone. He stared at the text messages still on the screen for a beat, then hurriedly swiped away. 'Why we bringing in Isaac, boss? I mean, obviously he's still in the frame, but why now?'

'The calls,' Logan said. 'In his previous statements, he said nobody had ever spoken. But, he repeatedly referred to the person on the other end as "he", and nearly let slip something they said.'

'"I know what you did",' Tyler said.

'We get them set up in two interview rooms. Play them off against each other. If we're lucky, one of them might crack.'

'My money's on Isaac,' Nidds whispered. 'Armand's going to be tougher.'

Tyler side-eyed the kitchen door. 'You did say we were looking for two people, boss. You think it's them?'

Logan's face gave nothing away. 'Maybe. Or one of them. I don't know, yet. I can't see the full picture.'

'Well, I can't see any of the picture yet, boss,' Tyler admitted, bringing his phone to his ear. 'So you're way ahead of me…'

Chapter 18

Understandably, neither Isaac Simpson nor Armand Holburn was particularly happy about being loaded into different police cars and driven ten miles back down to the police station in Fort William.

Logan didn't want to reveal his hand too early, so made no mention of the note, or the revelation that Armand had been behind at least a couple of the harassment calls.

Nidds dropped Armand's dog with the concrete frog lady on the other side of Isaac's house, then set off down the road in her own car.

Logan hung about in Armand's back garden, Tyler watching in silence as the DCI peered into the bins, then crossed to the metal sheds and rattled the heavy locks. There were no windows in either shed, and Logan's attempts to find a crack in the joins that might let him peek inside came to nothing.

'Remind me to ask him about these,' he said, running a hand up and down the galvanised steel. He rapped his knuckles on the wall. It was solid. Thick. Whatever was in there, he wasn't keen on anyone getting access to it. 'If the bastard's hiding something in there, I want to know what it is.'

When he got no reply, he looked back over his shoulder to see the detective constable staring at his phone screen.

'Tyler!'

'Eh?' DC Neish quickly shoved his phone into his pocket. 'Sorry, boss. Aye, eh, they're locked up.'

Logan's eyes narrowed. 'That's not what I was saying. What's the matter?'

Tyler's attempt to feign innocence only made him look more guilty. 'Nothing, boss,' he said. His voice sounded like a creaky floorboard.

Logan continued to glare at him for a few moments more, then tutted and shook his head. 'Fine. I'll take your word for it,' he said, striding towards the gate. 'Now, come on. I'll take you back to the station, then you can take your own car back up the road.'

Tyler fell into step behind him. 'Up the road, boss?'

'Aye. You're going home.'

'Home?' Tyler almost stumbled over the word, and the enormity of the argument that no doubt awaited him there. 'But, the case, boss. I'm needed here.'

Logan stopped at the driver's door of his car. Taggart bounced around excitedly in the back seat, his nose and tongue leaving smears on the inside of the window.

'Well, fortunately for us, the road goes in both directions,' Logan told him. 'You can head home tonight, then back tomorrow.' He opened the door. 'If you think I'm having Sinead give me an earful for keeping you here, you can bloody well think again.'

Fending off the DC's objections, Logan climbed into the car, begrudgingly acknowledged Taggart with a quick pat, then pulled on his seatbelt.

He had just started the engine when his phone rang, first in his pocket, then through the car's speakers as the Bluetooth connected.

'Ben Forde' flashed up on the dashboard screen, and Logan thumbed the button on the steering wheel that answered the call.

'Benjamin,' Logan said. 'We're just on our way back.'

'You've no' left yet?'

'No.' Logan shot Tyler a sideways look as the detective constable shut his door and strapped himself in. 'We were having a wee sniff around first.'

'Aye, well, there's something else for you to stick your nose into,' Ben said. 'We've got an address for Shayne Feasey.'

'Bloody Hell! Well done!' Logan gushed. 'Quick question, though. Who the hell's Shayne Feasey when he's at home?'

'Oh. Aye. You weren't here for any of that,' Ben said.

Once he'd finished explaining who he was talking about, and why tracking him down was so important, he gave them the address they'd been able to dig up.

'It's not definite. It's somewhere he was down as staying at before. Uses it as a mailing address. It's actually rented out to a guy who seems to be a mate of his, but according to that fella's social media, he's abroad for the next three months, which could mean the house would be empty.'

'And you think this guy we're after could be squatting there?' Logan asked.

'Squatting. Subletting. Maybe,' Ben said. 'But maybe not. It's grasping at straws a bit, but it's only at Torlundy, so you'll be passing the front door on your way down the road.'

'Won't hurt to check it out, boss,' Tyler said, a little too eagerly.

Logan eyed the younger officer with suspicion. 'If I didn't know better, son, I'd say you were trying to avoid going home.'

'Me, boss? No, boss. Absolutely not, boss.'

'Christ,' came the voice from the stereo. 'I'm not looking at him, and even I can see through that.'

Tyler shifted uncomfortably in the passenger seat, and Logan decided to let him off the hook.

'Text through the address. Tyler's right,' he said, pulling away from Armand's house. 'It won't do any harm to swing by and check it out.'

'Will do, Jack,' Ben replied. 'Oh, and, um… Would you mind if I nipped out for a bit this evening?'

Logan peered at the car stereo like he might somehow be able to read the expression on the DI's face over the airwaves. 'Nipped out? What do you mean?'

'Just, eh, just for a couple of hours. I'm, um, I'm… Just for a wee bite to eat.'

Logan's nostrils flared. 'Are you going on a bloody date?'

'Ooh, away you go! It's not a…' Ben began, his autopilot kicking in. He stopped himself, though, and the detectives in the car both winced when he said, 'Aye, actually. I am.'

'With that bloody dragon?'

'She's not a dragon, Jack, she's a human being,' Ben said with a sincerity that suggested her being a giant flying lizard had, until then, been within the realms of possibility. 'And she's not as bad as you think she is.'

'Well, there's a ringing endorsement, if ever I heard one,' Logan said. 'I know your memory's no' what it once was, but I'm sure I don't have to remind you that we're in the middle of a bloody murder investigation, Benjamin! And you want to go out gallivanting?'

'We'll still be in the middle of a murder investigation when I get back,' Ben countered. 'And it was Moira who identified Feasey, so maybe she'll be able to help. She might have more local knowledge that could be useful.'

Tyler grinned. There was something quite triumphant about it. 'So, are you saying you're going to pump her for information, boss?'

A hush fell over the car. It was a heavy, suffocating sort of silence that covered the vehicle like a blanket. Even Taggart, who had been happily panting away in the back seat, reeled his tongue back in and stared in mute disbelief at the detective constable.

The weight of all that quiet dragged Tyler's smile down several notches. Nobody was laughing, so clearly they hadn't quite grasped the joke.

Still, he could easily remedy that.

'By "pump" I mean—'

'Out,' Logan interjected, leaning over and pulling on the handle of Tyler's door.

Tyler snorted out an uncertain-sounding laugh. When, once again, nobody else joined in, he muttered a worried, 'Boss?'

'You heard. On you go. Stand out there,' Logan told him, pointing to a spot a few feet away from the car. 'Stand out there and think about what you've done.'

'Can I not just sit here and think about what I've done, boss?' Tyler asked. 'It's starting to rain.'

'Well, you should've bloody thought of that,' said Ben from the radio, 'before you came out with that filth.'

'It was just… I didn't mean…'

Logan cleared his throat and nodded towards the passenger door.

With a tut, Tyler got out of the car, ducking his head against the drizzle. He shut the door behind him, looked down at his feet for a few moments, then turned to look back in through the passenger window and shrugged.

'Can I come back in now?' he asked, his voice muffled. 'I've had a think, and it was wrong.'

'I'd give him a couple of minutes,' Ben suggested.

'It's for his own good,' Logan agreed. He gave Tyler a wave, fighting to keep the smile from his face.

'I mean, what a bloody thing to say. *Pump her for information*. Of all the bloody nerve!' Ben continued. 'Trust me, it's not like that at all. Honestly. It's no' that sort of date. Although, believe me, if I ever am pumping her, it'll no' be for information!'

Logan grimaced like he'd recently ingested poison and was now starting to feel the effects. He stared in mute horror at the stereo for a moment. Then, with an urgent prod, he turned it off, ending the call.

'Jesus Christ,' he whispered, fending off the mental pictures that were involuntarily painting themselves like murals across the walls of his mind.

Outside, Tyler wrapped his arms around himself as the drizzle shifted up a gear.

'I'll make you a deal, son,' Logan called, leaning across to the passenger side. 'I'll let you back in the car as long as we agree to never speak of that entire conversation ever again...'

—

The address Ben texted through was a couple of miles outside of Fort William, on the main A82 road to Inverness. It would've been quicker to send Uniform up to check the place out, although they were probably tied up ferrying around all of Logan's various suspects and interviewees.

It was a bungalow in a small gathering of white buildings just off the road, with a private car park that was boxed in by some threadbare patches of yellowing grass. Logan pulled up past the house they were looking for, tucking the car out of sight around the corner, where they could see the back door of the property.

He shut off the engine. The wipers nestled back into place at the bottom of the windscreen, and spots of rain immediately began to cover the glass.

'Right, stay here,' Logan instructed, unfastening his belt. 'I'll go round the front. You watch the back in case he tries to do a runner. If he does, get after him.'

'Will do, boss,' Tyler said. He hoped it wouldn't come to that, though. His last attempt at chasing anyone hadn't exactly gone well.

'Do *not* let him get away,' Logan warned, then he opened the door, ordered Taggart to stay where he was, and went marching back down the hill towards the bungalow's front door.

There were no signs of life from inside when Logan made his approach. Net curtains hung over the windows, making it difficult to see much of what was going on inside, but there was no movement from what he could tell.

It was quiet, too. He stopped and listened at the door for a moment, then hammered out a knock when he heard nothing.

Backing down a step, he scanned along the front of the bungalow, checking the windows for any twitch of the curtains.

Nothing.

It felt empty. The whole place did, in fact, all the other houses included. Were it not for the regular rumbling of the passing traffic, Logan would've felt utterly alone.

He went up the step again and was about to knock for a second and final time when he heard the clunking of a locking mechanism. The door opened a crack, until a security chain tightened and jerked it to a stop.

'Shit. Sorry. Hang on, mate.'

The door closed. Logan listened to the rattling of the chain.

He hadn't seen much of the man through the gap. Not enough to get more than a fleeting impression of him. The accent had been Manchester, though, he thought. But there'd been something else to it, too. A suggestion of something foreign.

The door opened again, revealing a man in his thirties with the most startling ears Logan had ever seen. It wasn't that they were big, necessarily—though they were—it was the shape and the angle of them. They were like two perfect semi-circles affixed to the side of his head so they stuck straight out at a ninety-degree angle.

They were the sort of ears that would've made life a living hell back where Logan had grown up. Bullies would've switched schools just to get a chance at tormenting a kid with ears like that. The bastards would've come from miles around.

Which maybe explained the build on the man in the doorway. He wasn't pumped up and over-inflated like a body-builder, but ripped and lean. Like a fighter. He wore a vest-style T-shirt that showed the cut of his muscles, and his sleeves of tattoos that covered both arms like the pages of a colouring book. Though, probably not one you'd want to give your kids.

While Logan was appraising him, he was doing the same to the detective, his gaze flitting up and down, getting the measure of the man on the doorstep.

'You police?' he grunted.

'What would give you that idea, son?' Logan asked. 'Why would the polis be turning up at your door?'

'You tell me. But you're definitely police. Can smell you lot a mile away.'

He didn't seem worried or even nervous, but his displeasure was obvious.

Logan produced his warrant card. 'Detective Chief Inspector Jack Logan.'

'A DCI! Bloody hell. A DCI out and about? I thought you lot just sat around in offices eating biscuits all day.'

'If only,' Logan said, returning his ID to his pocket. The other man hadn't even glanced at it. 'Are you Shayne Feasey?'

'Depends what I'm meant to have done.'

Logan nodded past him. 'Mind if I come in? Won't take long.'

Feasey's jaw clenched and his eyes narrowed while he considered the request. Then, with a tut and a sigh, he stepped aside, motioning for Logan to head on through. 'Living room's at the end of the hall.'

'Thanks,' Logan said.

He went inside and headed along the narrow hallway to the open door at the far end.

Behind him, Shayne stepped out, stole a quick look around in all directions, then returned to the house.

With the turn of a key, he quietly locked the door.

Chapter 19

Ben Forde was running out of interview rooms. He was also, more importantly, running out of time.

There were now three potential suspects being held in three different rooms, all of them still to be properly checked in, and all of them waiting to be spoken to.

And he had just over an hour until his big date.

Why the hell had he agreed to dinner tonight? What had he been thinking?

Maybe there was still time to call it off. Moira worked at the station. She knew what it was like. She'd understand.

Only she wouldn't. That was why she'd picked tonight, he thought. It was a test. Would he prioritise her, or would he put the job first?

He'd always put the job before Alice, his late wife. He'd never wanted to—he'd felt terrible every time he'd let her down, or arrived home late, or ruined their plans by letting an investigation become all-consuming.

She'd understood, though. She hadn't liked it, necessarily, but she'd understood.

He'd almost wished that she didn't. He'd almost encouraged her to leave, to be with someone who could give her their all. Give her everything she'd deserved.

But she'd stayed with him. She'd made do with second place.

And that had cost Alice her life.

The job had cost Logan his marriage, too, not to mention his relationship with his daughter. Ben looked over the top of his laptop to Hamza's desk. The DS was talking on the phone, chasing up some lead, or questioning some piece of evidence.

What he wasn't doing was tucking his kiddie into bed, or catching up on what his wife had been up to that day.

What he wasn't doing was living a life.

'Bugger it,' Ben muttered. 'They can spare me for an hour and a half.'

That was all it would take. A quick starter and main course, and he'd skip the dessert. He'd have to stay off the wine, too, but she could get ripped into the stuff to her heart's content.

An hour and a half. That was all. Surely all his years of service were enough to buy him ninety minutes of freedom?

Across at his desk, Hamza hung up the phone and practically jumped to his feet.

'Sir,' he said, and the urgency in his tone was impossible to miss. 'Just been following up on Shayne Feasey's army record.'

Ben raised an eyebrow. 'And?'

'Before his discharge, he spent a year in military prison for assault. Shattered a guy's arm in three places. Broke his ribs, leaving him with a punctured lung and other internal injuries. Tried to shove his thumbs through the poor guy's eyes before a couple of other squaddies jumped in to drag him away. He gave them a hiding, too.'

'Jesus,' Ben said.

'The first attack was almost an attempted murder charge, but it got reduced at the last minute,' Hamza continued. 'But by the sounds of things, he's a bit of a headcase. In fact, no. Not a bit of one, a full and complete headcase.'

The detective inspector ran a hand down his face. 'Shite.' He picked up his phone. 'Get Uniform around to the address. I'll get on to Jack. With a bit of luck, he hasn't engaged with the bastard yet.'

The door at the end of the hall led into a small kitchen that could generously be described as 'messy', but more accurately described as 'a global pandemic waiting to happen'.

Food festered on dirty dishes. Circles of stinking grease floated atop the murky grey water in the sink. A small pile of bulging black bags turned the air fetid and sour, the liquid seeping out from them further staining the already filthy linoleum flooring.

'I thought this was the living room,' Logan started to say, then something hit him on the back of the head. Heavy. Solid. His skull rattled, pain erupting, rushing outwards from the impact site.

He staggered, turned, fingers balling into fists, and just managed to deflect another blow from a wooden rolling pin before it could make contact with his head.

Feasey lunged, moving too quickly for Logan to fully comprehend what was happening, driving a fist directly into the centre of the detective's torso. The impact to his solar plexus made Logan's lungs cramp up. He swung wildly, gasping for breath, his fist finding nothing but air.

He was too slow to block another hit from the rolling pin. Too tired. Too old. It caught him a solid blow across the jaw, and he saw a flash of red as he spun, off balance, towards the sink. His fingers found a dinner plate, grabbed, slipped. He heard it thud against the floor. Too clumsy. Too old.

A flurry of punches pounded like hammer blows against his kidneys, drawing a hiss from his bloodied lips. He threw an elbow backwards. It made contact, but not properly. Not enough.

Fingers tangled in his hair. He gripped the edge of the sink, but not in time to stop his head being shoved violently forward. Once. Twice. The edge of a wall-mounted cupboard split an eyebrow, and blood poured down into an eye, half blinding him.

And then, he was falling, the world lurching up and around him, spiralling out of control. The floor knocked the last of the breath from him. It was sticky with spilled blood and filth.

He heard his phone ringing, but it was far away, down a dark tunnel, well beyond his reach.

He had to get up. Get moving. Get out. There was no saying how long he could stay conscious. No saying how far this bastard would go.

The door. The back door was just a few feet away. He could see the weak sunlight through a circle of frosted glass.

A light at the end of the tunnel.

Hands grabbed him by the back of the coat. His fingers found the wet plate he'd dropped, and he swung back and up with it. It shattered against the side of Feasey's head.

Logan didn't have time to enjoy the man's grunt of pain. He launched himself towards the door, caught the handle, and let his weight pull it down as he stumbled on his knees.

If it was locked, he was stuck here.

If it was locked, he was dead.

The door came off the latch, and he twisted himself enough to allow it to open. Legs failing him, chest tightening, he fell out onto the back step.

Feasey was on him immediately, his face a demon-mask of blood and rage.

'I bet you think you're so fucking hard. Don't you, big man?'

The words rushed at him like falling sand. Drowning him. Burying him.

'I bet you like to throw your fucking weight around.'

Logan tried to get up, but a foot slammed into his back, collapsing him onto the ground. The guy was fast. Strong. Ruthless.

And Logan was so very, very old.

A kick to the ribs flipped him over onto his back. Feasey's face was less than six feet away, but it was a blur. A smear against the sky above.

Logan saw a foot raise. A trainer. An Adidas Samba, with mud drying on the sole. It took aim at his head. Pain and exhaustion pinned him down, held him in place, left him with no option but to wait for the inevitable impact.

'Not so fucking tough now, are you?'

A dog barked. Shrill, and loud, and incandescent with animal rage.

And closing in fast.

Taggart.

Logan saw him over the swelling of his eye socket. Watched as the little dog hurled himself at Feasey.

Heard the sickening *thump* and the yelp of pain as the raised foot slammed down on the animal. Once. Twice.

'N-no!' Logan ejected, fury driving life back into his limbs. He grabbed at the leg just as Feasey swung back for another kick at the whimpering dog, dug his fingers into the flesh, and savoured the bastard's roar of pain.

He didn't see the other knee, just felt it as it smashed into the side of his head, filling it with noise and light and fog.

He fell back. Heard the crack of the stone step against his skull, and felt it a split second later.

Darkness rushed in like a stream of cold, filthy water. It poured into his throat, filling him up, dragging him down.

Through the fog, he saw Feasey looming over him. Grinning. Blood on his teeth. A vampire about to feed.

And then, there was movement. A rush of speed. A jarring impact.

A cry drifted past him in the dark.

'Got him, boss!'

Tyler.

No.

Please, God, no.

And then, the icy fingers of darkness fully took hold, and he was dragged, terrified, into the void.

Chapter 20

A blink.

A light.

Darkness.

Then, the pain.

Not one. Not specifically.

Pain in general.

Everywhere.

All at once.

…

A blink.

A light.

A shape.

Darkness.

Then, the worry.

Something had happened.

Something bad.

To someone.

To him?

No. Worse than that.

…

A blink.

A light.

A face.

Blood on its teeth.

He lunged, half-blind, roaring, lashing out. His hand found a throat. His fingers tightened, squeezed.

'Tyler!' he cried, in a voice that didn't sound like his own.

'Jesus Christ!' A man's voice. Sharp and urgent. 'Get him off him. Jack! Jack!'

Hands grabbed him roughly by the arm. He shrugged them off, and heard the crash of someone or something falling over.

His grip tightened, fingers locking into place around the throat.

And then, another voice. Softer. Kinder. The accent like music to his ears.

A familiar hand on his bare chest.

'Jack. Hey, hey, you're OK. It's me. It's me. You're all right. You're OK. He's a doctor. Just a doctor.'

A blink.

A light.

A realisation.

The hospital. He was in the hospital.

The purple-faced young man he was currently strangling wore a checked shirt and navy slacks, and was desperately trying to prise the iron bars of Logan's fingers from his neck.

Logan let go, and the junior doctor stumbled backwards, grasping at his throat, sucking down deep breaths.

Down on Logan's right, DI Forde pulled himself up off the floor using the bed rail and dusted himself off. The worried smile on Shona's face, and the fact that Ben didn't pass any remark about being knocked onto his arse, told Logan his injuries had to be serious.

They could wait.

'Tyler,' he rasped. 'Where's Tyler?'

A look passed from Shona to Ben. A look that said everything.

'Don't worry about that right now,' Shona urged. 'You need to concentrate on—'

Logan threw back his covers, gritting his teeth as the pain ramped up.

'Whoa, whoa!' Ben put a hand on the DCI's arm. 'What are you doing?'

'You shouldn't be moving yet, Mr Logan,' coughed the doctor, though he made sure to say it from a safe distance.

'Clothes,' Logan instructed.

He could see his coat piled up on a chair, his shoes below it, but his trousers and shirt were nowhere to be seen.

'Where are my clothes?' he asked, fumbling for the cannula in the crook of his arm that connected him to a bag of fluid beside the bed.

'Jack, wait,' Shona said, putting a hand on top of his. 'You're hurt. You need to stay where you are.'

'I can't,' Logan replied.

She moved her hand up to his face. Her touch sent electric shocks of pain through his jaw.

'I wasn't asking you. I'm telling you,' she said. 'You're no use to anyone right now. You need to rest. Recover.'

Logan held the IV line pinched between finger and thumb, but didn't yet pull it out. He turned to look at Ben on the other side of the bed, and felt like all his bones were grinding as he moved.

'Tyler,' he said. 'What happened?'

'We, uh, we don't know,' the DI replied. He spoke slowly, like the wrong word might turn out to be a landmine and blow up in his face. 'We found you out the back. No sign of Tyler.'

Out the back.

A blink.

A memory.

An animal squeal.

'Taggart!'

'He's fine. He's fine,' Shona assured him. 'He's at the vet, but he's going to be fine.'

Logan's eyes burned. He felt a pressure behind them, and lowered his head for a moment. They'd see his shoulders shaking, but they wouldn't see his eyes blurring with tears.

'I really must insist you get back into bed, Mr Logan,' the doctor said, still sounding a little croaky.

Ben winced. 'Oh, God. I wouldn't do that, son,' he said. 'I wouldn't insist. He doesn't take well to that sort of thing. *Insisting.*'

Shona turned to the younger man and smiled brightly. 'Maybe you could just give us a minute? You know, just to avoid any further strangulation–related incidents.'

She waited for the doctor to leave, then started to lift Logan's legs back into bed, fully expecting him to resist.

To her surprise, he didn't.

He groaned as his head sunk into the soft pillow. His eyes rolled for a moment, struggling to find focus, then they closed, plunging him back into darkness.

'*Got him, boss!*'

His eyelids snapped open. Ben and Shona had switched places. The light in the room had changed, the evening sunlight streaming through a gap in the clouds.

'Tyler?' he said.

'We're going to find him,' Ben said. 'I've spoken to Mitchell. She's authorised overtime and holiday cancellations. We're going to pull resources in from other areas. We'll turn the whole bloody country upside down, if that's what it takes. We're going to bring our boy home, Jack. It's a matter of when, not if.'

Logan struggled to form the next word. His mouth wouldn't make the shape at first. Not until he forced it to.

'Sinead?'

There was a moment of silence that felt like a gulf. Though his ears were still ringing from the beating he'd received, Logan heard the crack in the DI's voice.

'We spoke to her. Hamza and me. She was…' Ben looked down at his hands. He was wringing them together. 'Well, I'm sure you can imagine. She's going to stay home, though. With the kids. She's going to wait to hear.'

'Good,' Logan said. 'That's good.' He shut his eyes again, sleep returning to claim him. 'But, I don't believe that for a bloody minute…'

Sinead stood on the doorstep, rocking the double buggy back and forth, trying to keep the twins from rousing. They'd fallen asleep during the drive over, and had miraculously remained that way when she'd decanted them into the buggy and pulled the rain cover over the top.

She rang the doorbell again, holding her finger on it this time, and listened as the insistent *brrrr* rang through the house.

At the sound of footsteps, she stepped back, letting the rain hide her tears.

She started speaking even before the door had finished opening, the words tripping over themselves in their rush to get out.

'I'm sorry to bother you, I'd have gone to my aunt, but she's away, and I don't know who else to go to.' She glanced down at the sleeping babies. 'I need someone to look after them. Just for a little while. I have to go. Tyler, he's… Something's happened, and I need to go. He's in danger. I need to help him. Or try, anyway. I need to go to him. I have to.'

The rain was doing nothing now. Her tears were fully on show.

'But I can't take them. I need someone who can watch them for me. And it's stupid to come here, I know that, but I just… I don't know what to do. I didn't know where else to go.'

The man in the doorway looked her up and down.

'Boyband's got himself in fucking trouble again, has he?'

Sinead could only nod, her tears streaming down her face.

Robert Hoon regarded the buggy in silence as he sipped from a glass of whisky he'd been holding when he answered the door.

'Well, I know fuck all about looking after kids,' he told her. He scratched at his stubbly chin, then shrugged. 'But I know a woman who does.'

He set the glass down on the hall table, then turned his head enough to shout back over his shoulder.

'Berta! Get your fat arse up off that fucking couch and come make yourself useful.'

The reply was bellowed back at him from somewhere deeper in the house. 'I'll "make yourself useful" you, you arse-eyed daud of room-temperature dog shite!'

'Just get a fucking shifty on,' Hoon called back to his sister. He met Sinead's eye, and dipped his head in a nod that made her tears dry up. 'Me and this detective constable here are going on a wee road trip.'

—

They were whispering. Whispering about her.

She couldn't hear them, but she could see them. See the way they leaned in closer to one another. See the way their lips moved. See the way they tried not to be noticed when they shot their pitying looks in her direction.

They'd be arguing over who was going to come talk to her next. The skinny lad with all the plooks had been the first to come over and ask her if everything was OK. She'd given him a right bloody mouthful, and a well-deserved one at that.

So, her gentleman friend was running a little late. So what? Why did that matter? He'd booked the table. They knew he was coming. He was just a little behind schedule.

And besides, it wasn't like the restaurant was even that busy, was it? There were plenty of tables left. Plenty of room for any last-minute rush. What did another ten minutes of waiting matter? Stupid boy!

That had been half an hour ago. The restaurant's front door had opened five times since then, and though she'd tried not to look, her eyes had instantly been drawn towards it every time.

And every time, she'd quickly looked back down at the menu.

The waiting staff's whispering came to an end. The spotty-faced lad was clearly refusing to come over. A girl started shuffling towards the table, instead. She looked about twelve. She also looked scared, like she was walking into the dragon's den without a scrap of armour on.

She held her notepad in front of her as she approached. It was her shield, the pencil, her sword.

'Uh, hi,' she said. Her voice was teeth-grindingly cheerful. 'I'm really sorry, but we're going to need this table soon.'

She glanced around, indicating the now mostly full restaurant.

'So, do you, you know, do you want to order, or...?'

'No.'

The girl's smile faltered. 'No?'

'You deaf, young lady? All that bloody rock music gone for your ears?'

The waitress frowned. 'What rock music?'

Chair legs scraped on the floor as Moira Corson rose slowly to her feet. In her mind, it was a majestic and impressive display of authority. To everyone watching, it just looked like she was struggling with dodgy hips.

She could feel all their eyes on her. Judging her. Pitying her.

'No. I won't be ordering,' Moira declared.

And then, the scaffolding she'd erected around herself began to fail. Began to fall.

'I won't be ordering anything,' she said in a voice that was barely a whisper.

And with the judging looks of the staff and diners still on her, and with their sniggers of laughter ringing in her ears, she snatched up her coat and her handbag and walked out of the restaurant with her head held high.

And she knew that she'd never, *ever* return.

Chapter 21

An army of police officers had started to assemble in the briefing room, filling all the seats, and standing in lines along the walls. Most of them were in uniform, but half a dozen plainclothes CID officers stood together up the back.

Not one of them was holding a cup of tea—an indication of just how seriously they were taking the situation.

DI Forde stood at the head of the room, flanked by DS Khaled and DC Swanney. Hamza's face was tired and drawn. Even Tammi-Jo's energy levels seemed to have fallen through the floor.

A hundred-and-twenty-inch digital screen was fixed to the wall behind them, showing a larger-than-life photograph of DC Neish. In it, Tyler was cradling one of the twins in each arm, and grinning straight at the camera. Sinead had sent it to Hamza a few weeks after the babies had been born.

It was a decent enough picture of Tyler, though not the best. There were clearer images of him they could have used. His warrant card photo being the most obvious one.

But this one—a doting dad with his newborns—would have the most impact.

At a table beside them sat Chief Inspector Alisdair Lyle, better known to everyone in the room by what was widely regarded as one of the more unfortunate nicknames on the force—Praying Mantits.

The nickname had been a mash-up of two of the then-sergeant's most notable traits—his deeply held religious beliefs, and his ongoing battles with his fluctuating weight. Ironic-ally, although he'd slimmed down in recent years, it was the 'Mantits' bit that really stuck, and now most people only used the 'Praying' part if they were explaining the nickname's origins to the new recruits.

Ben shot the chief inspector a quick look to check that he was ready. Before the DI could say anything, though, Mantits got to his feet, rapped his knuckles on the table, and shouted, 'Right. Right! That's enough. Listen up.'

The crowd of cops had barely been making a sound, so the levels of noise in the room didn't really change.

'*Thank you*,' Mantits said, bowing graciously. He sat, then hurriedly stood again and gestured to Ben. 'Detective Inspector Forde,' he said, then he clapped as if to start a round of applause, before sitting down again in silence.

'Eh, thanks for that, Chief Inspector Lyle.'

Mantits smiled, rolled his eyes, and batted the offered grat-itude away with a wave of his hand.

'And thank you all for coming at such short notice,' Ben said, addressing the rest of the audience. 'As you may know, one of our own, Detective Constable Tyler Neish, is missing. This picture is of him after he recently became a dad. Of twins.'

He gave that a moment to sink in, his gaze flitting from face to solemn face.

'Earlier today, Tyler intervened in a serious assault on a senior officer. That's when we lost track of him. We believe he was taken by this man.'

He didn't need to look to know that Hamza had clicked through to the next slide. The focusing of the audience's atten-tion told him the image had changed.

'Shayne Feasey. I'm reliably informed that he's…'

Ben's heart skipped a beat, and he hesitated, just for a moment, remembering who had given him Feasey's details, and where he was currently supposed to be.

Shite.

That could wait. It would have to.

'A Grade A pain in the arse,' said one of the CID boys up the back, and there was some murmured agreement from various other parts of the room.

Ben looked around at the nodding heads. 'You know him, then. That's good. Because, as of right now, your most important job—your only job—is to find the bastard.'

Shona stood at the end of the hospital corridor, her hands in the back pockets of her jeans, her weight shifting anxiously from foot to foot.

She didn't want to leave him, but he'd insisted. He was fine. There was no saying what state Sinead was in. He wanted Shona to go to her and make sure she was OK.

Besides, someone had to go pick up Taggart from the vet. He was hurt and in a strange place, being poked and prodded by unfamiliar faces. He'd be scared.

Despite all his past protests about the dog, and his many objections to dog ownership, Logan's expression had darkened at the thought of Taggart being afraid and alone.

'I'll be grand,' he'd said. 'If anything changes, you'll be the first to know. Now, go do what you have to do. See if the dog's ready to come home, then make sure Sinead's got what she needs. She'll be going through hell.'

With some reluctance, Shona had agreed that he was probably right. She should get an update on Taggart, and she should go check in on Sinead.

There was also the matter of Alexis Maximuke's post-mortem. She'd thought about sharing that news with Jack, but decided that it really wasn't the time. He was unlikely to lose much sleep over the woman's death, but it still felt like an additional burden he could well do without.

And so, she'd given him a stern warning about getting plenty of rest and doing what the doctors told him, and then had planted a kiss on his forehead—the only bit of his face not swollen or covered in bruises—and headed out in search of a nurse.

'He's going to be a bloody nightmare,' she warned. 'He's not going to listen to anyone. He's a stubborn bugger.'

Nancy—a short but formidable-looking nurse with greying hair pulled back into a bun—smiled and put a hand on Shona's arm. 'We've dealt with our fair share of them, Mrs Logan. Don't you worry.'

'Oh, no. I'm not Mrs… We're not…' Shona shook her head. 'Doesn't matter. And yeah, I'm sure you have.' She glanced back along the corridor, to the door at the far end. 'But he's going to be worse than most of them. Possibly all of them. And I don't mean individually. I mean, put together.'

The nurse chuckled. 'Sounds like a challenge!'

'Oh, he can be that, all right.'

'Well, listen, here's what I'm going to do. I'll go pop in now and introduce myself. We haven't met yet. I'll gently stress the importance of recuperation—gently, mind, because I know what men are like when you try and tell them what to do—and then I'll keep a close eye. All right? I'll make sure he's behaving himself.'

Shona stopped dancing on the spot and let out a sigh of relief. 'Thanks. I just… I know what he's like. And something's happened at work that he's going to want to be there for. He's not going to be able to settle.'

'Don't you worry about a thing. He's a big bugger, so we'll see him sneaking about, and he doesn't have his clothes in there with him. He's not going anywhere,' Nancy promised, and Shona allowed herself to relax a little further.

'Great. Thank you.'

'No bother, pet. We've got your phone number, yeah?'

'Uh, no. I don't think I gave it to anyone. But Jack has it. Obviously, I mean. He has it. And I'm on the internal directory. Dr Shona Maguire.'

'Oh! You're a doctor?'

'Pathologist, actually. Based in Raigmore.'

'Ah. Well, we'll be able to find you if we need you. But it'll be fine. He'll be fine.'

Shona snuck a look back over her shoulder again, then came to a decision.

'Right. OK. Well, in that case… Good luck,' she said. 'I've a feeling you're going to need it.'

Nancy laughed at that, then escorted Shona to the door and waved her off with a promise to go back and 'check on the invalid' immediately.

The nurse's return along the corridor took a little longer than expected. One of the trainees had a couple of questions for her, and old Mrs MacAskill from Room 3 took it upon herself to wander into the corridor and hold eye contact while she released an impressively large gush of steaming hot piss onto the floor.

Nancy and another nurse had led her to the bathroom, though she insisted she no longer needed to go, and a clean-up of both the floor and the patient had got underway.

Once she was sure everyone was confident in what they were doing, Nancy had continued along the corridor and opened the door to the room at the far end.

'Hello, Mr Logan, your good lady asked me to—'

She stopped when she saw the empty bed and the open window.

'Oh,' she muttered. 'Bollocks.'

–

'Eh, now, hold your horses there, Detective Inspector.'

All eyes went to Mantits. Sensing the attention, the chief inspector got to his feet. He ran a hand down his front, over the curve of his belly, smoothing down his uniform.

'I know finding Detective Constable Neish is important, but I'm afraid it's not the be-all and end-all.'

'It is,' Ben shot back. 'Today, it is.'

Mantits' smile was thin gruel. 'No, I'm afraid it isn't. Need I remind you that you've got three suspects currently being held on these very premises?'

'They're part of it. They're connected. Don't you bloody worry. I'll be talking to them,' Ben said.

'Don't you bloody worry, *sir*,' the chief inspector corrected.

Ben ignored the rank pull, and gestured out to the crowd of coppers. 'But them, everyone else, they're focus is on finding Shayne Feasey, and bringing Tyler home. That's all that matters.'

'But it isn't, is it? Much as we might like it to be,' Mantits said, and the urge to punch that patronising smile clean off the bastard's face balled Ben's fingers into fists. 'The machinations of law and order don't stop just because one of our own is in trouble.' He held up his hands. 'Again, much as we might want them to. I'm not saying we don't. I'm saying we don't have that luxury.'

'With all due respect, *sir*,' Ben said, putting some venom behind the word. 'Detective Chief Superintendent Mitchell pulled holidays and authorised overtime specifically so we could—'

'Detective Chief Superintendent Mitchell isn't here, Detective Inspector. I am.' He pushed back his shoulders, straightening his usually stooped back. 'At this moment, I'm the senior officer in this station. Correct?'

Ben couldn't bear to look at him any longer. He glanced away, and saw Hamza and Tammi-Jo both biting their lips, like they wanted to say something.

He was right, of course. The bastard was the SO. He had the final say here. At least until Ben could get hold of Mitchell again and have her put him in his place.

With a sigh, he nodded. 'Aye. I suppose you are.'

'There's no "suppose" about it, DI Forde,' Mantits crowed. 'Here, we do things my way. Like it or not, I'm the highest-ranked officer. I'm in charge.'

'Well, you can get that idea right out of your fucking head.'

The voice was a boom from the back of the room. A thunderclap. The shifting of some ancient land mass.

Everyone turned to see Logan standing in the doorway, leaning unsteadily against the frame. His coat was buttoned up, covering most of him.

But not all.

As he walked into the room, his shoes *clacking* on the hard vinyl floor, all eyes were drawn to his bare legs.

'Jack?' Ben groaned. 'You're no' supposed to be here.'

'Aye, well, looks like I am,' Logan replied.

He stabbed a finger in the direction of Chief Inspector Lyle, who stood staring with his mouth hanging agape.

'You, sit down and shut up.'

'You can't—' Mantits began, before a look from Logan silenced him, and collapsed him back into his seat.

Logan turned. It was slow and awkward, and he was forced to grit his teeth against the pain. He aimed the next bunch of orders at the CID officers at the back of the room.

'You're on phone tracking. Tyler had his mobile with him. Where was it last pinged? What can the network get us? Feasey's, too. We must have a number for him. I want all CCTV in the area checked. Talk to the bank, find out if he's used his cards. Pull out all the stops. Anyone gets in your way, you point them to me and tell them to fucking brace themselves. Got that?'

'Got it.'

'Good.' The final command was issued to the rest of the room at large. 'And you. All of you. Get out there. Find this bastard. Bring our boy home. But for God's sake, be careful. He's dangerous. Minimum of twos, you think you're onto something, you call in backup. Do not—do *not*—tackle him on your own. Is that clear?'

A chorus of confirmation came back to him.

'Right. Then what the hell are you all still doing here? Go, go. Get a bloody move on.'

He waited until the stampede of officers had left, then sagged against the table Hamza had been sitting at. The DS, like Ben and Tammi-Jo, was now on his feet, fired up and ready to go.

'God. Are you all right, sir?' Tammi-Jo asked. 'You look like you had a proper kicking. Your face is really sort of...' She puffed out her cheeks. 'Have you ever seen that film, *The Mask*? Not the funny one with the Riddler in it. The Rocky Dennis story one. He had a big face that was a bit like yours, and I've realised I probably shouldn't have said that, and I'm sorry I did, and I wish I hadn't started talking in the first place.'

She smiled awkwardly, then gave him a playful fist bump on the upper arm.

'You look great,' she said. 'And you've got really good legs. You know, for an old... Not "old". For an *older*... Not much older, just, you know—'

She clamped her mouth closed before it could do any more damage, then whipped around like she'd just heard someone calling her name.

'Did anyone just hear...?' she said, before realising from their expressions that nobody was buying it. She quickly changed tack. 'You could probably use a cup of tea. I'll go put the kettle on.'

And with that, she slid over the top of the table like she was Starsky or Hutch sliding across the bonnet of their car, and went running, full tilt, out of the room.

'You shouldn't be here, Jack. You should be in hospital,' Ben said, once the detective constable had fled the scene.

Logan shook his head. 'I'm where I need to be. Are the husband, son and neighbour all still here?'

'They are, sir,' Hamza confirmed. 'DI Forde and I were going to interview them.'

'Good. I want DNA samples from them all, too. One of those men might be the key to finding Feasey. We find him, we find Tyler.'

'We got those already,' Ben said. 'Swabs all done.'

'Good,' Logan said.

He heard movement from Chief Inspector Lyle's desk, and spun around before the bastard could say anything.

'And you. Alisdair. Don't waste your time sucking up to Mitchell on this. She's behind us all the way on it. You'll only make yourself even more of a bloody laughing stock.'

'What the hell's that supposed to mean? I'm not a laughing stock!' Mantits insisted.

Logan's face remained impassive behind the mask of swelling. 'Aye. You keep telling yourself that,' he said. 'Now, how about you make yourself useful for once, and go find me some bloody clothes?'

—

Ben almost bumped straight into her on his way out of the briefing room. She stood in the corridor, dolled up in a navy blue coat that tied at the waist, and clutching a matching handbag in a way that suggested she could do some serious damage with it, and very well might be about to.

'Moira!' he yelped, warily eyeing the handbag. 'There you are. I was just coming to phone you.'

Moira was scowling. This was not anything new, of course, but there was a depth and richness to this particular scowl that set it apart from her standard everyday expression.

She waited until the last few uniformed officers had hurried past before replying.

'Were you? Were you really?'

'Eh, aye. Aye. I just… Sorry. I know we were meant to be meeting, but…' Ben glanced down at the paperwork in his hands, like he might find the perfect words written there. 'Something's happened. To Tyler.'

'I know. I heard,' Moira replied. 'Jennifer on the front desk couldn't wait to tell me all about it.'

'Oh!' said Ben, sensing that there may be a way out of this conversation that didn't involve too much suffering on his part. 'So, you understand, then.'

'Understand?' Moira parroted, her scowl plumbing all new depths of distaste. 'Understand that you couldn't take ten seconds to call me to let me know? Understand that you left me sitting there for almost an hour, left me feeling humiliated in front of all those people? Do you have any idea what a bloody idiot I felt like? Do you have any idea at all?'

'Moira, I'm sorry, I just—'

She wasn't ready to let him explain himself, though. She wasn't letting him off the hook that easily. 'And worse than that, worst of all, in fact, you didn't think to tell me that one of our own is in trouble. That, I'll never forgive you for. Never.'

He watched as she unbuttoned her coat, hung it over her arm, then straightened her back like she was standing to attention. The look of contempt on her face didn't budge an inch.

'If you need me, *Detective Inspector*, I'll be in the office until such times as we find that young lad of yours,' Moira said. 'After that, I think it'd be in everyone's best interests if we don't talk to one another again.'

Clutching her bag, she turned and walked off.

Ben called after her, but she didn't turn back, and as the door at the far end creaked closed behind her, the corridor was plunged into silence.

Though only temporarily.

'What the hell was that about?' asked Logan, appearing from the briefing room through the door at the DI's back.

Mantits was yet to reappear with a shirt or a pair of trousers in his size, and his coat and bare legs combo made him look like a flasher just waiting to expose himself to some unsuspecting passerby.

'Lover's tiff?'

Ben kept watching the door, as if expecting Moira to come walking back through it.

'Something like that,' he said.

'Good bloody riddance, if you ask me,' Logan told him.

Ben wheeled around at that, turning so suddenly that Logan stepped back in surprise.

'Aye, well, nobody did ask you, Jack,' the DI said, so forcefully that Logan shuffled back another step.

Then, without another word, Ben tucked his pile of paperwork under one arm, and went striding off towards the stairs.

Chapter 22

A string of bloody drool hung from Tyler's lips, stretching out, elongating until it joined the rest of the puddle on the floor at his feet.

His arms were hoisted above his head, his wrists bound together and tied to something hidden up there in the dark. The toes of his bare feet only just skiffed the uneven stone floor, so most of his weight was being taken by his wrists and shoulders. The muscles burned like they were on fire, but there was nothing he could do to extinguish the pain.

He'd stretched his legs out, searching for something he could stand on. A stool, or a box, or anything that might support him. If he could just take the strain off his arms, if he could just get higher, maybe he could unhook himself. Maybe he could get free.

Maybe he could get home.

He didn't want to die.

That shouldn't have come as any sort of revelation, but it was the overwhelming thought filling his head. Not the pain. Not even the fear, exactly, though he was definitely afraid.

It was the thought of no longer being in the world. Of not being around for Sinead. Of not being there to carry the twins on his shoulders while they ate ice cream. Of not being there to swing them around by the arms in the back garden, listening to their giggling cries of, 'Faster, faster!'

Of not seeing all their firsts. First day of school. First love. First job. First broken heart.

The thought of missing out on all of it...

Of them missing out on him…

He didn't want to die.

And he was damned if he was going to.

Gritting his teeth, blocking out the pain in his arms, Tyler brought his knees up to his chest. There was some give in the rope. If he could swing enough, maybe he could get his feet up high enough to hook over the beam, or whatever it was he was hanging from.

If he could do that…

Well, probably best to concentrate on that part first. No point in getting ahead of himself. One thing at a time.

He dropped his legs, swinging them back behind him. His wrists ground together, the rope burning deep welts into his skin.

He ignored it. He thought of Sinead. Of the faces of his children.

He brought his knees up again, riding the momentum of the swing, building it.

It was working. This could work. He could do this.

Something thin and solid struck him hard across the back of the thighs, instantly eclipsing the rest of his pain. A sharp cry of shock burst from his lips, and then the pain came again. Again. *Again.*

He heard the whipping of a cane through the air. The *crack* of it against his flesh.

'Don't. Fucking. Move!' hissed a voice from the darkness, punctuating each word with another strike.

'Stop! Stop!' Tyler said, choking on blood, and snot, and tears. 'Please. Please, stop. Just… Just stop.'

He did. The attack ended. Tyler's trousers had offered some protection, but now that he was no longer being struck, the pain began to intensify, swelling and growing until it was the only thing he could think of. The only thing in the world.

And then, just when he felt like he couldn't bear it any more, the cane struck him one final time, whistling through the air to announce itself just a split second before it made contact.

Tyler clamped his mouth shut, holding in the scream that would otherwise have escaped. Screaming might anger the bastard. Worse, he might take pleasure in it. Tyler wasn't about to give him that satisfaction.

When he felt confident that he could contain the pain, he opened his mouth and croaked into the darkness.

'Why are you doing this? What do you want?'

He flinched at the sound of the cane moving through the air, but it didn't hit him again.

'Here, you're the one who fucking attacked me, remember?'

The voice came from in front of him this time, and when Tyler squinted into the darkness, he could just make out the face and cartoonishly large ears of Shayne Feasey.

'You and your big fucking mate came to my place and started shit. I'm just defending myself. I wonder how he's doing, by the way? Looked to be in a pretty bad state when we left him there. Hope he's not dead.'

Tyler saw the bastard's teeth as he grinned.

'His little dog, too. Poor thing. I kind of felt bad about that. It's always the little ones that get it, isn't it? The weak ones. The runts. Like the dog, and you. And me, too, once upon a fucking time. No more, though. Not now. Now, nobody's pushing me around.'

He poked Tyler in the stomach with the end of the cane. His smile widened as he stepped back, flicking his wrist and bringing his arm out behind him.

'Shame you can't say the same, eh?'

He swung. The cane whistled.

And Tyler, once more, denied the bastard the satisfaction of hearing him scream.

Chapter 23

Back in the Incident Room, Ben had made his feelings about Logan's premature return very clear. The phrase, 'You're a bloody idiot', had been used more than once, coupled with some tutting, scowling and several disapproving shakes of the head.

Logan had taken all the feedback on board, then ignored every word of it.

The DI was right, of course. Sneaking out of the hospital and coming back to work this soon was an act of absolute madness.

But he'd messed up. He'd let that bastard get the drop on him. And now, because of that, Tyler was in danger.

Or worse.

'Right, if you're quite finished with your bloody whinging, let's get cracking,' Logan said. 'We'll start with the son, Struan Ward. Hamza, you and Tammi-Jo talk to him. I doubt he'll know much, so get done with him quick, then you'll both move on to Isaac.'

'The husband? You're giving us the husband?' Tammi-Jo gasped. Her eyes were like saucers. 'That's a big deal, sir. That's a big responsibility. I mean, for all we know, he might have done it.'

'That's generally the idea of interviewing him, aye,' Logan confirmed. 'But right now, our priority is finding Shayne Feasey and getting Tyler back. That's the focus. Why was Feasey targeting them? What is it he thinks they've done? Hopefully, who killed Sharon Simpson and why, will come out in the wash, but Tyler is our number one priority.'

'Understood, sir,' Hamza said, picking up a pen and pad. 'If Struan has anything to tell us we think is relevant, we'll report in before we talk to Isaac.'

'Do that. Ben and I will be in the other interview room. It's time we had a crack at Armand. That's a man who's hiding something if ever there was one. And he's no' leaving here until I know what it is.'

He turned, then ejected a sharp cry as pain went ricocheting up his spine.

'I'm fine,' he grunted, before anyone had a chance to ask. 'Ben, Tammi-Jo, go and get sorted. I want a word with Hamza.'

'You sure you don't need me to carry you through, Jack?' Ben asked. It was half reproachful, half concerned. 'Not sure you're going to be able to walk all that way.'

'Well, I climbed out a bloody window then over a wall, so I think I'll be fine,' Logan said. He ushered the DI and the DC towards the door, then shuffled himself around to face DS Khaled. 'You spoke to Sinead?'

Hamza flinched, just a little, the memory of the conversation clearly still painful. 'I did.'

'And?'

'And… It was rough. Not going to lie,' Hamza said. 'But she's, you know… She's Sinead. She's had her fair share of "rough", and she's always pulled through it. She'll get through this, too.' He hesitated, just long enough that his meaning was clear. 'Whatever happens.'

'What's going to happen is we're going to get Tyler home,' Logan insisted. 'That lassie's had quite enough grief for one lifetime, and those weans aren't growing up without their father.'

The reply came from over by the door. 'You're damn right they aren't.'

Logan had been expecting it. He was almost surprised it had taken her this long.

'Detective Constable Bell,' he said, turning to see Sinead striding across the room.

Sinead's nod was curt and businesslike. 'Sir.'

'You aren't supposed to be here.'

'By the looks of it, neither are you,' Sinead said, indicating his injuries with a flick of her eyes. 'But here we are.'

Logan sighed. 'Aye. Here we are,' he agreed. He ran his tongue across his lips. They'd been swollen for a while now, but they hadn't felt dry until now. 'Sinead, I'm sorry. This shouldn't have happened. I shouldn't have—'

'That's not helping Tyler,' Sinead told him. 'I know you, sir. I know you'd never have let this happen if you could've stopped it. If you want to feel guilty, or feel sorry for yourself, I can't stop you.' She stepped in closer, and for a moment, Logan felt like she towered above him. 'But moping isn't going to get my husband back, so, for the sake of him, and for my kids, maybe save the self-pity for another time.'

She was right, of course. Dwelling on what had happened wasn't going to help anyone.

'I assume you're reporting for duty?' he said.

'I heard all leave was cancelled,' Sinead replied. 'I took that to include maternity.'

'Right. Good. OK,' Logan said, his mind racing. 'I can put you in with Struan Ward. Son of the victim. Don't think he's connected to Tyler, but he might have something we can use against one of the other two suspects.'

'I'm up to speed, sir. I know who's who.'

Logan frowned. 'How the hell do you know…?'

The penny dropped, and he turned to Hamza, who was doing his best to look innocent. 'I may have forwarded on a couple of reports, sir. Just to keep her in the loop.'

'I should probably be annoyed at that, but bugger it,' Logan said. He faced Sinead again, deep in thought. 'We'll need to pair you up with someone. CID's tied up. Maybe Dave could sit in. Not ideal, but—'

'I might have a better idea, sir. Although, I'm not sure if it's technically allowed.'

Logan shrugged, and tried not to show how much it hurt. 'Aye, well, given the circumstances, let's not get too bogged down on technicalities. I'm open to ideas. What are you thinking?'

Before she could reply, the door to the Incident Room swung inwards. There was something about the way it moved that made everyone turn and pay attention. It wasn't just a door being opened, it was an announcement being made.

'Shitting Christ!' cried Hoon, recoiling in horror at the sight of Logan's face. 'What in the name of the wee man happened to your coupon? You look like Andre the Giant rage-fucked a meringue.'

'*He's* what I'm thinking, sir,' Sinead said. 'Technically, he is employed as a consultant, so there could be some leeway to—'

'Aye.'

Logan's response surprised the detective constable, who had already started to protest before his reply filtered through.

'Sir?'

'You sure about this, Jack?' asked Ben.

'Aye. What the hell? Let's do it.'

'Could be a career-ender,' Ben pointed out.

Logan met Sinead's eye. He thought of Tyler. He thought of their children.

'Aye. I suppose it could, at that.'

The door was thrown wide open again, missing Hoon by a matter of inches. Tammi-Jo rushed on through, almost walked straight into Bob's back, then managed to avoid him by pulling off a clump-footed pirouette at the last moment.

'Whoops! Sorry! Didn't see you standing there. Almost walked right into you. I mean, you are quite close to the door. Weirdly close, actually,' Tammi-Jo gushed. 'Like, I don't know, do you smell or something? Is that why you're standing over here? Or is that a personal question? I mean, obviously it's a personal question, but is it *too* personal? Oh! Hi, Sinead.'

Sinead gave the other DC a nod and a wave, but Tammi-Jo had already turned her attention back to Hoon. She took hold of one of his hands in both of hers and shook it, her smile so dazzling that even Hoon blinked in surprise.

'Hi. Sorry. Didn't introduce myself. I'm DC Swanney. Like the song about the river. Although, I think we decided that's racist.' She looked back at the others. 'Did we decide that's racist?'

She didn't wait for a response, and instead turned back to Hoon, who was staring at her with a look of growing horror on his face.

'DC stands for detective constable, by the way. In case you were wondering. Not sure how much you know about that sort of thing. Ranks. Acronyms. All that stuff. It's detective constable, not...' She seemed to physically strain for a moment, before saying, 'Devil Chicken', with a level of confidence that started high then diminished rapidly midway through the second word.

Undeterred, she readjusted her smile, then gave him a nod of encouragement. 'And you are...?'

Hoon looked down at his hand, which was still being shaken. 'Deeply fucking confused is what I am.' He leaned past Tammi-Jo until he saw Logan again. 'Who the fuck is she, and what drugs is she on? Because it's either way too fucking many, or nowhere near enough.'

'Bob, Tammi-Jo. She's our new DC, standing in for Sinead,' Logan said. 'Tammi-Jo, this is Bob Hoon.'

'Detective superintendent,' Hoon said.

'*Former* detective superintendent,' Logan corrected.

'Disgraced former detective superintendent,' added Ben.

'That's a bit fucking unnecessary, Benjamin,' Hoon said. 'Are you no' deid yet?' He realised Tammi-Jo was still shaking his hand, and jerked it away. 'Fucking quit that, you!'

'Sorry!' DC Swanney jumped back like his hand had given off an electrical charge. 'So *you're* Hoon? I've heard a lot about you.'

Hoon sniffed. 'All fucking positive, I'm sure.'

Tammi-Jo shifted awkwardly, then shook her head. 'Not really,' she said, her smile switching into apology mode. 'Pretty negative, for the most part. But still…' She bumped a fist against his upper arm. 'Chin up!'

With that, she walked out of the room again.

A moment later, she returned.

'Oh! Forgot to say, sir, that's everyone set up and ready!'

She gave double thumbs up to all the occupants of the room, going around them one by one, then left again.

'Right, two fucking questions,' Hoon said, the moment she was gone. 'One, has she had a recent fucking head injury or something? And two'—he pointed past Logan to the Big Board—'how come there's a drawing of a fucking frog up there?'

'Not that I'm aware of, and it's a long story,' Logan said, answering each question in turn. He looked over at the door the DC had just left through, then gazed thoughtfully at Sinead. 'Actually,' he announced. 'Forget that plan I mentioned a minute ago. I've just had a better idea.'

–

Logan nearly tripped over Dave Davidson on his way to the interview room. The constable was wheeling himself along the corridor, a stack of printouts balanced in his lap. The near collision toppled the paperwork over, scattering it onto the floor.

'Ah, bollocks,' Dave groaned. He stooped from his chair and retrieved the closest few pages, while Logan and Ben picked up some of the others.

'What's this?' Logan asked, scanning the list of numbers on the page.

'Shayne Feasey's phone records,' Dave said. 'Thought I'd go through them and see what landlines he's called, then get the addresses. See if anywhere looks like a likely hiding place.'

'Good idea, son,' Ben said, gathering up a few more of the sheets.

'Cheers. It's a right bloody boorach next door, though, so thought I'd go through it on my own. Easier to concentrate.'

'There's hundreds of pages here,' Logan said. 'It'll take hours.'

'I can rattle through it,' Dave insisted.

Logan finished gathering up the rest of the pages, then dumped them back in Dave's lap. Along the corridor, a Uniform turned the corner, surveyed the scene for a moment, then started to turn.

Logan wasn't letting her off that easily. 'Constable Niddrie,' he called, making sure he shouted loud enough that she couldn't claim not to hear him. 'You're with Constable Davidson. He'll explain.'

The look Nidds gave him was a pleading one. 'But, sir...'

'I'm not sure that's a great idea,' Dave said, anticipating the rest of her sentence.

'I don't care,' Logan told them. 'Whatever shite you two have going on, I don't care. It's not important. Right now, whatever else you were, whatever else you are, it doesn't matter. You're police officers. Fucking act like it.'

He wasted a second glowering at each of them in turn, then set off marching along the corridor, with Ben racing to keep up with Logan's much longer strides.

Once they were gone, Dave winced. 'Bit awkward,' he said, shooting Nidds a smile.

'He's right. We're police officers,' she replied. 'We've got a job to do.'

Her voice sounded almost robotic. She had her defences raised. But then, they'd been up since a couple of months into her and Dave's relationship, when she and him had first started to get closer.

'Right, then,' Dave said. He nodded to the pile of paperwork in his lap. 'Well, you can start by carrying these.'

Nidds seemed to struggle for a moment, like her feet were stuck to the floor. Then, she dragged herself over to Dave's wheelchair and picked up the paperwork.

And together, side by side, they headed into the Incident Room, and got to work.

Chapter 24

Armand Holburn had opted to have his lawyer brought in. He was a local guy, Donald Sinclair, and of an age that suggested he was probably fairly senior in whatever firm he worked for.

The man's demeanour backed that theory up. He was polite, for the most part, but made no attempt to hide his impatience, or to disguise the fact that he wasn't happy about being called out at half past eight on a Monday evening.

Logan was even more keen to get things all squared away. So, once all the introductions had been made and the recording was underway, he went straight in for the kill.

'You mind telling me what that is, Mr Holburn?' he asked, sliding over the evidence bag containing the note Nidds had found.

'What the hell happened to you?' Holburn asked.

He'd been studying the DCI's battle scars since the detectives had entered the room, occasionally wincing like he was imagining being on the receiving end.

'Just answer the question please, Mr Holburn.' Logan tapped the bag with a finger. 'What's that?'

'For the benefit of the recording,' Ben announced. 'DCI Logan has just presented Mr Holburn with Exhibit Seventeen.'

Holburn shot his lawyer a look. Sinclair gave him the go-ahead with a curt, weary nod.

'It's a note,' Holburn said.

'You mind telling me what it says?'

Holburn shrugged. 'I'm sorry, Detective Chief Inspector.' He patted the pockets of his shirt. 'I didn't bring my reading glasses.'

Logan kept his gaze trained on the man sitting directly opposite. Armand smirked, then shrugged.

'What can I say? Nobody told me I'd need them.'

'How about I just tell you what it says, then?' Logan suggested. He didn't look at the scrap of headed notepaper in the bag. He didn't need to. 'It says, "I know what you did."'

'So?' Armand said, just a beat too quickly. 'What's that got to do with me?'

'It was found in your bin,' Ben told him. 'We'd just like to figure out how it got there, that's all.'

'And what it means,' Logan said.

Ben conceded the point with a nod. 'And what it means. How it got there, and what it means. Just those two things.'

'I don't know,' Armand replied.

'To which one?' Ben asked.

'Either. Both. I've never seen it before. I don't know what it's referring to.'

'I don't understand,' Logan said. 'What was it doing in your bin?'

'Well, presumably someone put it there,' Armand replied. He settled back in his chair and folded his arms. 'I'm surprised a couple of detectives like you couldn't figure that out.'

Ben sensed what was coming and braced himself. Armand and his solicitor did not. They both jumped as Logan's reply crashed over them like a wave.

'Do you think this is funny, Armand? Do you see either of us fucking laughing here?'

'Steady on,' warned the solicitor. The look this earned from Logan dissuaded him from saying anything more.

'You shut your mouth and speak when you're spoken to,' Logan warned him, before aiming his wrath back in Armand's direction. 'The detective constable who was in your house with me earlier. DC Neish. Remember him, Mr Holburn?'

'Well, since I don't have a degenerative brain disorder, of course I do. What of him?'

'He's missing. Possibly dead,' Logan said. He gestured to himself. 'Same guy who did this has got him. Same guy who was photographed by your dead pal last year. Same guy we reckon was giving you grief. Making them funny phone calls.'

'Not all the funny phone calls, Detective Chief Inspector,' Ben interjected.

'No. True. But, we'll come back to that,' Logan said. 'Make a note. Remind me.'

'Done.'

'What's in those sheds of yours, Mr Holburn?'

Armand hesitated, thrown off by this sudden change in topic. 'What?'

'Your sheds. Big metal bastards. Heavy locks. What do you keep in there?'

'Just… stuff.'

'Stuff? What kind of stuff?'

'Shed stuff. Tools. You know? The garden hose. That sort of thing.'

'Must be a valuable bloody hose to need a shed like that,' Logan said.

'Big, too, to need both of them,' Ben added. 'Does it come in two pieces?'

'Obviously the security's not for the hose,' Armand said with an impatient sigh. 'It's for the tools. And I have a couple of shotguns. Fully licensed. As part of that licence, I'm required to store them securely, as I'm sure you're aware.'

'You know a gun cabinet would do, aye?' Ben told him. 'You don't need a giant shed per weapon. I mean, I'm assuming they're giant, based on how you described them, Detective Chief Inspector.'

'They're sizeable all right,' Logan replied, still eyeballing the man across the table.

'Big enough for a bike?' Ben asked.

'Plenty big enough. You have a bike in there, Mr Holburn? You a *cyclist*?' Logan spat that last word at him like it was an accusation up there with being a murderer.

There was a pause this time before Armand replied. 'What's that got to do with anything?'

'Just answer the question, please. Do you own a bike?'

Holburn's tongue flitted across his lips. 'I fail to see how that's relevant to—'

Logan held up a hand as large as the man's head, silencing him. 'You know what? It doesn't matter. We've got officers cutting their way into them now. We'll find out soon enough.'

'You can't do that,' Armand said, his cool facade slipping away. He turned to the solicitor. 'They can't do that!'

'We have a warrant to search the premises,' Logan said. 'The house, too.'

This was news to Ben, but he kept that fact to himself and just nodded along.

'I'll need to see it,' Sinclair said, writing a note in his legal pad.

'We'll get it to you,' Logan assured him. 'Want to tell us what we're going to find in there, Mr Holburn? Might as well do it now and get it out of the way.'

'Fine. I've got a bike. I don't see what it's got to do with anything, but yes, I used to cycle.'

'Used to?' Ben asked.

Armand's jaw tensed, like he was steeling himself. 'My wife and I used to ride. Before she…' The sentence ran out then. He shot a glance to his solicitor, who stepped in.

'Mrs Holburn passed away earlier this year.'

Logan's eyebrows crept up his forehead. The wife was news to him. Her death could be relevant. 'Passed away? How?'

'Cancer,' Armand said, his voice a flat line, carefully stripped of all emotion.

Logan was almost disappointed. A suspicious death would've been another piece of the puzzle.

'I'm sorry to hear that.' He allowed three whole seconds to pass in respectful silence. 'But you own a bike?'

'Yes! Yes, I own a bloody bike! What's that got to do with—'

'Does the name Shayne Feasey mean anything to you, Armand?' Logan asked, switching conversational tracks again.

Holburn frowned, caught off guard. He shook his head. 'What? No.' The blankness of his stare seemed irritatingly genuine. 'Should it?'

'Shayne Feasey's the man your dead pal managed to get a photo of. Sorry, can't remember his name.'

'Norman.'

'I don't care,' Logan said, throwing in a shrug to really hammer home the bluntness of the remark. 'Why would he be harassing the three of you?' He tapped the evidence bag again. 'Why would he be leaving you notes like this? What did you do to this man?'

'You don't have to answer that,' the solicitor said.

'He'll answer what I tell him to answer!' Logan spat. 'What did you do to him, Armand?'

'Nothing.'

'Who is he? Why's he leaving you notes?'

'I don't know who he is.'

'If you don't know who he is,' Ben probed, 'then how do you know you haven't done anything to him?'

'Well, because I haven't done anything to anyone, have I?'

'Never?' the DI asked. 'You've never done anything in your life that could've put you in someone's bad books? Rubbed them up the wrong way? Made them dislike you?'

'No.'

'Oh, I beg to differ,' Logan all but growled.

Holburn sat forward and clasped his hands together. He looked infuriatingly relaxed now, as if he'd suddenly realised that the detectives had nothing on him, and that he was holding all the cards. 'And I mean, come on, gentlemen. Think about it. I seriously doubt he left that note for me.'

'Oh? And what makes you say that?' Ben asked.

'Well, if you're to leave a note for someone, you don't generally put it in their bin.'

Ben and Logan both sat back at the same time, like this was a revelation that had knocked the wind right out of them.

'Christ. He's right, Jack,' Ben muttered. 'You wouldn't do that, would you?'

'No,' Logan admitted. 'No, you would not.'

'You'd only put something in the bin if you wanted rid of it.'

Logan nodded. 'You'd only do that if you didn't want anyone else to see it.'

'You don't use a bin to leave bloody messages for people!' Ben chuckled, but it died away just as quickly. 'You use a bin to dispose of things.'

'Hide things,' Logan agreed.

'Conceal them from others,' Ben concluded.

They both sat forward again with the timing of an Olympic synchronised diving team.

'That what you were doing, Armand?' Logan asked. 'Were you trying to hide this note from us?'

Across the table, Holburn scoffed, but his eyes flitted down to the note. Just briefly. Just for a moment.

Just enough.

'That's ridiculous,' he said. 'What are you suggesting? I steal a note from a crime scene and then "dispose" of it by scrunching it up and chucking it in my own bloody bin? What sort of moron do you take me for?'

His expression neatly straddled the line between a smirk and a sneer. He crossed his arms again, clearly convinced that his point was a good one.

The silence from the detectives was unnerving, though. They watched and waited until the smug look had fallen all the way off his face before responding.

'Who said anything about it coming from the crime scene, Mr Holburn?'

Armand made a valiant attempt to hide the sudden rush of panic. The look in his eyes, though, and the way his Adam's apple bobbed down and back up, gave him away. 'Oh, well, I mean, I just assumed.'

'Strange thing to assume. Why would you assume that?' Logan asked.

'Well, I mean...' Holburn began. He gestured vaguely at the evidence bag, like the rest of the sentence was self-explanatory.

'You mean what? How could you possibly know where this note came from? It did come from the crime scene, by the way,' Logan told him. 'It came from a pad on the bedside table in Sharon and Isaac's bedroom. How the hell would you know that?'

The solicitor, Sinclair, leaned forward. 'I'd like a moment with my client.'

'Tough,' Logan grunted. 'Answer the question please, Mr Holburn. How did you know this came from the room where Sharon Simpson was raped and murdered? How could you possibly know that?'

'The hotel!' Armand cried, and there was a note of triumph to it. 'The hotel. The Ambassador. In Wales. They went there last year. Isaac wouldn't stop talking about it.'

Logan's eyes narrowed. 'The hotel?'

'The hotel,' Armand confirmed.

'The Ambassador?'

Holburn nodded. He'd been on shaky ground there for a moment, but his confidence was returning. 'That's right. The Ambassador. Just outside Cardiff, I believe. I'm sure Isaac will be happy to fill you in.'

Logan eyeballed the man across the table in silence, then clicked his tongue against the back of his teeth. 'Detective Inspector?'

Without a word, Ben picked up the evidence bag, peered at the note for a few seconds, then set it back down again and folded his arms. 'Not a bloody clue,' he said.

'That is interesting,' Logan said. His chair gave an ominous moan as he sat back in it. 'That's very interesting.'

'What?' Armand asked, looking from one detective to the other. 'What's interesting?'

'You and DI Forde here have something in common, Mr Holburn,' Logan told him. 'He doesn't have his reading glasses with him, either. And the logo at the top of that page is a damn sight smaller than the message written on it. The message you claimed you couldn't see.'

Donald Sinclair, the solicitor, exhaled slowly through his nose, presumably realising that he wasn't going to make it back home anytime soon.

'So, how about you do us all a favour, Armand, and stop wasting our bloody time?' Logan suggested. 'The note. The message. I'm going to ask you the same question I asked you and Isaac earlier. You said you didn't know the answer, but I think you were lying, Mr Holburn. I think you both were. I think you know the answer only too well. And I think your dead pal knew the answer, too. So, here goes. You ready?'

He stabbed a finger down on top of the evidence bag, then slid it closer to the man sitting opposite. Armand didn't just avoid looking at the note, he actively recoiled from it, leaning back as it came closer.

'What exactly did you lot do to bring all this upon yourselves?'

Chapter 25

Hoon stood at the back of the interview room, leaning against the wall. He had his arms folded, and was currently wishing that his ears would spontaneously implode.

He'd been quite happy being paired up with Sinead. She seemed fairly switched on. Terrible choice in men, right enough, but he wasn't going to hold that against her.

And besides, they'd been through stuff together. They'd bonded over her spread legs and screaming weans, and while he could've done without the stains that were now very much a permanent feature of his car's back seat, that was the sort of thing that couldn't help but bring people closer together.

But Logan had decided to mix things up a bit. The bastard had reckoned Sinead would be more effective talking to the husband of the dead woman.

And so, Hoon has been saddled with the shite-chattering, though admittedly much hotter cousin of the fucking Energizer Bunny.

The guy they were interviewing wasn't much better. He had long flowing hair that he kept pushing back by running a hand across the top of his head, his fingers splayed wide. He'd probably dedicated more time to getting his twatty, Musketeer-like beard styled *just right* each morning than Hoon had dedicated to anything in his entire life, his police career included.

Especially his police career, in fact.

He was a smug-looking fucker, too, and he spoke with a condescending lilt that made Hoon want to storm over there and rip the beard off his face one hair at a time.

Between the smarmy self-importance of his answers, and the inane fucking babble of the DC's questions, Hoon's levels of patience and irritation were rapidly heading in opposite directions.

'So, the short story is, I've been travelling the world. Just, like, doing good, you know? Here and there. Where I can.' Struan Ward was practically reclining in his chair, one elbow resting on the back, his legs crossed. 'Sometimes small stuff—helping find a lost dog, maybe. Packing people's bags at a supermarket. Leading an old woman across a road, then taking her hand and telling her she's worthy of being loved. That sort of thing. Sometimes bigger. I helped build a drainage system for a village in Rwanda, for example.'

'Wow!' Tammi-Jo said. 'That must've been rewarding.'

'Oh, God, yes. It was. Not financially, of course. Nothing so vulgar. But the looks on their faces? The gratitude in their eyes?' He inhaled deeply through his nose and pressed a clenched fist against his chest. 'Those are the real rewards.'

'Fuck me! How is this the short version, you tedious bastard? Get to the fucking point!' Hoon cried.

Struan stroked his pointed beard, pinching it between finger and thumb. 'I feel it's important to establish a bit of backstory first, before we get to the meat of it.'

Hoon sprang away from the wall, marched over to the table, and stabbed a finger so violently in Ward's direction that the younger man recoiled as if he'd been poked in the chest.

'Listen, Arseholeimus, or whichever of the Three fucking Musketeers you're going out of your way to look like, we're no' interested in hearing all your self-congratulatory, "*Amn't I a great guy?*" verbal fucking masturbation. You carried a shopping bag and dug a fucking hole. Well done. No one gives a fuck. Just cut the shite, and answer the fucking question, before I take that fucking *Robin Hood, Prince of Thieves* hairstyle of yours and fucking hang you with it.'

Ward's confidence had immediately evaporated under the heat of Bob Hoon's stare. He swallowed, his shoulders stooping, his forefingers and thumbs pressing together so his hands formed a little figure eight on the table in front of him.

'What was the question again?' he croaked.

'Fuck knows,' Hoon admitted. He gestured to the detective constable as he returned to his spot by the wall. 'But I'm sure if you dig around in the next stream of consciousness that tumbles out of her fucking mouth, you'll be able to find one in there somewhere.'

Tammi-Jo felt her cheeks burn a little. She still didn't quite understand what Hoon was doing here, or what level of deference he was supposed to be afforded, so she was playing it safe and largely just pretending he wasn't present in the room.

In a small act of defiance, though, she scratched the back of her head with the middle finger of her left hand, and quietly hoped that he might notice. She was equally relieved and disappointed when he didn't.

'The question was pretty straightforward, *actually*,' she said, stressing the point for Hoon's benefit. 'I just asked why you chose now to come back?'

'And if you could try and answer this time without the four hours of tedious fucking preamble, maybe we'll get out of here sometime tonight,' Hoon added.

Struan had already opened his mouth to reply. It remained frozen like that while he carefully considered Hoon's warning.

In a well-judged act of self-preservation, he chose to cut right to the chase.

'The video,' he said.

'The video?' Tammi-Jo's eyes darted around the room, like she might find further explanation scribbled on one of the walls. 'What video?'

Struan reached a hand into the front pocket of his hoody, then quickly pulled it out again when he noticed that Hoon was positioning himself for a flying lunge. He held up a mobile phone and waved it, making it very clear that it wasn't any sort of weapon.

Once Hoon had relaxed again, Struan tapped the screen a few times, then set the unlocked mobile on the table and slid it across to the detective constable.

'That video,' he said.

The silky smooth confidence of a few moments before had gone. Now, his voice had a rough edge to it, like someone had gone at it with a cheese grater. He pressed his fingers into his ears and very deliberately averted his eyes as Tammi-Jo picked up the phone and Hoon stepped in closer for a better look.

'I really should warn you,' he said through a narrowing throat. 'It's disturbingly graphic.'

—

'No comment.'

Isaac Simpson sat bolt upright in his chair, his arms spread, hands flat on the table in front of him. He had pointed his eyes into the gap between Hamza and Sinead, and adopted the sort of thousand-yard stare that may well have worked during military interrogations, but which was going to do him bugger all good in here.

Hamza let out a well-rehearsed sigh. It was quite a good sigh. He was pretty proud of it. It was a carefully crafted blend of impatience and concern, with just a hint of amusement to give it some punch. It was a sigh designed to make the recipient— or the *sighee*, as he liked to think of them—feel a bit silly about their actions, while also suggesting that Hamza knew something they didn't.

Combined, those two thoughts would start worming away at the sighee's defences, bringing them down from the inside.

At least, that was the theory. Isaac Simpson, unfortunately, had thus far proved immune.

'It's not a difficult question, Isaac,' the DS said. He indicated the photocopy he'd made of the note they'd found in Armand's bin. 'We just want to know what this is about. You do want to find out who killed Sharon, yes?'

'No comment.'

'Wow.' Hamza sat back and shot a look of surprise across to Sinead, who sat on his left, biting her tongue. That look was almost as rehearsed as the sigh had been. 'I mean… Seriously? Wow. Listen, Isaac… Can I call you Isaac? Or is the answer to that going to be "no comment", too?'

The detective sergeant didn't wait to find out.

'Listen, Isaac, I don't know who's advised you not to answer any of our questions. It's absolutely your right to do so, of course, but I want you to think very hard about how this might look when relayed to a court. Here we are, offering you a chance to help us catch the man who killed your wife, and you're… what? Turning it down? Deliberately hindering our chances? That is not going to look good for you. You know that, right?'

Isaac continued to stare ahead through the gap between them. 'No comment.'

'Right, fuck this,' Sinead said, with a venom that caught Hamza off guard. She rifled through the paper in the folder in front of her, then held up the blurry photo of Shayne Feasey. 'Who is this? What do you know about him? We know you know something.'

The man across the table didn't even appear to notice the photograph, even when Sinead waved it in his face. 'No comment.'

'Look at it! Look at him. His name is Shayne Feasey. We know that means something to you. We know you know who he is!'

'No comment.'

'This man raped and killed your wife!' Sinead told him, the thin cords of muscle in her neck knotting as she swallowed back her growing rage.

Beside her, DS Khaled switched into damage control mode. 'We don't actually know that for sure.'

'Hamza,' Sinead said, shooting him a warning look.

For a moment, it looked like she was going to direct her anger towards him, but instead, the bottom fell out of it, and she let the photograph slip from her fingers. It landed face-up on the table.

She lowered her head, composing herself as best she could, then positioned herself somewhere within Isaac Simpson's line of sight. He didn't look away, but nor did he focus on her. Instead, he continued to stare through her, at a spot far away beyond the back wall.

'He has my husband,' she said. 'That man. Whoever he is. He has my husband. Tyler. That's his name. We have kids. Twins. A boy and a girl. They're only three months old. I had to leave them with a woman I barely know to come here, because I have to find him. I have to bring their daddy home, or how can I ever look them in the eye again?'

She slid both hands across the table and rested them on top of one of Isaac's. Hamza watched, but said nothing. His interview techniques were carefully practised, meticulously honed.

This, though, was neither of those things. This was honest. This was real.

And it was working.

Hamza could see Isaac's resolve wavering. He continued to stare directly ahead, but his focus was shifting. No longer was he gazing into the *way out there*. He was back in the room now, his attention directing itself—quite possibly against his will—at the solemn-faced young woman pouring her heart out to him.

'Armand said I shouldn't say anything,' he muttered. He sounded almost drowsy, the words slurring, as if he was gradually emerging from some sort of hypnotic trance. 'He said it was in our best interest.'

'In his best interest, maybe,' Hamza said. 'Not yours. Not Sharon's.'

'And not my husband's,' Sinead added. She slid both the photograph and the note an inch or two closer to Isaac, and fixed him with a pleading look. 'What is all this? Please. What can you tell us?'

'What does the note mean, Mr Simpson?' Hamza pressed. 'What is it you did?'

Across the table, the man's face was reddening. As his shoulders began to shake, the detectives realised he was fighting back tears.

Clearly not fighting hard enough, though. As one slipped past his defences and tumbled down his cheek, he spoke in a shrill, desperate whisper.

'Something *terrible*.'

Chapter 26

Shona's new assistant, Neville, had wisely buggered off for the night by the time she arrived back at the mortuary in Raigmore Hospital. She'd swung by Sinead's on the way there, but the house had been dark, and nobody had answered the door.

Hopefully, she was just at her aunt's house, though Shona had her doubts. Sinead was not a woman content to sit on the sidelines, especially when someone she cared about was in trouble.

They had taken her husband. God help them.

Shona had struck out in bringing Taggart home, too. He'd been sedated for some tests, and they wanted to keep him overnight for observation. She'd go back down for him tomorrow. No point worrying Jack any further.

There was a note for her on the counter when she got in. A quick glance at the bottom revealed it had been left by Neville.

'Christ, even his handwriting's attractive,' Shona mumbled, as she began to read.

Alexis Maximuke's body had been brought in, and was currently being stored in drawer three, ready for them to do the PM in the morning.

Usually, Shona would've cracked on with it now. She didn't like being home alone these days, and particularly now that she wouldn't even have Taggart for company.

But, she couldn't deny that having Neville here earlier had made things much easier. Maybe she didn't have to juggle half a dozen things at once now, and could focus just on the body.

Make sure she was giving the deceased the respect and attention they deserved.

A light was flashing on the phone on her desk, letting her know that a message had been left for her. She clicked on the kettle—she hadn't eaten in hours, and there was a Pot Noodle in the desk drawer with her name on it.

Literally, in fact. As soon as she'd heard she was getting an assistant, she'd started labelling all the food she brought in, because you could never be too careful.

The Pot Noodle was a new flavour. Kebab. While she loved both kebabs and pot-based noodle snacks, she'd been a bit wary of trying the combination until now. It was very much one of those things that could go either way. Either it would be delicious, or it would be an affront to God. There was, she reckoned, very little grey area in between.

After clicking on the kettle, she took the pot from the drawer, peeled back the foil lid, and hit the flashing button on the phone.

'Uh, hello, Dr Maguire.'

Shona tensed, recognising the voice at once. It was the nurse, Nancy, from the Belford Hospital in Fort William.

'I'm afraid we've got a bit of a problem,' the recording continued. 'You're, uh… Mr Logan. He's, um, well… I don't quite know how to say this.'

Shona lowered herself onto the desk. Just like the Pot Noodle, this could go one of two ways.

'He's climbed out a window,' Nancy announced. 'He's no longer on the hospital premises.'

'Oh, thank *Christ*,' Shona whispered.

She stopped the recording and fell into her chair. Jack escaping was not entirely unexpected. Jack escaping had been inevitable, in fact.

Jack escaping was a damn sight better than the other possible reason for the call.

The kettle rolled to a boil. Shona crossed back to the counter and started to pour the hot water into the Pot Noodle pot, carefully filling it, making sure not to pour past the line that indicated the—

'Jesus Christ!'

She jumped at the sight of the figure lurking just inside the doorway, then cursed as she sloshed boiling water all over the countertop.

Olivia Maximuke stood watching her. She was still in the same school uniform as earlier. Still had the same hollow, haunted sort of look on her face.

'Hey. There you are,' Shona said, setting the kettle down, the spilled water and her ravenous hunger both already forgotten. She smiled and spoke softly, sure she'd scare the girl off again. 'I was worried about you. I went looking, but I couldn't find you.'

Olivia said nothing. Her fists were clenched tightly by her sides, and her weight was rocking rhythmically from one foot to the other, while her breath came out in quick, shaky-sounding gasps.

The girl's eyes crept to the inner door of the mortuary, and the darkness pressing itself up against the glass.

'Is she there?' Olivia whispered. 'Is she in there?'

Shona hesitated, unsure of how to respond. She didn't know the right thing to say. She didn't know how best to ease the girl's pain.

And so, she settled for the truth.

'She is,' the pathologist confirmed. 'I'm so sorry that this has—'

'Can I see her?' Olivia asked. She was still looking at the door, but suddenly it seemed to blind her, and she was forced to avert her gaze. She turned to Shona, blinking. 'Can I go in and see her?'

'She's, um, she's not...' Shona shook her head and stepped a little closer. Olivia backed up the same distance. 'Listen, sweetheart, I don't think that's a good idea right now. All right? How about we—'

The girl moved quickly, running for the inner doors and throwing them wide, clattering into the darkness beyond.

'Olivia, wait!' Shona cried, racing after her.

She clicked on the lights, and found Olivia standing by the empty PM table, running her hands over the spot where a body would usually lie, like she was searching the empty space for her mother.

'Where is she? I want to see her. Where is she?'

'Olivia, listen,' Shona said, her voice a hushed and soothing melody. 'I know this must be hard. And you'll see her, I promise, all right? You'll see her. I just think it's best if—'

The girl moved again, this time charging across the room to the neatly arranged trays of equipment. She rifled through it, found a scalpel, and tore it from its sterile packaging.

'Where is she?!' she screeched, waving the blade in Shona's direction, arm raised and rigid. 'Where's my mum?! I want to see my mum!'

Shona bit back the urge to cry. Not for her own sake, but for the girl pointing the scalpel at her. Olivia's eyes were two dark holes of fear and pain. The knuckles of the hand holding the knife were white, the hand itself trembling like the warning tremors before some catastrophic seismic event.

'I know you're scared, sweetheart. I know you're upset. I know this is just the most awful bloody situation, and it's just not fair. It's not.' Shona took a step closer. Olivia stood her ground, the scalpel still raised. 'I know you feel like you're on your own, but you aren't. I promise, you aren't.'

She risked another slow step towards the girl. The blade was less than a foot from her face now. If Olivia lunged with it, there'd be very little Shona could do to avoid being sliced open.

'Stay back!' Olivia ordered. 'Stay the fuck back, I mean it! *I mean it!*'

Shona almost hesitated. Almost retreated. Almost believed her.

'Fine,' she said, shrugging. 'Cut my face off if you must. But I'm going to hug you now.'

'Don't! Stay back!' The knife hand—the whole arm—shook violently, like the effort of keeping it raised was proving too great. When Olivia spoke again, it was in the voice of a little lost child. 'Please, just stay back.'

Shona stepped in past the scalpel and threw both arms around the girl. Behind her, she heard the *thunk* of metal hitting the floor, then Olivia was holding onto her for dear life, sobbing against Shona's shoulder as her legs gave way.

The pathologist held her all the way to the floor, then kneeled there, the girl's full weight against her, rocking back and forth.

'How could she do this?' Olivia cried. Shona's shoulder muffled the words, but not the pain behind them. 'How could she leave me?'

'Shh. You're OK. You're all right. I've got you,' Shona whispered.

'What am I going to do? What am I going to do now?'

Shona stroked the back of the girl's hair and felt the grief spasming through her body.

'It's all going to be all right,' she whispered. 'Everything's going to be just fine. I promise.'

–

'Found anything?' Dave asked.

At a nearby desk, Nidds briefly looked up from the page she was working her way down, and shot the other constable a weary look.

'Again, no. Not really,' she told him. 'Most of these are mobiles. I've only come across one landline so far, and it's to a doctor's surgery here in town.'

'We can run the mobile numbers,' Dave said. 'If any of them are contract—'

'Then we can get an address. Yes. I know,' Nidds said. 'I'm the one who suggested that, remember? About ten minutes ago.'

'Oh. Aye. I know,' Dave said. He smiled, but it was a vague and uncertain thing. 'I was just, you know, agreeing with you. It's a good idea. That's all I'm saying.'

Nidds turned her attention back to the sheet. She continued to scan down it, moving her pen down the edge of the page, tracking through the numbers.

'Have I, eh… Have I done something?' Dave asked. 'It's just that you don't seem to be talking to me today.'

'I haven't talked to you in ages,' Nidds reminded him.

'Well, no. True. But that was more because we weren't in the same room. Or building, even. Now, we are. And you're not really saying anything.'

Nidds sighed, the tip of her pen pointing towards the next number on the list. Another mobile.

'We're working,' she reminded him. 'We're trying to find Tyler. I mean, I'm sure he's fine. I'm sure he's going to be OK, but… We're working.'

'We could have a drink after, if you fancy it?' Dave suggested. 'After we find Tyler, I mean. Or, you know, next week or something. It'd be good to catch up.'

'That's not a good idea.'

'Why not? What happened with us? I thought we were—'

'Did you tell him? Tyler, I mean?' Nidds asked, cutting Dave off. 'Did you tell him about my mum?'

'What? No!'

'But you told him I was adopted?'

The length and breadth of Dave's silence told her everything she needed to know.

'I knew it. I bloody knew it! That was private. That was between you and…' She set her pen down and pressed both hands to the side of her head, like she was trying to stop it from exploding. 'I knew I should never have said anything. I knew it.'

'I'm sorry, it just slipped out. I didn't mean to say anything,' Dave pleaded. 'Anyway, you're adopted. So what? It's nothing to be embarrassed or ashamed about.'

'Ashamed?' Nidds' head snapped up so quickly her hearing aids were almost yanked out. 'Who said anything about being ashamed? I'm not ashamed. I've got nothing to be ashamed of.'

'Of course not—'

'I just don't want things I share in confidence to be passed around like gossip. Is that really too much to ask?'

'It wasn't like that,' Dave insisted.

'Oh? Funny, because it sounds to me like it was exactly like that,' Nidds shot back.

'Well, to be fair, your hearing's not the best,' Dave said.

It was the kind of comment they'd made to each other a hundred times before. That's what they did. That was what they'd always done, taken the piss out of each other's disabilities and, by doing so, diminished them.

Today, though, she reacted like he'd plunged a dagger deep into her chest.

'Not funny,' she said. 'Not even remotely.'

Dave backtracked as hastily as he could. 'What? No. I didn't mean… That wasn't meant to be…'

He turned his chair to face her, wheeled himself over, and reached for her hand. They'd touched hands a thousand times before, long before they'd ever started a relationship. This time, though, she recoiled so violently that she shook the desk, causing a mini avalanche of paperwork to slide onto the floor.

'Shit,' Nidds groaned.

'Sorry. My fault,' Dave said, bending at the waist to pick up the paperwork. 'Shouldn't have done that. Totally on me.'

He shuffled some of the printouts together, then realised they weren't all from the same stack, and he was only making things worse. Among the pages and pages of phone numbers were other random documents that must've been sitting on the desk already.

One of them caught his eye as he flicked past it. He licked his thumb, then worked back through the pile until he found it again.

It was a photocopy that Hamza had made of the note Nidds had found in Armand Holburn's bin. The writing—'I know what you did'—was clearly visible.

Since, unlike Tammi-Jo, Hamza knew exactly how the scanner and printer worked, it was even possible to make out the outline of the indents the author's pen had left on the page.

Something about it made Dave pull it from the pile and sit it on his knee. He returned the rest of the bundle to the desk, his attention still focused on the copy of the note.

There was something about it that was unsettling him.

Something about the writing. About the indents.

The indents. Was that it?

Watched by Nidds, Dave wheeled himself away from the desk and over to the Big Board. All the evidence they'd gathered so far had been laid out there, albeit in a format that made very little sense to him.

He searched the jumble of notes, string and photographs until he found the image he was looking for.

It was another photocopy. This one showed the second page of the notepad—the one the Scene of Crime team had done the pencil rubbing on, revealing the text that had been written on the page above.

The same message as the one he currently held in his hand.

'Bloody hell,' Dave muttered. When Nidds didn't react, he tried again, only louder, and partly facing in her direction. 'Bloody Hell!'

'What?' she asked.

'Come see this.'

Nidds appeared reluctant, like she thought this might be some sort of trick. Begrudgingly, she got to her feet, and plodded over to join him by the board.

'What is it?'

'This note,' he said. 'Check it out.'

He passed her the photocopy of the headed hotel notepaper she'd found in the bin.

'Yeah. I've seen it. I found it. So?'

'So, the DCI reckons this is the note that was stuck to the wall in the dead woman's house. Right?'

Nidds eyed him warily, as if still suspecting this to come crashing down on her somehow. 'Right...'

'Well, if it's the same note,' Dave said. He pointed to the Big Board, and the other photocopy pinned there. 'How do you explain that?'

Nidds followed the finger until she found the printout amidst the descent into madness that was Tammi-Jo's organisational system.

For a moment, she said nothing.

Then, she didn't say very much.

'Oh,' was part of it. Then, 'Fuck.'

Chapter 27

He had left the room for a while, and Tyler had… Not slept, exactly. More flitted in and out of consciousness, lurching back and forth between twisted, terrifying dreams, and the all-too-real nightmare that was his current situation.

The last time, when visions of Eldritch horrors had given way to stark and painful reality, he'd heard the opening and closing of a heavy door, then the cheerful, upbeat whistling of a certifiable psychopath.

'Morning, gorgeous,' Feasey sang, shrugging off his jacket. He looked around for somewhere to put it in the sparsely furnished room.

Although, 'furnished' wasn't quite the right word, Tyler thought. He was yet to see any furniture, just objects. A couple of workbenches. The rusted frame of an old laundry mangle. Some wooden crates and metal buckets.

Wherever he was, it was somewhere industrial.

The place had been in darkness earlier, but now a single, old-style light bulb burned near the centre of the room. It hung from a long cord that vanished into the shadows overhead, and spilled a circle of red-orange light across the equipment, giving the place a demonic flavour.

Finding nowhere suitable to hang his jacket, Feasey opted to simply drop it where he stood on the rough stone floor. He then turned his attention back to Tyler, a furrowing of his forehead turning his smile into something cryptic.

'Someone's lost their manners,' he remarked. 'I just said, "Morning, gorgeous." And you… what? Don't say anything? Don't even fucking acknowledge me?'

Tyler didn't want to reply. Didn't want to give the bastard the satisfaction. Besides, he wasn't even sure it was morning. He didn't think he could possibly have slept that long, but the lack of windows in the room made it impossible for him to be sure.

'Morning,' the DC croaked. Because, while he didn't want to give in to the man, he wished to be beaten and tortured even less.

'There we are! That's more like it!' Feasey cried, laughing and rubbing his hands together.

There was a rustling sound, and Tyler noticed for the first time that Shayne was carrying a flimsy plastic bag. The 'Spar' logo was on the side. There were at least three of them in the Fort William area, as far as Tyler knew, including one in Spean Bridge, less than a mile from where Sharon Simpson had been murdered.

'I brought you some breakfast,' Feasey announced. He produced a bottle of banana flavoured Yazoo milkshake, and a multipack of Scampi Fries.

Tyler blinked, and found himself staring at the offered selection, thoughts crashing around inside his head like debris in a tornado.

No. Wait. Hold on.

That was weird.

Too much of a coincidence, surely?

Tyler hated banana milkshakes, and he fucking despised Scampi Fries. They were probably the only crisp-type snack that he didn't enjoy, and since you very rarely came across them in the wild these days without specifically hunting them out, it seemed unlikely that they'd been picked out by chance.

Had he chosen these things on purpose? If so, how did he know Tyler didn't like them? How *could* he know?

And if he did know, why had he brought them? Was it just to add another wee layer of cruelty to this whole idea?

Or was it to let Tyler know that he had no secrets from the man? That Feasey already knew everything there was to know about DC Tyler Neish?

Or was he just being a dick?

'Could you not have got Frazzles?' Tyler asked. It was a small act of defiance, but it made him feel a little better about himself. Like he wasn't just rolling over for the bastard.

He would, of course. If it meant getting home to Sinead and the twins, he would. And no doubt Feasey knew it, too. That was probably the only reason Tyler was still alive. Shayne hadn't tried to get information out of him yet, but he would. He was bound to. That had to be why Tyler was still here.

'Right, here's what's going to happen,' Feasey said, returning Tyler's 'breakfast' to the bag. 'I'm going to unhook you and stick you in that chair.'

Tyler hadn't seen a chair, and the other man had done nothing to indicate where it might be. The thought of sitting down, though, made the DC want to weep with joy. His arms had gone from aching, to screaming, to now feeling like they were completely dead. He could've been convinced that they'd been removed, were it not for the occasional hot flash of agony that ripped through them every time his legs fully gave way beneath him.

'If you try anything, I will fuck you up like I fucked up your big mate,' Feasey warned. 'You try and make a grab for me, you try and run, you try anything that isn't exactly as per my instructions, and you'll spend the final few hours of your life bitterly regretting your own stupidity.'

Final few hours.

What was he saying? Did he mean that this version of Tyler only had a few hours left to live, or the version of Tyler that tried to escape? Were both equally as fucked, or did he have a chance of getting through this if he just kept his head down and did as he was told?

He realised he'd zoned out through the rest of Feasey's speech, but didn't dare ask him to repeat himself.

Instead, he let his sore, stiff legs take his weight, and tried not to make eye contact with his captor as the ropes tying him to the hook overhead were loosened.

He was right there. Right in front of him. Once Tyler's arms were free, he could go for the bastard's throat. His eye, even. Blind him, at least temporarily. Buy himself an advantage. Take the chance to get the hell out of here.

That's what Logan would do, he thought. Logan wouldn't just go along with it. Logan wouldn't simply comply.

But Jack Logan was a bigger man than he was, in every sense of the word.

Besides, even if Tyler had wanted to fight, he couldn't. The moment his hands were unhooked, his arms became lead weights. They swung limply down, still tied together, and hung there in front of him, lifeless and limp.

All the blood that gravity had deprived them of rushed in, bringing with it sharp, hot pins and needles of pain.

A hand shoved him in the chest. Hard. Sudden. He staggered backwards, tripped, and fell onto an old kitchen chair with a rough wooden seat.

Instinct told him to get up, to run, to fight if he had to. Fortunately, other more sensible instincts overpowered that urge, and by the time he'd finished wrestling with the idea, a rope had been wrapped twice around his chest, and knotted between the spars at the back of the chair.

The lid of the Yazoo bottle was unscrewed, then discarded. The silver foil was peeled back.

'Drink,' Feasey instructed, and Tyler gulped, choked and spluttered as the flavoured milk was poured forcefully into his mouth.

It was awful stuff—thick like mucus, and with a taste so far removed from real banana that it wasn't even inhabiting the same continent.

He coughed on it, then gagged as two runny streams of the stuff came cascading down his nose, its chemical contents burning the lining of his nostrils.

'Not a fan?' Feasey asked, and the smirk on his face removed all doubt from Tyler's mind. The bastard knew. He had picked this stuff deliberately, knowing that Tyler hated it.

But how? How did he know? How could he?

'Scampi Fry?' Shayne asked, pulling open the top of the multipack. 'There's loads.'

'Not hungry,' Tyler said. He half expected Feasey to force-feed him a couple of bags, but instead he just shrugged, and helped himself to a pack.

'Suit yourself.' He opened the bag, and the fishy, lemony aroma of the snacks came wafting in the DC's direction. 'Bloody love these,' Feasey said, tossing one in his mouth. 'Hard to get these days, though.'

He smiled and crunched. Crunched and smiled.

Now that his blood was starting to circulate again, the feeling was returning to Tyler's arms. It brought pain with it, dull at first, but getting steadily sharper and more honed.

'What do you want me for?' Tyler asked.

Feasey chucked another Scampi Fry in his mouth and chewed, then spat soggy crumbs of the stuff when he spoke. 'Who says I want anything?'

'Then why are you doing this?'

Feasey paused with his hand in the bag, then shrugged. 'Just a laugh, innit?'

He broke into a little chuckling fit, like he genuinely saw the funny side. Tyler waited for him to finish.

'They're going to come for me, Shayne,' he said. 'They're looking now. They'll have brought in teams from everywhere, and they'll be going over the whole area with a fine-tooth comb. They're going to find me, it's just a matter of time, and then you're going to be in a lot of trouble.' Tyler managed something that, from certain angles, vaguely resembled a smile.

'But it doesn't have to be like that. We can fix this. We can sort it out, the two of us. Together.'

Shayne's chewing slowed. He swallowed, and the act seemed to take a lot of effort. 'Seriously? You think we can fix this mess? Because I don't want to get in trouble. I really don't.'

The reply seemed sincere. Far too much so to be real. Tyler went along with it anyway, just in case.

'We can,' Tyler assured him. 'We can sort all this out, me and you. I can talk to them. I can straighten it all out, tell them it's not what they think. But, for me to do that, you need to let me go, Shayne. Let me go, and we can get all this sorted. We can put it all behind us.'

'God. Right. Yeah, OK.'

There was a *paff* as the crisp packet fell to the floor. Feasey rushed around to the back of the chair, and Tyler felt him fiddling with the rope. He held his breath, hardly daring to believe that he might've got through to the other man, and that his plan might actually be working.

He was right not to.

A moment later, Feasey stopped messing with the rope. His voice poured into Tyler's ear like burning hot tar.

'Hang on. Hold on a minute,' Feasey began, and Tyler could smell his fishy breath. 'You're not lying to me, are you?'

'What? No. They'll be coming,' Tyler insisted. 'They'll be on their way.'

Shayne inhaled deeply through his nose. Tyler felt the draught of it.

'I think you're full of shit,' Feasey whispered. Something about the shrillness and the proximity of it made Tyler's body shudder uneasily. 'See, if someone was going to find you, Detective Constable Tyler Neish, they'd have found you already. But they haven't. And they won't.'

The whisper lowered, becoming something more akin to a growl.

'And I don't like being lied to. I fucking *hate* liars. You know that? They think they're so clever. They think they can get away with anything if they just deny, deny, deny. Don't they? You'll have seen it. Not just in the mirror, either, though you'll have seen it there. On the job, I mean. In the police. You'll have seen all those fucking liars. Dancing about. Strutting their stuff. You'll have heard the shit pouring out of their mouths. Smelled it. Fucking drowned in it, nearly, I bet. Liars. They're all liars. All of them. You, too.'

The response had started out coherently enough, but his anger had quickly built, and the words had come faster and faster, until he was spitting them at the side of Tyler's face.

Feasey's breath was a pungent odour of artificial seafood flavouring. The banana milkshake hadn't done much for Tyler's constitution, and the stink of the Scampi Fries was turning his stomach.

Part of him wanted to turn and throw up right in Feasey's face.

The suicidal part.

He resisted.

'I'm not lying. They're going to come looking. They'll find us eventually.'

'Shh,' Feasey urged. He placed a finger on Tyler's lips, silencing him. 'You just said it. You just said the magic word.'

He removed his finger, then stepped back, practically inviting Tyler to ask the obvious question.

'What magic word?'

'"Eventually",' Feasey replied. 'You said they would come "eventually".'

He slapped his hands hard on Tyler's thighs, then bent down low so they were face to face. Feasey's demented grin almost twisted Tyler's churning stomach the rest of the way around.

'I reckon there's an awful lot of crazy shit we can get up to between now and "eventually",' Feasey said, his voice becoming a whisper again. He squeezed hard, his thumbs digging into the muscles of Tyler's legs. 'What do you say we find out *exactly* how much?'

Chapter 28

'Are we going to fucking crack on with this or not? Boyband's no' going to fucking rescue himself.'

Sitting on one of the desks, Hoon fired a look at everyone else in the Incident Room—one look between them all—that dared them to keep pissing about.

Not that anyone was. They were hurriedly necking coffees, scribbling notes, handing them to Tammi-Jo to be pinned, apparently at random, to the Big Board.

Despite that, Logan clapped his hands together, and the bang they made drew everyone's attention. 'Bob's right. Let's get to it. We've a lot to get through. Dave, have the DNA samples from Isaac Simpson and Armand Holburn gone away?'

'They did. Lab boys have been called back in to rush them through. Should have results by'—he glanced up at the clock on the wall—'around midnight.'

'Good,' Logan said, then he asked the question he was almost too afraid to voice. 'Any update on Tyler?'

Constable Davidson flashed an apologetic smile at Sinead before replying. 'Nothing yet. His phone's off. Can't get one for Feasey, and no bank cards have been used. Helicopter's out, patrols are doing the rounds. We found a couple of possible addresses that they're checking out.'

'I want an update as soon as they've been checked,' Logan said. 'Sinead got the last ping on Tyler's *Find My Phone* thing on the road just south of Torlundy, which suggests he was heading back this way. Prioritise any that fit that area.'

Dave nodded his understanding, but PC Niddrie was quick to point out a potential flaw.

'He could've doubled back, though. Headed north if he realised the phone had been tracking him.'

'He could've,' Logan agreed. 'He could equally have chucked the phone in the back of a passing wood lorry and gone somewhere else entirely. We keep an open mind, but my gut tells me he went south.'

Logan's phone pinged in his pocket. He took it out and tapped on the message that was waiting there from Shona.

'We've no' got a number plate?' Hoon asked.

Logan frowned when he saw the message. It was brief and to the point. Worryingly so.

We need to talk x

'Eh, hello? Anyone fucking listening? Do we have a plate or what?'

It was DS Khaled who replied. 'Don't even know what kind of car he was driving, if any. Nothing registered to his name, or the friend whose house he's staying at.'

'Had to be in a vehicle,' Logan said, returning his phone to his pocket. Whatever it was, it would have to wait. 'No way he'd have got Tyler out on foot. Not without being seen.'

Unless he didn't get Tyler out, of course.

For all Logan knew, Feasey had slit the detective constable's throat the split second the DCI had passed out, and dumped him somewhere nearby.

He didn't voice the thought out loud. He didn't want to think it himself, let alone burden Sinead with it. Instead, he made a mental note to make sure a thorough search of the area surrounding the house had been carried out, then pressed on.

'Has CID briefed the press yet?' he asked Dave.

'They have, aye. Radio has already started running a bit, and it should be on the STV News at Ten. Papers will have it in the morning.'

Sinead ran her hands back through her hair and drew in a shaky breath. 'And what? Is that it? Is that all we can do?'

'Going out on the socials, too,' Hamza said.

'Great! We're Tweeting about it! That'll help.'

'We'll find him,' Logan promised her.

Nidds, who was sitting closest to Sinead, put a hand on the DC's arm. 'He'll be OK. He won't hurt him. The guy who took him, I mean. He knows Tyler's police. It would be crazy to hurt him.'

All eyes went to the increasingly mangled-looking face of DCI Logan, whose usual looming posture had been diminished by a sideways stoop brought on by at least one broken rib. He hadn't stuck around for the X-ray results to confirm exactly how many bones had given way beneath the force of Shayne Feasey's boots, but there were definitely a few.

'Aye, well, looking at the state of his fucking mush, your man doesn't exactly seem like the most level-headed bastard in the world,' Hoon reasoned. 'I mean, fuck me, Jack, you weren't an attractive man before, but you look like a burst arsehole.'

'Thanks for that, Bob.'

'Or the unholy offspring of Quasimodo and the fucking Elephant Man.'

Logan fixed him with what would've been a cool, hard stare, had all his facial features been their regular size and shape.

'You done?'

Hoon thought for a moment. 'Or like someone made a glory hole in a wasp's nest,' he said, then he nodded. 'There. Now I'm done. So, how about we all draw our fingers out of one another's arseholes and crack on, eh?' He tapped his watch. 'Time's fucking ticking here.'

Logan blew out his cheeks, then regretted it immediately because of how much it hurt.

'Right. Who's first?' he asked, swallowing down the taste of blood.

Hamza, Sinead, Hoon, Tammi-Jo and Dave all started to speak at the same time.

'Whoa, whoa, whoa,' Logan boomed, holding up his hands. He clicked his fingers and pointed to Hamza. 'DS Khaled. You were in with Isaac. What do we have?'

'A confession, sir,' Hamza said, getting to his feet.

'To the murder?' Ben asked, sitting forwards.

Sinead shook her head. 'No. To the reason behind it. Although, "confession" is a strong word.'

'True,' Hamza conceded. 'Not a confession. An explanation, then. It turns out that Isaac kept a lot of stuff out of his previous statements about the harassment.'

'Like?' Ben prompted.

'Like the fact the guy came to his door. Like the fact he made it very clear why he was doing what he was doing.'

Logan took a slurp of his coffee. 'And?'

'He said it on the phone, apparently. Not in person. When he came to the door, he just stood there smiling, saying nothing at all for a couple of minutes, then turned around and walked off,' Hamza said.

'Sounds like a total fucking headcase,' Hoon chipped in.

'On one of the calls, though, he told Isaac why,' Hamza continued. 'Why he was doing it all.'

'Bloody hell. Seriously?' Nidds asked, wide-eyed with surprise. 'He didn't mention it. Isaac. When I was there. He didn't mention any of this. What did the phone call say? Why did he say he was doing it?'

'Revenge,' Sinead said. 'He said he was getting revenge on all three men—Isaac, Armand and Norman.'

'For what?' Logan asked.

'He said they sexually assaulted his mother,' Hamza replied.

Ben frowned. 'What, all of them?'

'That's what he claimed on the phone call, apparently. Isaac completely denies it,' Hamza said. 'Feasey's mum was Bosnian. So was he. It was during the war. He said the three of them had raped her. Took it in turns. He'd been hiding under the bed, too scared to move. He just lay there listening to it. Listening to everything they did.'

'Jesus,' Dave muttered. 'That's grim.'

'Again, though, Isaac completely denies all this,' Sinead pointed out.

'You believe him?' Logan asked.

Sinead hesitated before shrugging her shoulders. 'Wouldn't like to say, sir. What he did or didn't do thirty years ago wasn't my number one priority during the interview.'

Logan nodded. 'Understood.'

Ben's chair creaked as he sat back in it, his fingers wrapped around his coffee mug like he was feeding off its warmth. 'It was a horrible bastard of a war that one.'

'Aye, you can fucking say that again,' Hoon agreed. 'That sort of thing was rife, too. On all fucking sides. Wasn't reported in the press about our boys, of course. Couldn't be having that. Kept well under fucking wraps, but some of the bastards were at it. You can mark my fucking words on that.'

'Doesn't matter if they did it or not. Not right now, anyway. We can deal with that later,' Logan reasoned. 'What matters is whether Feasey believes it, and by the sounds of it, he does.'

'So, all this… All the harassment, Sharon's murder, it was all just an escalation of some revenge plan?' Ben asked.

'Sounds very much like it, sir,' Hamza confirmed.

Logan asked if there was anything else of major importance that had come out of the interview, and after the DS had revealed there wasn't much else of interest, the DCI had moved on to the next pairing.

'Detective Constable Swanney,' he said, deliberately skipping over Hoon. 'You spoke to the victim's son. Thoughts?'

'He smelled a bit weird,' Tammi-Jo replied.

There was silence for a moment, which was eventually broken by a tut and muttered, 'For fuck's sake', from Hoon.

'Any other thoughts beyond that one?' Logan pressed.

'Not really, sir. Not thoughts, as such. But I can tell you what he said, if you like?'

'That's sort of what I was getting at, aye.'

'Oh! OK. Well, he was sent a video. Struan. Ward. The son, I mean. Sharon's son. He's not Isaac's son, by the way. Isaac's his stepdad. He was sent a video. Struan, not Isaac. To his phone. Well, no, he was sent the video to his email, but he read it on his phone.'

'He didn't read the fucking video,' Hoon interjected.

'Well, no. Obviously. He read the email,' Tammi-Jo said, shooting Hoon a sideways look that suggested that, despite only recently having met him, she already had quite deep-rooted concerns about his mental health. 'He *watched* the video.'

'And what did the email say?' Hamza asked.

'Nothing,' Tammi-Jo replied. 'It was blank.'

'Then how did he read…?' the DS began, before Hoon interrupted.

'See? You see what I'm fucking dealing with?'

'What about the video?' Sinead asked, cutting them both off. One of her legs was bouncing up and down, shaking her desk and the ones on either side. Nobody dared asked her to stop. 'What was on it?'

'It was a man having sex with his mum. With Struan's mum, I mean. A man having sex with Struan's mum, not a man having sex with his own mum. It definitely wasn't that. In case anyone thought that's what I meant.'

'I think I can safely say that nobody thought that, Detective Constable,' Logan intoned. 'What else? Go on.'

'Right, well, you don't see all that much of him. The… sexman. You just see his… You know? His… His John Thomas. And you also see Auntie Fluff.'

'The fuck?' Hoon ejected. 'Who the fuck's Auntie Fluff?'

Tammi-Jo's cheeks went so instantly red it was like a switch had been flicked. 'You know. The victim. You see her *Auntie Fluff*.'

'Saying it again with your eyebrows raised isn't exactly fucking clarifying matters,' Hoon told her. He turned to Logan, who had carefully lowered himself into a chair. 'You saw his cock, her tits, and her fanny. There. Terminology we can all fucking understand.'

'Uh, yes. Those,' DC Swanney said, her whole face now the colour of a ripe tomato. 'You saw all those bits that he just said. And they were… You know… The two of them were…' She winced, reaching for an appropriate description. 'Having *coitus*.'

'Fuck me. They were shagging,' Hoon translated. 'Some lad—big, too, if you know what I mean? It was a like a fucking baby's arm from that angle. Some lad was shagging her. Wasn't holding back, either. Really going at it.'

'Consensual?' Hamza asked.

'Oh, I'd say it was fucking consensual, all right,' Hoon replied. 'She practically gave him a round of applause at one point. Mind you, I was of half a mind to do the fucking same myself. The guy was a fucking champion. And I mean that literally.'

Tammi-Jo had now gone beyond the ripe tomato look, and into some hitherto unseen shade of red right at the edge of the visible spectrum. She quickly tried to bring the focus of the conversation around to more relevant matters.

'There were two videos,' she said, then she immediately shook her head. 'No. That's not right. There were two clips in the one video, edited together. You know, like they do in films? Or on the telly? Or—'

'What was the second clip?' Logan asked, cutting her off before she could launch into an explanation of the editing process.

'Um, just, you know. More of the same, really. The two of them. Doing it,' she said. 'In the first, the victim was on her back on the bed.'

Ben set down his coffee mug. 'What bed? The bed in her house?'

'Looked like it, sir, yes. She's on her back, he's standing over her with the phone, doing… That thing they were doing. She's, you know, having quite a nice time of it. And then, in the next bit, she's on her knees, facing away.'

'Handcuffed,' Hoon added.

Tammi-Jo pointed at him, either to confirm what he'd said was correct, or to thank him for not making her say it. 'Face down on the bed.'

'Wait, what?' Logan asked, hauling himself up onto his feet. 'What are you saying? That the video was from when she was killed?'

'It doesn't show it happening,' Tammi-Jo said. 'But it looks like it was recorded just before. Stops before it gets violent, though.'

'You see a face?' Ben asked. 'His, I mean?'

Tammi-Jo shook her head. 'Not that I noticed, sir.'

'No fucking wonder. She had her hands over her eyes for most of it, going, "Oh, no, no, no. Don't put that there",' Hoon revealed. He shrugged. 'I didn't see a guy's face, either, though. Mind you, I can't say I was really on the hunt for one.'

'Struan thought he recognised the clothing the man was wearing, though. Thinks it could've been Armand Holburn. You get a wee flash of a cravat in amongst all the… nonsense.'

Logan hadn't yet sat back down. The effort it would involve didn't really feel worth it.

'OK. That's interesting. Who sent it?' he asked. 'Who was the email from?'

'His mum,' Tammi-Jo replied. 'Well, his mum's account. It was sent after she was killed, so it probably wasn't her sending it.'

'Fuck me,' Hoon muttered. 'Aye, you're probably right. Probably wasn't her. Never know, though. Maybe we should go fucking ask her to make sure?'

'So, someone with access to her email account sent it to her son,' Hamza said before Hoon could fully go off on one.

This revelation had them all a bit stumped. There could be no connection between Struan Ward and the alleged attack in Bosnia. Struan wasn't born until years later, long after the war had ended.

'I don't get it. I don't see the logic to it,' Logan admitted. 'What's the *why* here? What would he have to gain by sending her son that video?'

'Maybe the person who sent it wasn't the same man as in the video?' Hamza suggested.

'Or maybe it was, and he's just a nasty bastard,' Ben reasoned. 'Maybe he just likes the idea of people suffering. That fits with what we know of Shayne Feasey.'

'Does it fucking matter?' Hoon barked, jumping down from the desk he'd been sitting on. 'Some shagger sent a guy a homemade porno. So fucking what? How the fuck is any of this helping us find Boyband? We're no' going to find him pissing about here. We've got more chance of huffing the steam off a dodo's pish. We should be out there tearing the fucking town apart to find that useless wee plastic-haired bag of fucks.' He shot Sinead a glance. 'No offence.'

Sinead dismissed the remark with the tiniest shake of her head.

'We're doing everything we can,' Logan insisted. 'We've got hundreds of Uniforms out there looking for him. Dogs. Helicopters. Blanket press coverage starting now, wall to wall. We've got the tech bods just waiting for his phone to ping. If there's so much of a sniff of Tyler, we'll pick it up.'

He stabbed a finger down on the desk beside him, hard enough for it to make an audible *thunk*.

'This. This is what we can do. What we always do. Put the pieces together. Build the picture. Figure out everything we can about this bastard, so we can work out where he took him, and why.'

'I know why, sir,' Sinead said. She got to her feet, then crossed to stand by Hoon's side. 'Because he could. Because nobody was able to stop him.'

Logan opened his mouth to protest, but the DC raised a hand to silence him.

'I'm not saying it's your fault, sir. I know it isn't. I know you'd have stopped it happening if you could,' she continued. 'But Tyler put himself in danger to protect you. He risked his life to save yours. And, much as I hate to admit it, Hoon's right.'

'Too fucking right I am.'

'We can't just sit here waiting for some miracle to happen. We can't just act like everything's normal,' Sinead said. 'We can't just go about business as usual. *I* can't. I won't.'

'What are you saying?' Logan asked.

Sinead looked around at the faces of her colleagues—of her friends—then indicated Hoon with a tilt of her head. 'I'm going with him.'

'You're on duty, Detective Constable,' Logan reminded her. 'You cancelled your maternity leave, remember?'

Sinead straightened herself up. 'Permission to uncancel it, sir?'

'Permission denied,' Logan shot back. 'Chasing your tail out there isn't going to help anyone. Not Tyler, and not you.'

'Then I quit, sir.'

Hamza blinked, shocked. 'Sinead, don't.'

'Quit?' Logan looked the DC up and down, like he was seeing her for the first time. 'You can't bloody quit!'

'You're upset, Sinead,' Ben said, inserting himself between her and Logan. 'That's all. We get it. You're just upset, you don't mean that. You're not thinking straight.'

'Oh, I know I'm upset, sir,' Sinead agreed, doing an excellent job of standing firm in the heat of Logan's glare. 'I'm very upset. And maybe I'm not thinking straight, but it doesn't matter. I've never been more sure of anything in my life. Tyler's out there, not in here. And out there's where we'll find him.'

Hoon jerked a thumb in the DC's direction. 'Aye. What she fucking said.' He looked around at the others. 'Anyone else with me? Ben? Detective Sergeant?' He looked from Ben, to Hamza, then on to Tammi-Jo. 'Human Shite Tornado?'

DC Swanney glanced behind her, as if expecting to see someone else by that name standing there. When she didn't, she pointed to herself.

'Wait, am *I* the Human Shite Tornado?'

Hoon scowled. 'Are you in or are you out, princess? We've no' got all fucking day here.'

'Nobody's going anywhere, Bob,' Logan said, answering for them. 'They know I'm right on this.'

Hoon gave the team another once-over, then his lips drew back over his teeth in a sneer. 'Suit your fucking selves, but if anything happens to the calamitous wee fucker—again, no offence—then that's on all of you. It's on every fucking last one of you.'

With his warning still ringing in their ears, Hoon marched out of the Incident Room.

'Sinead,' Logan said as she stepped past him. It wasn't an order. It wasn't much of anything, in fact.

'Sorry, sir,' she told him. 'I have to.'

And with that, just like Hoon a moment before her, she was gone.

Logan watched the door for a few moments, expecting—hoping—that it would open again.

It didn't, and so he turned himself around, limping, and faced the others.

'Right, then. Where were we?'

'Shouldn't we go after them?' Hamza asked.

Logan carefully prodded his bloated bottom lip with his tongue a few times before replying. 'No. Not our priority. Our priority is here. It's finding Tyler.'

He looked across at the Big Board, then down at his own scribbled notes. There was something desperate about the way his head jerked up and down.

'Now, for the love of God, someone tell me we've got something else.'

Dave Davidson opened his mouth to respond, but Nidds jumped in before he had the chance. 'Actually, sir, yes. We do have something. It's about the notes, sir.' She stole the quickest of glances at her fellow constable. 'Dave noticed it.'

Dave wheeled himself towards the Big Board, a sheet of paper resting in his lap.

'And,' he said, the wheels of his chair squeaking, 'it's going to blow your mind!'

Chapter 29

Hoon sat behind the wheel of his Honda CR-V, holding back on starting the engine until Sinead had climbed into the passenger seat and shut the door. He eyed her carefully, and there was a look on his face that didn't sit comfortably there.

Uncertainty.

Usually, Hoon was unshakably confident that he was right, even in the face of significant evidence to the contrary.

Especially then, in fact.

He had a cast-iron confidence in his own decision-making ability that rarely wavered, even when it very probably should have. This rock-solid self-belief had rubbed a lot of people up the wrong way over the years.

It had also kept him alive.

Seeing the flicker of doubt on his face stopped Sinead midway through putting on her seatbelt. 'What?' she asked. 'What's wrong?'

'You sure about this?' Hoon asked. 'Doing this. With me. Could be a career-ender.'

There was a firm *click* as the metal clasp of the seatbelt was inserted into the connector.

'There's always Tesco,' she said.

Hoon grimaced. 'Fuck. Been there, done that,' he said. He started the engine and the old car coughed into life. 'Would not fucking recommend.'

'Where are we going?' Sinead asked. 'What's the plan?'

Hoon raised his eyes upwards, either deep in thought or seeking divine inspiration. 'Can you still get into the shared inbox?' he asked.

'Think so, yeah.'

'Can you get the list of addresses that big bastard was on about? The ones this Feasey guy's connected to.'

Sinead nodded. 'I'd imagine so.'

'Happy fucking days.' Hoon floored the accelerator, and the Honda's tyres screeched, lurching them towards the exit of the car park. 'Then, I reckon we start by working our way through them.'

Logan stood staring at the printout on the board. Ben, Hamza and Tammi-Jo all gathered a pace or two behind him, their mouths slack with disbelief. Even DC Swanney seemed to be lost for words.

'You see it?' Dave asked. He was holding up the scan of the note that Nidds had found in Armand's bin. 'Took me a minute.'

They weren't the same. The position of the writing on the crumpled note didn't match with the imprint that Scene of Crime had been able to take from the pad in the bedroom.

It was close in a few places. The shape and size of the block capital letters were similar.

Similar, but not identical.

They'd been working on the assumption that the note taken from above the bed in Isaac and Sharon's bedroom had been the same one they'd found in Armand's bin. That would've suggested that Armand had found it, taken it, and disposed of it.

And *that* would've placed him at the crime scene.

But these weren't the same notes. From what Logan could tell, they weren't even the same handwriting.

'Two notes,' he said, though he wasn't quite sure who he was saying it to. 'They're two different notes.'

'Bingo!' Dave said. He lowered the printout he was holding. 'No idea what it means, mind.' He looked up at the detectives, hoping it might mean something to them. 'Any clue?'

Ben looked like he might be about to offer a suggestion, but then he thought better of it.

'Beats me,' he admitted. 'Doesn't fit our picture at all. Jack?'

Logan continued to stare at the note, though it was hard to say if he was looking at it or through it.

'Leave it with me,' he said, after a moment. He wheeled around, suddenly all business. 'Good spot, Constable Davidson. Detective Constable Swanney, that video Struan Ward was sent?'

Tammi-Jo winced at the thought of it. 'What about it, sir?'

'Get it to DS Khaled. He can go through it. I want the man in the footage identified.'

The DC looked sceptical. 'Unless we're going to be doing an ID line-up of men with their John Thomases hanging out, I think he'll struggle, sir. And, if we are doing that, I don't want to be on the other side of the glass, if that's all right with everyone? I've seen quite enough of it for one day, thank you.'

Hamza gave her a second to make sure she was finished, then nodded to Logan. 'I'll get on the case, sir. See what I can find out. Might be able to pull an IP or something from the email headers, too.'

'I don't know what that means, but I like the sound of it,' Ben said.

'Aye. Do that,' Logan agreed. 'We got a warrant for Armand's place yet?'

'I thought you told him we already had one?' Ben said.

'Oh. You're right. I did tell him that, didn't I?' Logan said. He turned to Dave. 'Don't make a liar of me, Constable.'

'Came in a few minutes ago,' Dave said. 'Detective Superintendent Mitchell must've worked some magic on it.'

'Thank Christ,' Logan said. He looked around for his coat, then snatched it up. 'Send Struan Ward away once we've got the video, and he's signed a statement. Get an address for him while he's here. He can't go back to his mother's house until we give it the all-clear. Ben, get back in there with Holburn. Let him know we're turning his place over. Ask him about the rape claims. Tell him that Isaac corroborates it. Basically, rattle the bastard's cage and see what he shits out.'

'With pleasure,' Ben replied. He watched the DCI struggling into his overcoat. 'What about you?'

'I'll be the one turning his place over.'

'Not on your own. Take someone with you, for God's sake.'

With some difficulty, Logan finished wrestling his arms into his sleeves. He shrugged on the coat, then pulled the collar into place with a flick.

'No. I'm going alone,' he said. 'I've put quite enough officers in danger for one day.'

Chapter 30

Adrenaline had kept Tyler conscious long after the beating he'd received at the hands of Shayne Feasey.

It hadn't been too bad, all in all. He'd had worse. A fight back in high school, for one. Hell, even that time he'd been hit by that car, and that had barely hurt at all, even if he'd milked it a bit afterwards.

Feasey hadn't been out to do any lasting damage, just to slap him around a bit. He appeared to have viewed it as some sort of light entertainment, and had eventually grown bored of it.

Now, he sat on a rectangle of scuffed, dented metal—part of an old air duct, Tyler thought—munching his way through his fourth packet of Scampi Fries. Tyler sat opposite, still tied to the chair, too exhausted to do anything but sag there with his head hanging down.

'What are we going to do with you?' Feasey asked.

It was a rhetorical question, of course. Tyler answered it anyway.

'Let me go,' he said, raising his eyes just enough to meet those of the other man.

Feasey snorted, shook his head like he'd just heard something unbelievable, and went back to his scampi-flavoured snacks.

'I've got kids,' Tyler said. He regretted it at once—the idea of revealing to this man that he had children suddenly making him feel sick. It was a desperate hand to play, but the only one he had left. He lowered his head again, ashamed at himself for bringing even mention of his children into this.

Feasey's chewing slowed. His hand dipped thoughtfully into the pack, making the foil bag rattle. 'That's news to me,' he said, looking genuinely surprised by this revelation. 'You winding me up?'

Tyler bit his tongue, saying nothing. A Scampi Fry bounced off his forehead.

'Don't clam up on me now. Tell me, or I'll break a finger,' Feasey said. When this still got no response, he sighed. 'I'm just making fucking conversation here. It's not like I'm going to go after them. Jesus. What do you think I am?'

He waved his forefinger back and forth between them, pointing to them both in turn.

'And anyway. This is what you're meant to do in this situation, isn't it? Bond. You and me. Form a connection. That's what they tell you to do, isn't it?' He ran his tongue around the inside of his mouth, scooping up the vaguely seafood-flavoured mush. 'So, go on, then. Do it. Connect. What's the worst that could happen?'

Feasey grinned, showing the clumps of orange matter clinging to his teeth.

'Maybe, if you're persuasive enough, you might even convince me to let you go home to see them. That's got to be worth a try, right?'

Tyler's tongue dragged across his dry lips. It felt like a long time since that gulp of banana milkshake, though he couldn't begin to guess. According to his captor, he'd been here all night, but the lack of windows, and his earlier dipping in and out of consciousness, meant he wasn't sure how true that was.

'They're twins,' he ventured.

'Twins? Wow. How old?' Feasey asked.

Tyler wrestled with himself over giving a response. 'Three months,' he finally said.

'Wow. Bloody hell. Young, then.'

'Just babies.'

'In that case, I doubt they'll miss you,' Feasey reasoned. 'I mean, they might, but it'd pass. They don't exactly understand anything at that stage, do they? They'd get over it. That's what kids do, isn't it? They get over stuff. They bounce back. So everyone says, anyway. That's what we tell ourselves. "'Kids are resilient.'"

He looked down at the puddle of blood and spit Tyler had left on the floor.

'And they are. Way more than adults. Adults whinge all the time, but kids just get on with it. They're made of tougher stuff.'

Something about the way he was talking told Tyler he may have found a weakness.

'What about you?' he asked. 'You have kids, I mean?'

'Fuck that,' Feasey spat. 'No chance.'

The thought of it clearly agitated him. He grabbed the final bag of Scampi Fries and got stuck into the contents. He was yet to offer his prisoner any. Tyler was quite happy with that.

'Why not?' Tyler pressed. Feasey was right about the whole 'forming a bond' thing. The more kidnappers got to know their hostages, the less likely they were to hurt or kill them.

Not *much* less likely, but Tyler would take anything he could get at this point.

There was a pause. It was so heavily pregnant, its waters were at risk of breaking.

'None of your fucking business. That's why not,' Feasey eventually said.

He picked away at his teeth for a few moments, seemingly deep in thought.

'Anyway, how come you're here, and not with them?' he asked. 'Don't you get, like, family leave or something? Isn't that a thing now? Because dads are apparently so fucking important these days.'

He all but hissed that last part through gritted teeth. There were some daddy issues there, Tyler suspected. Maybe he could find a way to play on that, he thought.

Although, he had no idea how he might actually go about doing that.

'First day back,' he said.

This drew a whoop of laughter from Feasey. His face lit up like he'd just landed six numbers on the lottery.

'Fuck off! No way! First day back, and you end up here with me? Jesus Christ. That is unfortunate. I mean, what are the chances?' He shook his head, chuckling. 'I almost feel like I should be apologising or something. I won't, obviously. But I feel like I should.'

'Why are you doing this, Shayne?' Tyler asked. 'What have you got to gain from this?'

'That's not the question you should be asking, Mr Policeman.' He dragged out the last word, emphasising every one of its syllables. 'It's not about what I've got to gain. It's about what I've got to lose.'

'What have you got to lose?' Tyler asked.

Feasey scrunched up the half-full bag of scampi-flavoured snacks, and tossed it back over his shoulder. It landed with a *paff* in the shadows at the edge of the pool of light.

'Nothing,' he said, through a grin. 'Not a thing. See, that's the whole point, isn't it? Those fuckers, they already took everything from me. They did this to me. They made me like this.'

He thumped himself in the middle of the chest. There was an air of disgust to the gesture, like he hated himself almost as much as Tyler did, though the DC didn't see how that was possible.

'They took everything from me, so that's what I'm doing. I'm taking everything from them. Eye for an eye, and all that. I'm taking everything. And then, that's me, I'm done. I'm bowing out.'

He brought his arm up so sharply and suddenly that Tyler flinched. Instead of hitting the DC, though, Feasey snapped off an exaggerated salute.

'Mission accomplished. Sir, yes, sir!'

He laughed. It was a loud, throw-the-head-back sort of laugh that rolled around the junk-strewn room for several long, uncomfortable seconds, before he eventually ran out of steam.

'Sorry. Why am I doing it? That's what you asked, isn't it?' Feasey said, wiping away tears of mirth on his sleeve. He shrugged. 'Because someone has to. Someone has to make them pay for what they did. Someone has to hold those fuckers accountable. And that someone's us.'

'Us? What do you mean?' Tyler asked.

Feasey's face fixed itself into a cold, immobile mask. He leaned closer to Tyler, and rested a hand on the detective constable's leg.

'All in good time,' he whispered. 'All in good time.'

Tyler managed to hold eye contact with the bastard, trying to show as little fear as possible. That plan went right out the window when Feasey's phone suddenly blasted out a melody, and the unexpectedness of it almost made the detective constable shit himself.

Feasey sat back and checked the screen of his mobile. The ringing tone was an upbeat, slightly sleazy-sounding jazz arrangement so downright catchy that it made Tyler's captor tap a foot in time with it.

Tyler, unsurprisingly, didn't feel the same urge to succumb to the rhythm.

'I have to take this, but I promise I'll be right back,' Feasey announced, getting to his feet. He fired a grin back over his shoulder as he made for the door. 'Don't you be going anywhere, now!'

Tyler caught a glimpse of darkness outside just before the door closed at Feasey's back. It wasn't morning, then. His instincts had been right. The prick was just playing mind games.

The ropes binding him were strong, but the chair wasn't. Tyler pulled, twisted, wrenched his arms. He leaned forwards as far as he could, straining against the ropes. Pain burned deep grooves into his wrists and his arms.

He heard the old wood groan.

Felt it bend. Bow.

His head swam with the effort. Foamy flecks of blood bubbled on his lips.

Just a little further. Just a little more.

And then—with an almighty *crack*—something snapped.

His momentum sent him tumbling forwards, spilling onto the floor. His hands were tied at his back, and he could only close his eyes, roll a shoulder, and brace himself for the impact with the floor.

He wasted half a second assessing the damage from the fall. Not bad. Could've been much worse.

With some effort, he managed to get himself up onto his knees, then to his feet. The stone was cold and rough against his bare soles. He wouldn't be able to run far or run fast.

With his hands bound, he wouldn't be able to fight back, either. He knew, though, that the ropes were too tightly tied for him to be able to get free.

Escape was the only option. And since a straight sprint was out of the question, he'd have to try and sneak away.

Turning, he scanned the rest of the room. It was definitely some sort of industrial storage shed or something, though the walls were hewn from rough stone, and it didn't seem to have been used in a long time. There were no windows, and no other way in or out.

The door Shayne Feasey had left through wasn't locked, but it still took Tyler a few tries to turn the handle while facing the other way. A wind came whistling in through the gap as he eased the door open, sounding for all the world like some shrill distant scream.

When it died down, Tyler heard Feasey's voice. It was nearby, but not right outside. Close enough, though, for him to hear most of what was being said.

'You didn't tell me he had kids.'

There was a pause while he listened to quite a lengthy reply.

'Course it doesn't make any difference. Why would I give a shit? Just interesting that you chose not to mention it. I could've used that, and you know it.'

Another pause. Feasey's voice, when he spoke again, sparked with anger.

'No, *you* listen. It is the plan. I made the plan, and I can change it. And this—him—he's now part of it. No, he's the part that stops me getting bored. That's all.'

Feasey listened for a moment. When he spoke again, there was anger behind it.

'Well, we'd better hurry it the fuck up, in that case, so I don't have to start killing time with him.'

Midway through his last reply, Feasey had started to sound a little muffled and more distant. Tyler hoped that meant he'd turned his back. There was no way of knowing without stepping outside, though. Tyler had no choice but to risk it.

Hooking a bare foot around the bottom of the door, he eased it slowly inwards. He could hear the crunching of slow footsteps, and Feasey's voice was becoming quieter still. He was walking away. It was now or never.

Pulling the door so it was just wide enough to fit through, Tyler slipped out into the darkness. Sharp gravel dug into the soles of his feet, and he bit his tongue to stop himself gasping at the pain.

The darkness was almost absolute, a layer of cloud blocking out the light from the moon and stars. He got the impression of tall trees towering above him somewhere up ahead, and a suggestion of a dirt road running beneath their branches.

There were lights somewhere off on his left. The sound of traffic, or machinery. Keeping low, he crept towards it, each stony step agony on his bare feet.

It took him just a few seconds to reach the corner of the low, squat stone building he'd been imprisoned in.

It took a single second more for him to realise he could no longer hear Feasey talking on the phone. A glance back revealed nothing but darkness. Nothing to indicate where the bastard was.

Shit.

Tyler hobbled on, head down, hands bound at his back, heart rattling inside his chest like it had shaken itself loose of its moorings and was now bouncing around freely in there.

He wanted to throw up. He *would* throw up, he was sure of that. Just not now. Not yet. Not until he was out of there. Not until he was safe.

There was another building, similar to the one beside him, a hundred feet away. He could just make out the edges of it in the orange glow from somewhere beyond. Streetlights, maybe? God, he hoped so. Streetlights meant cars. Cars meant people. People meant help.

Getting to the next building from this one meant being out in the open. It would be a mad, frantic dash across the gravel. Thirty seconds, maybe more. Thirty seconds of running for his life. Thirty seconds of pain.

He thought of what would happen to him if he was spotted.

He thought of Sinead and the twins waiting for him back home.

The decision was easy.

Tyler ran.

And the crunch of each agonising footstep rang out through the darkness.

Chapter 31

Logan checked in with the guards stationed at Isaac Simpson's house, made sure nobody had tried to access the scene, then 'borrowed' one to help him at Armand's place next door.

'I want these two open,' he instructed, pointing to the metal sheds in Armand's back garden.

The uniformed constable gave the heavy locks a doubtful look. 'Not going to be easy, sir,' he remarked.

'There might be keys inside,' Logan told him. 'Either that, or I've a set of bolt cutters in the boot of my car. It'll take a bit of welly, but they'll do the job.'

The Uniform nodded, then trotted after Logan towards the back door of Armand's house. 'You got a key for there?' he asked.

The officer stopped and jumped back when Logan raised a foot, took aim at a spot near the door handle, and shattered the frame with a single kick.

'More or less,' the DCI said, trying not to show how much the move had taken out of him.

He took a moment to catch his breath on the step, then led the way into the kitchen and pointed to a terracotta pot on the windowsill.

'Check that for keys. Otherwise, have a hunt around, but be careful. You find the keys, or you see anything out of the ordinary, you shout.'

'Got it, sir,' the Uniform confirmed. He crossed to the window, and Logan continued on into the house.

He headed for the living room first, where he and Tyler had interviewed Isaac earlier. Isaac and Armand's whisky glasses were still on their respective tables—Armand's on a side table beside his armchair, Isaac's on the dining table where he'd been questioned by the detectives.

The fire had burned itself out now, and most of the room's oppressive heat had escaped through the gaps in the rickety old bay window, which looked badly in need of replacing.

What was he looking for? He wasn't sure yet. He was sure there was something here, though. Something that would reveal another piece of the puzzle.

Something that would help him put the whole thing together.

Something that would somehow bring Tyler home.

A bookcase stood against the back wall. It had been behind where Logan had been sitting while talking to Isaac, so he hadn't checked it out.

Most of the books on it were non-fiction, and the theme was heavily military-centric. There were whole volumes about specific battles from most of the major wars of the last century, and quite a troubling number of thick, heavy tomes about tanks.

What he'd thought was a leather-bound journal when he'd excitedly pulled it from one of the shelves turned out to be a series of fold-out maps showing the locations of all the major events of World War II, and the estimated casualty count for each one.

Logan slotted it back into the place he'd found it, then crouched, reading the spines of the books below. Some of these also detailed a battle, albeit a very different one.

Eight of the books were about cancer. Four were about ways to fight it. Three were about ways to live with it, and the last—and smallest—was about how to deal with the grief of losing a loved one to it. The spines of all but that last one were lined with creases, while it remained untouched and pristine.

The rest of the shelf was taken up by crime fiction, a few romance novels, and a couple of Hilary Mantels. None of them felt like something Armand would be reading—none of them centred on military machinery or genocide—so Logan assumed they had belonged to his late wife.

If so, it was the only hint of her he'd seen in the place so far. There were no photographs of her anywhere. No keepsakes or treasures that she might once have called her own.

This was the home of a man who liked to sit in his worn leather armchair, drinking expensive whisky in front of a roaring log fire. The furniture was all antique oak, and Logan knew that if he opened the carved wooden box sitting on the coffee table, he'd find it contained several obnoxiously large cigars.

He checked.

It did.

This was a man's house. A very specific type of man, at that.

He wondered if it had always been that way. Or had Armand cleared out everything of his wife's the moment she'd died, leaving only half a shelf of well-thumbed genre fiction as a reminder that she'd ever been there?

There was nothing of obvious interest in those books. Logan leaned on the table and hauled himself back to his feet. From the way he was aching, he reckoned the painkillers he'd been given at the hospital must be wearing off.

Maybe Holburn would have some in a cupboard somewhere that he could nab. Paracetamol was unlikely to knock the pain on the head, but it might take the edge off it.

'Found them!'

The shout came from the kitchen. A moment later, the PC popped his head around the living room door and jangled a bunch of keys.

'This is them. I checked,' he said, then he frowned as he looked the DCI up and down. 'You all right, sir? Besides the obvious, I mean. You want a sit-down?'

'I'm fine,' Logan told him, though he was annoyed that his discomfort was that obvious. 'You open the sheds yet?'

'No, sir. Just undid the padlocks. Thought you'd want to be there.'

'Good. Don't suppose you spotted any painkillers while hunting for the keys, did you?'

The constable unfastened the top pocket of his vest, produced a pack of Ibuprofen, and passed it over with the satisfied air of a man who had spent his entire career to date carrying the packet with him in the hope of just such a moment.

'Take as many as you want, sir,' he said. 'I mean, two's the recommended, obviously. I'm not saying you should take an overdose or anything. I'm not suggesting that. I just meant, you know, feel free to take some for later. If you want. Keep them. Keep the pack. I don't mind.'

Logan pressed two tablets out of the foil, swallowed them with a jerk of his head, then handed the packet back. 'Thanks. That'll do me,' he said. 'Now, let's get a look inside those sheds.'

'Right you are, sir,' the PC said, returning the Ibuprofen to his pocket.

He left the room. The DCI followed, but as he reached the door, something nagged at him. Some part of his subconscious wasn't happy about leaving. There was something else to be found here, it insisted.

It could wait.

He headed back out through the broken door of the kitchen and found the PC standing in front of the sheds. The padlocks had been undone and placed on the ground beside each door. The constable smiled when Logan emerged from the house, and gestured to the sheds like he was presenting the DCI with his choice of prizes.

'There you go. Ready when you are, sir.' He rubbed his hands together. 'It's like that show, isn't it? *Storage Wars.* When they bid on the shite that people have left in old lock-ups. It's amazing some of the stuff they leave behind. Have you seen it? It's a fun show. I think it's on one of the satellite channels.'

Logan tuned him out so he could, for all intents and purposes, no longer hear him. This was a skill he'd had for years, and one which had been forced to evolve rapidly ever since Tammi-Jo had joined the team.

He went to the shed on the left first. The heavy bolt took a bit of work to slide all the way to the left, but once it did, the door sprang outwards a few inches like it had been just waiting to be set free.

The inside of the shed was dark, but the constable stepped up quickly and shone his torch over Logan's shoulder, illuminating everything inside.

There were two bikes propped against one wall, with helmets hooked over the handlebars. The smaller bike was closest to the wall. The tyres looked a bit deflated, and a few cobwebs gave it a general air of abandonment.

The bike leaning against it was larger, and notably cobweb free. The tyres had been fully pumped up, and when Logan asked the constable to direct his torch at the front one, he saw a slick of mud still in the process of drying out.

He'd put good money on it being a match for the track they'd found outside the victim's house.

There wasn't much else of interest in the shed. There was a workbench and various tools. Assorted pieces of gardening equipment leaned against the wall behind an old petrol lawn-mower that made the whole place smell like cut grass.

The bike would need the tyre tread checked, then have to be swabbed and fingerprinted to make sure Armand had been the one riding it. It was hardly a smoking gun, though. They were neighbours. Armand could argue that he was in and out of Isaac's all the time, and he'd probably be telling the truth.

Ordering the constable to secure the door again, Logan took the man's torch and went to the next shed.

The niggling in his subconscious was still there. There was something he'd missed in the house. Something he should've seen.

The bolt on the second shed slid aside more easily. Logan pulled open the door, shone the torch in, then muttered a,

'Fuck!' of surprise at the sight of a woman standing by the back wall, staring at him.

Half a second later, when the blinding light in her eyes failed to make her blink, he realised he was looking at a mannequin.

It had been kitted out in a shoulder-length brown wig and a red dress that came down to around its knees. Its feet were a little too big for the matching red heels, despite someone's best efforts to cram them in.

Logan swept the light around the shed. There were four freestanding racks of women's clothes—everything from jeans and T-shirts to what he guessed was a wedding dress in a pearlescent protective bag.

Several cardboard boxes lined the walls. Logan poked around in one and saw nothing but shoes. The next one along was full of perfume bottles, lipsticks, and trays of coloured makeup.

Another box held vinyl records and CDs. Alanis Morissette. Eva Cassidy. Some miserable looking cow in a beret that had chosen not to put her name on the front of the record sleeve.

He realised what he was looking at. This was where Armand's wife had been relegated to after her death. He hadn't got rid of anything of hers, he'd just shunted it out here to this halfway house between their former shared home and the local dump or charity shops.

Logan felt the lifeless stare of the mannequin and had to fight the urge to pass on his condolences.

'Christ on a bike,' remarked the constable, appearing in the doorway. 'Almost shat myself there. Thought that was a ghost.'

Logan regarded the mannequin, with all its belongings gathered around it. 'I think maybe it is.'

He took another quick look around, but there was no smoking gun here. Hauling himself outside, he returned the constable's torch to him. 'Same again. Secure that, then head back to the scene. Leave the keys in the kitchen. I'll hang onto them.'

'Right you are, sir. You, eh, you sure you're OK, though?'

Logan ignored the question. Ignoring it meant he didn't have to lie. 'Thanks for your help. If there's anything else, I'll shout.'

'Right you are, sir.' The constable spun the keys around on his finger like a cowboy with a six-shooter. 'I'll fire on and lock this one up, then pop the keys on the draining board inside.'

'Aye, fine,' Logan said.

He took a step towards the house, then stopped as the subconscious thought that had been prickling away at him howled in celebration.

Fire on.

Logan rushed in through the damaged door, across the kitchen and the hallway, and back to the living room.

The room had been too hot earlier. Stiflingly so. It had been daytime in May, and while that wouldn't necessarily prevent someone from switching the heating on—it was Scotland, after all—a raging fire was a bit much.

Logan kneeled by the hearth. The wood and coal had mostly turned to grey ash. He found a poker hanging from a brass rack at the side of the fireplace and carefully prodded away at the remains of the fire.

And then, blackened by soot, he saw it.

The thing he'd missed.

The thing that had been nagging at him.

There, in the burned-out remains of the roaring log fire, lay the smoking gun.

Chapter 32

'Let me do the talking,' Sinead said, stepping back from the door of the second-floor flat, her warrant card already out and ready to be flashed.

She'd had the forethought to pick it up before leaving the house, though she hadn't quite known why at the time.

Maybe she'd known it would come to this.

To her surprise, Hoon didn't argue. 'I'll just stand back and look like a scary bastard,' he suggested, folding his arms and arranging his face into an intense lopsided squint that made him look like Popeye having the worst day of his life.

This place was the last one on the list of addresses Shayne Feasey had called. It was also one he was believed to have lived at once, though he didn't appear to have stayed for long. The house was a private rental that sat in The Plantation housing estate above Fort William, an area with a reputation for being rough.

Sinead was familiar with *the Planny* from her time on the beat here, and while it did indeed house its fair share of bams, there were just as many decent folk.

She hoped whoever it was she could hear plodding down the stairs on the other side of the door would turn out to be the latter. All they had to go on was the name on the council tax records—Donna Bruar.

The footsteps reached the door, then there was silence. Sinead held her warrant card up to head height so it could be seen through the peephole, then lowered it again as a lock was undone.

The door opened a few inches, then stopped when two different security chains went tight. The woman who appeared in the gap was in her twenties, with straggly hair, sunken cheeks and a black eye that her cack-handed attempts with concealer had failed to hide.

'Hello. Did you forget something?' she asked, with all the self-assurance and confidence of a mouse pinned beneath the paw of a hungry cat.

'Sorry?' Sinead asked.

'You were just here. Well, not you, obviously. The other police.'

'Right. Yes. Donna, is it?' Sinead asked. When the other woman nodded, she continued. 'I'm Detective Constable Bell. We were hoping to ask you just a couple more questions about—'

'I already told you, I don't know nothing. I can't help. I don't know where he is. And my kid's asleep, so you can't come in.'

'It would be good if we could just chat with you for a few minutes, all the same,' Sinead pressed. 'Maybe there's something you don't realise could be helpful.'

Donna wasn't listening. Instead, she was staring past Sinead to where Hoon stood lurking. 'Hang on! You're him! You're that guy!'

'What guy?' Hoon asked, his eyes narrowing further. 'What the fuck have you heard? Were the bastards who were here talking about me?'

'You were at the Eastgate centre. At Christmas. With the Santas!' Donna said, the pitch of each sentence creeping higher and higher, her face igniting into a big beamer of a smile. 'That was you, wasn't it?'

'Oh. Aye. Aye, that was me, right enough,' Hoon said. His arms uncrossed themselves, then fell to his side. 'You heard about that, then? No' a bad day's work, if I say so myself.'

'Heard about it? I was there. I was shopping for my daughter. It was her first Christmas.' Donna's voice cracked a little. 'You totally saved my life.'

'Oh. Right,' Hoon said. 'Well, in that case, maybe you could let us in for a quick chat, eh?' He winked at her. 'I'll even do you an autograph.'

The door was slammed closed in their faces.

Sinead tutted. 'Oh, nicely done.'

'Hold your fucking horses,' Hoon muttered.

The door was pulled open again. This time, the chains had been unfastened, and it opened all the way to reveal Donna hopping from foot to foot with excitement.

'My mum's not going to believe this!' she cried. She stepped aside and gestured for them both to come in. 'Come on. In you come. Don't mind the mess.'

It was hard not to mind the mess. There was what seemed to be a full set of dirty women's underwear hanging from the bannister at the bottom of the stairs. A kid's clothes and toys were strewn across every step that led up to the living room above.

Most of the houses on this street were laid out in the same split-level style, with the living room and kitchen upstairs, and the bedrooms down at basement level. The front door was situated slap-bang between them, with stairs leading off in each direction from the tiny hallway.

Sinead had been in dozens of them over the years, and yet was always slightly surprised by the layout. She and Hoon followed Donna up into the living room, and were instantly hit by the smell.

Quite what the smell was, they couldn't say. Dirty nappies made an appearance, along with the pungent aroma of overfilled bin bags that should've been chucked out days ago. The odour wafted through from the adjoining kitchen, and though she'd made some attempt to mask it with a plug-in air freshener, the notes of cinnamon it produced only made the whole thing smell even more sickly.

'I couldn't believe it when that guy blew up,' Donna said, grinning at Hoon. 'I mean, God, you don't see that every day, do you?'

Hoon shrugged. 'You'd be surprised.'

'It was crazy, though. I thought we were done for, and then you… God. Wow. I can't believe you're here! I mean, you're famous!'

'Fuck. Don't tell me that,' Hoon muttered.

'It's true. You are. They even did a bit about you on *Loose Women*.'

Hoon's expression became a bitter, hate-filled thing. 'Aye. I fucking bet they did. Cackling pack of bastards that they are.'

Donna thrust her mobile phone into Sinead's hand, then hurried over to stand by Hoon. 'Here, can you do a picture of us?'

Sinead stared numbly at the phone. Then, like she wasn't fully in control of her own body, she took aim with it, and snapped off half a dozen photos of a very excited-looking Donna standing with an arm around the shoulders of a bemused, though not entirely unhappy, Hoon.

'Yes!' Donna cheered, swiping back through her gallery. 'They're going on Insta.'

She started to type out a post there and then, her thumbs continuing to fly across the screen even when Sinead addressed her.

'Donna, we're hoping you can help us. I'm sure the other officers mentioned that we're looking for Shayne Feasey,' the DC said. 'Your ex-boyfriend. We believe he stayed here for a while. It's urgent we find him.'

At the mention of the name, Donna's thumbs froze in place. She tried to smile, and came reasonably close to pulling it off, but nowhere near close enough.

'Like I told the last lot, I haven't… I don't know where he is,' she said. 'I've not seen him in yonks.'

'But you must have some idea of the sort of places he might be?' Sinead urged. 'Please. It's important.'

All Donna's excitement at having Hoon in the house had gone now. The mention of Feasey had stooped her, shrunken her down.

'I don't want him back in my life. I can't,' she said. Her voice was flat and level, but there was a pleading note to it. 'I don't want to get mixed up with him again.'

'Why not?' Sinead asked.

Donna lifted her eyes to meet the detective's. 'Because he's a fucking psycho. That's why.'

She put her phone away, all thoughts of posting on Instagram now forgotten.

'Who gave you the shiner?' Hoon asked.

When she looked blankly back at him, he indicated her black eye.

'Oh. That. That was James.'

'Is James your boyfriend?' Sinead asked.

Donna laughed. 'No! No, I'm young, free and single. Just the way I like it. Believe me. I've had quite enough of men. James is my daughter.'

Hoon bristled. 'What?'

'James,' Donna repeated. 'She's my daughter. She hit me with the TV remote. Properly clocked me one.'

'You sure "daughter" is the word you're fucking aiming for here?' Hoon asked.

'What do you mean?'

'I mean that there's very few fucking people with a daughter named James.'

'Ha! Yeah. It can be a boy or a girl's name,' Donna said.

'I hate to fucking break it to you, sweetheart, but no, it can't,' Hoon replied. 'And whoever told you it could, is a fucking liar.'

'It can! She's named after Lily James. You know, the actress?'

A vein bulged on the side of Hoon's head. 'Then why no' fucking call her Lily, then?'

'Ryan Reynolds' daughter is called James,' Donna added, in a manner that implied this was the big *mic drop* moment of the discussion.

Hoon was quick to counter her point, though. 'Who the fuck's Ryan Reynolds?'

Sinead cleared her throat. 'Sorry, can we…?' She directed a stern look in Hoon's direction, then turned to Donna. 'You described Shayne as "a psycho".'

'He is. Totally.'

'In what way?' Sinead asked, bracing herself for the answer.

'He's just… He's mean. Like, properly mean. Hurt people for fun, kind of mean,' Donna said. 'At least, that's what he always said. When I asked him why he did that stuff. To people. To… me. I asked him why, and he said he did it for fun.'

She sat down on her couch, half her arse on the cushion, half on a copy of a true crime magazine that lay open and abandoned on the seat.

'But I don't think that was true. I don't think it was fun,' she said, frowning through the memories she was being forced to dredge up. 'I don't know if anything's fun for him. I don't know if he even understands what it is. He just… He hurts people because he can. Almost like, *why not*? You know? Like there's no difference to him between hurting someone and not hurting them. Like, it makes no odds.'

Acid bubbled up in Sinead's stomach. She felt an urge to throw up.

'It's vital that we speak to him,' she said, swallowing her nausea back down. 'Do you know where he is?'

'No. Thank God. I haven't seen him in months. And that suits me fine. I'm well shot of him. Fucking lunatic that he is.'

'You don't know where he could be now?' Sinead pressed.

'I heard he left the area. Went back to England. Not far enough for my liking.'

'Aye, well, he's back,' Hoon said, and Donna's eyes instantly became two beacons of raw panic.

'What? When? Oh, God. Oh, God!'

'Does he have any friends or family living locally?' Sinead asked.

'What? Oh. Uh, no. I don't think so. He doesn't have many friends. None, really. No family, neither, far as I know. He was in homes, an' that. Care homes. Orphanages, or whatever. Think that's what sent him a bit...'

She pressed a finger to the side of her head, then twisted it like a screwdriver.

'Though, saying that, I'm sure they're not all mental, are they? Kids like that, I mean, I'm sure they're not all nutters,' Donna reasoned. 'But he is. He's off his bloody head.'

Sinead ran a hand through her hair. She wasn't sure what she'd hoped to find here, but whatever it was, it was more than this.

Still, there were other addresses they could go to. Other known associates they could check out.

But it all took time. And there was no saying how much of that Tyler had left.

'He's got my husband.'

She didn't mean to say the words, but suddenly there they were, hanging in the room between them.

Donna looked confused. 'What? How do you mean?'

'My husband. He's a detective constable. Earlier today, Shayne took him. We don't know where he is.'

'Oh. God.' Donna got to her feet, a shaky hand held over her mouth.

To Sinead's surprise, the woman stepped in closer and threw her arms around her.

To Sinead's even greater surprise, she let her, and found herself sagging into the hug, a prickly heat bringing tears to her eyes.

They stood like that for a while, two strangers, connected only by a man that one of them had never met, and the other wished they'd never encountered.

Until, finally, Donna released her grip and stepped back. She sniffed, wiped a tear away on her sleeve, then set her shoulders back and nodded.

'I, uh, I might have a number,' she said, taking out her phone again. 'But please, God, *please* don't let him know where you got it.'

'We won't,' Hoon said, stepping in while Sinead fought to compose herself again. 'I guarantee that wee fuck won't be coming anywhere near you. Or Jamie.'

'James,' Donna corrected.

Hoon grimaced. '*Jamie*'s a gender-neutral name.'

'So's James.'

'Is it fuck,' Hoon spat, then he tutted as Sinead elbowed him aside before the argument could be settled to his satisfaction.

'Thank you, Donna,' she said, taking out her pad. 'I promise, he'll never know where we got it.'

'Here you go,' Donna said. She held up her phone, showing off a mobile number listed under the name 'DO NOT ANSWER'. 'I just really hope you're not too late.'

Chapter 33

Tyler could hear traffic. Heavy works vehicles, he thought, with big diesel engines. A few hundred yards away through the darkness. Maybe less.

The soles of his feet were being ripped to ribbons by the sharp stones and gravel. Had there been daylight, he'd be easy to track. Feasey would just have to follow the bloody footprints.

But the dark gave him a fighting chance. Hindering his escape though it was, the dark was also his ally. He was a bit like Batman, he thought. Albeit the kind of Batman who shat himself and ran away from danger, rather than confronting it head-on.

A much more sensible Batman, all in all.

Sensible. There was a word that hadn't been used to describe DC Tyler Neish very often. But he wasn't the same man who'd left on paternity leave all those weeks before. He was a parent now. A father. He had to be sensible these days. He had responsibilities.

Despite his fear, as he limped across the gap between the two buildings, head down, he found himself thinking of all the final demands and debt collector letters in his jacket pocket.

He'd hidden it all from Sinead. He'd been ashamed by it.

He'd been a bloody idiot.

If he made it out of this, he'd tell her. They'd deal with it together. She'd understand. She always did.

The engines were growing louder. He was headed in the right direction.

Still running, he looked back over his shoulder, but saw no sign of Feasey in the darkness. There were no shouts, either. He couldn't have noticed that Tyler was gone yet. Even when he did realise, he'd have no idea which way he'd gone.

Tyler snorted out something that was part-laugh, part-sob. He was going to make it. He was going to bloody make it!

He faced front again. A shape moved in the shadows just ahead of him.

There was a glint of metal.

An eruption of pain.

Tyler didn't remember falling. He just found himself sprawled there on the ground, blood filling his mouth, flooding backwards down his throat.

The light from a torch hit him in the face, blinding him, forcing him to screw his eyes tightly closed.

Just before he did, he caught a glimpse of a hand.

Of a gun. A shiny silver revolver, aiming directly at his head.

'I thought I told you,' Feasey said with a cold matter-of-factness that was more chilling than any raised voice could ever be, 'to stay where you fucking were?'

Nidds yawned and pressed a forefinger and thumb into her eyes, massaging them awake. When her vision cleared, Dave was across the desk from her, a printout in his lap, his face a picture of concern.

'You're knackered,' he said. 'You should go and get some kip.'

'I'm fine,' Nidds countered. 'I'll get some more coffee.'

'Nobody's going to mind if—'

'I said I'm fine! Jesus.'

Dave held up his hands in surrender. 'OK, OK. Sorry. Just worried about you.'

'Well, don't be. You don't get to worry about me. That's not your job.'

She turned away from him, directing her attention back to a stack of paperwork she had been sifting through. Dave hesitated for a moment, then sighed and wheeled himself away from her desk, and over to where Hamza was staring, unblinking, at his monitor.

'Is that the shagging video?' the constable asked.

Hamza nodded, his eyes still trained on the screen.

'Well, you can probably stop watching it now,' Dave announced.

He slipped the sheet of paper he was carrying onto Hamza's keyboard. The detective sergeant clicked his mouse, pausing the video footage, then looked down at the page.

'DNA results on the Johnny found in the bedroom. It's a match.'

'Wait, what? For who?'

'For Armand Holburn.' Dave nodded at the computer screen. 'Looks like that confirms it's him on the tape.'

Hamza picked up the page and sat back. He scanned the report quickly, then went through it again more slowly. His brow remained furrowed in confusion the whole time.

'Tammi-Jo?'

DC Swanney looked around from where she was fixing some more notes to the Big Board. 'Sarge?'

'Is DI Forde still through with Holburn?'

'Think so, yeah. Haven't seen him come back in, anyway. Why?'

Hamza looked from the DNA results to his screen. He rocked in his chair for a few seconds, then sat forward.

'I think we better go get him. I'm pretty sure he's going to want to see this.'

Logan strode into the room, already ridding himself of his coat. 'See what?'

'DNA results,' Dave said. 'The condom. It was—'

'Armand Holburn's,' Logan concluded.

'Bingo,' Dave said.

'I found something else, though, sir,' Hamza said.

'Aye, well.' Logan produced an evidence bag containing the charred corner of a piece of paper. 'Lot of that going around at the moment. Any word on Tyler?'

The silence in the room spoke volumes.

'Damn.'

'He'll be OK,' Nidds said, though there was a hint of desperation in it. 'It's Tyler. He's going to be fine. He's always fine.'

'I wish I had your confidence, Constable,' Logan told her. He nodded to Tammi-Jo. 'Go get DI Forde. Call him out of the interview. We'll do a briefing on new developments, then he and I will go back in and get to the bottom of all this.'

He placed the evidence bag on Dave's desk to be checked in, then cracked his knuckles.

'Armand Holburn has been filling us full of shite,' the DCI declared. 'And I'm going to get the truth out of the bastard. Even if I have to reach down his throat and tear it out of him with my bare bloody hands.'

–

Tyler tasted the metallic tang of the metal on his tongue. Felt it grinding between his teeth.

He'd thought about shouting for help, but the revolver had been pressed against the underside of his jaw, and he'd had no choice but to let himself be led back to the low, squat building he'd escaped from just minutes before.

While running away, he'd been able to block out the pain in his feet. Trudging back, every step had been agony, every inch of progress a test of endurance.

Now, he kneeled on the floor, his hands still bound behind him, the barrel of Feasey's gun jammed in his mouth.

'You shouldn't have done that,' Feasey told him, in that same unsettlingly reasonable tone as before. 'I told you I might let you go. All you had to do was behave yourself. That was it.

Play along. Do as you're told. Keep your head down, and we could've got on like a house on fire.'

He tilted his head, gazing down at Tyler like a kindly primary school teacher. Not angry, just *disappointed*.

'Funny phrase that, isn't it? *Getting along like a house on fire.* You ever seen a house on fire?' Feasey asked. He sniffed. 'I have. Long time ago. Not exactly a barrel of laughs.'

Something painful manipulated the otherwise slack lines of his face, then was gone again before it had a chance to take root.

'Sorry, getting sidetracked there. Don't know what put that in my head,' he said.

The apology sounded sincere. Tyler might even have swallowed it, had his mouth not been full of gun.

'The point is, I don't actually need you for anything. Never have. You came looking for me. I could've just run, but I had a bit of time to kill, and I get bored easily. ADHD, probably. Never been diagnosed, but I've read a bit. Watched some TikTok videos. Describes me to a tee. Impulse control. That's always been my problem. I've always been sort of spontaneous. Never been much of a planner.'

He shrugged. The gun rattled against Tyler's teeth, straining the muscles of his jaw.

'Well, not until this, anyway. I had this all planned out. For months. Years, actually,' Feasey shook his head. 'No. Not years. I've been dreaming about it for years. Fantasising about it. But I only started planning it properly a few months ago.'

Tyler wanted to ask him about the plan. Not so he could stop it, necessarily—that felt like a bit of a stretch right now—but the longer he could keep Feasey talking, the better his chances were of getting out of this alive.

'But you? Taking you, I mean. Tying you up. Sticking this gun in your mouth. That's the old me doing that. That's the *spontaneous* me. I see something, I have an idea, and I just do it.' He laughed. 'Or sometimes I don't! Because, if I always do whatever shit pops into my head, that's not spontaneous, is it?

262

That's predictable. That's why I had no idea if I was going to kill you or not. Genuinely. I mean that. I might've let you go.'

He kneeled and yanked the gun out, drawing a yelp of pain from Tyler. A fine mist of blood sprayed in Feasey's face, but he didn't seem to take notice.

'Now, though, I have to kill you. I told you to do something, you didn't do it. Consequences. That's what all this has been about from the start. People facing the consequences of their actions.'

'What about you, Shayne?' Tyler asked, his voice barely a croak through the raw meat of his mouth. 'What about your consequences? Or does it not apply to you?'

Feasey grinned at him. It was a demented, rubbery thing that showed too many of his teeth.

'Oh, it applies. To them. To you. And to me, too.'

He pressed the gun against the side of his head, gazed deep into Tyler's eyes, then shouted, '*BANG!*'

Despite the suddenness of the shout, and the volume of it right in his face, Tyler didn't flinch. There wasn't enough left of him to be frightened now. Not by something like that, at least.

'Once it's done, I'll do the decent thing,' Feasey said. 'I'll blow my fucking brains out.'

He stood up.

'But you first,' he said.

The gun was pressed against the detective constable's fore-head.

'No, wait!' Tyler cried. 'Don't, don't!'

A single gunshot rang out.

And the world was filled with smoke, and fire, and noise.

Chapter 34

Donald Sinclair, Armand Holburn's solicitor, had just made the mistake of interrupting.

Logan had been in full flow at the time, stressing to the suspect that time was of the essence, and that any attempts by either Holburn or his lawyer to 'piss them about' would not end well for anyone.

This was the point when Holburn's lawyer had chosen to try and piss them about.

'I want my client released, on the understanding that we reconvene back here tomorrow morning at a time of his choosing.'

'No,' Logan said, barely so much as glancing in the solicitor's direction.

'I'm sure I don't need to remind you that Mr Holburn isn't actually under arrest? He's here of his own free will, so he's equally free to leave whenever he likes.'

'Fuck it, then. He's under arrest,' Logan replied. 'DI Forde?'

Logan sat back with his arms folded while Ben read Holburn his rights and made the arrest on suspicion of the murder of Sharon Simpson official.

Sinclair ejected a few half-hearted protests during it, but the sheer force of the DCI's glare kept him from objecting too much.

'You've got this clown to thank for that, Armand,' Logan said once Ben had finished. 'See what happens when you let these guys talk for you? Never ends well. He doesn't care, he gets to go back home to his family. He's not the one with his balls in a vice, and a very uncertain future ahead of him.'

He uncrossed his arms, tapped his fingers on the table, and sat forward, his mouth contorting into the sort of smile that sharks wore, right before they made a hearty snack out of one or more of your limbs.

'So, if it was me—if I was in your shoes—I'd be worrying less about what he's telling me to say, and concerning myself more with telling the truth.'

He continued to stare at the man across the table for a few moments, really trying to hammer that point home. Then, he sat back again and gave Ben a nod.

'Mr Holburn,' Ben said, picking up the printout he'd been given by Dave. 'Armand. This document does not do you any favours. That's the first thing I'm going to say.'

Armand's eyes flitted down to the paper, but it was angled in such a way that he couldn't read what it said.

'I'd say, in fact, that it puts you in a very difficult position, indeed,' Ben continued. 'See, at the scene of Mrs Simpson's murder, someone left a condom. A used condom.'

There was very little reaction from Holburn. 'And?'

'And it contained your DNA,' Ben continued.

'A full two bollock loads of it,' Logan added.

'What? Bullshit. No way. No, that's not possible! That's not possible. I didn't… I wasn't…' Armand turned sharply to his solicitor. 'Someone's stitched me up. Someone fucking…'

He suddenly sat up straight, clicking his fingers and pointing at Logan.

'That woman.'

'What woman?'

'The other night. A few days ago. Um… Thursday. I went out for a drink. She came up and said hello. Younger. Much younger than me. I thought it was odd she was interested in someone my age, but she was. She came back to my place. We… you know.'

He ran his hands down his face, the truth of that encounter hitting him.

'She must've taken it. The condom. She must've...' He clicked his fingers again, his brow furrowing. 'Anne. Annie! That was her name. Annie something.'

'Seems awfully convenient,' Ben said. 'Don't you think, Detective Chief Inspector?'

'Very convenient,' Logan agreed. 'I think you're lying, Armand. I think that condom was left in Sharon's bedroom because you ran out of there in a hurry.'

'That's not true! I didn't do anything to Shazz. I didn't touch her, let alone shag her, for Christ's sake!'

'But you were there, though?' Logan said. 'You're admitting that much?'

'No! I didn't... That's not what I said.'

'Mr Holburn didn't mention being at the scene,' Sinclair chipped in.

'But you were. Weren't you, Armand?' Logan drummed his fingers on a folder sitting before him on the desk. 'You were there. That's how you got your hands on that note.'

Holburn scoffed at the suggestion. 'I thought I'd made it clear, I'd never seen that note. If I'd wanted to hide it, I wouldn't have stuck it in my bloody bin!'

'You'd have destroyed it,' Ben said.

'Exactly!'

Logan opened the folder. There, in an evidence bag, was a charred corner of a sheet of notepaper bearing part of the logo of the Ambassador Hotel. Most of the page had been consumed by the flames, but a few letters were visible on the left.

'There's not much of it, but it's a match for the imprint we took from the pad in the bedroom,' Logan said. 'This page was taken from the wall above Sharon and Isaac's bed. By you, Mr Holburn. You rode over there on your bike, didn't you? You rode over there, you had sex with her, and then you killed her.'

'No! That's not... I didn't kill her!'

'Here, look, we're not saying it was deliberate,' Ben told him. 'Accidents happen. Things got a bit… vigorous. She couldn't breathe. You didn't realise until it was too late.'

'What?' Holburn recoiled, the legs of his chair scraping on the floor. 'No! That's not… That didn't…'

'I disagree. I reckon you did it on purpose,' Logan said. 'I think maybe she was going to tell Isaac about you. About what you two had been getting up to together.'

He sat forward, interlocking his fingers, eyeballing Armand in a way that dared him to disagree.

'Or maybe she was going to grass on the pair of you,' he said. 'Maybe she'd found out what the two of you and your pal Norman did to that lassie in Bosnia.'

For a moment, it looked like Holburn was going to cry. His mouth tried out a variety of shapes as it searched for a response. When it finally settled on one, there was very little conviction behind it.

'I don't know what you're talking about.'

'I'm afraid Isaac's told us everything, Mr Holburn,' Ben revealed. 'About the attack. The three of you. How you took it in turns to rape that poor woman.'

The length of Armand's pause told them everything. Isaac may have denied the accusation, but his partner in crime had more or less just confirmed it.

'He's lying,' Holburn croaked. 'He's full of shit.'

'What is this? This is the first I've heard of any of this,' the solicitor said. He looked between his client and the detectives, his head tick-tocking left and right. 'What's the claim?'

'The *claim*, Mr Sinclair, is that while serving with the British Army in Bosnia, Mr Holburn here, along with Mr Simpson and the late Mr…' Logan hesitated. Ben picked up on it right away.

'Todd.'

'…sexually assaulted a civilian while, unbeknownst to them, her young son was hiding under the bed, too terrified to make a sound. Isn't that right, Armand?'

'No. No, that's not… It didn't happen like that. I didn't do those things. I didn't do that, and I didn't kill Sharon!'

'Cut the shite! You killed her, Armand!' Logan shot back.

'No!'

'You went round there on your bike, you had sex with her, and you murdered her!'

'That's not true!'

'You smothered her. You forced her head into the covers so she couldn't breathe! You pushed so hard you broke her neck!'

Armand's response was shrill and piercing. He jumped up, knocking his chair over. 'She was already dead when I got there!'

Silence fell. Quite a smug, self-satisfied sort of silence at that.

A look of dread rose like the dawn across Armand's face, as he realised what he'd just said. He tried to distract from it with a babbled, 'I didn't kill her!' but the damage had already been done.

'Sit down, Mr Holburn,' Logan intoned.

Holburn slowly stooped and picked up his chair. 'I didn't kill Sharon,' he said again, as he returned it to its position by the table.

'Oh, we know you didn't,' Logan told him.

Armand gawped at him in surprise. 'What? Then why…?'

'I told you to sit down,' Logan reminded him.

He waited until Armand had lowered himself onto his chair before continuing.

'There was a video sent to Sharon's son, Struan.'

'Of a sexual nature,' Ben added.

Armand blinked. 'Sharon?'

Logan nodded. 'Someone was wearing clothes not dissimilar to yours. Between that and the used condom at the scene, it very much looked like you were the one in the footage. Clearly, that's what we were meant to think, but luckily, we have a secret weapon they didn't know about.'

The solicitor frowned. 'Secret weapon?'

'Detective Sergeant Khaled,' Ben said. 'Knows a lot about computers. Video editing. All that stuff. He went through the footage one *whatchamacallit* at a time.'

'Frame,' Logan said.

'One frame at a time,' Ben confirmed. 'And there's a glimpse—blink and you'll miss it—of a man significantly younger than you, Armand. Bigger ears, too. Much bigger.'

'Shayne Feasey,' added Logan.

'The man who's been harassing you,' Ben clarified.

'The boy hiding under that bed.'

Holburn's pallor had taken on ghostly levels of whiteness. There was a good chance that none of this was new to him—if Isaac knew who Feasey was, then almost certainly Armand did, too. But no doubt, with the dredging up of his past deeds, he could sense a net closing around him.

'I can't say I fully understand his endgame,' Logan began. 'But it seems to me that Shayne Feasey is fully committed to getting revenge on you three. Well, you two now, I suppose. And one of my officers is trapped in the middle of it.

'It's you he wants, though, Armand. And make no mistake, if it comes down to a choice between saving you and saving DC Neish, I know who I'm choosing. And, in case that's not clear enough, it isn't you.'

The solicitor interjected. 'You have a duty to protect him.'

'I have a duty to a lot of people,' Logan replied. 'So, Armand, let's rattle through this, so we're all on the same page. Last night, you cycled over to Sharon and Isaac's house. Why?'

Holburn was looking down at the table now, unable to make eye contact with either of the detectives. He crossed his arms and shifted his weight around, looking for all the world like a petulant child.

Just when Logan and Ben thought he wasn't going to respond, he surprised them.

'She texted me. Photo message. She was... semi-undressed,' Armand revealed, speaking slowly, like he was being very careful with his word choice. 'She said she wanted me. You know'—his eyes raised, just for a moment—'sexually. We've always been a bit flirty, Shazz and I. Nothing's ever happened. I mean, I've thought about it. We've made a few drunken jokes, but I never thought it would come to anything.'

'So, you get the text saying what? Inviting you over?' Ben asked.

Armand nodded. 'Yes.'

'What time?' Logan asked.

'Late. Midnight, maybe? I deleted the message after... everything.'

He took a deep breath. Rather than lighten his load, the confession seemed to be weighing him down, sinking him into the chair.

'I took the bike. There's no lights on the road, so walking at that time's not ideal. There are lights on the bike, though. I went over. The door was unlocked. I went in. Shouted. She didn't answer. I mean, obviously, she didn't answer.'

'Then what?' Ben prompted.

'I went upstairs. Thought maybe she was waiting for me.' Armand swallowed twice, like he was trying to force down the memory. 'And I suppose she was, in a way. I could tell she was dead straight away. Her eyes. They were open. She was just... she was staring. Just staring at nothing.'

'What about the note?' Logan asked. '"*I know what you did.*" That must've freaked you out, after all the phone calls and harassment. You must've known who did it. You must've known *why* he did it, too.'

'I just... I panicked,' Armand admitted. 'I didn't know what to do.'

'So you took it,' Logan said. 'You took it, and you burned it.'

Armand said nothing, but his expression said everything.

'Please answer out loud for the tape, Mr Holburn,' Ben said.

The response, when it came, was practically a sob. 'Yes. I took it, and I burned it. And I didn't tell anyone. About Shazz. About what had happened to her. I should've, but I couldn't. I just couldn't.'

'And the note in your bin?' Ben asked. 'Where does that fit in?'

'I don't know. I've never seen it before,' Armand said. 'I don't know who put it there.'

Before either detective could drill any deeper, there was a knock at the door. It opened almost immediately, and Hamza poked his head around the frame.

'Uh, sir. Urgent one.'

Logan was already on his feet before he started talking. 'Interview paused at'—he checked his watch—'eleven thirty-six p.m. DCI Logan and DI Forde leaving the interview room.'

With a promise to Armand that they'd be back soon, Logan and Ben joined Hamza in the corridor.

'What have we got?' the DCI asked.

'Sinead's been on the phone, sir,' Hamza told him. 'We've got a possible number for Shayne Feasey.'

Hope fluttered in Logan's chest. The force of it made his broken ribs ache.

'Mobile?'

Hamza nodded. 'CID and the network are running it now. Looks like it's switched on.'

'Christ!' Logan ejected. He set off marching along the corridor, Armand Holburn instantly forgotten. 'Can they get a location?'

Hamza and Ben hurried to keep up with the DCI's enormous strides. 'Won't be too precise out here, given how spaced out the base units are, but should give us a starting point,' the DS said.

'Better than nothing. In the meantime, I want a list of all incoming and outgoing calls.'

Logan barged through a set of double doors, throwing them open with such force that the handles left circular imprints on the plasterboard where they hit the wall.

'If that bastard's been talking to someone, then I want to know who!'

Chapter 35

Smoke curled lazily from the barrel of Feasey's revolver. He stared down at the motionless figure of Tyler on the floor, his chest rising and falling like he was barely containing his excitement.

'Get up,' he instructed.

Tyler shifted on the cold concrete, one hand clamped over his ear. Feasey had aimed wide at the last moment, swinging the gun to the side of the detective's head before pulling the trigger.

He'd watched with a detached sort of amusement as Tyler had writhed on the ground, screaming in pain. He'd watched as the screams became pitiful groans. He'd watched as the detective constable had fallen silent and still, his eyes trained on the gun that Feasey continued to hold pointed at him.

'I'm not going to tell you again,' Feasey said. 'Get. Up.'

Glaring defiantly at the bastard, Tyler struggled up onto his knees.

'That's far enough.'

Without a word, Tyler planted first one foot, then the other. With a grunt, he stood upright.

Feasey let out a throaty little laugh, then drove the butt of the pistol into the top of Tyler's shoulder, buckling him back down onto his knees.

'Stay down,' he instructed.

Tyler did.

But not for long.

'What the fuck are you trying to prove?' Feasey asked, his brow furrowing as Tyler hauled himself back up onto his feet.

'If you're going to kill me,' Tyler wheezed. 'Just kill me.'

'Fucking hell. Melodramatic, or what?' Feasey shrugged. 'Fine. I was getting bored, anyway.'

He drew back the hammer of the pistol.

'Wait,' Tyler said.

Feasey sighed. He stared expectantly at the DC for a few moments, then waved the gun. 'Well, hurry up, then.'

Tyler's bottom jaw shook, like he was standing firm against the urge to break down in tears. He drew in a breath before he spoke again.

'Can I ask a favour?'

This caught Feasey off guard. He used the muzzle of the gun to push out one of his already huge ears. 'Come again,' he said in disbelief. 'A favour? What the fuck are you talking about, *a favour*?'

Tyler didn't flinch. Didn't back down. 'If you're going to kill me. There's something I want you to do for me first...'

—

They'd all gathered in front of the big screen in the briefing room—Logan's whole team, including Sinead and Hoon, and some of the boys from CID. Only Dave and Nidds had remained back in the Incident Room, chasing up the rest of the phone records for Shayne Feasey.

Even Mantits had stuck around. He took the floor, enjoying his few minutes in the sun.

'Network reckons he's got to be somewhere in this area,' the chief inspector announced, indicating a fairly substantial portion of the on-screen map. It took in both local retail parks, a factory, an old castle and even the police station itself.

Not to mention around half of Fort William town centre, and the hundreds of houses in between.

'That's about twenty fucking square miles,' Hoon piped up. 'Is that the best we can fucking do?'

'It's not an exact science,' Mantits ventured, though he bowed his head in deference to the former detective chief superintendent. Or, more likely, in fear of him. 'But it tells us that he's still in the area, at least.'

'Or that his phone is,' Sinead said.

'Get all resources redirected to that circle,' Logan instructed. 'Start at the centre, and work outwards.'

It was the obvious next step. The only one he could think of.

But Hoon was right, he knew. There had to be three or four hundred houses within the area the network had given them, and Feasey and Tyler could be in any one of them. Going door to door would take too long.

'I want the chopper out there with IR cameras. And boots on the ground. Get the dogs there, too.'

'It's a big patch, Jack,' Ben cautioned.

'It's a fucking huge patch,' Hoon spat. 'Are you sure we can't zoom the fucking thing in?'

'Jesus, Bob. How long did you do this bloody job?' Logan spat. 'I know it's a big area. But this is how we find him. All right? This is all we can do.'

Hoon squared up to him like he was challenging the DCI to a fight. On paper, Logan, with his longer reach and definitive size advantage, was the obvious favourite. But Hoon fought hard and fought dirty, so it could go either way.

Throw in the fact that Logan had recently had the living shit kicked out of him by a man half his size, and Hoon looked likely to come out on top.

'Well, I'm no' fucking sitting here twiddling my bollocks, waiting for something else to happen,' the former detective superintendent declared. 'I'm going out there and hunting for the hopeless wee bag of shite.'

Logan glowered down at him. Both men clenched their fists. Ben stepped forward, getting ready to intervene, then stopped when the DCI nodded.

'Aye,' he said.

The well-worn scowl lines on Hoon's brow deepened. 'What?'

'Good plan. Let's get out there and find him.' He turned away from Hoon and met Sinead's eye. 'Let's get out there and bring our boy home.'

'Now you're fucking talking!' Hoon boomed.

'You'll never find him,' Chief Inspector Lyle said. 'It's too big an area. You'll never find him.'

'Here, Mantits!' Hoon barked.

The chief inspector recoiled, shocked to hear his nickname being spoken to his face. He turned to find Logan and Hoon standing side by side, glaring back at him.

'Going to shut the fuck up?' Logan said. 'The more of us are out there, the quicker we can narrow it down.'

He turned to the other officers—not just his own, but the CID boys, too.

'We all OK with this plan?'

'Hundred per cent, sir,' Hamza confirmed.

'Totally. Didn't even need to ask,' Tammi-Jo said. 'Well, I mean, obviously you had to—'

'Shite Tornado!' Hoon barked. 'Button it.'

Logan pointed to him. 'You—don't talk to one of my officers like that,' he warned. 'The rest of you, pick a street. We work in pairs. Stay together. Ben'll stay here and coordinate with Uniform.'

'My arse I will,' Ben said. 'I'm coming. Mantits... I mean, the chief inspector can do that. You said it yourself, Jack, If we're going to find him, we need all the help we can get. Even a doddery old bastard like me.'

The sound of a throat being cleared cut short any protestations from the DCI. He and Ben both turned to see Moira

Corson approaching, a torn notebook page in her hand. She walked with her head held high, striding towards Logan while ignoring Ben completely.

'Detective Chief Inspector,' she said. She stopped directly in front of him, and though Ben was right next to her, she didn't so much as glance his way. 'Just saw this. Thought it might be relevant.'

She thrust the page out to him. Logan, like everyone else in the room, had picked up on the tension between Moira and Ben.

Now wasn't the time to worry about it, though.

In fact, he thought, he'd almost certainly *never* get around to worrying about it.

Instead, he took the page and scanned the handwritten note on it.

'A gunshot?' he said, his head snapping up so he was staring directly into the old dragon's eyes.

'Or something like one, yes.'

'When did this come in?'

'Just a few minutes ago. 101 call. They reckoned it came from out the back.'

Logan practically threw the note at Sinead. 'You know the area. Where is this?'

Sinead's eyes widened as she read, then she turned to the screen and pointed to a row of semi-detached houses that backed onto a railway line, and not a whole lot of anything else.

'It's there. Right there.'

'Couldn't be a car backfiring,' Logan reasoned. 'No roads out there.'

'Trains wouldn't be running this time of night, either,' Hamza said.

Sinead pointed to a cluster of buildings on the map. 'The BA. It's an aluminium factory.'

Mantits rolled his eyes. 'It's not called that any more, actually. British Alcan no longer owns it. It's actually Rio Tinto, I believe who—'

'Who gives a flying fuck?' Hoon barked.

'He used to work there.'

All eyes went to Moira again. She looked around at everyone, but skipped right over Ben.

'Your man. Shayne Feasey,' she explained. 'He did a wee spell there a few months back. They let him go after his trial period. Attitude problem.'

'How do you know that?' Ben asked.

'I phoned them,' Moira said. She didn't look at the DI, and it wasn't clear if she was answering the question or just making a coincidentally related statement.

Logan looked the woman up and down, like he was suddenly seeing her in a whole new light. 'Moira, I could bloody kiss you!'

'Please do,' Moira retorted. 'Then I can have you done for sexual harassment. And I'll have your bollocks off, while I'm at it.'

'Oh, I fucking like this one!' Hoon announced.

Logan stabbed a finger at Mantits. 'I want the helicopter over that factory. Get every unit in the area there now. They don't move in until we get there.'

'We're half a fucking mile away,' Hoon pointed out. 'Quit spouting shite and we'll be there in three fucking minutes.'

'OK, then,' Logan said. He pulled on his coat on his way to the door, and the others—even Hoon—fell into step behind him. 'Then what the hell are we standing around here for?'

–

'I want to see them,' Tyler said.

Feasey glanced around, like he was expecting to find someone else standing there.

'See who?'

278

Tyler steeled himself. He was in a fair amount of pain, but nothing could possibly hurt him worse than the next part.

'My kids,' he said, and he almost choked on the words. 'I want to see my kids.'

His captor shrugged. 'Fine.'

Tyler's eyebrows shot upwards in surprise. He hadn't expected Feasey to agree quite that easily. He'd had a whole spiel worked out to try and convince him.

'What?' he heard himself asking, his shock getting the better of him. 'I mean… great. Thank you.'

'Just tell me where they are, and I'll go pick them up,' Feasey said. His smile crept higher as Tyler's heart sank. 'They can watch you die.'

'No. No, I didn't… I just meant… Their photo. I want to see their photo.'

'Aw, I bet you do, mate. I bet you do,' Feasey said, all mock concern and crocodile tears. 'But even if I wanted to help you out—which I don't—where the fuck am I meant to conjure that up from?'

Tyler glanced very deliberately at the rectangular bulge in Feasey's left pocket. Shayne had taken his own phone from his right pocket, and since Tyler didn't have his on him, he was guessing Feasey had taken it.

'Please.'

Shayne rocked his weight back onto his heels, then waved at Tyler with the gun. 'You're smarter than you look. I mean, that's not exactly saying much, but I'm almost impressed. Well spotted.' He shook his head. 'But no can do.'

'Please,' Tyler begged. 'Just… I just want to see them. Just once. Just for a minute.'

Feasey snorted out a laugh, but said nothing. He tapped the gun against the side of his leg and tilted his head from side to side, like some tiny part of him was wrestling with the rest.

Kids. There was something about kids, Tyler thought. Some instinct to protect them, maybe.

Logan would use that.

Maybe he could, too.

'Please. You're taking their dad from them.'

'Dads are overrated,' Feasey shot back.

'You're going to hurt them. You're going to ruin their lives.'

'Fucking hell. High opinion of yourself, eh? And, maybe you haven't noticed, but I don't actually give a shit.'

'I think you do. I think someone did something to you, Shayne,' Tyler said. 'Someone made you like this.'

The gun began to tap more quickly against Feasey's leg. His head was rolling around on his shoulders now, like a boxer limbering up for a fight.

'Shut up. You don't know anything about me, all right?' His voice rose in volume, becoming a roar. He lunged at Tyler, jamming the gun against his forehead and screaming into his face. 'You don't know anything about me!'

'OK, OK. Sorry. You're right. You're right, I don't,' Tyler admitted. He took a steadying breath. 'But I know you're going to shoot me.'

'No points for that one. I think I've made that pretty fucking clear,' Feasey said.

'You have. You have. Just, *please*, let me see my babies first. Just let me see them. Just for a second, Shayne. That's all. Please.'

Feasey's eyes darted left, right, up, down, searching the DC's face. The cold metal of the gun continued to press against Tyler's forehead, imprinting a little red circle into his skin.

Then, so slowly as to almost go unnoticed, Shayne's hand slid towards the front left pocket of his jeans.

Chapter 36

Despite the station's proximity to the aluminium factory, the road leading up to it was an impressive light show by the time the detectives' cars arrived. Although, it would've been even more spectacular had the lights not all been blue.

Overhead, a helicopter hung in the dark night sky, its spotlight sweeping the grounds around the main factory building.

A set of train tracks ran across the road, though there were no gates to block traffic, just a set of lights that would presumably flash if anything was due to come trundling past.

As Logan's car reached the tracks, Hoon piped up from the back seat.

'What's down that way?'

Sinead, sitting up front, turned to her left. A metal gate blocked a side road, and there were no signs to indicate what lay beyond it. She knew the route well, though. She used to run it back in the day, while training for her police fitness test. On a good day, she'd run all the way to the car park at the north-face side of Ben Nevis. Once, she'd even gone beyond that, all the way up to the restaurant at the Aonach Mor Ski Resort, where she'd promptly collapsed into a thoroughly delicious chocolate brownie.

Beyond that, a few miles further on, lay the route through Leanachan Forest where, years later, she had first met DCI Logan.

'It's just a track. Goes on for miles,' she said.

'Any buildings?' Hoon asked.

Sinead thought. She'd usually run past with her head down and earphones in. She couldn't remember any buildings, but nor could she rule them out. There was a dim recollection of some ruined old shack, but that had been years ago, and it was unlikely to still be standing.

'Don't think so. Not sure,' she said. 'Maybe.'

The car *thu-thunked* across the railway tracks, and the gate was lost once again to the darkness.

Up ahead, Ben, Hamza and Tammi-Jo had already parked up. Ben was the first one out of the car, and Logan could see him taking charge of the army of assembled Uniforms.

From the corner of his badly swollen left eye, Logan clocked the expression of terror on Sinead's face. This was it, he knew. This was their one chance at getting Tyler back.

'He's going to be OK. We're going to get him,' the DCI told her. 'Everything's going to be all right.'

—

Tears rolled down Tyler's cheeks, carving narrow trenches through the dirt and dried blood. Feasey hadn't given him a choice of photos and had just brought up the first one he'd come across.

Tyler didn't care. Any photo of them would've done.

This one showed Sinead propped up in the bed in hospital, holding both twins, one in each arm. She looked exhausted—the birth hadn't exactly gone as planned, and the bedside manner of the makeshift midwife had left a lot to be desired.

But she had looked more beautiful than Tyler had ever seen her look before. And now, months later, captured as a picture on his phone screen, he still felt the same.

The twins were swaddled in crisp white blankets that made them look like marshmallows. They were both asleep—they actually slept back then—and looked completely at peace.

The moment hadn't lasted long. Tyler had accidentally sat on one of the 'Congratulations' balloons that DI Forde had brought in, and the subsequent explosion had woken them both up screaming.

In that photo, though, it was a perfect moment that would last forever. Long after he'd gone.

Tyler, too, felt at peace. Seeing them, just knowing they existed in the world, had that effect on him. His wife. His children. His wee family. The three things he loved most in the world, presented there before him.

'Thanks,' he whispered, and he meant it.

'This your missus? She's pretty tidy,' Feasey said, turning the phone away from Tyler so he could study the screen. He pinch-zoomed in, and then raised his eyebrows suggestively. 'Maybe I'll pay her a wee visit after you've gone.'

Tyler's gaze shifted from the phone to the man holding it. His sense of tranquillity was swept aside by a rising swell of rage.

'Don't you fucking dare. You stay away from her!'

Feasey let the phone fall to his side, then stepped in closer so he was nose to nose with the detective constable.

'Or what, mate? Eh? Or what? What the fuck are you going to do? How are you going to—'

Tyler's forehead connected with the bridge of the bastard's nose. Feasey roared, stumbling backwards, clutching at his face too late to stop the gush of blood cascading down over his mouth and chin.

'That,' Tyler told him. 'That's what I'm going to do.'

Tyler's phone landed on the floor, the screen cracking as it hit the concrete.

'Oh, now you've fucking done it,' Feasey seethed, hacking up blobs of dark blood and snot. 'Now you've fucking done it! I was going to kill you quickly, but not now. Not now. Fuck that! Now, I make it slow! Now, I make you suffer!'

He unfastened his belt, veins bulging at his temples as he wrapped the leather around and around his clenched fist.

'And then, I'm going to make your bird suffer, too.' He spat a big wad of blood out onto the floor. 'And them little fucking brats of yours, too.'

Mantits sat alone in the briefing room, fully engrossed in his mobile phone. He tapped at the screen, studied the results, then repeated the action a second time.

The trick, apparently, was to try and clear away all the blue diamonds first. Those were worth the most points. Clear all them, and you were over halfway to the score required to unlock the next level.

Annoyingly, he was out of the wee bomb things that would make clearing the blue diamonds that much easier. With the wee bomb things, he'd be able to make quick work of the next few stages.

He could buy a pack, of course. It was only a couple of quid. But he was already a few hundred in the hole on this game, and was secretly starting to suspect that he might have some sort of problem.

What was he even trying to achieve? He'd flown past level one hundred in a matter of days, and was now closing in on double that. Did it ever end? Was there an actual purpose to be achieved? Or was it just an infinite futile quest to get further and further without ever actually getting anywhere at all?

It didn't really matter, of course. Either way, it was bloody addictive.

Bu-bleep.

Mantits frowned at the screen. That was a new noise. He'd never heard the game make that one before.

Plenty of *patwings* and *cha-chings*, and the occasional fanfare of triumph whenever he bought anything.

But *bu-bleep*?

No, that was a new one.

He was tapping around the various icons, trying to figure out where the sound had come from, when it came again.

It wasn't coming from his phone, he realised.

It was coming from the big screen that currently showed the network data and estimated location for Shayne Feasey's phone.

A second circle had appeared. It more or less overlapped with the first, so it took him a moment to notice it, but when he did, he checked the information readout on the bottom right of the screen.

There were two numbers there now. Both active. Both connected to the network.

'Fuck!' Mantits yelped.

He swiped away his game, opened up his contacts, and frantically began to scroll.

-

Logan's phone rang while they were still driving down the hill towards the factory and the sea of flashing blue lights. The name 'Praying Mantits' appeared on his dashboard, and Sinead pressed the button to answer before Logan could even react.

'What have you got?' she demanded, with enough authority to immediately put the chief inspector on the back foot.

'Uh, Jack?'

'I'm here, Alisdair. What is it?'

'His phone,' Mantits said. 'DC Neish. His phone.'

'What about it?' Sinead asked.

'It's on. It's been turned on.'

Logan hit the brakes. Hoon ejected a, 'Fuck's sake!' as he was slammed against the back of the passenger seat.

Chief Inspector Lyle continued to talk, but Sinead was already pulling out her mobile, calling up the *Find My Phone* app, and tapping furiously on Tyler's photo, trying to force it to refresh. It used the same technology as the tag Shona had put on Taggart's collar. If active, it should give them an accurate reading of where Tyler was.

'It's more or less the same region as the suspect's,' Mantits said. 'So I'm not sure how useful it's going to be, but I thought it was worth—'

Logan jabbed the icon that ended the call and turned to Sinead. 'Anything?'

'No. No, it's not connecting! It's not…' She let out a gasp as the map of the Fort William area suddenly zoomed in on the little round icon that represented her husband. 'Got him! I've got him! Back up, back up!'

Logan slammed the BMW into reverse. The tyres screeched, billowing smoke, as the car skidded a full one-eighty in the road.

'Bit of fucking warning would be nice!' Hoon hollered from the back, as his head clunked against the side window.

'Across the tracks, then take a right. He's past the gate,' Sinead instructed.

'Oh, so just where I fucking asked about, then!' Hoon said. 'But did you listen? Did you fuck!'

'Shut up!' Logan and Sinead both shouted, their voices almost harmonising.

Ahead of them, the lights signalling an approaching train began to flash. There were no passenger trains at this time of night, but this stretch of track was used almost exclusively by the factory. Through the trees on the left, Logan caught a glimpse of an old diesel picking up speed as it raced towards the junction.

'Hold on,' he warned, jamming his foot to the floor. The BMW shot forwards, throwing them all back into their seats. Logan gripped the wheel. Sinead held the handle above the side window.

Even Hoon, sitting in the back, quietly clipped on his seat-belt.

The car powered up the incline. The suspension thudded as the wheels hit the tracks. Light flooded the cabin. A horn screamed at them. Two different diesel engines roared.

And then, with a sudden violent twist of the steering wheel, Logan careened the car onto the side road and ploughed straight into the metal gate just as the train went thundering by behind them.

He killed the engine and the lights. Sinead and Hoon leaped out of the car. Logan took a second to rattle off a text to Ben, updating him and calling for reinforcements, then he joined the other two outside.

They all left their doors open. The passing train might just have masked the sound of the impact with the fence, but it was a distant rumble now, and there was no way it would disguise the sound of three car doors closing.

'Where?' Hoon mouthed.

Sinead checked her phone, then pointed ahead along the track. 'Thirty yards. Maybe less,' she whispered.

They should wait for backup, Logan knew. There was strength in numbers. But Feasey may well be within earshot, so he daren't phone, and Ben was yet to read the message the DCI had sent.

Besides, Hoon had already vaulted the gate, and was sneaking along the single-track road, sticking to the trees so as not to suddenly find himself silhouetted by the headlights of traffic passing on the factory road.

Sinead was also in the process of clambering over it. There'd be no calling either of them back now.

And there was no way he was letting them go alone.

'Fuck it,' Logan muttered. He approached the gate, swung one leg straight over the top of it, then the other, and hurried onwards into the dark.

Chapter 37

There was a light. A faint one, just visible through a crack at the bottom of a boarded-up window.

But a light, all the same.

Hoon had already done a search for exits and entrances, and then performed a complicated hand gesture that either suggested there was only the one he was now standing in front of, or that whoever was on the other side of it was a wanker.

It was also possible that he was insinuating both those things.

Cupping his hand over his phone screen to block the glow, Logan checked his text messages again. The one to Ben was still showing as having been delivered, but not yet read.

Shite.

Sinead was tucked in low against the side of the derelict building, staring up at the DCI like she was waiting for him to give the order.

Hoon, however, wasn't hanging about to be told what to do. He flew at the door, a boot raising, and drove a kick into the old wood. The whole thing disappeared inside the building, promptly followed by Hoon himself.

Sinead launched herself to her feet.

There was some shouting. Hoon. Feasey.

Tyler, too.

He was alive! Christ, he was alive!

Logan ran for the door.

There was a scuffle. A grunt.

A gun fired. Once. Twice.

Fire lit up the room like the flash of a camera. A spray of blood hit Logan just as he reached the door, Sinead just a step or two behind.

He saw Hoon spinning, red spilling down his front and spurting from his thigh, his face contorted, an outburst of swearing stuck somewhere at the back of his throat, blocked by the pain.

By the time Hoon hit the floor, the gun was trained on Logan.

'Bloody hell. You again?' Feasey said. 'I didn't think you'd be on your feet for a while. I'm impressed.'

Shayne beckoned him in with his free hand, his chest rising and falling in slow, steady breaths.

'That bitch, too,' Feasey said, stabbing a finger at DC Bell.

Tyler stifled a sob at the sight of his wife, but he didn't acknowledge her. He didn't dare. She looked different from how she had in the photo. Far harder and less vulnerable. Maybe Feasey wouldn't recognise her.

Please, God, don't let him recognise her.

At the door, Logan and Sinead both raised their hands and took a couple of slow, tentative paces into the room.

'All right, son. Easy, now,' Logan said. 'Let's all stay calm here.'

'I'm perfectly fucking calm,' Feasey replied.

'That's good to know. Bob. How you doing?'

'I've had better fucking days,' Hoon hissed, one hand clutching his shoulder, the other clamped down on his thigh. There was a lot of blood coming from the leg wound. Way too much. 'I'm going to chew through this Dumbo-eared kettle of shite's ballsack, and gnaw his stunted wee cock off at the root.'

He considered this image for a moment.

'Aye but, you know, no' in a fucking gay way, or anything.'

Sinead's gaze went to Tyler. He saw the fear in her eyes when she looked at him. The worry. He bit his lip to stop himself crying out to her, gave the slightest shake of his head, then he quickly turned his attention back to the man with the gun and hoped that she took the hint.

'You shouldn't be here,' Feasey spat, waving the weapon in Logan's face. 'How are you here? That's not the plan. How the fuck did...?'

His eyes narrowed. Tyler's phone on the floor grabbed his attention long enough for him to process what had happened, but not nearly enough for Logan to grab for the gun.

'You!' Feasey spat, turning on DC Neish. 'You little prick! I was nice to you! I let you see your fucking kids!'

Despite the fury in Feasey's gaze, Tyler refused to turn away.

'It's over, Shayne,' he said. There was a calm authority to his voice that nobody in the room—not even Tyler himself—had ever heard before. 'Don't make this any worse for yourself.'

'He's right, son,' Logan added. 'Put down the gun.'

'Could you no' have fucking told him that thirty seconds ago?' Hoon muttered.

'Over? It's not over,' Feasey insisted, swinging the revolver back in Logan's direction. 'It's not over until I say it is. It's not over until those evil pieces of shit are both dead! You know what they did? You know what they did to me? To my mum?'

'We do,' Logan told him. 'We know, and I promise you, son, they're going to face justice for it.'

'Justice?' Feasey scoffed. 'There's only one sort of justice for what they did, and they sure as shit won't get it from you!'

'Killing them isn't the way, son.'

'Oh, and what is *the way*? What are you going to do, arrest them? What evidence have you got? My mum can't testify. You know why? Because she killed herself a year and a half later. Couldn't stand living with the shame of it. Couldn't even look me in the eye. You know when she did that? My birthday. I was ten. *Ten*. Left me alone. Saddled me with a horrible little bastard who never listened to me. Got me bounced from care home to care home. Do you know what happened to me in some of them places? No, you don't, do you? You don't fucking care.'

He pointed at the wall with the gun, indicating some random location beyond the building's boundary. 'They did that! Them! And there's nothing you can do to make them pay for it.'

'You don't want them dead, son. You want them in jail,' Logan reasoned. 'That's why you tried setting Armand Holburn up for the murder of Isaac's wife, isn't it? Why you made those phone calls to the other two from a phone you'd registered in his name. Why you arranged that woman to get the condom from him. Why you seeded all those clues for us. You wanted him put away. You couldn't get him for what he did, so you tried to get him for something else.'

Feasey stared at him for a few moments, blinking rapidly, an incredulous smile spreading across his face.

'Seriously? You think that's what that was?' he scoffed. 'Jesus Christ, you don't know anything, do you? You've not worked it out.' He laughed. It was a sharp, piercing sound, like the rattle of machine-gun fire. 'I knew it was a good plan. I said. I said that. "It'll work", I said. "They'll never work it out!"'

'And yet here we are,' Logan said.

'By total chance!' Shayne spat. He waved the pistol. 'And I'm the one holding the gun!'

'You think that's the only gun, Shayne?' Logan asked. 'You're here, stuck in a corner, with polis swarming the place just right outside. And you hear that helicopter? Whatever happens here, it ends tonight. It ends now. We can walk out of here together, son, you and me. We can talk about what happened to your mother. We can figure out a way forward.'

Logan lowered his arms to his sides.

'Or, the armed response unit can put a bullet between your eyes the moment you step outside. Those are your two choices.' He shrugged. 'I know what one I'd be going for.'

Feasey stared back at him over the top of the pistol. It was pointed directly at the DCI's head, and while Shayne's chest was rising and falling like he'd just finished a sprint, his hand was barely shaking at all.

'Not much of a choice,' he said.

'Not great, no,' Logan said. 'But it's the only one you've got.'

'Can we get a fucking move on here?' Hoon demanded through gritted teeth. 'Unless anyone's got a spare blood transfusion kit and a couple of pints of O-fucking-Negative on them that I can borrow?'

Logan ignored him. Hoon still had the energy to rant. When he stopped, that was when the DCI might start to get concerned.

'What's it to be, son?' Logan asked. 'I can't keep the rest of them away forever. It's decision time.'

Feasey said nothing. Not for a while. His tongue moved around inside his mouth, like it was chasing something that had got loose in there. His breath whistled in and out through his nose.

He looked from Logan to Tyler, glanced at Sinead, then turned his attention back to the DCI.

It lingered there on Logan.

But only for a second.

'Wait,' he said, returning his gaze to Sinead. 'Wait. You're her, aren't you?'

'No. It's not her,' Tyler said, urgently.

Feasey's smile returned. 'Yes, it is. That's her. You're his wife, aren't you? We were looking at your photos. You and the babies. Bless. You guys looked adorable.'

'Shut up,' Tyler spat. 'Leave her out of this.'

Feasey side-eyed the detective constable, his smile ramping up into a full-blown grin.

'I told you I'd get her,' he said.

He shifted his aim.

Sinead gasped.

And the world crashed down into slow motion.

—

Ben had just finished sending another search party to check around the back of the factory when it finally occurred to him that Logan should've been there by now.

'Hamza, you seen Jack?'

'No, sir,' the DS replied.

Ben sucked in his bottom lip. 'Huh.'

He turned slowly in the pool of light from the overhead street lamp, peering past the flashing blues to where he'd parked his car.

'I thought he was right behind us.'

'He was, sir,' Tammi-Jo confirmed. 'I waved at them a couple of times on the drive over. They didn't wave back, though Mr Hoon did make some quite rude gestures. I think he's got a bit of an attitude problem.' She held up her hands. 'There, I've said it, and I stand by it. I think Mr Hoon has a bad attitude.'

'No flies on you, Detective Constable, eh?' Ben said.

He put his hands on his hips, clicked his tongue against the roof of his mouth a few times, then reached for his pocket.

'I'll give him a ring,' he announced, taking out his mobile. 'Hang on. There's a...'

He pulled on his glasses, squinted at the notification on the screen, then tapped to read the full message.

'Oh,' he muttered, his eyes widening. 'Oh, bugger.'

–

Tyler flew. That was how it felt, at least. One moment, he was standing there, the next he was soaring through the air, shoulder first, some primal sound roaring out of him from deep in his gut and millennia before.

It was the sound of a wild animal.

No. More than that.

It was the sound of a monster.

Tyler flew, and he howled, and he roared.

And he prayed. He pleaded. Begged.

Just this one thing.

Just let him do this one thing right.

He hit Feasey with all his weight. Drove everything he had into the bastard.

The gun roared.

No, no, no!

Tyler and his captor fell, flailing, all arms and legs. The gun clattered against the concrete, sliding all the way into the corner.

Before the detective constable knew what was happening, a knee connected with his chin, snapping his head back and bringing a flickering checkerboard of black and white down over his field of view.

He called her name. Pitifully. Desperately.

'Sinead?! *Sinead?!*'

Feasey slid out from under him, but there was nothing Tyler could do to stop him.

'Get the fucker!' Hoon bellowed, then a *whumpf* and a pained exhalation of breath silenced him.

The darkness began to clear in time for Tyler to see Feasey ducking past Logan, avoiding the DCI's grasp.

Shayne raced out through the open door. From somewhere out there came a shout.

'Stop! Police!'

Lights flashed. The beam of a helicopter spotlight encircled the bastard. He looked up, shielding his eyes, blinded by the light.

'It's over, Shayne!' Logan barked. 'There's no point in… Fuck!'

Feasey lurched into the darkness on his right and vanished. The light of the helicopter swept after him. Footsteps raced past outside, giving chase.

'Get after the bastard!' Logan ordered.

Tyler blinked. It had all happened so fast. Too fast for his still-rattling brain to process.

It didn't matter. None of it mattered. Not yet. Not now.

Steeling himself, he shifted his gaze to where Sinead had been just a moment before.

She was no longer standing there. She was down on the floor. Beside him. Blood on her face.

'Hey,' she said, and he realised she was holding his hand. That the blood on her face was his, not her own. 'It's OK, babe. It's OK.'

And then, her arms were around him, and he collapsed against her, sobbing and coughing up all the fear and pain of the past few hours as she rocked him back and forth.

'Shh. It's OK. I've got you. I've got you,' she whispered.

'Aw. This is a touching fucking moment,' Hoon wheezed. 'But if someone could spare a wee fucking second to call me an ambulance, that would be greatly fucking appreciated.'

Outside, Logan watched as the Uniforms went racing past. Feasey was nowhere to be seen, and so it looked like they were all chasing the circle of light cast by the helicopter as it swooshed overhead, its downdraught waving the branches of the nearby trees.

'What the hell kept you?' he asked, shooting Ben an unimpressed look.

'It's not my fault you bloody texted! Who texts at a time like this?'

'We were too close, I didn't want him to hear,' Logan explained.

'Then back up a bit and phone, man!' the DI shot back. 'Don't bloody text! And especially don't text *me* of all bloody people! You're lucky I didn't delete it by mistake. You know what I'm like with all that bloody stuff.'

Hamza jogged up the track to join them. 'I've opened the gate, sir. Ambulances are on their way.'

'You'll need to shift my car or they won't get past,' Logan told him.

'Tammi-Jo's moving it now.'

'Christ,' Logan grunted.

'To be fair, sir, the front's already caved in. Couldn't really see the harm.'

'Aye, I know the front's caved in, but there's three other bloody sides to the car, Detective Sergeant,' Logan reminded him.

He shot an exasperated look in the direction of the gate, then spun on his heels and marched back into the building beside them.

'Still with us, Bob?' he asked.

'Oh, aye, I'm tickety-fucking-boo,' Hoon said. He gestured to the bloody mess that was his leg. He'd whipped off his belt and tied a makeshift tourniquet just above where the bullet had gone through. 'Have you got that jug-headed fuck yet? If you have, can I stick my fucking thumbs through his eyes?'

Logan sniffed. 'Aye. You're fine. Ambulance'll be here soon.'

'It'd fucking better be! If I die here, I'll be fucking haunting the lot of you.'

'Pretty sure that's already the case,' Logan muttered.

He shifted his attention to Tyler, still lying in Sinead's arms. She'd untied him, and he was gripping onto her for dear life, like separation might kill them both.

For a moment, Logan didn't quite know what to say.

Just for a moment, though.

'I'm sorry, son. I should've stopped this. This should never have happened,' he said. 'But you're all right now. We've got you. Everything's going to be OK.'

A hand unclamped itself from Sinead's back.

A thumb raised shakily.

Somewhere in the mess of blood and bruising, a smile appeared.

'Cheers, boss,' Tyler said.

And Logan turned away before anyone could see his eyes filling with water.

Chapter 38

Logan went with them to the hospital. Tyler and Hoon were whisked off to different parts of A&E to have their respective wounds taken care of.

A nurse informed them that they were in luck. There was a room available with two beds in it. They'd get to be roommates.

Both of them complained. Bitterly.

They were still moaning when Logan left them to it.

'You going to be all right?' he asked Sinead, as she helped herself to a depressingly weak coffee from a vending machine that looked like it could no longer be arsed with its lot in life.

'I'll be fine. Honest,' Sinead said, smiling at him through the steam from her plastic cup. 'I called Berta. The twins are fine. They're sleeping, amazingly.'

'Must be a night for miracles, eh?'

She let out a little laugh at that. 'Aye. Must be.'

After a sip of her coffee, and a wince of disappointment, she let out a long, shaky breath.

'I'm sorry about what I said,' she ventured. 'About, you know, quitting, and that. I, uh, I fully understand if you want me to stand by that and—'

'Detective Constable?' Logan said, cutting her short.

Sinead straightened up. 'Sir?'

'Gonnae shut up?'

She looked down at her cup for a moment, then saluted. 'Sir.'

'That's more like it,' Logan told her. He nodded to the double doors behind her, through which Tyler had been wheeled away in a hospital chair. 'Let me know when he's out.'

'Could be late, sir.'

'Doesn't matter,' Logan told her. 'I suspect that Mr Feasey and I have a long night ahead of us back at the station.'

—

'What do you mean, "*he got away*"?'

Mantits looked tired. Scared, too.

Mostly scared, in fact.

He tried polishing the buttons on his uniform by blowing on the fabric of his sleeve and buffing them up. It was a nonsensical gesture that said volumes about his current state of mind.

'He, um, it seems that he was able to evade capture,' he said.

'No, I get that bit, Alisdair. I understand what "he got away" means,' Logan growled. 'My question is *how* did he get away? There was a bloody army after him!'

'He had a motorbike. A trials bike sort of thing. Off-road,' the chief inspector offered.

'A motorbike?' Logan ground his teeth together. They still felt odd from his beating at the hands of Shayne Feasey, like everything was slightly out of place. 'Correct me if I'm wrong, Alisdair, but did we no' have a fucking helicopter? Helicopter beats motorbike. So, again, how did he get away?'

To Mantits' immense relief, DI Forde intervened.

'He got away *for the moment*, Jack,' Ben said. 'There's a full-scale hunt on for him. Motorbike or no motorbike, he's going nowhere.'

Logan thought of a number of terrible things to say to Chief Inspector Lyle, then decided against any of them. Instead, he turned to the big screen that took up a chunk of the Briefing Room's back wall.

It still showed the map from earlier, though there were now no circles of mobile signals overlaid.

'He turned off his phone. Maybe ditched it,' Mantits said. He produced a laser pointer from somewhere about his person, and waggled at a few tracks and back roads. 'He headed in this direction. Bit of a maze of forestry roads. Obvious exits are here, here, and here. We've got Uniform in force at all of them, and the chopper sweeping the whole area. I'm confident we'll find him.'

'Oh, you're confident. You hear that, Detective Inspector? Alisdair's *confident*.'

'There's no need to say it like that,' Mantits protested.

'I want guards at the hospital right now,' Logan instructed, aiming the order at the chief inspector. 'Make sure they're visible. I want them at every entrance, and on the ward, too.'

'You don't think he'll try anything, do you?' Ben asked. 'There's no way he'd get away with it. It'd be madness.'

'I'm not prepared to take the risk,' Logan said. He clicked his fingers and pointed at Mantits. 'Why aren't you on the radio yet? Go! Get a bloody move on!'

'Sorry! Sorry!' the chief inspector trilled. He seemed to jog on the spot for a moment like he was a character in a cartoon, then he dashed out of the room without daring to glance back.

'We'll get him, Jack,' Ben said, once the door had finished swishing shut. 'He's not going to get away.'

'Aye, well,' Logan grunted, striding off in the same direction that Mantits had gone running. 'That's if he's even trying to.'

Chapter 39

Dave was sitting alone in the Incident Room tagging the last of the exhibits when Logan and Ben arrived back. The place was in near darkness, with the only light coming from Dave's desk lamp and the screens of a few computers.

'All right?' the constable asked, sealing a bag and studiously writing the serial number on the first of many pages of paperwork.

'Where the hell is everyone?' Logan demanded.

'I sent them home,' Ben said, hurrying to catch up with him.

'Home?' Logan frowned, like he wasn't sure what the word meant. 'What do you mean?'

'It's one in the morning, Jack,' Ben told him. 'It's been a long day. Uniform's got this now. We've done our bit. They needed to go home and rest. Even Tammi-Jo, and she's powered by some sort of nuclear fusion reactor. They need to rest. We all do, especially you.'

Logan wanted to argue. He wanted to give the DI a bollocking for packing the rest of the team off.

But he knew his old friend was right.

'I'm surprised the hospital didn't try and keep hold of you when you went in with Tyler and Hoon.'

Logan sunk into a chair. The glow of the computer screen picked out all the bumps and bruises on his face.

'They tried,' he admitted. 'I told them I'd think about it and get back to them.'

Ben chuckled. 'You spoken to Shona?'

Logan remembered the text message from earlier. If he'd had the energy, he would've winced. 'Shite. No. Not yet. Bit late to call now.' He let his head fall backwards and groaned. 'Bollocks.'

'What's up?' Ben asked.

'Still got Isaac Simpson and Armand Holburn to deal with.'

Ben sat across the desk from Logan. There was a cautiousness to it that the DCI picked up on right away.

'What?' he asked. 'What have you done?'

'I sent them home, too,' he said.

Logan almost exploded out of his chair. 'What?!'

'Well, no, not exactly that,' Ben said. 'Given that Feasey's still out there, and Isaac's house is off limits, they've sorted a hotel.'

'What the hell were you thinking?' Logan demanded.

'The solicitor was pretty adamant. And, really, what did we have to hold them on? We've got tampering with evidence on Holburn, aye. But he's not going anywhere. And we've got nothing at all on Isaac.' Ben sighed. 'Even if they did do what Feasey claimed they did, what can we do about it? Honestly? After all this time, what can we actually do?'

Logan deflated, all the anger leaving him in one big breath. 'Aye. Suppose,' he conceded. 'Maybe that bastard was right. Maybe we should've just let him kill them.'

'You don't mean that, Jack,' Ben said. 'Anyway, if he'd wanted to kill them, he had plenty of chances.'

Logan nodded. This was true. He'd been stalking the men for months, maybe longer. He'd turned up on their doorsteps. If he had wanted to kill them, he'd had ample opportunity.

He hadn't wanted them dead, then.

Not at that point, anyway.

'He didn't want them in jail, either,' the DCI mumbled out loud.

Ben raised his eyebrows. 'What was that, Jack?'

Logan sat forward. 'Feasey. In that room, with Tyler. I thought the condom was a set-up. I thought he was using it to put Holburn in the frame, to try and get him put away, but he laughed that off. Said I wasn't seeing the bigger picture.'

'Which is?' Ben asked.

Logan shrugged. 'Fucked if I know.'

He looked across to the Big Board. Someone, probably Tammi-Jo, had stuck a photo of Shayne Feasey up on the right-hand side. Her chocolate factory had finally produced its first bar.

Although, now that he thought about it, and with Feasey's mugshot staring back at him, the DC's analogy made even less sense.

The finished 'product' wasn't what was intriguing him, though. He was more interested in all the 'ingredients' DC Swanney had pinned up on the left. There was something in there. He could feel it niggling away at him. Some explanation. Some reason for all of this.

It wasn't just revenge. If it was, he'd have killed them. Maybe tortured them a bit first.

Sure, he might've been building up to it. Maybe he enjoyed toying with them. He was cruel, they knew that. Maybe killing Sharon was the final step. Isaac would be heartbroken. If the murder was pinned on Armand, the men's friendship would be destroyed.

Was that it? Was that all?

Maybe Feasey thought one of them might confess to their sexual assault back in the Nineties, even if only to spite the other.

That would be a stretch, though. There was no saying it'd pay off. The odds were stacked against it, in fact.

Not that, then. He'd planned it too well to leave that to chance.

What, then?

Bones creaking, Logan rose from the chair and crossed to the board.

'What have you seen?' Ben asked.

'Nothing yet.' Logan glanced back over his shoulder. 'You get off. You're right, we need to get some rest.'

'Aye. *We* do,' Ben agreed. 'I'm not leaving you here stewing all night on your own.'

'I won't be,' Logan said. 'Dave's here.'

Ben groaned, but it became a chuckle. 'Aye. Fair enough,' he said, gathering up his briefcase and coat. 'I think I'll check into a hotel myself. Can't face that drive up the road at this time of night.'

'You no' going to stay with your fancy woman?'

Ben sucked air in through his teeth. 'Eh, no. No. I think that's done and dusted.'

'Thank Christ for that!' Logan said, but the muted reaction from the DI soon wiped the smile off his face.

'Heh. Aye,' Ben said. He tapped a finger to his brow. 'Night, Jack. Night, Dave.'

'Night!' Dave said, looking up from his paperwork.

'Aye,' Logan said, watching the older man shuffling towards the door. 'Good night.'

'Ah, love, eh?' Dave said once the door had closed. He sniffed, shook his head, then went back to writing. 'Better off without it.'

Logan's eyes were drawn to the seat where Nidds had been sitting. The computer was still on, a report of some kind still on the screen, but the chair was empty. It had been rolled back a few feet from the desk. Presumably, she'd gone home, and in a bit of a hurry, too.

'You don't have to stick around,' Logan said. 'You get off.'

'Ach, I'm fine here,' Dave said. He placed another now-registered evidence bag into the filing box on the floor by his desk. 'Nearly done, anyway.'

Logan shrugged. 'Suit yourself.'

He turned his attention back to the board, and settled on the two notes that had been left—one at the crime scene, the other in Armand Holburn's bin—each saying the same thing.

'I know what you did,' he muttered, his gaze flitting between the photo of the SOC team's rubbing from the pad, and the scan of the crumpled note Nidds had found.

Two notes, the same, but different.

Armand had taken the one from the scene, because he knew it would lead to questions being asked about what precisely Isaac—and by extension, Armand—was being accused of.

He'd taken it, and he'd tried to destroy it.

He denied all knowledge of the one in the bin, and Logan was inclined to believe him.

So, who put it there? When? Why?

Did someone know he'd destroyed the other note? Did they plant a second one to make it look—correctly—that Armand had tampered with the scene? Did they put it there to connect him to the murder?

Did that fit?

Logan ran a hand down his face.

Maybe. It might fit. But he didn't like it.

If that had been the plan, they wouldn't put it in the bin, would they? What were the chances of anyone actually finding it in there? It was sheer luck that Constable Niddrie had spotted it amongst the rubbish.

Good job she did, too. If she hadn't, they wouldn't have had enough to pull Armand in.

They wouldn't have got him to confess to being at the scene.

They wouldn't have done the DNA test and linked him to the used condom.

The floorboards groaned as Logan shifted his weight from the ball of one foot to the other.

The condom. The DNA test.

There was something there. Something darting around the fringes of his mind. An itch that he couldn't quite reach to scratch.

He found his attention returning to the scan of the crumpled note. The printing issues had mostly been resolved by Hamza, so Logan could make out every one of the dozens of creases and folds in the original Post-it.

It had been properly scrunched up.

What were the chances of someone finding that note in that bin?

If he'd seen it, balled up like that, he wouldn't have given it a second thought.

The odds of Nidds not only spotting it, but recognising its importance...?

He puffed out his cheeks. He'd told Sinead it had been a day of miracles, but that one felt like a step too far.

Something sour brought a tide of saliva up into his mouth. He swallowed it down as he turned to Constable Davidson.

'The harassment. Armand and Isaac,' he said. 'We ever find out who the Uniform was that they say went out to talk to them?'

'Nah,' Dave said, barely looking up from his writing. 'Some woman, apparently, but she hasn't logged it. God knows. Probably just got overlooked.'

'Aye,' said Logan, after a pause. 'Probably.'

He turned to the board, but then continued around in a full three-sixty so he was facing away from it again.

Constable Niddrie's computer was still open. Her chair still pushed back.

She'd left in a hurry.

And she'd been so sure that Feasey wouldn't hurt Tyler. Logan had thought at the time that she'd been staying positive for Sinead.

And maybe she had been.

Maybe that was all it was.

Maybe.

He made his way over to the workstation. His legs, like the rest of him, had been painful since his fight with Feasey, but now they felt heavy, each step sinking them further and further into the quicksand of the carpet.

Something Feasey said back in that building with Tyler started to rattle around inside Logan's head. It hadn't made much sense at the time, but he hadn't thought too much about it. He'd been more concerned with the gun that had been pointed in his face at the time.

Now, though, as he approached the computer, he got a sense of the significance of it.

'*Left me alone, saddled me with a horrible little bastard…*'

Logan had assumed he'd meant an adult carer, but what if he was being literal? What if he'd meant it in the old-fashioned sense?

What if he'd meant a child?

One born out of wedlock?

Logan felt a rib shifting painfully as he bent to look at the report on the computer Nidds had been using.

To a layman like him, the text wasn't particularly easy to understand, but he recognised a DNA report when he saw one, even if he didn't really grasp many of the details.

There were two of them open in different tabs, one for Armand Holburn, the other for Isaac Simpson. The summary at the bottom of Armand's linked him to the condom found at the murder scene, but the raw data was there, too. The sequencing of the samples provided a full breakdown of both men's genetic makeup, if you knew what you were looking for.

Logan put a hand over his mouth, his fingers and thumb tracing all the new bumps and lumps he found there.

'Dave?'

There was no answer from the constable. He had his evidence box on his lap, and was rifling through it, his wide brow furrowed in concentration.

'Dave!' Logan said again.

The man in the wheelchair quickly raised his head. 'What?' he snapped, then he quickly corrected his tone. 'Sorry. I meant… What?'

'Constable Niddrie,' Logan asked. 'She go home?'

'Aye,' Dave confirmed.

Logan breathed out. 'OK. OK, good.'

Dave returned his attention to the box. 'She was just dropping off your two fellas at the hotel first.'

The sentence seemed to toll like a funeral bell. Logan's stomach tightened all the way up to his throat.

He'd heard the whole conversation between Dave and Tyler earlier, when they'd both incorrectly thought they were speaking quietly.

Nidds had done a degree. 'Science stuff', Dave had said.

She was adopted.

'Saddled me with a horrible little bastard who wouldn't listen to me.'

Logan swallowed. 'What hotel?' he asked.

Dave's rummaging was becoming more frantic now. He had taken half of the evidence bags from the box, and was digging around in what was left.

'Dave!' Logan barked in a voice that was impossible to ignore. 'What hotel did she take them to?'

'Uh, I don't know. One of the ones just outside of town, I think. Glasgow road. Why?'

Logan debated on whether to say anything to him.

But only for a moment.

'I think she might be mixed up in this,' he said, searching his pockets for his car keys. 'In the case. I think she might be connected.'

'Connected?' Dave let out an incredulous little laugh. 'What do you mean?'

Logan looked back at the DNA results on the screen. 'I don't… I'm not sure. Not fully. But I need to know where she is. I think she might be going to do something stupid.'

All amusement drained from Dave's face. He set the box back on the floor and wheeled himself out from behind the desk.

'What do you mean? How stupid?'

'I think she might want to hurt them. I think she's working with Feasey.'

'No. No way. Not Nidds,' Dave said, though there wasn't the fire behind it that Logan would've expected.

The constable glanced back down at the box on the floor, and the stack of evidence bags piled on his desk.

'What? What's the matter?' Logan demanded.

Dave cleared his throat. He was a man who Logan had, until that moment, considered to be utterly fearless. But now, when he spoke, there was a shake to his voice.

'The, uh, the gun. The gun you brought in. Feasey's gun,' he said. 'It's gone.'

'Fuck!'

Logan did another search of his pockets, before remembering that his car had been towed away with the front caved in.

And some of the back, too. He knew he should never have let Tammi-Jo drive the bloody thing.

'Do you know what kind of car she drives?' Logan asked.

'Aye. Wee Mondeo. Blue.'

'Right. Get your keys,' Logan instructed. He clamped his hands on the handles of Dave's chair and started racing them towards the door. 'You're driving.'

Chapter 40

They found Nidds' car parked up outside the Clan Macduff Hotel, just south of Fort William. There was no sign of Nidds, Isaac or Armand.

The hotel's front door was locked for the night, but a few rings of the bell, a bit of hammering, and a flash of a warrant card granted Logan and Dave access to the building. A disgruntled night porter locked the door behind them, then stood in front of a floor-to-ceiling map of the west of Scotland, with a double power socket roughly where Tobermory was meant to be.

He didn't hesitate in answering Logan's questions. This was clearly all just some inconvenience he wanted dealt with as quickly as possible.

Yes, a constable had come in with two men.

Yes, he'd got them both booked in.

No, nobody else had been with them.

No, nobody seemed distressed.

Yes, he could cut them a master key that would let them into both rooms, as long as they promised he wouldn't get landed in the shit for it.

Logan wasn't really in any position to promise that. He did it anyway, then snatched the keys from the porter's hand, before being directed through a door to a couple of ground-floor rooms deeper back in the darkened hotel.

The lights were on a sensor and clicked on a few seconds after Logan and Dave entered the corridor.

He'd called for backup the moment they'd seen the car. An actual phone call this time, not a text, so he was confident it would be here. They'd been instructed to keep the sirens off and to avoid any radio chatter. For all they knew, Nidds could be listening in to all of it, although she'd failed to respond to either a radio check or a phone call from Dave on the way over.

Logan stopped at the first door the porter had directed them towards. He listened, his ear pressed to the wood, but heard nothing but the thudding of his own heart.

'Anything?' Dave whispered.

Logan shook his head. He tapped the key to the lock, and a strip of light flashed green.

Easing the handle down, he nudged the door open just enough to get an impression of the room beyond. It was in darkness, the bed still made, the tea-making facilities and biscuits untouched.

He let the door close again, pressed a finger to his lips, then pointed along the corridor to the next door along.

Once there, he repeated the process, bringing his ear in close to the door and listening for any signs of life on the other side.

Voices. Murmuring. It could be a TV on low, or it could be a conversation. It sounded calm, though. Friendly, even.

Was he wrong on this? Christ, he hoped so.

But it all fit.

And the gun was missing.

He brought the keycard to the lock. It flashed and whirred, and he opened the door to find Armand and Isaac sitting alone at a small table, half the contents of the minibar already demolished in front of them.

'Jesus Christ. What the hell is this?' Armand demanded. 'You can't just walk in here. You shouldn't be here!'

'Oh, thank God,' Dave whispered, rolling into the room at Logan's back.

'You're OK?' Logan asked, looming over the two men at the table.

'What the hell are you talking about?' Armand demanded.

'We're fine,' Isaac added. 'Why?'

'Eh… Nothing. Maybe nothing,' Logan said.

He looked around the room for any sign of Constable Niddrie, but there was nothing to indicate she'd ever been there.

Let him be wrong. Just this one time, let him be wrong.

Across the room, behind the door of the en suite, a toilet flushed.

A snib lock *clacked*.

On the other side of the bed, the bathroom door opened.

Nidds took a single step, then stopped, her feet registering her shock before her face had a chance to. She stared, first at Logan, then at Dave.

'What?' she asked, as if failing to properly hear a question that hadn't actually been asked.

Dave wheeled himself a little closer, but the bed blocked his way. 'Nidds,' he said, and the pleading tone to his voice sent her eyebrows creeping up her forehead.

'Constable Niddrie,' Logan intoned. 'I'd like a word.'

Nidds shifted her weight from one foot to the other. She was still gripping the handle of the door, like she might slam it closed at any moment.

'What about, sir?' she asked.

'We'll discuss it in private,' Logan told her.

He held a hand out to her. She was too far away to reach for it, but he hoped the gesture might be enough to coax her closer.

'Come on,' the DCI urged. 'Let's get you home. We can talk on the way.'

She knew. She knew why they were there. Of course she did. Her bottom lip trembled for a moment, then stopped as the muscles in her jaw went tight.

He was losing her.

311

'She's off duty,' Armand said. He waved his glass, sloshing around the measure of Scotch he'd poured from one of the minibar miniatures. 'If she wants to stay, she can stay. She's the only one of you people to ever take our complaints seriously.'

Nidds hadn't moved. She was showing no sign that she was about to, either.

'Mr Simpson, Mr Holburn, I'm afraid I'm going to have to ask you to leave,' Logan said, his gaze still trained on the constable standing in the bathroom doorway. 'There'll be uniformed officers out front any minute. Go wait out there.'

'What?' Isaac snorted out a half-laugh. 'What are you talking about? We just got here.'

'My solicitor made it very clear that I'll come back in the morning,' Armand added. 'I'm buggered if I'm going back to a bloody cell when I could be here.'

Logan diverted his attention to the two seated men. The table they were sitting at was between him and Nidds, off to his right. He stepped aside, leaving the door behind him clear.

'You need to leave. Both of you. Now.'

Constable Niddrie's voice rang out. 'Don't.'

Logan shut his eyes, just for a moment.

Why? Why couldn't he have been wrong?

Why not just this once?

'Nidds! Fuck's sake!' Dave cried. 'What are you doing?'

Logan wasn't surprised to see the gun in her hand. The men sitting at the table, on the other hand, both leaped to their feet in alarm. Considering their military backgrounds, the sight of the revolver spooked them far more than Logan would've expected.

'Jesus Christ! What is this? What's she doing?' Armand wailed, his voice a shrill hiss of terror.

'Sit down,' Nidds told him, swinging the gun in his direction.

Armand threw his hands above his head and practically curtseyed back down into his seat.

Beside him, Isaac—who was the closest person to the constable and, by extension, the gun—eyed up the gap between where he and Nidds were standing. It was just a few feet. Not far.

'Please don't,' Nidds said, pointing the gun at him. 'Just sit down. All right? Everyone just sit down.'

She waited until Isaac had taken his seat, then nodded to Logan.

'You too, sir.'

'Give me the gun, Constable. You don't have to do this.'

'I do, sir,' Nidds replied. She turned the gun his way, and there was a steely coolness in the way she looked at him. 'Now, please, sit down, or I'm going to have to shoot you. And I don't want to do that. I really don't.'

Logan believed her. On both counts. She had no reason to want to shoot him, but everything about her demeanour told him she would if he tried to get in her way.

There was nowhere to sit but the bed, and he didn't think she'd let him get that close. Instead, he shoved aside a large, ugly lamp that had been placed on the room's small desk, and perched himself there.

'Backup is on the way, Constable,' he told her. 'Everyone's coming.'

'It's OK, sir. It's not going to take long,' Nidds said. The calmness in her voice was chilling.

'What the hell is this?' Armand demanded. He was the only one in the room to have his hands raised, and he seemed to have no intention of taking them down again. 'I don't understand what the fuck's going on.'

'I do,' Logan said. 'Or, I think I do. Maybe you can fill in some of the blanks, Constable?'

Nidds said nothing. The gun was no longer trained on the DCI. It wasn't really pointed at anyone, and was instead bobbing in a compact figure of eight, aimed somewhere in the space between Armand and Isaac.

'I think this all goes back to what you did in Bosnia,' Logan told the men. 'The woman you raped.'

'We didn't rape anyone!' Armand said. It was out of him in an instant, like an always-ready automatic response. 'I'm sorry, young lady, but if you think—'

'This is her daughter,' Logan said. He looked to Nidds for confirmation. She didn't give it, but the lack of denial told Logan he was right.

The penny dropped for Isaac first. 'Oh. Oh, God.'

'Daughter? She didn't have a daughter,' Armand said, before catching himself. 'Uh, the… I mean… If it's the woman I'm thinking of. The one who falsely accused us of—'

'Armand,' Isaac said. He sighed, a weariness overtaking him and making his muscles go slack. 'Just… Just stop. All right? Please. Just stop. Jesus. Norman was right. He was right. We should've listened to him. We can't pretend it didn't happen. We can't pretend we didn't do those things.'

Holburn stared back at him, his eyes all but bulging out of his head, his mouth moving around like he was chewing on something that was proving very hard to swallow.

'Good. Thank you. Maybe now we can get somewhere,' Logan said. 'You raped that woman. And you're right. She didn't have a daughter. She did have a son. The man who was harassing you. The man who murdered Sharon. He was just a kid at the time. He was hiding under the bed. He listened to what you did. He heard it all.'

Isaac let out a shaky breath. 'Oh, Christ. Oh, God, Sharon.'

'Maybe not just Sharon. He may have killed Norman, too,' Logan added, further twisting the knife.

'He didn't,' Nidds said quickly. Her expression was giving nothing away. It was mostly blank, like she had detached herself from the emotion of the moment. Like she was an impartial observer, watching on. 'They did. They killed him.'

'What?!' Holburn spluttered. 'That's… No. No, no. How dare you? How can you even…?!'

'Oh, shut up, Armand,' Isaac hissed.

He picked up his glass, drained the contents in one gulp, then pressed it to his forehead like he was trying to cool a rising fever.

'He was dying,' Isaac began. 'Norman. He'd found God towards the end. Got right into it all. Born again. He was worried if he didn't confess… If he didn't own up to what we'd done… He, uh, he started to talk about coming forward. Owning up, sort of thing.'

'But you couldn't have that, could you? So, you killed him,' Logan said. 'You killed him to stop your dirty little secret getting out, then you dumped his body somewhere. Made everyone think he'd done himself in.'

Isaac ground his teeth together for a moment, then nodded in response.

Armand lowered his hands from above his head to just above shoulder height. 'I had nothing to do with that,' he said. 'I knew nothing about this. This is all news to me. I want that on record.'

'Oh, shut up, Armand. It was your idea. It was all your idea!'

'My God! How dare you? How fucking *dare you* say that? Really, Isaac, that sort of accusation is—'

'I've got you on tape, Armand!' Isaac bellowed.

That shut Holburn up. He sat there, completely motionless, staring across the table at the other man.

Isaac exhaled, and it was like a weight lifted from him. 'All right? I recorded it. Everything. Everything you said. Everything we planned. I recorded it, because I knew one day you'd try this shit. You'd try and put it all on me. Christ, you're bloody pathetic.'

'That's… No. You're lying. That's…' Armand said, but then he took on a sort of distant and vacant look, like he had gone into low-power mode while his brain tried to figure out a way out of this situation.

'They've confessed, Beatrice,' Logan said. 'They're going to go to jail now.'

315

'Put the gun down, Nidds, eh?' Dave said. 'He's right. We've got them now, bang to rights. They'll go away for what they did.'

'They'll go away for killing Norman,' Nidds said, her voice still unnaturally calm.

'Exactly,' Dave said. 'They'll do life for that.'

'And what about my mum? How do they get punished for that?'

'They'll be in prison,' Logan assured her. 'They'll be in prison, and if I have anything to say about it, they won't ever get back out.'

'For killing their horrible bastard rapist mate,' Nidds stressed. 'Not for what they did to my mum. To Shayne. To me.'

'We didn't do anything to you!' Armand cried. 'I don't even understand who you are. He literally just said that she didn't have a daughter, so…'

And there it was. The moment of realisation.

The moment when Armand Holburn caught up with everyone else in the room.

'Oh. Oh, Christ.'

'There are far easier ways of getting hold of DNA,' Logan told Nidds.

She shrugged. 'Shayne wanted to do it this way. Make them suffer through it. "Kill two birds with one stone", he said. He wanted to humiliate them. Punish them, a little bit at a time. He said it was right that we make them pay as much as possible.'

Her blank expression gave way to uncertainty and concern for a moment.

'I, uh, I eventually realised he just enjoys it. He gets a kick out of being cruel. Just for the sake of it,' Nidds continued. 'He seduced Sharon Simpson. He'd been screwing her for weeks, just because he could. That wasn't even part of the plan. He just did it because it would hurt him.' She pointed at Isaac with the gun.

'What? No,' Isaac said, but his protest was a weak one. 'No, no. I don't believe that. She wouldn't! She loved me!'

'Oh, Jesus Christ, now who's being pathetic, Isaac?' Armand spat.

'He ran over your dog, too,' Nidds said, looking him dead in the eye.

'What?!' The word caught in Armand's throat. 'Molly? He killed Molly?'

Nidds ignored his sob of outrage. Her gaze shifted from Logan to Dave and back again. 'But I told him not to hurt Tyler. I made him promise he wouldn't.'

'He did,' Logan said. 'He beat him. Nearly killed him. Tried to murder Sinead.'

'Shot Hoon,' Dave added.

Logan blinked, like he wasn't sure what the constable was on about, then he nodded. 'Oh. Aye. That, too.'

'I didn't know he was going to do any of that, sir. I swear,' Nidds said. 'He promised me he wouldn't. He said he was just holding onto Tyler for insurance. Said he thought we might have to trade him for these two. I didn't want Tyler in danger. I didn't want you hurt either, sir.'

Her eerily calm exterior was cracking now, flaking away like dead skin, revealing a trembling mess below. That wasn't good. Calm people thought rationally. Scared people did not.

Calm people could be reasoned with.

'It's OK, Constable. You're all right,' Logan assured her. 'We believe you. You didn't want any of that to happen.' He took a chance and stood up. She narrowed her eyes, but otherwise didn't react. 'And I don't think you want any of this, either. Do you? I don't think you want to be here doing this.'

'No,' Nidds admitted. 'I don't, sir. I really, really don't.'

'Then give me the gun, Constable,' Logan told her. From outside, blue lights flickered across the fabric of the curtains. 'Come on. Let's get the hell out of here. Uniform can take these two in.'

'They raped her. All three of them. Shayne had to listen,' Nidds said. Tears welled up, then made a mad dash for it down her cheeks. 'She tried to kill herself when she was pregnant with me, you know? Twice. She couldn't bring herself to get rid of me, so she tried to get rid of us both. Her boyfriend at the time, he kicked shit out of her when he found out what had happened. Called her a dirty slut. Stamped on her stomach, over and over, trying to get rid of me. They think that's what happened to my hearing.'

'Nidds, please,' Dave said.

'He chucked her and Shayne out before I was born. Onto the street. I was eight months old when she killed herself. I was there. Don't remember it, of course, but Shayne does. He heard me crying. Screaming the place down. He'd been out trying to get us food. Came in, and found her there. Hanging.'

'Oh, God,' Isaac whispered. He cupped both hands over his mouth, trapping a shaky breath. 'I'm sorry. I'm so sorry.'

'Sorry?' Nidds frowned, but one corner of her mouth tugged up, like she'd just heard a joke she didn't quite understand. 'You're sorry?' The suggestion of amusement evaporated, the lines of her face all hardening at once. 'You don't get to be sorry. Not after what you did. What you *all* did! All you get is to pay for it. Finally, you get to pay for it.'

'And he will, Constable,' Logan reasoned. 'We'll make sure of it. And I need you around to see it happen. You can testify. You can help put them away. You just need to put down the gun, and let me and Dave take you out of here.'

Nidds stared at him for a few seconds, then slowly nodded. At first, Logan thought she was responding to him. But it soon became apparent that it was a reaction to some inner voice only she could hear.

'I can't do that, sir,' she said.

'Nidds, come on,' Dave pleaded. 'Don't be daft.'

Her face screwed up. Not with anger, but with something like grief.

'I'm sorry, Dave,' she told him in a breathless whisper. 'I liked you. I *like* you. A lot. I do. But I knew this was coming. I knew someday soon I'd be here. With them. With a gun in my hand. I didn't want you to be a part of that. I never wanted any of you to be involved.'

'Well, I am involved,' Dave said. 'I'm right here. And I'm telling you, I can help. I'm telling you…'

While he was speaking, she reached up and turned off first one hearing aid, then the other.

'Nidds? Nidds, don't do that. Listen to me,' Dave begged. 'Please, listen to me.'

Nidds gripped the pistol with both hands. Its earlier stillness was gone, and it bobbed wildly in the air.

'Jesus Christ!' Armand wailed, covering his head with his hands. 'Don't shoot us! Don't shoot us!'

'Constable Niddrie! Put down the gun, that's an order!' Logan bellowed. 'Put down the gun now!'

She wasn't looking at him, so couldn't read his lips. Her attention, and the gun, was trained on Armand, who had stuck his hands straight up above his head again, and was now bawling his eyes out.

'Look, please. Please, I'm sorry, all right? I'm sorry!' Armand sobbed. A thought struck him. He almost bounced out of the seat with excitement, sensing a way out of this. 'Anyway, anyway, it can't be me! It isn't me! I can't be your father! I'm not capable, see?! I can't have kids. I'm not able to! I'm firing blanks!'

Thunder roared. The muzzle flash from the gun painted the walls in orange, then the bullet sprayed them red.

'I'm not,' Nidds said, and that steely calmness was back again.

Logan closed his eyes and pinched the swollen bridge of his nose.

'Nidds! Oh, God. Nidds. No,' Dave wailed, as some imagined future he'd been clinging to for them went up with the smoke from the gun.

At the table, the partially headless body of Armand Holburn slid sideways onto the floor, one eye missing, the other gazing blankly into the eternal void.

From out in the corridor, there came the sound of panicky voices and running footsteps that faded as they raced for reception, and the car park beyond.

Outside, Logan heard the urgent clipped tones of the assembled Uniforms, and the sound of boots fanning out across the tarmac.

'It's you, by the way,' Nidds said. She turned the gun on Isaac. 'In case you were wondering. You're my dad.'

Logan launched himself forwards, praying that Nidds' reluctance to shoot him might buy him the time he needed to wrestle the gun from her.

It fired before he was halfway to the bed. The bullet hit Isaac in the chest, slamming him back against the wall, then sideways into the table. Glasses and bottles crashed to the floor. Blood spurted from the hole where his heart should be, then popped as burbling bubbles on his lips.

Logan stood frozen for a moment, watching a dying man sink to the floor. Then, he charged again, diving for Nidds just as she jammed the pistol against the side of her head.

'Nidds, no!' Dave howled.

Logan wasn't close enough. Not fast enough. He wasn't going to make it.

She screwed her eyes shut, whimpered out an, 'I'm sorry', then pulled the trigger.

Click.

Her eyes opened.

'No, no, no!' she wailed.

And seventeen stone of flying detective slammed her against the wall.

Chapter 41

Everything hurt. This was not surprising. The few hours of sleep he'd managed to get in the hotel bed had been fitful and restless, and had simply served to make all his muscles seize up so that dragging himself out of it again had been a Herculean task.

Still, he'd been lucky to get a hotel at all, given that everyone at the Clan Macduff had to be decanted to other accommodation at two in the morning.

The shower had helped a bit. The assortment of painkillers he'd knocked back had taken the edge off it further.

But everything still hurt.

And he was getting very little in the way of sympathy.

'I told you, you should've stayed in the hospital,' Shona said, her Irish accent sounding thin and tinny over the speaker of his phone.

She was munching her way through a bowl of Coco Pops. And while a few months ago the sound of anyone slurping up chocolatey milk the way she was might have incited him to cause them actual bodily harm, he found he didn't particularly mind it these days.

At least, not when she did it.

'But thank God you didn't,' she conceded, before wiping the milk off her chin with the back of her hand.

'Aye. Well. For all the good I did,' Logan muttered.

'Tyler's alive,' Shona reminded him. 'That feels like a pretty big win.'

Logan nodded. 'That's true, I suppose. But, still. I just... I should've seen what was happening. I should've... I don't know. Done it better. Seen it sooner.'

'You did it all in one day, Jack,' Shona pointed out. 'While beaten to a pulp, too.'

'I wouldn't say "beaten to a pulp", exactly,' Logan protested. 'And he clocked me from behind.'

Shona smiled. 'Either way, you did good.'

The DCI remained unconvinced. 'That bastard's still out there somewhere. No saying where he is.'

The manhunt had gone nowhere. Feasey appeared to have vanished off the face of the Earth.

'They'll find him. He won't get far,' Shona said. 'You've done your bit. Just get organised and come home. You need time to rest. Recover.'

Logan blew out his cheeks. His nose was still plugged up with dried blood, so no air was able to escape that way.

'Aye. You're right.'

'Obviously,' Shona agreed. 'I mean, that's just par for the course.'

'Oh! How was your new fella?'

'Neville?' Shona almost dropped her spoon. 'God, Jack, you should see him. He's like a male model, or something. His face is, like, forty per cent cheek bones. He's handsome, charming, *and* competent. You don't get that very often. Smart. Attractive. And his teeth, Jack! Christ on a bike, but he's got great teeth.'

Logan suddenly became aware of his own slightly yellowing gnashers. 'Should I be worried here?' he asked.

'What? God, no! He's not my type at all.'

'I feel like I should be taking offence at that...'

'You know what I mean!' Shona said, smirking. 'Don't you be getting paranoid on me. Just get your arse home.'

'Fair enough. I'll go by the hospital first. Check in with Tyler and the rest of them. Then, I'll pick up the dog.'

'Ah, grand!' Shona said. 'I don't know about you, but I've missed the daft little bugger.'

Logan made a show of thinking this over. 'No,' he finally said. 'No, not really.'

'Liar!' Shona laughed. She glanced back over her shoulder at the kitchen door, then faced the camera again.

'What's up? Something wrong?' Logan asked, picking up on the look. 'Neville's not about to come walking in, is he?'

'Ha! What? No, of course not!' Shona said, before quickly changing the subject. 'What's going to happen? With Constable Niddrie, I mean.'

'Hamza and Tammi-Jo are bringing her up to Inverness. We'll interview her up there. But Dave and I saw her kill them both. Not really much more to say about that part, but maybe we'll find out more about her brother. Maybe she'll be able to tell us where to find him.'

'You don't sound hopeful.'

'I'm not,' Logan replied. 'I doubt she'll know much. My instinct is that he used her. Got her to get all the contact details for them, got her poking around in their lives so he could put all this in action. I think maybe the whole thing was done partly to punish her, too.'

'Jesus. Why?'

Logan shrugged. 'Maybe in his mind, if she hadn't come along, his mum would've still been around. Maybe he blames her as much as the men who did it.'

Shona sighed. 'Aw. Jesus. It's a mess, isn't it?'

'It is,' Logan confirmed. He thought of Dave, and the look on the poor bastard's face when Nidds had been bundled into the cage in the back of the police van. 'It really is.'

He remembered something else from the day before, too.

'Your text,' he said. 'You sent a text. Sorry, I didn't get a chance to get back to it.'

'What? Oh, no. It's fine,' Shona said, dismissing the apology. 'Don't even worry about it. The text? *That* text? It was nothing. Seriously.'

Logan didn't need his detective instincts to know she was hiding something.

'You said we needed to talk,' he reminded her, shuffling a little closer to where the phone was propped up on the bedside table. 'What was it?'

'Nothing! I forget,' Shona said.

She quickly scooped up another spoonful of Coco Pops and shoved it in her mouth so she couldn't say anything more.

Behind her, just as she started to chew, the kitchen door opened.

Logan watched in silence as a girl shuffled past wearing a pair of Shona's pyjamas. Her eyes were half shut, and her hair looked like she'd recently lost a fight with a particularly surly hedge.

'Morning,' she mumbled, leaving the shot.

Shona chewed on her mush of cereal. 'Morning,' she said from the corner of her mouth.

Behind her, the girl walked past again in the opposite direction, carrying a glass of orange juice and yawning.

Logan watched as she left the room again.

Shona swallowed.

'Was that…?' Logan began. He frowned as he tried to process what he'd just seen. 'Was that Olivia Maximuke?'

'Was who Olivia Maximuke?' Shona asked, stalling for time.

Logan pointed to the screen. 'The girl who just walked into the kitchen and left again.'

'Oh! Right. *Her.* Yes. Yes, that was Olivia. She slept in the spare room last night,' Shona confirmed. She bit her lip. 'Like I said in that text—which you completely ignored, by the way, shame on you—there's something we really need to talk about…'

'Fuck me!' Hoon ejected when Logan ducked into the hospital room. 'If it's no' Mr Potato Head. Can I get an autograph? I fucking loved you in the *Toy Story* films!'

Hoon was propped up in one of the room's two beds, one arm in a sling and his leg partly cocooned in bandages. A yoghurt pot and an apple sat untouched on his bedside tray, suggesting breakfast had recently been served.

Clearly, Hoon hadn't liked what he'd been given. Then again, Logan was fairly confident that his former boss's usual breakfast of a quarter bottle of Famous Grouse whisky would not have been one of the menu options.

'Aye, very funny, Bob,' the DCI intoned. 'At least I'm up and about.'

'With a fucking coupon like that, maybe you shouldn't be,' Hoon shot back. 'No' when you're no' under the cover of fucking darkness, anyway. I hope you didn't pass any kids on the way here. Wee shites'll be traumatised for fucking life.'

DI Forde, who was sitting by the other bed with his back to the door, turned to the DCI and grimaced.

'Jesus. Aye. He's not wrong. That bruising's fairly coming out. You do look pretty rough, Jack.'

'Rough?!' said Hoon. 'He looks like there should be a mob of angry villagers with pitchforks chasing him through the fucking streets.'

Logan elected to rise above the remark, and continued across the room to where Ben and Sinead sat by Tyler's bed.

'All right, boss?' Tyler asked.

'Not bad, son. You?'

Tyler shrugged. 'All right, boss,' he said, his tone flattening out. 'I mean, I've had better days, obviously.'

'I'd imagine so, aye.'

'Most of them, actually,' Tyler replied, but there was a suggestion of a smile in there. 'But, still, way better than yesterday.'

'It's early fucking days, son,' Hoon called over. 'Mind you're stuck in here with me all day.'

Tyler winced. 'Shit. Aye. Forgot about that, right enough. Might've spoken too soon. I'll get back to you, boss.'

'You learn to tune him out,' Logan said, tilting his head back in Hoon's direction.

'I fucking heard that! And here, wee man, don't listen to that big burst oyster,' Hoon said, shifting around in his bed until he could see Tyler through the gap in his visitors. 'If you're going to take advice from anyone, maybe don't take it from the guy who looks like a horse's cock that got caught in the fucking stable door.'

'See?' Logan said. He pointed to one of his ears. 'No idea what he just said.'

They spent a while just chatting. They managed a couple of laughs at Hoon's expense, and then the tone changed when Logan filled them in on all the details of the night before. They'd known some of it—Ben had already shared what he knew—but hearing it first-hand from someone who had been there made it all the more real.

'God,' Sinead said. 'It's so...'

She fumbled around, searching for an appropriate word to describe the awfulness of the whole situation. It was possible, however, that such a word didn't even exist.

'Aye,' Logan agreed. 'Aye, it is.'

'How's Dave doing?' Tyler asked.

'About how you'd expect,' Logan said. 'Blames himself. Not sure why. He wanted to go up the road with them all, but she didn't want him there. Don't think she can face him. Not after everything.'

'Poor Dave,' Sinead said.

Tyler nodded. 'Aye. And, you know, poor me, too. Let's not forget that I've had a hell of a time,' he said, and it was somehow enough to lift the mood, just a little.

'Oh, of course,' Ben said.

'I mean, *obviously* you've had it way worse!' Sinead agreed.

'Thank you,' Tyler said. 'Though that sounded a wee bit sarcastic for my liking. I properly did have it worse. I'm all for fun and games, but let's not lose sight of the fact that I was kidnapped and tortured.'

'Jesus Christ,' Hoon said. 'He slapped you around a bit. Is that what you fucking snowflakes call torture these days? Try boiling water up your arsehole, son! Try wee fucking sheets of sandpaper rubbing at your fucking eyeballs. Then we'll talk.'

There was a moment of silence around Tyler's bed. It was eventually broken by the detective constable himself.

'God, you're right, boss,' he said, his trademark cheerfulness ringing around the room. 'You totally can just block it out!'

–

Twenty minutes later, Logan pulled up outside the vet's surgery in his borrowed car, spent a few moments trying to figure out how to apply the handbrake, then unfolded himself from the driver's seat.

The vet shared a building with a dental practice that sat in the shadow of Cow Hill, a several hundred-foot-high dome-shaped, tree-covered mound with a TV mast poking up from the top.

As far as Logan could work out, it had got its name from the Highland cattle that either used to roam the hillside, or currently did. Ben had been the one to tell him about it, and he hadn't been entirely clear on the current state of affairs.

The hill's winding tracks were mostly used by hikers looking to get one of the best views of the area, dog walkers wanting to get away from the people and traffic down below, and off-road cyclists who, quite frankly, needed their bloody heads examined.

He heard dogs barking as he approached the vet's front door. In the waiting room, a golden retriever was being scared shitless by a couple of yappy wee Yorkshire terriers who were tag-teaming the bigger dog, undaunted by its size.

The retriever glanced up at Logan as he entered, and there was a note of exasperation in the look.

The Yorkies, startled by the detective's sudden arrival, turned on him and started barking, then stopped when they discovered that, no matter how far back they craned their necks, they couldn't see all the way to the top of him. They shrank back a little in fear at his sheer scale.

Logan winked at the golden retriever, then approached the reception desk and rang the bell.

A conversation through in the back office fell away into silence, and a woman in a shapeless pale blue outfit emerged.

'Hello! Can I help?' she asked, then she grimaced in horror. 'Oh!'

The sight of his face almost took the legs out from under her. She clamped her hands on the back of the empty receptionist's chair and leaned her weight on it, like it was the only thing holding her up.

'I'm here to pick up my dog,' Logan said.

'Right! Yes.' She searched his face, taking in his injuries, then gave herself a shake. 'Right. OK. Name?'

'Jack Logan.'

'Weird name for a dog.'

Logan frowned. Or, at least, the various lumps and bumps of his face arranged themselves into an expression that could be read as confusion.

'What?'

The woman smiled. 'The dog's name, I meant. What's the dog called?'

'Oh. Aye. Right. It's Taggart.'

Across the desk, the woman's eyebrows dipped into the beginning of a frown. No real surprise. She was barely out of her twenties, by the looks of her. She'd probably never even heard of the TV show that inspired the choice of name.

'It's from the telly,' he explained. 'Old detective programme. Inside joke.'

'Eh, right. OK.'

328

This didn't seem to ease her confusion, though. She pulled out the chair and sat down, then slid around some paperwork that sat on the desk.

'Is he ready to go?' Logan asked.

'Um. Yes. No.'

Logan shifted his weight from one foot to the other. Behind him, the Yorkshire terriers resumed their tormenting of the golden retriever.

'That's some mixed signals you're sending there,' Logan told the woman. 'Is he ready to go, or is he not? Has something happened? Is he all right?'

'I, um, no. Yes! He's fine. He's absolutely fine. He's been keeping us all entertained.'

Logan realised that his hands had balled into fists. He relaxed them, and let some of the tension that had suddenly built up in his shoulders ease off again.

'Right. Good. So I can take him?'

'Uh, that's the thing,' the woman said, looking up from the scattered notes. 'Someone already did.'

'What? When?'

'About five minutes ago. A man. He said he was a detective. Said he worked with you. He said you'd asked him to come pick Taggart up.'

'What did he look like?' Logan demanded.

Though, he knew. He already knew.

'Um, thirties. Short hair. Quite, uh, quite intense looking. Said his name was DC Neish, I think.' She nodded. 'Yes, that was him.'

'No, it wasn't,' Logan said. He turned to the door. It offered a narrow view of the road leading up to the building, and not a whole lot else. 'Did you see what way he went?'

'Uh, no. Sorry,' the woman behind the counter replied. 'But he hasn't been gone long. If you hurry, you might still be able to catch him.'

Chapter 42

From the way she answered, Shona had been waiting for his call.

'Jack. Hi. Listen, I know it's all a bit of a shock. I just didn't know what else to do.'

'What? What do you mean?' Logan asked. He was standing in the vet's car park, a sudden downpour of rain skelping across his bruised cheeks and broad shoulders.

'Olivia. Staying here last night. She had a bit of a shock.'

Logan didn't waste time setting her straight on his reason for phoning. 'The dog's gone. He's taken him.'

'What? What are you talking about? Gone where? Who's taken him?'

'Feasey. The killer. He's been at the vet's. He's taken Taggart.'

'Oh, God. What? Christ Almighty, Jack!' Shona replied, her panic rising. 'Have you tracked him yet?'

'Tracked him? Of course I haven't bloody tracked him. I'm no' a Native bloody American hunter here, Shona. I'm going to call it in, but—'

'On your phone! Have you tracked him on your phone, I meant?!'

'My phone?'

Wait.

His phone.

The collar.

'Christ! Hang on.' He tapped the button that put her on speakerphone. 'You'll have to talk me through it.'

He listened and followed her instructions as she explained how to open the app and check the location of the tag. As soon as he saw where it was, his heart sank.

'It's here,' he said. 'It's right here. It's more or less overlapping my wee icon.'

'Are you sure?' Shona asked. 'Here, let me check.'

There were some muffled noises as Shona took her phone from her ear and started tapping at the screen.

'You're right. He's right next to you,' she confirmed.

'Aye, but he's not.' Logan looked around, scanning the car park. 'He must've ditched the collar somewhere. Under one of the cars, maybe.'

'Shite. Yeah. He must've done,' she said. Logan could tell she was trying hard not to panic. 'Unless he's right below or above you.'

'Aye, well, unless he's dug a big hole that I can't...'

Logan blinked several times, as if a punch had just stopped a few millimetres from his face. The tail end of the sentence filtered through.

Slowly, with his heart rising into his throat, Logan turned and looked up at the looming mound of Cow Hill disappearing into the mist and rain overhead.

'Call Ben,' he said, powering off towards the path that connected the car park to the hillside. 'I know where Feasey's taken Taggart.'

–

Various parts of Logan felt like they were on fire by the time he crested the first rise of the hill. His thighs and calves, mostly, but his lungs, too. Every rasping breath made his ribs shift around in the meat of his chest, and the exertion of the climb was making every one of his cuts and bruises come alive with pain.

He was barely a tenth of the way to the top, by his estimation, but his body was already begging him to stop.

He should, of course. Carrying on through all this pain was bound to be causing damage.

But Shayne Feasey was up here somewhere.

And the bastard had his dog.

The path took a sharp turn to the left, zig-zagging up the hillside. He hauled himself up it, enjoyed a few moments of respite when it dipped down for a few paces, then steeled himself for a final push up to what he hoped would be a flatter, more level stretch above.

The rain had stopped as quickly as it had started, and the sun was now poking through the clouds. Logan would've preferred the rain. A cool wee drizzle would be just the very dab right now, he reckoned, as he powered his way up the incline.

He was just below the ridge when he heard the growling. It was Taggart. He recognised the sound of the dog right away, even if he'd never heard him making that particular one before. He'd never heard the animal sound so cornered. So scared.

Anger ignited his aching muscles, flooding him with adrenaline. He crested the top of the rise and there, a dozen yards away, was Shayne Feasey. He was perched on a rocky outcrop that overlooked a steep drop into the car park below. The roofs of the buildings were fifty feet down, maybe more. A fall from this height would kill a man.

Or a dog.

Feasey was kneeling on a huge, rounded boulder five times the size of himself, gazing dispassionately at Taggart, who was trapped beneath one of the bastard's knees. The dog's legs kicked, his back end wriggling as he desperately tried to free himself.

Logan tried to run, but the ground was too steep, the stones of the path too loose and slippery. No way he'd get to them before Feasey noticed. A stealthy approach was out of the question, then.

Which left him only one alternative.

'Oi, ya prick!' he bellowed. Despite the burning in his lungs, his voice rolled across the hillside like an oncoming storm. He pointed to Taggart. 'Get your fucking hands off my dog.'

Feasey raised his head and stared. For several seconds, he just stared, his eyes and mouth all gradually opening wider.

He watched, saying nothing, as Logan hauled his heaving, sweating carcass up the hill towards them.

Down on the ground, Taggart let out a series of frantic yelps. He sounded terrified, and yet at the sound of Logan's voice, his stubby tail had gone into overdrive, spinning like a helicopter rotor.

'Holy fuck,' Feasey finally said. Clearly, he had not been expecting the DCI to appear.

Logan took a moment to savour the horror on the other man's face, before it twisted itself into a grin.

'Look at the fucking state of you. How are you still alive?'

'It'll take more than you to do me in, son,' Logan said.

Feasey laughed. 'I meant the hill. You look like you're going to pass out, old man. You should sit down before you have a heart attack.'

'Get off my fucking dog. Now.'

Taggart yelped sharply, then the sound was cut off as Feasey pressed down with his knee. He held a hand up, warning Logan to stop.

'That's far enough, big man. Any closer and I collapse his windpipe. Which, I'll be honest, I'm probably going to do anyway.'

'Why?' Logan asked. 'Why are you doing this?'

Feasey looked to his right, out over the town squatting below him, out along the shimmering loch to the hazy greens and purples of the rolling mountains beyond. He stared for a moment, like he was going to find the answer out there.

Finally, he turned back to the detective and shrugged. 'Why not?'

'Your sister's right, son. You really are a sick bastard.'

'Yeah. Me and the rest of the world,' Feasey agreed. His eyes sparkled with mischief. 'So, you know, then? It's all out in the open?'

'It is. We know. She's in custody.'

'Haha! Good. Good enough for the daft wee bitch. Did she do it? Did she kill them?'

'Give me the dog, son,' Logan said. 'I'm warning you.'

'You don't get to fucking warn me. Don't you see? All I have to do is lean, and your wee dog's dead.' He rubbed at Taggart's head, tousling his hair. 'Isn't that right? Yes! Yes, it is! Aren't you a dead boy? Yes! Yes, you are! *Dead* boy. Dead boy!'

He turned back to Logan, his playful tone becoming deathly serious again.

'Did she do it? Did she kill them?'

'Did you kill Sharon Simpson?'

Feasey smirked. 'I asked you first.'

'Why'd you climb the hedge?' Logan asked.

Logan shifted his weight onto the balls of his feet, calculating his chances. He was still downhill. Still too far away. If he moved, Taggart was done for. Maybe if he kept Feasey talking, he could get closer.

'She knew you were coming, didn't she? Sharon. You'd arranged to meet her. So why climb the hedge?'

Feasey regarded him in silence for a moment, then shrugged. 'Fine. Because I knew that was the night I was going to do it,' he said. 'That I was going to kill her. Didn't know how. Not exactly. But I knew it was going to happen, so I didn't want to be seen.'

He nodded to Logan, and applied a little more pressure on the dog's neck.

'Now you. My sister. Did she do it? Did she kill them?'

Logan's only hope was to keep stalling.

'She did,' he said. 'She shot them both.'

'Fucking hell!' Feasey seemed genuinely shocked by that. Pleased, too. 'Didn't know she had it in her. Which one was it? Which one was her old man? My money's on Armand. Right?'

Logan shook his head.

'Isaac? Fuck. Well, there you go. That's surprised me.' He shrugged. 'Not that I really give a shit. I just wanted all of them fucking punished. Those three rapist fucks and her. Those four ruined my life.'

He ran a hand back across his head, his fingers splaying through the short crop of his hair.

'You want to know why I am the way I am? Why I do all this shit?' he asked. 'Because why should everyone else get it easy? Why do they get to have a nice time, when all I get is pain and misery? That's all I've ever got.

'You know what one of the foster dads said to me once? You won't fucking believe this. He said—and I've never forgotten it—"For some of us, our lot is to suffer." Can you believe that? Saying that to a twelve-year-old? Just after you'd fucking touched him up, no less. Can you fucking believe that?'

Logan's breathing was steadier now. His lungs no longer felt like two shrivelled balloons. For all the good it would do him if he couldn't get any closer.

'I'm sorry, son. I'm sorry life was shite. Doesn't mean you get to inflict the same on everyone else.'

'Yeah, but it does. I do. I am,' he said, gesturing down to the dog.

'Let him go,' Logan said. 'Last warning.'

Feasey, to Logan's surprise, looked worried. He sized the detective up, like he was calculating his chances, then he slowly lifted his knee.

'All right, fine,' he said.

As soon as the pressure was off his neck, Taggart wriggled up onto his feet. He was panting furiously, his tongue flopping down, his eyes just about bulging out of their sockets. He tried to run for Logan, but then jerked to a stop.

'You want him?' Feasey said, tightening his grip on the dog's collar. He leaped to his feet, spinning, whirling Taggart around by the neck. 'Go get him!'

He launched the squealing dog towards the sheer drop.

'No!' Logan bellowed.

There was a *clack* of breaking plastic as the clasp of the collar snapped. Taggart flew sideways, hit the ground hard, and rolled several feet across the rocks before coming to rest on the grassy verge beside the path. He lay there, whimpering and wheezing, his eyes locked on Logan, pleading for help.

'Jesus! Cheap bastard!' Feasey spat. 'Where did you get the collar, the fucking pound shop?'

He tossed it over the edge, then turned towards the dog, his face knotting up in glee.

Logan's voice was a baritone from right behind him.

'Don't. You. Fucking. Dare.'

Feasey spun and found himself face to chest with the much taller detective. Logan's fists were clenched so tightly that the knuckles shone like little nuggets of white.

The younger man looked him up and down, then his face cracked into a smile.

'Seriously? You think you've got a fucking chance, old man?' he said, squaring up. 'Look at the state of you.'

Logan indicated Feasey's face with a nod. His eyes were black, his nose bloated from where Tyler's head had connected with it.

'Could say the same for you, pal.'

Feasey laughed. 'Yeah, but have you forgotten? Not twenty-four hours ago, I kicked the absolute living shit out of you. Did I give you amnesia, is that what this is? Did I hit you so hard you forgot the whole thing?'

'No.'

'So what the fuck makes you think you can fight me today, eh?' Feasey demanded. 'You were in decent shape yesterday, but today, you're injured. No, you're fucked is what you are. You're injured, you're old, and you're completely fucking ruined.'

'I'm something else, too,' Logan told him. 'Something I wasn't yesterday.'

'Oh yeah? And what's that? Angry? Determined? Full of righteous indignation?'

Logan shook his head. 'No,' he said.

A fist connected with the centre of Feasey's chest. It struck like a sledgehammer, launching the bastard backwards off his feet.

'Facing forward,' Logan said.

The punch had been perfectly placed. All the air had been ejected out of Feasey's lungs in one big gasp, and they weren't in any position to start filling up again. He clutched at his chest, eyes bulging, as he struggled up onto his knees.

A shadow fell over him as Logan approached.

'See, it's one thing to clock a guy on the back of the head and then lay into him,' the detective said.

He clamped a hand on the back of Feasey's neck and dragged him up onto his feet.

'But looking him in the eye as you do it?'

He drove another punch into Shayne's stomach with enough force that, for a moment, he was sure his knuckles touched spine. The DCI released his grip and Feasey fell onto the rocky ground, coughing up a greasy smear of semi-digested Scampi Fries.

'That's another matter.'

Finding some inner source of strength, Feasey launched himself back to his feet, fists flying. He was out of control, though, his movements uncoordinated.

Logan's hand clamped over his face, almost enveloping his entire head. He held the bastard there at arm's length, beyond the reach of his flailing punches.

'You know the big difference between you and me, Shayne?' Logan tightened his claw-like grip, and most of the fight went out of the man on the receiving end. 'I don't say this often, so listen up. The difference between you and me is that I only *pretend* not to care about people. That's my big secret, Shayne. That's the skeleton in my closet. I only pretend to hate everyone. And seeing you—seeing what being a hate-filled arsehole looks like from the outside—I'm thinking maybe I should stop.'

He shrugged, his hand still clutching Feasey's skull. This drew a whimper from somewhere behind his palm.

'Or, you know, at least on the odd occasion, anyway.'

He released his grip. Feasey staggered. Breathing was still proving difficult for him, but he remained standing, albeit with a bit of a sway.

'I don't care about what you did to me, Shayne. That's part of the job.' He stepped in closer. So close that he blocked out the sun, and his face was cast into deep, dark shadow. 'But you hurt my friend. And you hurt my dog. And that? That I do care about.'

There was no big roar from Feasey. No dramatic battle cry. Instead, he just swung with a right hook, pouring all his remaining strength into it. All his decades of rage.

Logan jabbed him in the throat before his punch could land. It was the final straw for Feasey's struggling respiratory system, and he sank onto his hands and knees, hacking and coughing up mouthfuls of spit.

A nudge from an enormous foot rolled him over onto his back. He squinted in the sun, staring up at the giant figure silhouetted above him.

'You think you're something special, Shayne. You think because you've had it hard, you get to take that out on everyone else.'

He pressed his foot down on the other man's throat, pinning him there, just like Feasey had done to the dog.

'But here's the thing. You're no different to anyone else. You're just like the rest of us. Everyone has it hard. Everyone's dealing with their own awful shite. It might not look like it sometimes, but we are. We all are.'

He pressed his foot down harder. It would be easy, he thought, to push all the way.

Far too easy.

'But what sort of world would it be if we all went around taking it out on someone else?' Logan muttered.

He lifted his foot. Feasey rolled onto his side, clutching at his throat, coughing, gagging, and sobbing on the rocks.

A shout from down the hill made Logan turn. Half a dozen Uniforms, all younger and fitter than him, were charging up the hillside, the steepness of the climb proving to be very little challenge.

'About bloody time,' Logan remarked to the world in general.

He limped over to where Taggart lay in the grass. Muscles burning, broken bones screaming, he kneeled and scooped the little dog up into his arms. As Logan cradled him against his chest, Taggart twisted his head and coated the detective's face in big, sloppy licks.

'Jesus!' Logan protested. 'Enough, enough!'

Taggart yelped. The sound was raw and sore, but happy, too. Mostly happy, in fact.

'Right, come on then, boy,' Logan said. He saw Feasey rising up onto his hands and knees, and helped him back down into the dirt with a foot to the back. 'Let's get you home.'

Chapter 43

Ben and Logan stood in the car park of Fort William Police Station, watching Shayne Feasey being loaded into the back of a squad car. There had been an obligatory trip to the hospital to get him checked over, but as soon as they'd confirmed he wasn't going to die on them anytime soon, he'd been whisked back to the station for processing, before being bundled up to Inverness.

Moira Corson had helped check him in. In many ways, Logan reckoned, that was almost punishment enough.

'Good work, Jack,' Ben told him. He patted his old friend on the arm, drawing a grimace of pain. 'Shite. Sorry. Does that still hurt?'

'It's just that arm,' Logan said. 'And, you know, pretty much all my left side. And ninety per cent of the right.'

'Get to the bloody hospital!'

'Aye, aye. I will,' Logan said.

He wouldn't.

'How's the dug?' Ben asked.

Logan pointed over to the car he'd been loaned by CID. Taggart bounced around excitedly in the back, his nose leaving streaky marks on the rear windscreen.

'Vet checked him over. He'll be fine.'

'Oh well,' Ben said. 'And to think, you almost managed to rid yourself of him, too.' He smirked, like he knew a secret. 'Better luck next time, eh?'

Logan gave a noncommittal sort of grunt. 'Aye,' he said. 'Fingers crossed.'

Ben glanced back at the front of the station. Through the glass, he could just make out Moira standing behind the reception desk, pointedly ignoring him like she had been all morning.

'Right. Well, are we fit?' he asked. 'If we hit the road now, we'll miss the dinnertime rush at Inverness.'

'Aye. All set,' Logan said. He looked down at his hands, as if realising something that was supposed to be in them wasn't there. 'Shite. The Big Board box. With all Tammi-Jo's...'

'Nonsense?' Ben guessed.

'Close enough, aye,' Logan said. 'I said I'd bring it back up the road.' He shuffled on the spot, making a show of having a limp. 'Could you...?'

Ben tutted. 'Oh, aye. Leave it to the old fella to climb the bloody stairs and lug the heavy boxes around, why don't you?'

'I'm injured!'

'You're a malingering bastard is what you are,' Ben told him. He took a breath like he was steeling himself for battle, then set off for the door. 'But, aye. I'll get it. Just have the engine running and be ready to go in case I get cornered.'

'Will do,' Logan confirmed. He watched Ben enter the building and head for the reception desk. Moira didn't look up, but the internal door buzzed, so the DI changed direction halfway there and carried on through into the station proper.

Logan puffed out his cheeks.

He cracked his knuckles.

'Right, then,' he said.

And with that, he stepped inside.

–

Ben entered the empty Incident Room, looked around for the box, then stopped when he spotted the two styrofoam clamshell trays sitting on one of the tables, their lids closed over.

Each was positioned in front of a chair, a knife and fork set out on either side.

A single unlit white candle had been stuck in an eggcup in the centre of the table, a long-handled lighter placed beside it.

'What the hell is…?' Ben mumbled, taking in the metal teapot and the chipped china mugs that had been set out beside the candle, along with a little pot of milk, some packs of sugar and an assortment of sauces in colourful sachets.

He made his way over to the table, and the heady aroma of a piping hot fry-up came to meet him halfway.

He put a hand to the teapot, then quickly pulled it away again.

Hot. Burning hot. It had been put here recently.

He turned when he heard the door opening. Moira bustled her way in, then stopped as soon as she saw him.

'Well?' she demanded.

Ben blinked in confusion. 'Well, what?'

'These boxes. That lazy big idjit downstairs told me you needed a hand.'

She looked around the room, just as Ben had done. Just like the DI, her gaze eventually settled on the styrofoam trays.

'What the hell is this meant to be?' she asked.

'Just what I was wondering,' Ben said. He flipped open the lid of the closest tray, then found himself staring deep into the sunshine yellow egg yolk of a full cooked breakfast. 'I think… I think it's a JJ's.'

'A JJ's?' Moira came closer, peering at the arrangement of items on the table like they might be some sort of trap. 'What do you mean *you think it's a JJ's*?'

Ben gestured to the breakfast. 'Look.'

'Oh! I see what this is,' Moira snapped. 'Aye, very good. I see what you're doing.'

'I'm not doing anything!' Ben protested. 'It wasn't me. It was… *Bastard*.'

He hurried over to the window, parted the blinds with two fingers, and peered down into the car park. Logan stood by the car, his hands in his pockets, smiling up. He nodded, tapped a finger to his forehead in salute, then climbed into the driver's seat and was immediately set upon by an overly excited mongrel.

'I'm sorry, Moira, this wasn't...' Ben began, turning away from the window.

Moira sat in one of the chairs, swirling the teapot around, helping the tea inside it come to full strength.

'Well, it'd be bloody daft to let it go to waste, wouldn't it?' she said, noting his look of confusion.

She didn't seem happy about the situation.

But then, she never did.

The DI smiled. 'Aye,' he said. 'Aye, I suppose it would, at that.'

And as DCI Jack Logan drove away from the car park, Ben Forde pulled out his chair, took his seat at the table, and reached for the lighter to light the candle.

CANELOCRIME

Do you love crime fiction and are always on the lookout for brilliant authors?

Canelo Crime is home to some of the most exciting novels around. Thousands of readers are already enjoying our compulsive stories. Are you ready to find your new favourite writer?

Find out more and sign up to our newsletter at canelocrime.com